Dear Reader,

What would you do if you... day and discovered a bouquet of roses from a secret admirer? Depending on what kind of woman you are, you might be delighted, surprised—or even afraid. In this groundbreaking anthology, bestselling authors Sharon Sala, Paula Detmer Riggs and Peggy Moreland present to you all the possibilities in three romantic tales that start from the same premise—and explore all the exciting opportunities life and love have to offer.

In Sharon Sala's "Sudden Danger," the mysterious gift represents a very definite threat. Kristie Samuels has every reason to believe the roses are from a deadly admirer. All the more reason why she puts herself under the protection of sexy detective Scott Wade.

Bryce Hunter is "Fighting for His Wife" in Paula Detmer Riggs' emotional tale of a husband who pursues his soon-to-be ex-wife as a secret admirer in order to prove that he is her one and only.

And finally, in Peggy Moreland's "It Had To Be You," a plucky heroine believes her romantic dreams have come true when she discovers the romantic gift. Now Jamie Tyson wonders if the flowers are from her dream man—or someone else....

We hope you enjoy all the twists and turns these exciting new tales take you on!

Happy reading!

The Editors

Silhouette Books

SHARON SALA
is a child of the country. As a farmer's daughter, her vivid imagination made solitude something to cherish. During her adult life, she learned to survive by taking things one day at a time. An inveterate dreamer, she yearned to share the stories her imagination created. For Sharon, her dreams have come true, and she claims one of her greatest joys is when her stories become tools for healing.

PAULA DETMER RIGGS
discovers material for her writing in her varied life experiences. During her first five years of marriage to a naval officer, she lived in nineteen different locations on the West Coast, gaining familiarity with places as diverse as San Diego and Seattle. While working at an historical site in San Diego she wrote, directed and narrated fashion shows and became fascinated with the early history of California. She writes romances because "I think we all need an escape from the high-tech pressures that face us every day, and I believe in happy endings. Isn't that why we keep trying, in spite of all the roadblocks and disappointments along the way?"

PEGGY MORELAND
published her first romance with Silhouette in 1989 and continues to delight readers with stories set in her home state of Texas. Winner of the National Readers' Choice Award, a nominee for the *Romantic Times* Reviewer's Choice Award and a two-time finalist for the prestigious RITA® Award, Peggy's books frequently appear on the *USA TODAY* and Waldenbooks bestseller lists. When not writing, you can usually find Peggy outside, tending the cattle, goats and other critters on the ranch she shares with her husband. You may write to Peggy at P.O. Box 1099, Florence, TX 76527-1099, or e-mail her at peggy@peggymoreland.com.

Sharon
Sala

Paula
Detmer
Riggs

Peggy
Moreland

Turning Point

Silhouette® Books
Published by Silhouette Books
America's Publisher of Contemporary Romance

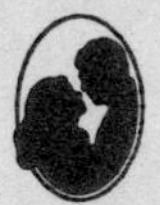

SILHOUETTE BOOKS

TURNING POINT

ISBN 0-373-48481-X

This edition published by arrangement with Harlequin Books S.A.

Visit Silhouette at www.eHarlequin.com

Printed in U.S.A.

CONTENTS

SUDDEN DANGER

Sharon Sala

I'm dedicating this book to three women
who are very dear in my life.

The first, my daughter, Kathy, who endured and survived
a vicious act of random violence.

The second, my daughter-in-law Kristie Ann,
who has learned a different kind of survival,
but one that is no less heart-wrenching.

The third, my niece Christina,
who at the age of five, had to learn to survive
without the mother who'd given her life.

I'm so proud of them all and of the mothers
they have become. It is my fervent prayer that
the powerful strength of will they all possess
has been passed on to their children.

They are living proof of what I believe, and that is
that all things come full circle and that love never ends.

Thank you, my dears.
You are always in my heart.

Dear Reader,

I was pleased to be asked to be a part of the *Turning Point* anthology. I think we can all agree that there comes a time in everyone's life when something must change. Some people call it coming to a crossroads. Others refer to it as the last straw. Whatever you call that moment, it is one in which you realize that life will never be the same, and therein often lies the problem. There are many people who live out their lives in a rut—who not only don't want things to change, but resist it with every ounce of their being. For them, change is traumatic, even devastating.

However, the truth of the matter is that change is a part of life. From the moment of our birth, we are in the constant act of change. Nothing stays the same... not our appearance or our experiences. Or the stories we write. And while our stories are fiction, the love with which they are offered to you is our truth. At this point in my life, the fact that I am sharing my stories with people who love to read is my dream come true.

Enjoy, and know that you are appreciated.

I can be reached at P.O. Box 127, Henryetta, OK 74437 or at sharonsala@romanticfiction.com.

All the best,

Sharon Sala

Chapter 1

Kristie Samuels stepped out of the cab and pulled the collar of her full length blue coat a little tighter around her neck. Ducking her head against the cold, December wind, she made a dash toward the front door of the office building where she worked. It was the day after Christmas, and in her opinion, the time when all good girls should still be warm in bed. However, no one at Shay, Tremaine and Weller had asked her opinion, so here she was, trying to outrun a wind chill of ten below just for the privilege of being employed in one of Chicago's premiere advertising firms.

The security guard at the front desk looked up as she entered the building, and waved a greeting at her before he returned to the morning paper.

"Good morning," Kristie replied as she headed for the elevators, then flinched as she saw movement out of the corner of her eye. It was only after she realized she was seeing her own reflection in the highly-polished metal of the elevator doors that she relaxed.

She shook off the spurt of anxiety, took a deep breath and pushed the up button, reminding herself that she had nothing to fear. The crazy letters and weird phone calls she'd been getting over the past few months had turned her into someone she didn't like. She was jumping at shadows and becoming afraid to answer her phone. And then just as suddenly as they began, they had stopped. It had been three days since she'd had any contact from this stalker and she was praying that it was over. Last night was the first night in weeks that she'd had a good night's sleep. For whatever reason, the nut who'd been bugging her must have moved on to greener pastures.

And since he'd never called her at the office, or indicated that he even knew where she worked, she had no earthly reason to assume she was in danger here. She got on the elevator, absently punching the tenth-floor button as she ran a practiced hand over the slick chignon she'd made of her thick, red hair. On a good day, it was very, very curly. On a day like today, with the wind and the threat of snow, it was out of control. Thus the need for the somber hairstyle, which in a way, matched her mood.

This was the first Christmas of her life that she hadn't spent with her family back in Texas. Not only that, but she'd spent all day yesterday alone, trying to remember exactly why she'd ever wanted to move so far away. Between the loneliness and the stalker, she was a hair away from calling it quits and moving back to Midland. Midland wasn't exactly the cosmopolitan city that Chicago was, but it had its own allure, especially if you were partial to mesquite and pump jacks on an ever-flat horizon.

The elevator stopped. Kristie exited quickly and as she entered the office, had already slipped into the mind-set of what needed to be done today. But as she approached her desk, she stopped in mid-step and stared. There was a huge vase of red roses on each secretary's desk and neither the receptionist or her co-workers were in sight. Not unusual, since she had a habit of getting in to the office about an hour earlier than everyone else. Her bosses appreciated her eagerness, as they were earlybirds themselves. Curious, she hung up her coat, still eyeing the flowers.

As soon as she got back to her desk, she lifted the card from the bouquet. Maybe they were from her parents. When she'd called them yesterday to wish them a merry Christmas, she'd been feeling sorry for herself. They'd probably heard the tears in her voice and sent her a pick-me-up. She leaned down and smelled the bouquet, thinking to herself that hothouse roses never smelled as sweet as the ones that climbed up the trellis on her mother, Shelly's, back porch.

Still thinking of her parents, she glanced at the note.

This is going to be our year.

Love...your secret admirer.

Her heart skipped a beat as she read it again, and as she did, the blood drained from her face. Secret admirer? She didn't even have a boyfriend. It had to be him. The stalker.

Without thinking, she dropped the note as if she'd touched something filthy, shuddering as she tried to draw a decent breath. Her heart was pounding, her mouth had suddenly gone dry. This had gone on too long. Either she called the police now or she quit her job and went home. But not to her apartment here in Chicago. She meant home, as in Texas. There the neighbors were not strangers, but friends of long standing, and family was only a phone call away.

Detective Scott Wade leaned forward, resting his elbows on his desk, and rubbed the back of his neck with both hands. The day was just starting and he already had the beginnings of a headache. He stood abruptly and strode into the break room to refill his coffee cup. Maybe another dose of caffeine would help.

"Hey Wade…Fisk is looking for you."

Scott grabbed a doughnut from the box on the table and picked up his coffee. The fact that the lieutenant was already looking for him didn't bode well for the headache he was trying to lose.

"What does he want?" Scott asked.

"You," the detective said, and then grinned and dodged as Scott flicked sugar from the doughnut on his arm.

Scott ate the doughnut in three bites and washed it down with a quick sip of coffee before he headed to the lieutenant's office.

"You wanted to see me, Lieutenant?"

Joe Fisk looked up from his desk and handed Scott a piece of paper.

"Go check this out," he said.

Scott glanced at the name and address. "What's it about?"

"Some woman is claiming she's being stalked. I don't like stalkers. See what you can find out."

Scott took the paper, glancing briefly at the name of the caller. K. Samson.

"Tucker's not coming in today," Fisk said, referring to Scott's partner, Paul Tucker.

"What's wrong with him?" Scott asked.

"His ex-wife had an emergency appendectomy last night."

"Oh man…who's got the kids?" Scott asked, thinking of the two little boys that Paul had every other weekend.

"Her parents."

"That's good, but if it's all the same to you, I'd rather work alone until Tucker comes back," Scott said.

"Okay for today, but if he's still gone tomorrow, you take someone else with you. I don't want my men going out alone. You always need someone at your back."

Scott nodded, then grabbed his coat as he headed for the parking lot. The wind was bitter, and not for the first time, he thought about relocating somewhere further south. It wasn't like he had any ties to the area. His parents had moved to Florida his senior year in college and he couldn't remember the last time he'd dated a girl more than two or three times before calling it quits.

It dawned on him as he pulled into traffic that

part of his dissatisfaction with the weather had to do with being lonely. If he had someone special to come home to every night, he probably wouldn't care how cold it got.

A short while later, he pulled up in front of the office building and got out, his strides long and hurried as he ducked through the revolving door, grateful to be out of the wind. The security guard looked over his newspaper long enough to tell him to sign in.

Scott flashed his badge and asked what floor Shay, Tremaine and Weller was on.

At that point, Barney the guard dropped the paper, jumped to his feet and put his hand on his gun. "Is there a problem?"

"As you were," Scott said. "I'm just here to investigate a complaint."

The guard blustered and puffed. "Well...if you need any help, just let me know."

Scott shook his head as he moved toward the elevator. Something told him that guard wasn't worth the lead he was carrying on that gun belt. He stepped on the elevator and then combed his fingers through his hair as the car began to move, trying to put a semblance of good grooming to his windblown hair. Moments later, he exited on the tenth floor and started looking for the office. It was halfway down the hall on the right. He pushed the double glass doors open. There was a woman standing with her back to the door. As he walked into the office, she turned around. At that point, Scott froze, staring at her in disbelief. When he felt the floor shifting beneath his feet, he knew it was time to speak.

"Kristie?"

For a moment, the world was put on hold. "Scotty?"

"I'm looking for a K. Samson? Something about a stalker?"

Scott pulled his badge out of habit. Kristie stared at it in disbelief, trying to assimilate the fact that her high school sweetheart, whom she hadn't seen in years, was working for the Chicago P.D.

"You're a cop?"

"A detective, but that's not important right now. I was given to understand there was a stalking complaint. Where is this K. Samson?"

Kristie started to hedge. It seemed embarrassing to be admitting what had been happening to her, especially to him. He'd been her first love, her first lover, and the first boy to break her heart. Of course that hadn't really been his fault as much as the fault of his parents for moving away during his senior year. It had been slightly disappointing to her that she hadn't died from the grief of losing him. He wrote a couple of letters, one of which she had answered, but the last one he'd written had been more of a farewell than their actual parting had been. After that, she'd given up her youthful dreams of living happily ever after with Scott Wade and finished growing up without him. Looking at him now, with no traces whatsoever left of the gangly teenager that he'd been, she was consumed by a new set of anxieties. That bone-straight chocolate brown hair had been cut to frame a face that had turned into a mixture of hard angles and planes and his dark, brown eyes were giving nothing of his emotions away. He was all man in every sense of the word.

"I'm the one who made the call," she said.

"Someone must have written the name down wrong."

Scott looked at Kristie again, and this time saw past her surprise to the fear in her eyes.

"Tell me," he said.

Kristie sighed and then gestured toward the vase of roses on her desk. "It's just so ugly."

"These are from your stalker?"

"I think so."

Scott eyed her closely. "No husband?"

She shook her head.

"No significant other?"

Kristie sighed. Again, admitting this was embarrassing. It made her sound like such a loser.

"No, Scott. I'm not married, nor have I ever been. There is also no partner, no significant other, no boyfriend. Not even an acquaintance with a crush."

Scott stifled a rush of pleasure at the news and made himself focus on the business at hand.

"This is surely not the only thing you've received?"

She leaned against the edge of her desk and folded her arms across her breasts in an odd, protective manner, as if the act alone might somehow keep her safe.

"There are letters at home, as well as a half-dozen tapes from my answering machine."

"Have you ever seen him?"

"No."

"How long has this been going on?"

Kristie looked up at him, her eyes welling with tears.

"Too long."

Scott couldn't resist. He slid his hand beneath the

weight of her hair and gently squeezed the back of her neck.

"I know this is rough, honey, but could you be more specific?"

His affection was so familiar, and yet every time she looked at him, it was like looking at a stranger. She was having a difficult time keeping her memories of her Scott separate from this big, intimidating man with a badge.

"I don't know...four...maybe five months?"

He exhaled sharply. "Why didn't you call the police before now?"

"Because I didn't think they'd take me seriously."

Scott cupped her chin, tilting her face until she was forced to meet his gaze.

"Well, you were wrong. My lieutenant has a big hate for stalkers. I'm sorry you've been so afraid, but we'll see what we can do about stopping the harassment before it goes any further, okay?"

"Very okay," Kristie said, and for the first time in months, felt as if there was hope after all.

The office doors opened and two men walked in.

"Oh great," Kristie said.

"Who are they?" Scott asked.

"My bosses. This is such a mess."

However, Kristie need not have worried. Scott took over.

"Miss Samuels is going to be leaving with me," Scott said, when he was introduced. "I need the letters and tapes she's been accumulating at her home to begin an investigation."

Ben Tremaine and Michael Shay were suitably horrified. They expressed their concerns to Kristie.

"Of course, of course," Ben said, and Michael

echoed the sentiments. "Take whatever time you need to get this cleared up."

Before Kristie knew it, she was back on the street and being ushered into the passenger seat of Scott's car. Scott slid behind the wheel, looked at her once again as if he was looking at a ghost, and then smiled for the first time.

"Damn, Kristie Ann, I can't believe you're here in Chicago. How long have you lived here?"

"Six years. I came straight out of college and up until this mess started, was satisfied with my decision. However, I will be honest when I tell you that during the past few weeks, I've thought about moving back home more than once."

"I can understand why, but selfishly, I'm glad that you didn't."

"Are you married?"

Her question came out of nowhere. He glanced at her once before starting the car, but her expression was closed and the question could have been nothing more than curiosity.

"No."

"Have you ever been?"

"No."

"Any significant other?"

He smiled to himself. She was grilling him much as he'd questioned her a few minutes earlier.

"No significant other, or anyone closely resembling the same."

Kristie glanced at him once, caught a glimpse of his smile and sighed.

"Just curious."

"Where to?" he asked.

She gave him her address.

Chapter 2

Scott pulled into the parking lot of Kristie's apartment complex and then stared in disbelief.

"I don't believe this."

"What?" Kristie asked.

"I used to live here."

"You're kidding? When?"

"Oh, about ten years ago. Right after I got out of college. I was going through the police academy and my parents had just moved to Florida."

"How are your parents, by the way?" she asked.

"They're fine, and yours?"

She thought of Blaine and Shelly Samuels and felt homesick all over again.

"Still in Midland."

Scott nodded. It seemed bizarre to be making uncomfortable small talk with Kristie. There was a time when everything had been easy between them, including sex. The uneasy silence continued to stretch until he pulled the keys from the ignition.

"Are you ready?" he asked.

"This feels so strange."

He turned to face her. "What do you mean?"

"I didn't think I'd ever see you again and now...to see you again in the middle of this mess." She sighed and then shrugged. "It's just weird, you know?"

"Yeah...I know." He reached across the seat and clasped her hand. "We'll find who's doing this and we'll put him away. Then you won't have to be afraid anymore."

"I hope so."

"It's a promise, from me to you...okay?"

Kristie hesitated a moment and then smiled. "Okay."

A few minutes later they were in the building and exiting the elevator. As they started down the hall, Scott commented, "When I lived here, I had a sixth-floor apartment. I would have been right above you. How long have you lived here?"

"About four years. Before that, I was on the east side of the city. The drive was too long and parking was difficult so I moved closer to work. Even now, I still rarely drive my car. I usually just take a cab or the bus."

Kristie paused in front of apartment number five twenty.

"This is it," she said, and unlocked the door.

As they entered, Scott swept the room with a practiced gaze, taking in the family pictures and the warm, homey furniture. The scent of her morning coffee still lingered in the air and there were some gardening magazines on the coffee table. Her home was a far cry from the apartment in which he lived. He had furnished his apartment with a display of furniture right off the showroom floor without any thought as to whether or not it fit his personality. And even though it was comfortable, it had never made him feel as welcome as this room did.

He fingered a soft, white-chenille throw pillow and then bent to sniff the bouquet of fresh flowers sitting on an end table. He didn't know their names, but he recognized some of them from the garden his mother used to have when they'd lived in Texas. As he straightened and turned around, he caught her looking at him.

"You have a great place."

She nodded her thanks, but then added, "You don't know how surreal it seems for you to be standing here in my living room."

"I used to know the way to your bedroom better."

Her mouth dropped. The fact that he'd just alluded to their teenage years and the stolen nights of making love was more than she'd expected.

"I can't believe you just said that," she muttered.

"Why? It's the truth."

She felt herself blushing. "Well...that was a long time ago and—"

"We're still the same people, Kristie Ann. Older maybe, but still the same."

"Still—"

"Show me the letters, okay?"

Scott's abrupt change of subject was a rude reminder of why he was really here.

"Yes, of course," she said, then waved toward

the sofa. "Take off your coat. Make yourself comfortable. I'll be right back."

She walked out of the room with her fingers curled into fists and a knot in her stomach. It wasn't enough that she was being terrorized by some unknown stalker. Scott's reappearance in her life was something like coming face-to-face with a ghost. She dug through her dresser, grabbing the letters and tapes in short angry motions, reminding herself that there was no need to get upset. It had been a surprise to see Scott Wade again, but there was no need to make a big deal out of the fact. They'd been in love, sure, but that had been years ago. It had nothing to do with now. She strode out of her bedroom and back down the hall.

"Here they are," she said, and dumped them onto the sofa.

Scott's eyes widened. "There's got to be at least thirty letters and a half dozen tapes. Why in God's name did you wait so long to call the police?"

Kristie burst into tears.

Scott felt like a heel. He took her in his arms and pulled her close, and as he did, realized how truly fragile she was beneath the bulk of her winter clothes.

"I'm sorry, kid, it was just a surprise, okay?"

"I'm sorry, too," Kristie mumbled, and pretended for just a moment that the years between them had never passed.

Scott gave her a quick hug and then pulled her toward the sofa.

"Sit with me," he urged as he gathered up the letters and tapes and laid them aside.

Kristie sat. Scott pulled a couple of tissues from

a nearby box and handed them to her, then pretended to ignore her as she wiped her eyes and blew her nose.

"Now. Down to business," he said, and took out a notebook.

Kristie sat with her hands folded in her lap, unable to meet Scott's gaze.

"Which came first...a letter or a phone call?"

"Letters...maybe four or five before I first heard his voice. I've marked the tapes by date. The letters are postmarked so you can see the order in which they came, also."

"Very good," he said, and sorted through the letters until he found the first one. He slid it from the envelope and began to read.

"'I know you're alone. A beautiful woman like you should not be alone.'"

Scott looked at the drawn expression on her face and knew she was fighting back a fresh set of tears. He'd worked hundreds of cases during his years with the Chicago P.D., but this was the first time one had struck this close to home. He hated the fear in her eyes and wanted to take it away. He winked at her and then grinned.

"Well, now...see, he's already given away a facet of his personality."

Kristie leaned forward in disbelief. "Like what?"

"He said you are beautiful. Now we know he has good taste." She rolled her eyes and fell backward against the sofa.

"For Pete's sake, Scott! I thought you were serious."

Without thinking, he leaned forward and kissed her full on the mouth.

It was hard to say who was more surprised, him or her. When he pulled away, he slid the letter back into the envelope before he spoke.

"Don't expect me to apologize. I've been wanting to do that ever since I saw you in your office."

Kristie's heart fluttered softly and then settled into a normal rhythm as she stood abruptly.

"I'll get a bag for that stuff."

Scott watched her walk out of the room and closed his eyes on a sigh. *What in hell had he been thinking?* He looked up when he heard her returning.

"I think this is big enough for the letters, but I didn't have one big enough to hold your ego," she said, dropping a clear plastic bag into his lap.

Scott felt heat on his cheeks and knew that his face was red. He picked up the bag, dropped the letters and tapes inside and then sealed it up.

"Just for the record, I suppose I had that coming. But I've never been able to see you cry, and you know it. Kissing you was just the first thing that came to mind. However, since it so obviously disagreed with you, rest assured it won't happen again." Then he dangled the bag in front of her. "I'll take these to forensics. Maybe they can get some evidence from them."

"I don't see how," Kristie said. "I've handled them. You've handled them. God knows how many other people who work for the U.S. postal system have handled them, too."

"How do you seal your letters?" he asked.

"Why...I lick them and— Oh."

"DNA can be retrieved from saliva and thanks to the self-stick stamps, if we're lucky, we might even get a fingerprint off the underside of one. It's a place to start, okay?"

"Wow! I had no idea."

"Kristie Ann, is there anyone...anyone at all who you might suspect?"

Her shoulders slumped. "No. Not a soul. I haven't had a serious relationship in ages and especially one that went bust. There's no one I know who could be holding a grudge against me. As for strangers, I've noticed no one."

"What about people you do know?"

"What do you mean?"

"Is there someone who is overly friendly with you. Maybe someone who's asked you out and you refused? Think hard. Maybe at the cleaner's where you take your clothes...or the garage where you park your car? It could be someone who means nothing to you other than the person who regularly takes your money for a service. Do you see what I mean?"

"Yes, I do, but honestly, Scott, I've been going over this in my mind for weeks. I can't think of anyone."

He handed her his card and then impulsively took it back and wrote a second phone number on the back before laying it in her hands.

"This is the number at the department where I can be reached and the one on the back is my home phone. Call me anytime...day or night if you're afraid, or lonesome, or if you think of something you think might help."

She curled her fingers around the card as if it was her lifeline to sanity.

"Yes, all right, and thank you," she added.

"You can thank me after we catch the bastard," he said, and picked up his coat from the back of the sofa. "I'm going straight to the crime lab. If we get a hit on anything, I'll let you know."

He paused. "Are you going to be all right?"

She straightened her shoulders and then nodded. "Of course, but I suppose you should know that I don't think I'm going to go back to work for a few days. At least not until after the new year."

"Good idea," Scott said. "And remember...be careful who you let into your apartment."

"I always am."

"Right."

She opened the door for him and then stepped back, waiting for him to exit.

Scott frowned. He didn't want to leave her, but he had no choice.

"Remember what I said...call me anytime."

"Yes, I will."

He started to touch her in passing and then remembered how ticked off she'd been about the kiss and decided against it. He was all the way into the hall and heading for the elevator when Kristie called out to him.

"Scott."

He pivoted sharply. "Yes?"

"Just for the record, I wasn't disgusted by your kiss and it didn't disagree with me. However, rest assured that I will be properly pissed if it never happens again."

Before he could answer, she shut and locked the

door. He stood there in shock, absorbing the promise of what might come, and as he did, a silly grin began to spread across his face.

Properly pissed. He hadn't heard that expression since he'd left Texas and it made him suddenly homesick for all the things of his youth, including Kristie Ann.

Meanwhile, Kristie was heading for the phone to call her office. Michael Shay answered.

"Shay, Tremaine and Weller."

"Mr. Shay, this is Kristie."

The concern in his voice was obvious. "Are you all right?"

"Yes, sir, but I have a favor to ask."

"Anything," he said.

"I'd like to take a few days off...maybe until after New Year's? I don't want to drag this awful thing into your business."

"It isn't about that at all," Michael said. "Our concern is your safety. Just give us a call from time to time to let us know you're okay."

"Yes, sir, and thanks so much."

As soon as he had disconnected, Kristie knew there was one more call she had to make. She dialed again, only this call would be long distance. The phone rang once, twice, then three times, and just as she thought the answering machine was going to come on, she heard her mother's breathless voice.

"Hello."

"Mama, it's me, Kristie."

The lilt in Shelly Samuels's voice made Kristie smile.

"Kristie Ann! I'm so glad you called. You won't guess what."

"Probably not," Kristie said. "What's up?"

"Loretta and Billy had their baby last night! It's a boy. They named him Daniel Elliot."

Kristie clutched the receiver and tried not to cry. Her little sister had just become a mother and she was half a country away trying not to get herself killed. Besides that, she was a far cry from having a family of her own.

"That's wonderful...and unexpected. I was just talking to them yesterday at your house."

"Yes, I know," Shelly said. "Christmas just wasn't the same without you. Try to get some time off and come home for Easter, why don't you?"

"Yes, Mama, I'll try," she said.

"Are you calling from work?"

"No. I'm home."

The tone of Shelly's voice shifted. "Are you sick?"

Kristie laughed and then bit the inside of her lip as tears spilled down her cheeks.

"No, Mama. I'm fine. I just wanted to hear your voice again."

"Then why are you home?"

"Oh...uh, I spilled something on my dress at work and came home to change."

"That's too bad. I hope it didn't ruin your outfit."

"No, it will be fine."

"That's good. Oh, honey, if you could only see that little boy. It looks like he's going to have red hair...just like yours, and he's got the longest fingers and feet. Loretta says he's going to be tall like your daddy."

Kristie swallowed past a lump in her throat. "How is Daddy?"

"Wild about the baby. He went out and bought the cutest little pair of cowboy boots and the tiniest Stetson I've ever seen."

"That's great," Kristie said. "Give Loretta my love and tell her I'll send a gift."

"Okay, sweetheart. Well, I've got to go. I don't want to miss visiting hours at the hospital. Let us know about Easter when you can."

"Yes, I will...and, Mama?"

"What, honey?"

"I love you."

"I love you, too, Kristie Ann. Take care."

The line went dead in Kristie's ear. She hung up the receiver then sat within the silence of her apartment, staring at the loneliness that had become her life.

It was the middle of the afternoon and Kristie had just finished running the vacuum cleaner when she heard a knock on her door. She stood for a moment, wondering if she should even answer it. And then a second knock came, along with the sound of a woman's voice, and she relaxed. It sounded like Mrs. Petrowski from upstairs. When she looked through the peephole, her suspicions were confirmed. She opened the door with a smile.

"Mrs. Petrowski. How nice to see you."

Marjorie Petrowski gave her blue-gray hair a firm pat and swished inside before Kristie had a chance to invite her. Kristie stifled a grin.

"Do come in," she said, then added, "Have a seat."

But neither had been necessary since Marjorie was already in and seated.

"I was worried about you, dear," Marjorie said. "Are you ill?"

"No, ma'am. Why would you think that?"

"Because you're home and it's a workday. You're never home in the middle of the day. I know because I pay attention to what goes on where I live."

"Oh...yes, well I'm fine, but thank you for asking. Actually, I just decided to take a few days off. I'll be going back the day after New Year's."

Marjorie nodded forcefully. "Good idea. I always say that everyone deserves a breather now and then."

"May I offer you something to drink? Maybe coffee or hot chocolate. It's pretty chilly outside today."

"No, dear, but thank you just the same." Then she gestured toward the heavy jogging suit she was wearing. "As you can see, I'm about to do my daily walk. Do you exercise?"

"Not as religiously as you, I'm afraid."

Marjorie leaned forward and patted Kristie on the hand. "You should try it sometime. It's quite invigorating." Then she stood abruptly. "I must be off. I have a dinner engagement this evening and don't want to miss my appointment with the hairstylist."

"Who do you see?" Kristie asked.

Marjorie waved her hand vaguely. "I don't frequent any particular salon." On her way to the door, she suddenly stopped and turned. "I just had the most marvelous idea. While you're off, you must come and have lunch with me sometime. I'm quite a good cook, you know. Just let me know if you have any dietary restrictions."

Kristie wasn't sure whether she wanted to get too chummy with Marjorie. Even though she was always nice, she was a bit overbearing.

"Thanks so much for the invitation. I'll have to let you know later."

Marjorie frowned. "You don't date much, do you?"

Kristie was a bit taken aback by the change in conversation.

"I'm particular, that's all."

Marjorie stared for a moment, then smiled.

"That's smart. Don't rush into things, I always say. Take care and I'll give you a call."

Smiling politely, Kristie locked the door behind her neighbor and then went back to the bedroom to put away the vacuum.

The digital clock on his nightstand clicked over to 12:00 a.m. but Andrew McMartin was a long way from sleep. The fire in his belly burned slow but steady. She'd finally contacted the police. He'd been expecting it for weeks. In fact, he'd been slightly surprised that she'd waited so long. Most of the time they panicked immediately. He liked it when they freaked. It was part of his high.

He rolled over and sat up on the side of the bed, reached for the shot glass of whiskey he'd poured a while back and downed it in one gulp. It was part of the ritual—feeling the heat of the liquor sliding down his throat and into his belly—picturing the blood in his veins getting thinner—flowing faster.

His nostrils flared as he sat the glass down with a thump and reached for the phone. He needed a fix.

The shrill and unexpected ring of the phone beside her bed yanked Kristie out of a deep, dreamless sleep. She answered without thinking, her fingers curling around the receiver as she dragged it to her ear.

"Hello?"

He heard the quiver of uncertainty in her voice and started to smile.

"Kristie, darling…you've been a very bad girl."

Immediately, Kristie threw back the covers and leaped out of bed. The intrusion of just his voice within the sanctity of her bedroom made talking to him an obscenity.

"Leave me alone," Kristie said, and slammed down the receiver.

Almost immediately, the phone rang again. She refused to answer, instead, counting the rings until the answering machine would pick up. If he wanted to talk, he could talk to himself. She wasn't having any of it, but she still wanted to hear. She ran from the room and down the hall into the living room just as she heard the machine pick up.

"Now, Kristie, surely your mother taught you better manners than that?"

Her stomach lurched. The drawl in his voice was too intimate. So strong was his presence that it was almost as if they were standing face-to-face.

"You called the police, didn't you?"

She gasped. How had he known?

"Now you've muddied the waters, my darling, and you're going to have to pay. You belong to me, beautiful lady…only me. And if I can't have you, nobody will."

The click sounded, indicating he'd ended the call.

Kristie stood within the silence of the room, her heart pounding, her body trembling from shock. Her first instinct was to run to the phone and call Scott, but reason told her there was nothing he could do. Not at this time of night and maybe not at all. It was a phone call and it was over. There was no way to trace it and nothing to indicate who it was. Just the blood-chilling sound of a stranger's voice, promising to end her life.

She ran to the front door just to reassure herself that it was firmly locked. The heavy metal of the dead bolt and the chain on the other lock was still in place. She leaned forward, resting her forehead on the solid weight of the door, and wanted to wail. But breaking down would serve no purpose other than to give herself another headache. Besides, it would be even more proof that her stalker was winning—and she would have none of that.

Determined not to lose her faith or her focus, she pushed herself away from the door and strode back through the rooms, taking comfort in the familiarity of the shadows. This was her sanctuary and Scott would find out who was terrorizing her. She knew, because he'd promised, and for now, it had to be enough.

Chapter 3

It was five minutes after 8:00 a.m. when Kristie finally woke up. Her disbelief that she'd overslept was soon gone when she remembered that she wasn't going to work. Not today or tomorrow, and here in Chicago, maybe never again. Somewhere around three this morning, she'd made up her mind that if this stalker wasn't found soon, she was going home—back to Texas. She didn't want to die before she'd had a chance to live. Besides, she was an aunt now. She had familial responsibilities that meant more to her than any hotshot job in the big city.

She rolled over and sat on the side of the bed, contemplating her next step. She had to call Scott. That was a given. But that meant he would come over, and she needed to have her game face on before she faced him again. That parting shot she'd given him yesterday had come out of her mouth before she'd thought and while it was a bit embarrassing, it was still the truth. Like it or not, there was still chemistry between them.

She dragged herself to the bathroom, exiting a short while later with a better attitude and freshly washed hair. She was going shopping for a baby gift after Scott came and went. There was a brand-new baby named Daniel back in Midland, and she wanted him to know that, from the very first day, she considered him special.

Once she had dressed and had her first cup of coffee, she found Scott's card and gave him a call, but the man who answered wasn't Scott.

"Chicago P.D."

The unfamiliar voice took her aback. It took her a moment to change what she'd been going to say.

"Uh...may I speak to Detective Wade?"

"Sorry, ma'am, he's not in. Want to leave a message?"

This wasn't what she had expected. If she left a message, she would have to wait for him to return the call, which meant shopping for her new nephew would have to wait.

"Yes, I guess so," she said. "Just tell him that Kristie Samuels called. Tell him I got another call last night. He'll know what it means."

Paul Tucker frowned. "Are you the lady with the stalker?"

Kristie was surprised that he knew. "Um, yes, I am."

"I'm his partner. Does he have your number?"

"Yes."

"Then hang tight, Miss Samuels. I'll page Scott and have him call you right back, okay?"

"Yes, thank you," she said. As she hung up, she

realized she'd misjudged the police by not contacting them sooner.

She stood by the phone for a moment, thinking that she would soon hear Scott's voice. It bothered her a little that she was making too much of his reappearance in her life but she told herself it meant nothing. She was probably transferring her fear over what had been happening to some sort of fixation on Scott, simply because they had a past. Satisfied that she'd figured out what was wrong with her, she went to make some toast.

She had just spread peanut butter on her first slice of toast and taken a bite when the telephone rang.

"Oh, great," she muttered, and reached for the phone while trying to swallow. "Hello?"

Scott frowned. "Kristie...are you all right?"

"Mmm," she said, still trying to get the peanut butter off the roof of her mouth. "Wait a minute," she managed to mumble, then took a sip of coffee to help wash it down. "Okay...I'm fine, now. Thanks for waiting."

"What were you doing?" he asked.

"Eating peanut butter and toast. It stuck to the roof of my mouth."

Scott sighed. After the message he'd just received, he'd imagined something dire.

"I hear you got another call."

Kristie sighed. "Yes. Last night just after midnight."

"What did he say?"

"He knows I called the police. It made him angry. He said if he couldn't have me then he'd make sure no one else did."

Scott's heart sank as he thought back over the

tapes that he'd listened to at the office, as well as the text of the letters she'd received.

"Has he ever threatened you physically before?"

"No."

"Damn," he said, more to himself than to her. "I'm not far from your place. I'll be there soon."

"Want some breakfast?" she asked, and could tell from the sudden silence that she'd taken him aback.

"Well...yeah. That would be good."

"How do you like your eggs?"

"Got any picante sauce?"

She chuckled. "Scott, I was born and raised in Texas. What do you think?"

The sound of her laughter went all the way to his heart, and he found himself smiling.

"Right. Sorry, what was I thinking?"

"So...the eggs?"

"Well-done and scrambled."

"See you soon," she said, and by the time she hung up, found herself thinking that the stalker would probably go ballistic if he knew she used to make love on a regular basis with the cop who was working her case.

Scott found himself moving rapidly as he got out of his car and headed toward Kristie's apartment building. He didn't bother to lie to himself as to the urgency of his movements. It wasn't just about the most recent threat to Kristie's life. It was because he wanted to see her—to find out if yesterday the pull between them had been more about surprise at seeing one another again.

Ignoring the elevator, he headed for the stairwell

and started up the stairs, taking them two at a time. Just as he came upon the third-floor landing, the exit door opened and a tall, thin man in drab olive coveralls stepped through.

He saw Scott almost at the same time Scott saw him and stopped abruptly before they collided. Scott noticed the coveralls the man was wearing, as well as the toolbox, and took him to be the maintenance man for the building.

"How are you doing?" Scott asked, more in the way of a greeting than an actual question, but the man obviously wasn't in the mood to visit.

He gave Scott a nervous look and then moved past him, the toolbox bumping against his leg as he scurried away.

Scott paused on the landing, curiously watching the man's descent. He didn't know why, but there was something in his behavior that set off all sorts of alarms. He made a mental note to ask the building superintendent about him later and then continued on his way up to Kristie's apartment. A couple of minutes later he was knocking on her door. When she opened it with a smile of welcome, one question he'd been asking himself was just answered. It would be too damned easy to fall in love with Kristie all over again.

"You made good time," Kristie said. "Come in."

Scott shed his coat and laid it on a nearby chair as he followed her into the living room.

"Your breakfast is ready."

"I want to hear the tape."

"But your eggs will get cold," she said.

Scott frowned. "They'll reheat, Kristie Ann. The tape. Please."

Kristie sighed and pointed toward the answering machine on the sideboard.

"It's on that tape," she said. "It's a new tape and the message is the only one on it. Feel free to take it with you when you go. I have another I can put in."

Scott knew that matter-of-fact manner in which she was behaving was to cover up. She was trying to hide her true feelings, but it wasn't working. At least not for him. He knew her too well.

He looked at her once and then punched the play button. Within seconds the ugly threats of Kristie's stalker filled the room. Scott listened, his mouth a thin, grim line. When the call ended, he popped the tape from the machine, dropped it into a small bag and then put it in his pocket. When he turned toward Kristie, it was as if the call had never happened.

"About those eggs..."

Kristie relaxed. At least Scott wasn't going to quiz her about things she couldn't answer.

"In the kitchen, along with that picante sauce you asked for."

Scott slid a hand across her shoulders and gave her a quick hug.

"Did you get any sleep?"

Kristie shrugged. "Enough. Do you still drink your coffee black?"

Scott took her by the arms and turned her around, making her face him.

"Kristie."

"What?"

"Talk to me."

Kristie's frustration over the situation suddenly boiled over.

"And say what, Scott? That I'm afraid to go to work? That I close my eyes at night and wonder if I'll wake up to live another day? I talked to my mother last night. Loretta and her husband recently became parents. They have a son. They have a son and each other and I have a job in a city that is hundreds of miles away from everyone I love and someone has decided I don't deserve to live. Is that what you want to hear?"

"Yes."

She glared.

He gave her back look for silent look, then leaned down and kissed her.

The shock of what he'd done passed almost immediately as Kristie melted beneath the touch. It was so familiar and yet different. She'd known Scott the boy, but not Scott the man. Even as she was telling herself to slow down, she wrapped her arms around his neck and leaned into his embrace.

It took everything Scott had to pull back when his heart was telling him to take everything she would give him and beg for more.

"Oh, honey...that felt so good," Scott whispered, and pulled Kristie close, cupping the back of her head as she rested her cheek against his chest.

"To me, too," Kristie said, then looked up at him. "What are we doing here, Scott? We can't go back to what we had. We were kids."

"Old enough to make love," he said softly.

She sighed. "No we weren't. We weren't old enough, but we did it."

"And it was so good between us. You have to give me that much."

She hesitated, then nodded. "Yes, I'll give you that. It was just about perfect."

Scott heard the hesitancy in her voice and frowned, then reminded himself she had a lot more on her mind besides renewing an old love. And so should he.

"About those eggs?" he said.

Kristie wanted to say more but held her tongue. Like Scott, she was confused as to her priorities. She should be out of her mind with fear that she was the victim of a stalker, but ever since he'd walked into her office, all she'd been able to think about was the past that they'd shared.

A few minutes later Scott was sitting at the table, pouring hot picante sauce over his scrambled eggs and sausage as Kristie slid a plate of hot buttered toast in front of him.

"This smells fantastic," Scott said, and then took a big bite, chewed and swallowed then rolled his eyes in appreciation. "Oh, man…talk about a little taste of home and heaven."

Kristie grinned. "Well, good grief, Scott. It's only scrambled eggs."

"Honey, do you remember the time I cooked for us?"

Kristie frowned, thinking back over the years. Then her expression lit.

"Are you talking about the night that your folks drove to Odessa to the Gatlin Brothers concert and gave us free run of the backyard grill?"

He grinned and nodded as he took another bite.

"I remember that you *tried* to cook."

"Exactly," Scott said. "My point is, I haven't gotten any better. I eat out a lot."

"Then I'm glad you're enjoying your food," Kristie said.

Scott paused, a forkful of eggs and sausage halfway to his mouth.

"I'm enjoying a whole lot more than your cooking," he said softly.

Kristie looked at him and then sighed. "When this is over—this stalker thing, I mean. What happens then?"

"What do you want to happen, Kristie Ann?"

"What do you want?" she countered.

"You. I want to call you and to take you out to dinner. I want to laugh with you and to make love to you. I can't make up for the years we lost, but we can start from now and see where it goes."

Kristie felt light, as if she'd suddenly gone weightless. It was more than she'd hoped for.

"If you're going to do all of that, then you need to finish your breakfast and go catch my bad guy."

Scott grinned. "Does that mean I've got a chance?"

"Want some more coffee?"

"I already told you what I want," Scott said, and then finished off his eggs and sausage.

He was swallowing his last sip of coffee when his cell phone rang. He took it out of his pocket, glanced at the Caller ID and frowned.

"This is Wade," he said as he answered.

"This is Leslie, from the lab."

"What do you have for me?" Scott asked.

"We got DNA off the envelope, just as you expected. Give me a suspect and I'll be able to tell you yea or nay."

Scott frowned. Therein lay there problem. At the present time, there were no suspects.

"What about fingerprints?" he asked.

"Oh...there were prints all over the envelopes, as we expected, and you were right on the money about the stamps. We got three partials from underneath three different stamps. Two partial forefingers, one partial thumbprint."

"I'm not liking the sounds of this. Do we have enough of a partial to make an identification?"

"It's not likely, but we're going to give it a shot."

"Damn," Scott muttered. "Thanks for letting me know, and if you come up with something definite, give me a call immediately. We're working against time here."

"You know it," she said.

Scott hung up.

Kristie could tell by the look on his face that the call hadn't been good news.

"Bad news?" she asked.

"Not exactly," he said. "We got DNA off the envelopes, but unfortunately we have no suspect to match it to. There were three partial prints from under the stamps, but we don't know if there was enough to make a match."

Kristie felt as if she'd been kicked in the gut. All the previous joy she'd been feeling was gone and she was back to square one.

"So what now?" she asked.

Scott dropped his phone back into his pocket.

"You don't worry about it. You're going to have to trust me on this. Can you do that, honey?"

Kristie clutched her fists to her stomach. "I don't have any other choice."

"That's not true, Kristie. You always have choices."

Kristie looked at him then, at the cool, confident expression on his face and the light in his eyes.

"You're right, and I'm sorry. I don't mean to sound so pathetic. I do trust you, Scott, and I'm thankful for your presence."

"That's what I wanted to hear." Then he took her by the hand and tugged until they were standing face-to-face. "Thanks for breakfast."

"You're welcome."

Scott couldn't quit looking at her—so familiar, and yet a stranger.

"You are so beautiful," he said softly, tracing the soft curves of her cheeks with his thumbs, then tangling his fingers in the thickness of her hair. The color always made him think it would be hot to the touch, and yet he never ceased to be amazed at the cool, silken texture, instead.

Kristie smiled. "You always did talk pretty, Scotty."

He smiled, satisfied for now to let her change the subject. "What will it get me?"

"For now…a goodbye kiss."

"I'll take it," Scott said, and took not only Kristie's kiss, but her breath, as well.

"I'll call," he said as he headed toward the door moments later. "Stay safe for me, honey."

"I thought about going shopping for a baby present for Loretta and Billy's baby."

Scott frowned and then made himself relax as he picked up his coat and put it on.

"Yeah, well, it should probably be all right, but take a cab, okay, and stay out of the parking garage until this is over. The less you're alone in places like that, the safer you'll be."

"Yes, I will."

"And call me when you get back in your apartment so I'll know you're okay."

She smiled. "I'll do that, too."

He opened the door and stepped into the hall. Kristie followed him, reluctant to say goodbye. As she did, they both heard someone running down the stairwell. Instinctively, Kristie stepped toward the door of her apartment as Scott's hand slid beneath his coat to his shoulder holster and the gun within. Moments later, the door flew back and Marjorie came out at a jog.

Immediately, Kristie relaxed, although Scott was still uneasy.

Marjorie saw them standing in the hallway and smiled as she jogged past.

"Morning," she said to Kristie, while eyeing Scott curiously as she jogged in place. "Aren't you going to introduce me?"

Kristie smiled. Subtlety, it seemed, was not one of Marjorie's virtues.

"Marjorie Petrowski, this is my friend, Scott Wade. Scott, this is Marjorie. She lives on the floor above me and is quite the avid athlete."

Scott let his hand fall to his side. "It's a pleasure," he said, and tried not to grin at the blue-gray curls bouncing against her forehead as she jogged in place.

"Indeed," she said.

"On your way outside for your morning run?" Kristie asked.

"Not today, my dear. It's threatening rain and I just got my hair done yesterday. I'm taking my morning constitutional indoors this morning. See you later," she said, and started off down the hall at a brisk stride, aiming for the other stairwell at the far end of the hall.

"Quite a woman," Scott said.

"I guess," Kristie said. "I don't know her well, but she seems nice."

"Okay, honey, I'm out of here. Don't forget to call me when you get home."

"Yes, all right," Kristie said, and stood in the hall, watching until Scott got on the elevator.

As the doors closed Kristie realized she was standing in the hallway alone. There was a thump at the far end of the hallway where Marjorie had disappeared. She turned to look, half expecting to see Marjorie on a return jog, and instead saw a tall, thin man carrying a toolbox. Almost immediately she recognized him as the maintenance man. For a moment they stared at each other—Kristie at one end of the hall, the maintenance man at the other.

He started toward her, his toolbox bumping against his leg. Suddenly, Kristie realized that she didn't really know him. She began backing toward her doorway and then abruptly turned and ran into her apartment, slamming and locking the door behind her.

She stood with her ear to the door, her heart pounding as she waited for him to pass by. Moments later she heard the faint clank of metal against metal and knew he was coming closer. She looked out the peephole just in time to see him pass by and then he was gone.

Determined not to let that ruin her shopping trip, she hurried to her bedroom to change clothes. The stores would be crowded with after Christmas shoppers but there was nothing to be done for the fact. She wanted to get the baby's gift in the mail as soon as possible.

As she was changing, Scott was downstairs, talking to the building superintendent.

"The maintenance man," Scott asked. "How long has he been with you?"

"Almost a year. He's a good worker. Never late and knows his stuff."

"Does he live on the premises?" Scott asked.

"No, why?"

"Just checking," Scott asked, then started to leave when he noticed a huge stack of pornographic magazines on the floor by the sofa. "Do a lot of reading?" he asked.

The super caught the drift of Scott's gaze and grinned.

"Oh, yeah...I've got a real intellectual mind."

Scott looked at him again, seeing the grease spots on the belly of his shirt, the stub of an unlit cigar hanging from the corner of his mouth and the dissolute expression in his eyes.

"How do you spell your name?" he asked abruptly.

The smile froze on the man's face. He blinked twice, as if trying to come to terms with the question, and then yanked the cigar from his mouth.

"That's Abrams. Pete Abrams. A-b-r-a-m-s."

Scott wrote it down without speaking, gave the man another long, studied look and then left.

Pete Abrams shuddered slightly as he shut the door, then jammed the cigar back into his mouth. To hell with cops. Who needed them?

Chapter 4

The shopping bags in Kristie's arms were getting heavy as she came out of the last store. It had been impossible for her to stop at just one gift for the baby and the longer she'd looked, the more she'd bought. It was only after she realized she'd bought more than she could comfortably carry that she'd decided it was time to go home.

As she came out to the street, the rain that Marjorie had warned about was just starting to fall. Kristie dashed toward the curb to hail a cab. Luckily, one was just unloading a passenger in front of the department store. She ducked into the cab, her lap full of shopping bags, and leaned back against the seat, gave the driver her address, then breathed a slow sigh of relief. By the time the cab arrived at her apartment building, the rain was coming down in sheets.

"Driver, would you please pull into the parking garage. I'll take the elevator up from there."

"Yes, ma'am," he said, and accelerated past the front door to the parking area a hundred yards ahead.

He turned right and took the tunnel into the garage. As he did, the cessation of rain upon the cab was abrupt and welcoming.

"There," Kristie said, pointing toward a single elevator to their left. "I'll get out here, and thank you," she added as she paid him and gathered up her bags.

He drove away, leaving her to make her way to the elevator on her own.

Kristie punched the button on the wall and glanced back toward the street as she waited for the elevator car to arrive. She knew it was deceiving, but from where she was standing, the rain looked solid. Visibility was nil beyond the entrance to the garage. As she stared into the downpour, she thought she saw someone step out from the street, start into the garage, then stop abruptly.

At that moment she remembered Scott's warning not to drive because there would be an inevitable time when she'd be alone in the garage. She hadn't driven, but she'd still wound up in the parking garage, and she was still alone. A little nervous, she punched the up button again, although she knew from experience that the car would not arrive any sooner. When she turned around to look back at the street, the figure that she'd seen was gone.

Breathing a quick sigh of relief, she readjusted the bags she was holding and settled down to wait. As she did, one car came down from one of the upper levels and took the exit out onto the street. A short while later a second car did the same, and still she waited. Just as she was about to decide that the elevator was out of order, the doors opened and two men exited. She recognized them as residents in the building and nodded cordially as she entered the car. She punched the fifth-floor button, then braced herself against the back wall as the car jerked, then started its ascent.

She was picturing the look on her sister's face upon opening the baby gifts and wishing she could present them in person when the car suddenly shuddered to a halt. Thinking that had been a shorter ride than normal, she waited for the door to open. When it did not, she looked up at the number display above the door and frowned. The display was off. She knew it wasn't a power failure, because the light was still on in the car. She had no sooner thought it when the car suddenly went dark.

"Oh, no," she muttered. Dropping her packages where she stood, she felt her way toward the floor panel and used the flat of her hand to push at the buttons in the hope that one of them would be the alarm. But nothing sounded.

It wasn't the first time this had happened in the building, but it was the first time Kristie had been involved. Feeling her way toward the doors, she began pounding on them with her fists and yelling as loudly as she could.

"Help!" she yelled, and pounded on the door of the car. "Somebody help me."

"What's wrong, Kristie Ann? Are you beginning to feel a little trapped?"

Kristie froze. She knew the voice. She'd heard it

before, in the middle of the night, on her phone. She plastered herself against the back wall of the car and willed herself not to scream.

"I'm up here," the voice said.

Although it was pitch-black in the car, she looked up instinctively, remembering the trap door in the ceiling. Fear shot through her body, piercing her like a knife and leaving her feeling helpless and trapped. With nowhere to run and no one to help her, she was at her stalker's mercy.

Suddenly she thought of the cell phone in her purse. She dropped to her knees and began digging through the bags until she found it on the floor beneath the sacks.

Her stalker laughed. "I hear you, Kristie. Are you on your knees? That's good. One should always pray before dying…just in case that fairy story about a heaven is really true."

Kristie's hands were shaking as she finally felt the phone beneath her fingers. She yanked it out, shielded it with her body so he wouldn't see the face when it lit up, and dialed 911, mentally counting the rings until the dispatcher answered.

"Nine-one-one. What is your emergency?" a woman asked.

Kristie's voice was shaking so hard it was all she could do to speak.

"Help! I need help! I'm trapped in the elevator of my apartment and a man who's been stalking me is on top of the car."

"What is the address?" the dispatcher asked.

Kristie blurted out the address and then started to cry.

"Please...please... Oh, God...don't let him get me."

A soft, evil chuckle drifted down to her from above. Then he spoke, his voice little more than a loud whisper.

"Why, Kristie, why did you go and do that? We don't need anyone else for our little party. Besides, it's already too late. I already have you. You're mine. Anytime. Anywhere."

Bile rose in the back of her throat as she crawled on her hands and knees into the opposite corner of the car.

"Ma'am! Ma'am! Are you still with me?"

Kristie put the phone back to her ear. "Yes. I'm here, oh, hurry. Please tell them to hurry."

"There's a patrol car less than two blocks away," the dispatcher said. "Just stay with me. They'll be there in minutes."

"I'm stuck between floors and the power is off."

The dispatcher relayed the information, then got back to Kristie.

"What's your name?" she asked.

"Kristie Samuels. Tell Detective Scott Wade. He knows about the man. He knows I'm being stalked."

Immediately, the dispatcher had another person relay the information to the Chicago P.D. while Kristie waited with one ear tilted toward the ceiling, praying she didn't hear the sound of that panel coming off, praying that her stalker would not suddenly drop into her lap.

There was a loud thump, as if someone had hit the top of the car with a fist, then the voice, taunting her once more.

"Kristie...my Kristie. You had no right to drag someone else into our world. Our relationship was special and now you've ruined it," he said. "You have to be punished."

"You're crazy!" Kristie screamed. "Do you hear me? How can there be an us when I don't even know your name. You're nothing to me but a bad dream. Leave me alone! Just leave me alone."

"Kristie! Is he still on the car, above you?" the dispatcher asked.

"Yes."

"The officers are pulling up in front of your building. They're on the way. They're on the way."

Scott had been worrying about Kristie for more than an hour. Finally he'd gotten tired of waiting for her to call and was on his way to her apartment. Unfortunately, the weather was impeding the flow of traffic and it was getting worse by the minute. He'd expected to hear from her hours ago and had called her apartment three times already, but gotten nothing but the answering machine for his troubles. How long could it take to buy a baby gift?

He was less than five blocks from her apartment when his cell phone rang. Pausing at a red light, he answered absently, but his focus shifted as Kristie's frantic plea for help was relayed to him. At that point, panic set in. It didn't take long for him to realize his promise to protect Kristie might have been futile. He slapped the portable police light onto the dashboard just as the traffic signal turned green, then accelerated through the intersection, trying not to think of the danger she was in.

He reached the building in record time, pulling

up right behind a police cruiser that was skidding to a stop. He got out on the run, flashing his badge at them as rain beat against his face.

"Kristie Samuels! What's her status?" he yelled.

One officer answered as they ran. "She's stuck in the parking garage elevator. The power is off and there's some nut on the roof of the car who's hassling her."

Scott pushed past them and ran into the building. He hit the door to the stairwell with the flat of his hand and bolted up the stairs. Halfway up the first flight, he heard Kristie screaming and his blood ran cold. The two officers were right behind him, their footsteps thundering as the men raced to save her. With the car stuck between floors, they needed to cover all their options, so one of the officers exited on the second floor while Scott and the other one kept going. They went up to the third-floor landing and were about to head up to the fourth when Scott stopped and listened. He could still hear her screaming, but the sound seemed to come from below him now.

"What do you think?" he asked.

The other officer pointed. "I think she's below us."

"Me, too," Scott said. Taking a chance that she was stuck between the second and third floors, they exited the stairwell on the run.

The maintenance man was coming down the hallway.

"The elevator!" Scott yelled. "Which way to the elevator?"

The man pointed behind him and then stepped aside as Scott and the officer ran past. Seconds later, he took off down the hall, running in the opposite direction. Scott didn't see his reaction to their appearance, and at that moment, wouldn't have cared. His focus was on the ear-piercing shrieks coming up the elevator shaft.

He reached the doors and punched the button, but it was obvious that the power was still off.

"Kristie! I'm here!" he shouted. "I'm coming to help."

He thrust his fingers into the crack between the doors and started to pull, but before he could make any headway, the car began to move upward. He banged on the doors and then punched the button, trying desperately to make the car stop, but it moved past the floor and continued to go up.

Panicked, he and the officer dashed back to the stairwell and started up. By the time Scott reached the fifth floor, his heart was hammering against his chest and sweat was running down the middle of his back. He burst into the fifth-floor hallway while the other officer was still negotiating the stairs. He turned a corner and looked for the doors. The car was just coming to a halt. He heard the familiar ping signaling that the elevator car was at this floor. The doors were opening just as he dashed into the small foyer, but when he realized that Kristie was no longer screaming, his heart sank. Was he too late? Had the stalker already done his worst?

"Please, God," Scott muttered as he dashed forward and grabbed at the doors, forcing them open faster than they were meant to go.

To his relief, Kristie was not only alive, but standing in the corner of the car. He started toward her then realized that she didn't even know he was there. Her face was devoid of color, her gaze fixed upon the ceiling of the car and the gaping hole above her head.

Scott saw the screened panel from the ceiling lying on the floor in front of her and immediately pulled his gun. He could only imagine her fear when it had hit the floor of the car, believing that the stalker would follow suit.

Only a second passed before he put himself between her and danger. Moments later, the other officer arrived, took stock of the situation and radioed his partner on the floor below that the stalker had escaped.

"Seal off the building and call for backup," Scott said, holstering his gun as he turned to Kristie. "Honey... Kristie Ann..."

She shuddered and then swayed on her feet.

Scott reached for her. "Kristie...it's over, honey. He's gone."

She looked at him then, her gaze shattered and unfocused.

"It won't ever be over," she mumbled, and then fainted in his arms.

Kristie awakened in her bed and for a moment couldn't remember what had happened or how she'd gotten here. Then suddenly everything came flooding back.

Scott was coming out of the bathroom with a wet washcloth when he saw her eyes opening. Remembering what she'd just gone through, he tossed the washcloth back into the sink and then called out her name, wanting her to know she wasn't alone.

"Kristie."

She gasped, then turned toward the sound of his voice. Within seconds, she was out of the bed and in his arms.

"He was here...in my building...on top of the elevator car. I heard him, laughing, taunting me. Oh, God... Oh, Scott...how did he know I'd be in the elevator? How could he know? Is he following me everywhere I go?"

Scott held her close because it was all he could do. Never had he felt so helpless or so afraid.

"I'm so sorry. I'm so sorry," he kept saying. "Halfway up the stairs I heard you screaming. Dear God, Kristie...I was so afraid I wouldn't get to you in time."

She laid her cheek against the front of his shirt, wrapped her arms around his waist and just held him. There was no way to describe how safe she felt within his arms. She didn't want to ever let him go.

"I'm not safe anywhere anymore," she said. "Oh, God...I don't want to die."

Scott tunneled his fingers through her hair and then tilted her head until they were looking into each other's eyes.

"I won't let that happen," he promised.

"You can't stop it," Kristie moaned. "He knows where I live, where I work, what I'm doing, where I'm going. He's playing with me, Scotty. He's waiting for the moment when it's no longer fun and then he'll kill me. That's what I believe."

"Believe in me, Kristie Ann. I need you to believe that we're going to find him and we're going to put him away for a long, long time. I need you to trust me when I tell you that I won't let you die."

Kristie shuddered, then closed her eyes and leaned forward, resting her forehead against his chest.

Scott's lips thinned into a hard, angry line as he wrapped his arms around her and held her close.

"We're going to make this okay. I don't yet know how, but we will."

He felt her go limp as she stood within the circle of his arms. Silence lengthened between them. Kristie was the first to pull herself away. She looked around the room in some confusion.

"What are you looking for?" Scott asked.

"The baby presents. They were in the elevator with me."

"The officers brought them in for you. They're in the living room."

"Okay. Thanks." She looked at him and sighed. "I'm sorry. That must seem like such an inconsequential thing to worry about after what just happened."

"You don't apologize for anything," he said.

She shuddered, then straightened. "I'm suddenly so cold," she said. "I think I'll make some coffee. Want some?"

"Yes, but let me do it," he said.

She looked at him and managed a wan smile.

"Your coffee tastes like mud."

"Well, I told you I couldn't cook, but with that much caffeine, I damn sure don't go to sleep on the job."

"I'll make the coffee. You can watch," Kristie said.

"Deal," Scott said, and put his arm around her as they walked out of the room.

But the good mood lasted only until they walked into her kitchen.

There, written in red on the door of the refrigerator were the words You Can Run But You Can't Hide.

Her heart stopped and then resumed its beat in a rapid and irregular rhythm. He'd been inside her home. He'd touched her things. She felt as violated by the message as if he'd put himself inside her body. She covered her face with her hands.

Scott grabbed her and pulled her out of the room as he took his phone from his pocket.

"This is Wade. I need a forensic team sent to the Mercury apartment building, Apartment 520—and make it fast." Then he pulled her hands from her face and turned her around to face him.

"Look at me."

When she didn't respond, he grabbed her by the shoulders.

"Look at me, damn it."

She lifted her head. The unfocused look in her eyes said it all—it was only a matter of time.

"You're coming home with me," Scott said. "You'll be safe there. He doesn't know anything about me...about us. He won't know where you are and it will buy us some time."

Kristie's gaze wavered as Scott's face came into focus.

"Home with you?"

"Yes, baby...home with me. Now go pack some things. We'll leave as soon as the forensic team shows."

* * *

Scott unlocked the door to his apartment and then stepped aside for Kristie to enter.

"Home sweet home," he said as he walked in behind her and then shut and locked the door.

Gauging the degree of her lingering shock, he decided that a stiff drink and a long nap were in order. But getting her to agree to either was going to be tricky. The Kristie he'd known from before hated alcohol in any form. He set her bag down on the floor and then gently turned her around and helped her off with her coat.

She acquiesced without comment, and when he led her to the sofa, she sat with a plop, as if the bones in her legs had suddenly turned to mush.

Scott took off his coat and tossed it on the back of a chair before running his hands through his hair in frustration. He needed to call in to headquarters, but he hated to leave her alone. He looked at her again, seeing the muscle jerking in her jaw, and figured she was clenching her teeth to keep from crying.

Impulsively he strode to a nearby cabinet, opened the doors and poured some bourbon into a shot glass.

"Drink this," he said, and thrust it into her hands.

Kristie blinked slowly, then realized what he'd handed her.

"I don't like whiskey."

"I know, but drink it anyway."

She downed it as if it were medicine, shuddering as it slid down her throat.

Scott knelt at her feet and began to remove her shoes.

Kristie shuddered again as he slid his arms beneath her and laid her in a prone position on the cushions.

"Are you going to seduce me?" she asked, and then laughed.

To Scott, it sounded more like a sob and he wanted to sit down and cry with her.

"Not right now," he said, pulling the afghan from the back of the sofa to lay over her. "I've got to call my lieutenant. Close your eyes. I won't be far."

Kristie looked up at him, studying the steady gaze and the firm jut of his chin, and knew he meant what he said.

"Okay." She dutifully closed her eyes.

Scott watched her just long enough to see tears seep from the corners of both eyes before exiting the room to make his call.

Kristie heard the angry stride of his footsteps as he left the room, then the low murmur of his voice from another room. Secure in the knowledge that now she was as safe from the stalker as she would ever be, she let herself relax. Within moments, she was asleep.

The police were everywhere, banging on doors in the apartment building, questioning everyone in residence. McMartin had seen them drive up. But they could look forever and never find him—not in a million years. It hadn't been easy getting out of the elevator shaft ahead of the police, but he'd done it. He still couldn't believe his luck when he'd seen Kristie standing alone in the parking garage.

For a moment he'd thought about grabbing her there, but the chance of being discovered before he'd had time to enjoy her had been too great. Almost immediately, he'd realized that his chance to make contact with her again would have to be the elevator, which he knew how to disable. It had been a race to get back into the building and to find just the right moment to hop on the car. It was dangerous as hell, but something he and his friends had often done when they had been teenagers. The high for him had come when the power had gone off and he'd heard the fear in her voice. He was still rocking from the adrenaline surge.

Of course, there had been that brief moment of insanity when he'd considered jumping down into the car with her. She wouldn't have been able to see him and he wanted to put his hands on her, to see if her skin was as soft as it appeared, and how quickly her flesh would yield to his knife. But reason had overcome the urge and he'd escaped from the shaft just ahead of the arrival of the police.

The rain had stopped and he was back on the streets and walking briskly while trying not to strut. Just to prove to himself that he was invincible, he found a pay phone, stepped into the booth and dropped in the necessary coins.

He waited in anticipation, expecting to hear Kristie's voice or at least her answering machine. But when the phone rang and rang without an answer from either, he hung up in frustration. So she'd turned off the machine. Picturing her holed up in her apartment alone and frightened was enough for now. He'd pay her a visit later, when he was certain there were no police around. Maybe tonight was the night he would finish what he'd started. He thrust his hands into his pockets and pulled the collar of his coat up around his ears as he exited the booth. A coffee shop across the street beckoned him with the enticing scents of freshly brewed coffee. The thought of a cappuccino and some biscotti sounded good, especially after the strenuous day that he'd had.

He darted across the street, dodging a pair of cabs that seemed hell-bent on racing to the next red light, then winced as water lapped at the tops of his shoes as he stepped into a puddle at the curb. The thought of biscotti was making his mouth water as he moved toward the coffee shop. A young couple was exiting as he reached the door. The woman smiled at him. He looked at her mouth as he smiled back, wondering if she was a screamer, or if she was one of the women who froze from fear. The man with her nodded cordially, then held the door open for him as he moved inward. He didn't bother to acknowledge the young man's deed as he strode past on his way to the counter.

Chapter 5

Scott had gotten the okay from his lieutenant to finish out the day with Kristie, but tomorrow would be another matter. He was going to have to go back to work and he wasn't certain she was going to be able to stay alone. Whether she knew it or not, she was still in shock. There was a wide-eyed, almost-blank stare in her eyes and a muscle jerking at the side of her mouth that had yet to stop. He was a little uneasy about taking her out of the apartment in full view, but he figured that even if she'd been seen leaving with him, no one would ever imagine that he'd taken her home. It was his ace in the hole to keeping her alive until the stalker was caught.

He'd put her bags in his bedroom and decided he would be sleeping in the extra bedroom, which he used as an office/workout room. There was a twin bed in the corner of the room, though he knew from experience that his feet would hang off the end.

However, discomfort didn't matter as long as he knew Kristie Ann would be safe.

Now here he was, sitting in the living room in a chair opposite the sofa where she was sleeping, studying the shadows on her face and remembering when they were teenagers and the way she'd come undone in his arms when they'd made love.

When her lower lip suddenly trembled, his gut knotted. Damn the sick bastard to hell and back for scaring her this way. He didn't want to think about what he would do when he caught him. For now, making sure she was safe was enough.

And then in the middle of his reverie, he realized that Kristie was awake and staring at him. He jerked, surprised that he'd missed the moment of her awakening and wondering what she'd seen on his face in the unguarded moments. It was when she sat up from the sofa and came toward him that he knew she'd seen all the way to his heart. She held out her hand without speaking and then pulled him to his feet.

"What is it, honey?"

"If I asked you a favor, would you grant it?"

"Anything for you."

"Make love to me, Scotty. Today I thought I would die. Now I need to remember what it feels like to be alive."

The shock of her request ricocheted through his mind as he opened his arms and pulled her into his embrace. There was no thought of refusing her or himself. It wasn't as if he hadn't dreamed of doing this very thing since the moment she'd walked back into this life, but he hadn't planned it quite this way.

He didn't talk, and neither did she as he took her

by the hand and led her to his bedroom. She paused just inside the door long enough to see the king-size four-poster with the plain blue spread, before she started removing her clothes.

At that point time stopped and then began to rewind. It was as if they'd both stepped backward to the innocence of their youth when loving each other came easy and the future extended no further than tomorrow.

Scott undressed right beside her, stopping often just to touch her or to help her off with a particularly stubborn bit of clothing. She accepted his help as if they'd done it countless times before, but when she started toward the bed, he turned and scooped her off her feet, then carried her the rest of the way.

Scott laid her down and then stood for a moment, staring at the lushness of her body, admiring what maturity had done for her.

Kristie was oblivious to the breadth of Scott's shoulders or the hard, flat planes of his belly. She didn't see anything but his face and the hungry look in his eyes. It was a need that mirrored her own. She reached for him then and he came to her, stretching out beside her. Almost frantic, they reached for each other and then suddenly, they paused. For a few silent moments their gazes were locked as they lay face-to-face, without moving, barely breathing. Then Scott touched her hair, letting his hand trail through the soft auburn curls.

"You were always pretty, honey girl...but the years have been good to you. You are so, so beautiful."

The chill that Kristie had lived with for so long began to melt under Scott's tender gaze. She took his hand into hers and pulled it to her lips, gently kissing his palm, then the tips of each finger.

Scott inhaled sharply as he rose up on one elbow. "I'm so sorry that this is happening to you, but I will be forever grateful that you came back into my life. Once we had something really special. I'd like to think that there're enough feelings left between us to build on."

"You want that?" Kristie asked.

Scott sighed. Admitting it left him wide open to hurt, but he didn't have it in him to lie. Not to her. Not ever.

"Yes, sweetheart, I want that very much."

Kristie curled her fingers around his neck and pulled him close—so close that he could feel the warmth of her breath against his cheek.

"So do I, Scotty, but you have to keep me alive to make that happen."

Scott's expression darkened. "Count on it."

"I am," Kristie said. "And I'm counting on you."

The weight of his promise rode heavy on Scott's heart as he took her into his embrace. At first their touches were tentative, as if testing to see if their memories of each other were still the same, but within minutes of the first kiss, their embraces reached fever pitch.

Kristie felt as if her skin was on fire. Every touch of Scott's hand on her body was almost painful, but not nearly as painful as the ever-tightening coil of heat between her legs. She'd forgotten how swiftly he could make her come undone.

She wanted him. Now. Hard and fast. All she had to do was catch her breath long enough to tell him.

"Scott... Scotty..."

The desire in her voice was but a shadow of the need in him and he'd almost waited too long to maintain control. Hurriedly, he raised up and then lowered himself between her legs. Before he could think past the next breath, she had wrapped her legs around him.

"Please, Scotty...in me...now."

He made one tentative move at the apex of her thighs and then slid inside.

Kristie inhaled slowly and closed her eyes, knowing that what she'd been feeling was nothing to what was about to come next. She wanted it—and him—and when he began to move, she knew joy and a wonderful, settling peace.

For Scott, thought ceased. He was operating on instinct, lost in the heat and the motion. Time passed in excruciating sweetness as they made new memories from an old love.

One minute they were locked in a rhythm and the next it was as if they'd come to an impenetrable wall that they couldn't go past. They both hit it at once, shattering every ounce of cognizance they'd had in the blinding heat of climax. A few moments later they lay still and mindless within the warmth of each other's arms, waiting for their breathing to steady and their heartbeats to settle into a normal rhythm.

But as perfect as it was to savor the aftermath of their lovemaking, Scott knew he couldn't stay here forever. Finally, he rolled off of her with a groan, then took her with him. When she would have gotten out of bed, he pulled her against him instead, spooning her against his body and then closing his eyes.

"Don't move," he begged, then pulled covers up over them both. "I just want to hold you."

Kristie sighed, then pulled his arm around her as if it were a blanket and settled. It had been so long and it still felt so right.

Within minutes they'd both fallen asleep. When they woke it was evening. To be exact, it was ten minutes after five on December twenty-seventh.

Kristie opened her eyes, felt the weight of Scott's arm across her belly and smiled as she turned to face him.

"Hey, you," she said softly.

Scott's eyelids fluttered and then opened. He lay for a moment, savoring the sight of this woman in his bed and knew he would be a lucky man if he could wake up like this for the rest of his life.

"You all right?" he asked softly.

She nodded, then smiled.

"We've still got it going on, don't we, honey?"

She sighed and then nodded again.

"Don't you have anything to say?" Scott asked.

"You didn't just get older, you got better?"

He laughed and then raised up and kissed her soundly before rolling out of bed.

"Where are you going?" Kristie asked.

"To shower and then get dressed. I don't know about you, but I'm starving."

Kristie sat up in bed, unmindful of her nudity, and watched him disappear into the bathroom.

"Scott?"

"Yeah?" he yelled back.

"Are we having pizza?"

He stuck his head out of the bathroom and grinned. He knew that some people had a good smoke after sex. They'd always had pizza.

"Don't we always?"

"Thin crust supreme?"

"Is there any other kind?"

"Hurry," Kristie said. "You're making me hungry."

"You want to call it in?" he asked.

She nodded, smiling to herself as he winked at her and then disappeared. Moments later she heard the water running and knew he was taking that shower. She smiled to herself as she got out of bed, then caught herself choking back tears. This had been too sweet—too perfect—and maybe too late. She couldn't quit thinking about all the years she'd spent alone, wondering why she had never been satisfied with the men that she'd met. Now she knew. All this time and it had been Scott who'd still had the claim to her heart. Only a relationship with him wouldn't be as simple this time. A stranger stood between them and happiness and until they found him, her life was in limbo.

But for now, she wouldn't let herself dwell on the hopelessness she was feeling. By some strange twist of fate Scott was back in her life, and she was going to do everything in her power to keep him there.

She found a phone book in the bedside table, looked up the number to her favorite pizza parlor and called in their order. Delivery would take about forty-five minutes. That was just long enough for her to clean up and get dressed. Tonight was going to be all about them. Tomorrow would have to take care of itself.

* * *

It was three o'clock in the morning when McMartin reached Kristie's apartment. His pulse was pounding as adrenaline shot throughout his system. The high he was on was not chemically induced. It came from the power he had over her life. He knew she was afraid. Her screams in the elevator had been a big turn-on as had the fear in her voice when he'd talked to her on the phone. Now the only thing separating them was this door and he was about to make quick work of that.

Glancing up and down the hallway to make certain he was still unobserved, he took a lock pick from his pocket. In seconds, it was open. Thinking he would have to cut the chain that she always put on the door, he took a small pair of bolt cutters from his pocket. However when he turned the knob and pushed, the door swung inward. Startled, he paused on the threshold and stared into the darkness of the foyer. When he was satisfied that he was still undetected, he slipped inside the apartment and shut the door behind him.

The thrill of the hunt was upon him. He knew the layout of the rooms from being in here before, so he started forth with cool assurance. His thoughts were racing, picturing Kristie in her bed, imagining the fear on her face when she saw him standing in her room.

Kristie…my Kristie.

Giving the living room and kitchen only a cursory glance, he continued down the hall to her room. The door was ajar. The room, as the rest of the apartment, was dark. His heart skipped a beat as he put the flat of his hand on the door and then pushed.

The door swung inward, revealing the interior of the room. Her bed was against the wall to his left and there was a faint glow from a night-light in the adjoining bathroom. Enough light to let him know the bed was empty.

She was gone.

The knowledge hit him hard, like a fist to the gut. This was to have been the night—his night—but once again she'd messed up his plans.

He turned on the light and quickly searched through her closet, then moved on to the bathroom. From what he could see, a few things were missing that indicated she was somewhere overnight, but he didn't think she'd be gone for long. Her toothbrush and toothpaste were gone, as was a hair dryer and hairbrush. He knew because they'd been here before when he'd left her the little message on the refrigerator. He had no way of knowing what clothes she had taken, but it didn't appear to be many. Also, the full-length blue coat that she usually wore to work was nowhere to be found.

Rage borne of frustration made him want to destroy everything in sight, but that would be counterproductive to what he intended. All it would prove to the police was that he'd been thwarted; he wasn't going to give them the satisfaction.

Instead he took a deep breath, slammed his fist into the palm of his other hand and headed for the door. Just as he stepped into the hallway, he heard footsteps coming down the stairwell. He stepped back into the apartment and closed the door, listening carefully until he was certain that whoever it was, was gone.

Now that the plan had changed, he was anxious

to get away. He needed to find out where she'd gone and how long she was going to be gone. There were decisions to be made and places to go. Once this was over, he was ready to move on. He didn't like this cold weather and was thinking about moving to a warmer climate. There were available women everywhere. It was just a matter of picking the right one.

He opened the door again, listening carefully to make sure he was alone, then slipped into the hall, taking care to lock the door behind him as he left. A few seconds later he was gone.

Scott woke up to the smell of coffee and bacon and then looked at his alarm clock. It was ten minutes after six. He couldn't remember the last time he'd awakened before the alarm. But, he reminded himself, he hadn't had anyone to wake up for except himself. He grabbed a pair of sweats and put them on as he headed for the bathroom. A few minutes later he came out smelling of aftershave and toothpaste, his hair still damp but neatly combed.

"Wow...this place has never smelled this good," Scott said, and then kissed Kristie on the back of the neck.

Kristie leaned against him, savoring the feeling of being held.

"Still like your eggs well done?" she asked.

"Yes, ma'am, that I do." Then he leaned down and whispered in her ear, "I could get used to waking up like this."

She smiled to herself. "Yeah, I know what you mean," she said just as a timer went off.

"What's that for?" Scott asked.

"Biscuits."

He rolled his eyes and then groaned as she took them out of the oven.

"Have mercy, Kristie Ann. This isn't playing fair, and you know it. I'm already putty in your hands."

Kristie set the pan of biscuits on a hot pad and turned around.

"I'm not playing, Scotty. I'm serious. You may think this is too soon, but I'm going to say it, anyway. I'm falling in love with you all over again. If you don't want that, just say so now and I'll back off. We'll call last night one for old time's sake and when this is over, part as friends. But know this…it's not what I want."

The teasing smile on his face disappeared. He took her into his arms and laid his cheek against the softness of her hair.

"It's not what I want, either, baby."

Kristie leaned back and looked up. "What do you want, Scotty?"

"You." His mouth brushed the surface of her lips. When she sighed, he swallowed the sound as well as her breath. "I'm falling in love with you, too, honey girl."

"This is good," Kristie said.

He grinned and then reached over her shoulder and snagged a hot biscuit from the pan.

"And so is this," he said, taking a big bite.

She smiled. "Okay, okay, I get the message. You're hungry."

"Starving."

"So pour us some coffee and I'll fix the eggs. Everything else is done."

He did as he'd been told, and by the time she had the food on the table, he knew something dramatic was beginning to happen. His apartment—the place he'd been paying rent on for a good number of years—was starting to feel like a home.

They ate the meal together with the ease of people who'd known each other for years. It was as if the time they'd been apart had never happened. It wasn't until Scott was finishing his second cup of coffee that the phone rang. He glanced at Kristie and then shrugged an excuse as he went to answer the call.

"Wade," he said.

"Hey, Scott, it's me, Leslie. I thought you'd be interested to know we got a hit on that partial."

Scott's pulse kicked. It was the criminologist from forensics and she'd just given him a new lease on life.

"Tell me," he said.

"His name is Andrew McMartin, last known address, Los Angeles, California."

"Has he got a sheet?"

"Yes, but this is the biggie. There's an open warrant for his arrest out of L.A."

"What for?"

"Wanted for questioning in the death of a twenty-seven-year-old woman named Lucy McKee. It seems he'd been stalking her for almost six months, but they couldn't make anything stick. Then she turns up dead and he's missing."

"When was this?"

"About six months ago."

Scott turned to Kristie. "Honey, when did you tell me the first letters started arriving?"

"About four or five months ago."

Scott's focus heightened. The time line fit.

"Thanks, Leslie, I owe you."

"I know. I won't let you forget."

He hung up and turned to Kristie. "Do you know a man named Andrew McMartin?"

"No."

"You're sure?"

"Positive."

"Okay...he's probably using another name anyway. I'll get a mug shot and bring it home with me this evening. Maybe you'll recognize him."

"Oh, Scott! Could it be this easy?"

He grinned. "Sometimes we get lucky."

"Do you know where he lives? What he does?"

"I don't know anything yet, but I'll start the ball rolling the minute I get to work."

Then he frowned. "I don't want to leave you alone."

"I'll be fine. I promise not to leave or to answer the door to anyone."

"Yes...okay." Then he reached for her, needing to hold her, if for no other reason than his own reassurance. "I don't think anyone could possibly know that you're here, but you know we can't be sure."

"I'm sure, Scott."

He hesitated still. "Do you remember when you used to go rabbit hunting with me?"

She nodded.

"How long has it been since you fired a gun?"

Kristie's eyes widened. "Since I last went with you."

He frowned. "Okay...here's the deal. I'm leaving you here alone, but not without protection."

"You have a rifle in the apartment?"

He laughed. "No, it's a pistol. Come with me. I'll show you how to take off the safety. After that, just aim and fire."

Kristie's stomach lurched at the thought of shooting at someone, never mind killing them. And then she remembered the elevator and that horrible voice taunting her in the dark and knew that she'd do whatever it took to stay safe.

A few minutes later Kristie was on her own—except, of course, for the black, semiautomatic weapon that Scott had laid on the sideboard. She glanced at it several times as she finished cleaning up the kitchen. When she moved to the bedroom to make up the bed, she took it with her. Within a short time, she'd done all the chores and settled herself in the biggest overstuffed chair in the living room. She could tell from the imprint in the cushion that this must be Scott's favorite chair. It was also in direct line to a big-screen television and a most amazing entertainment center.

Men and their toys, she thought as she turned on the TV. After settling on a program on the food network, she leaned back and put her feet up on the ottoman, then took a sip of the coffee she'd brought with her from the kitchen. Everything seemed ordinary—even normal—except, of course, for the gun she'd laid beside the remote.

By noon Scott felt as if he was caught in a whirlpool. They had all kinds of information on Andrew McMartin, including a four-year-old mug shot, a rap sheet that had started when he was a teen, his last known address and the phone number and address of his only living relative, a woman named Frannie Howell who's last known address was a Chicago suburb.

The only problem was that McMartin hadn't been seen since he'd disappeared from L.A. They had no proof that he'd ever been in Chicago except for the fingerprint on the stamp and the Chicago postmark. It didn't prove conclusively that he was here, but it was a good start toward building the case. In Scott's opinion, he had to be near, or how else would he have fixated on Kristie?

He'd read the file on Lucy McKee's murder, and it made him sick to his stomach all over again. He couldn't help but transpose Kristie's face onto the pictures taken from the crime scene. The brutality of the poor woman's death was extreme, which only enforced the urgency of the department to find McMartin before he got to Kristie.

Lieutenant Fisk was on a mission to catch the stalker and had already put more detectives on the case. They were out now, trying to locate a woman named Frannie Howell, who had the distinction of being the only sister of McMartin's deceased mother.

It was almost noon and Tucker had gone out to get himself and Scott some sandwiches from a nearby deli. While Scott was waiting, he picked up the phone and dialed the number to his own home. The answering machine picked up and he immediately began talking so that Kristie would know to pick up.

"Kristie...it's me. Pick up, honey. I've got some more news."

He waited, expecting to hear her voice, and was a little disconcerted when he didn't. He knew there were any number of reasons why she hadn't answered. Maybe she was in the bathroom or had the washing machine running. She'd teased him this morning about the pile of towels needing to be washed. That had to be it. He told himself he'd wait a bit and then call again. But the longer he waited, the more nervous he got.

Again he made the second call and again there was no answer. Frowning, he hung up and tried not to worry. She'd promised not to leave. He was certain she wouldn't go out and take a chance on a repeat of yesterday's event in the elevator. But if that was the case, then where the hell was she?

He stood abruptly and was reaching for his topcoat when Tucker came back with their food.

"Hey, Wade...I just heard a call on the radio. There's a fire in the building next to your apartment. They've evacuated everyone in the buildings on either side."

"Hell," Scott said, and headed for the door, with Tucker right behind him.

Chapter 6

Kristie had been herded across the street with the rest of the apartment residents and was watching the arrival of the fire trucks in the same manner one watches an accident happening—in mounting horror but unable to look away. The intensity of the fire seemed to be growing and it appeared to her that nothing would save the building. The police had cordoned off the area, but onlookers were still gathering. Ever so slowly she was being pushed to the back of the crowd until she found herself sandwiched between the back of the building and a short, elderly woman holding a shopping bag full of groceries.

A stiff gust of wind whipped around the corner of the building in front of where the crowd was standing. Kristie shivered as she pulled the collar of her coat up around her neck and then huddled beneath the awning above them. Even though they were a block away from the fire, the wind blew the mist from the spray of the water hoses right in their faces.

If it wasn't for the fact that Scott would panic, she would have already called a cab and gone to her own home. At least there she wouldn't be so cold and wet.

Suddenly a dark blue car came speeding around the corner of the opposite street and stopped at the curb. Two men got out on the run, flashing their badges at the street cops who were guarding the area. When Kristie saw Scott she began to push her way through the crowd, trying to let him know where she was.

Scott's heart was in his throat as he saw the flames coming out of the building next to where he lived. It had been under renovation for over a year and the owners were just about ready to start leasing apartments. He could only imagine the losses they were going to sustain. And while his sympathies were with the company who was suffering the loss, his concern was for Kristie. A quick glance of the area told him where the evacuees were being detained. He yelled at his partner over the noise of the trucks and sirens, then pointed toward the people on the opposite side of the street, indicating that that was where he was going. His partner nodded, then got back into the car, away from the wet and the cold.

Scott hadn't gone more than ten feet when he caught a flash of red hair and saw Kristie break free of the crowd. She ducked under the yellow tape and ran toward him. A uniformed officer yelled and started to grab for her when Scott waved his badge and called out an okay. The officer grinned and nodded as Kristie jumped into Scott's outstretched arms.

Scott held her close, feeling the dampness on her hair and face, and guessed she was probably freezing. He gave her a big hug and a quick kiss and then held her at arm's length, just to assure himself that she was really okay.

"Are you all right?" he asked.

She nodded. "Just cold."

"Come with me," he said. "You can sit in the car with Tucker until we figure out what to do."

He sheltered her under his arm and started walking her toward the car, unaware that the on-the-spot reporter had recognized him or that their reunion had been witnessed and broadcast live.

"I tried to call you," she said. "But they wouldn't let us linger in the building. All I managed to get was my purse and coat."

"I tried to call you a couple of times and when I didn't get an answer, I got worried. Then Tucker came in and told me what was going on."

When they reached the car, Tucker jumped out and shook her hand.

"Hello, Kristie. We spoke briefly on the phone earlier. I'm Scott's partner, Paul Tucker, but you can call me Tucker."

Kristie smiled. "Nice to meet you, Tucker."

"Get in the front with Scott," Tucker said. "I always wanted to be a back seat driver."

The interior of the car was warm and still, a welcome relief from the sharp wind and cold mist coming off the water from the hoses. She leaned back in the seat and closed her eyes as a shiver engulfed her.

"Honey?"

She turned to look at Scott. "What?"

"Are you sure you're okay?"

"Yes...just so cold. I can't feel my toes."

"Kick off your shoes," he said. "I'll turn up the heater."

Kristie did as he asked and moments later felt a rush of hot air on her chilled body.

"Oo-oh, that feels heavenly," she said. "Thanks." Then she glanced toward the building that was completely engulfed. "Those poor people."

"At least no one was living there, and they're bound to be insured. It's the buildings on either side of it that I'm worried about."

Kristie leaned forward, her hands clasped around her knees.

"Do you think we'll be allowed to go back into the building tonight?"

"Who knows?" he said, then glanced back at his partner. "Stay with her, okay? I'm going to see what I can find out."

Tucker nodded.

As Scott was closing the door, he heard Tucker asking Kristie if she had any sisters. He grinned. Tucker had been divorced twice already, but was a hopeless romantic and always ready to give love another try.

Kristie watched Scott move through the melee of firemen and emergency personnel and knew she was blessed to have him on her side, as well as back in her life.

"You're pretty gone on him, aren't you?"

"Yes."

Tucker chuckled. "You don't mince words, either, do you?"

"No."

"Good girl. If my second wife had been more like you, we'd still be together. Although I'm not going to say anything bad about her because she's just recovering from an appendectomy."

"Ouch," Kristie said as she smiled to herself. She could really like this man. She just hoped they found her stalker so her life could get back to normal.

"For what it's worth," Tucker said, "I've been partners with Scott for over seven years and I have never seen him this gone over a woman."

"We grew up together," Kristie said.

Tucker leaned over the seat, his voice high with excitement.

"You're kidding! He didn't tell me that. All I knew was that he'd picked up your case the day I was gone. I thought...well, never mind what I thought."

There were a few moments of silence and then Kristie heard Tucker mumble, "So you've known each other a long time."

The warmth of the heater warmed Kristie's bones, but it was the truth of what Tucker had said that warmed her heart. It felt as though she'd known Scott forever, even though she'd lost track of him for those years, but their time apart had only made their reunion that much sweeter.

She looked up just as Scott came jogging toward the car.

"He looks soaked," Kristie said.

"He'll dry. He's tough, you know," Tucker said.

Kristie eyed the length of his stride and the arrogant tilt of his chin, and smiled. He might be tough in the world, but in bed, he was as tender as they came.

"They are going to let people back into the buildings within the hour," Scott said.

"Okay...I can wait around until—"

Scott grabbed her arm. "No way, honey. You're coming with us. We're off duty in about four hours. We'll come back together."

"But won't your boss mind if—"

Tucker piped up from the back seat. "Shoot no, the lieutenant won't care. He's the one who sicced Scott onto your case to begin with."

"Then I'm glad to be going back with you because I want to thank him personally."

Scott looked at her and then frowned. "Just don't go and ruin my tough guy image."

"You can count on me," she said.

Scott's gaze darkened and for a moment it seemed difficult for him to speak.

"I always could, couldn't I, honey girl?"

She nodded. "Just like I'm counting on you."

A huge groan came from the back seat. "Lord, save me from all that sugar."

Scott glanced up into the rearview mirror and grinned.

"Partner, if you hadn't shared your sugar with someone besides your wife, you wouldn't be doing your own laundry."

"*Touché,*" Tucker muttered, then chuckled. "Point taken."

"Buckle up," Scott said, and made a U-turn before moving back into traffic.

Unknown to them, the news crew who'd shot the film had been broadcasting live from the scene, and anyone who happened to be watching their channel had witnessed the touching reunion of the big cop and the pretty red-haired woman.

For most of the viewers it had been a touching and heartwarming moment, but not for Andrew McMartin. He'd been heating a bowl of soup in the microwave when the news bulletin had interrupted regular programming. He'd turned to watch out of curiosity, but when he recognized the woman coming out of the crowd and running toward the big man in a dark blue overcoat, he'd started toward the set, as if he would be able to stop the man from embracing her. But he couldn't. Instead he was impotent to do more than watch her fall into the man's arms. It took another minute for it to sink in that he'd seen the man before. It was the cop who was working her case.

The microwave dinged, signaling that his soup was heated, but he walked away, no longer hungry. His plans had changed—drastically. But he wasn't quitting. Not when he'd invested this much time into a relationship and not before he made Kristie Samuels pay for breaking it up.

Kristie was sitting at Scott's desk and trying to remain inconspicuous, but found it difficult not to stare. Lieutenant Fisk had not only welcomed her to their department, but had brought her a cup of coffee and a jelly doughnut from his personal stash. She'd thanked him kindly, sipped at the coffee that tasted curiously like battery acid smelled, and eaten enough of the doughnut so as not to hurt his feelings.

Now she was left with nothing to do but watch the unfolding proceedings. A detective on the other side of the room was interrogating a woman wearing two small pieces of pink satin that were supposed to pass for a blouse and skirt. Her coat was some sort of fake fur and looked as if someone had skinned a big wet dog and made some wild kind of coat. From the expression on the detective's face, Kristie couldn't help but wonder if the coat didn't smell like one, too.

There was a female detective across the room. The man sitting in the chair beside her desk was crying. Kristie felt guilty for even noticing and quickly looked away. She didn't want to think about what news he might have been told. It reminded her too much of how her own parents would react if they received the news of her demise.

No sooner had she thought it than she remembered she had yet to mail the baby gifts to Midland, and she needed to check her messages. She hadn't told her mother anything about what was going on, or that Scott Wade was living in Chicago, never mind that they were already involved again.

She glanced up, checking Scott's whereabouts, and saw that he was still in the lieutenant's office. She took out her cell phone, dialed her home number and then waited for the answering machine to come on before she punched in her code. According to the machine, she had six messages. As the first one started to play, she grabbed a pen from Scott's desk and held it poised above a pad of paper, ready to write.

I know you're gone. It doesn't matter. You still belong to me.

Startled, Kristie dropped the phone and then realized what she'd done and scrambled to pick it up before the message was over. She got the phone just in time to hear the click as the call disconnected. Her good mood was swiftly disappearing. The second call began to play and she took a deep breath, making herself concentrate. To her relief, it was her dentist, reminding her of an appointment that she realized should have been this morning. The third one was a hang-up. The fourth was from the girls at the office, asking if she was okay. The fifth was from her mother, as she'd feared, and she made a mental note to call her as soon as she hung up.

Expecting that the last one would be as innocuous as the other four, once again, she was taken aback when she heard her stalker's voice. What bothered her the most about this call was the undisguised fury in his voice.

You cheated on me, Kristie. I don't like that. I don't like that at all. I saw you today on television, running toward that man…throwing yourself in his arms. How do you think that made me feel?

"Honey…what's wrong?"

Kristie looked up, only now aware that Scott was standing by the desk. Pale and shaken, she handed the phone to him.

"Who is it?" he asked.

"Just listen."

He put the phone to his ear.

You're a whore…cavorting with that cop. You

thought I wouldn't know, but I saw it. The whole world saw it. And now you're going to pay.

The call disconnected, but not before Scott slammed the phone closed in anger, then turned and yelled at his partner.

"Tucker! Was there a news crew at the fire scene today?"

"A couple, I think. I know I saw Mel Stewart from Channel 19 doing some on-scene stuff."

"Son of a bitch," Scott said.

He and Mel Stewart had gone head-to-head a couple of years back and Mel had come out the loser when Scott had forbidden him to air some footage he'd gotten in a place he shouldn't have been. It would have meant busting a case wide open before they were ready; as a result of Scott's order, Stewart had been scooped by a rival station two days later. He hadn't gotten over it and Scott figured he'd just been paid back.

"Can you find out if there was some footage of me with Kristie that aired?"

Tucker frowned. "From the fire?"

"Yeah."

"Damn," Tucker muttered, then headed for the phone as Scott turned to Kristie.

"Okay, Kristie...this is not a big deal. So he knows where you are. So what? We'll fool him again, okay?"

Kristie's voice was barely above a whisper.

"But how?"

"Just because he found out where I live doesn't mean we'll be there again."

"What do you mean?"

"Just trust me," he said, and then headed for the

lieutenant's office again. When he came back, he had a look on his face that she'd never seen. "Honey, get your coat."

"Where are we going?" she asked.

"Where is the last place he'd think to look for you now?"

Kristie wondered if she looked as defeated as she felt.

"I don't know."

"Home. I'm taking you home."

"Back to my apartment?" she asked.

Scott smiled, but it was the coldest smile she'd ever seen.

"Only long enough to get some of your clothes, then I'm putting you on a plane to Midland. I want you out of this city until we find McMartin and put him behind bars."

"But if he knows I'm gone, he'll—"

"We're putting a female cop in your apartment and—"

Kristie froze. "You're going to put someone else in danger because of me?"

"It's what we do," Scott said. "Her name is Melissa Franks. She's about your height and size and has long red hair. We'll set her up in the apartment and she'll be waiting for him when he makes his move."

"I won't do it," Kristie said. "What if he hurts her?" Her voice broke. "What if he kills her, thinking it's me?"

"And if we don't, he could kill you," Scott said. "I couldn't live with myself if I let that happen."

"But you said—"

"I said I'd keep you safe, and I'm going to do

just that. We still have a couple of leads to run down and a possible suspect to question.''

"Like who?'' Kristie asked.

"Like the maintenance man in your apartment. I've seen him hanging around your place more than once. We've got a couple of men out looking for him now, but we haven't been able to find him.''

"Why don't you just talk to him at work?''

"Because he hasn't been seen since the day of the elevator incident, and because the address he gave the building superintendent doesn't exist.''

"But he doesn't look much like that picture you showed me of Andrew McMartin.''

"They're the same height and have the same facial structure. McMartin's head was shaved in the mug shot, but he could have grown his hair back and lost a little weight. Criminals do it all the time.''

Kristie shook her head in disbelief. "It's the twenty-eighth day of December. In four days, it will be a whole new year. I should be planning my new year's resolution, not my getaway.''

"As long as it's not your funeral, I don't give a damn what you plan,'' Scott said. "Now let's go. We've got a lot to do and not much time to do it.''

Kristie frowned, still battling her own feelings about what he'd just said, and then surprised herself and him by what she said next.

"No. I don't think I should leave. He'll find out, I just know it. Then that would just delay the inevitable, or worse yet, it would drag this ugly mess home to Midland, and I won't have it. I won't have my parents or any members of my family put in danger by this nut.''

"Damn it, Kristie, you don't—''

"Wait. Before you get mad, just listen. Please."

"I'm listening, but this better be good."

"This female cop..."

"Yeah, what about her?" Scott asked.

"She can stay with me...like a bodyguard. And no one will know she's there, see? This McMartin will think I'm alone and when he makes his move, she can make hers."

Scott hesitated. It wasn't the best of the plans, but he understood her not wanting to put her family in any danger, even if there was only a remote chance of it happening.

"Maybe. I'll have to talk to my lieutenant."

"So go talk. Tell him I'm not budging and he has no choice."

"You are nuts...you know that?" Scott growled.

Kristie laid her hand on Scott's arm. "Maybe so. But I'm also getting mad—real mad. I'm tired of being afraid. I'm tired of hiding behind the walls of my own home. And most of all, I'm tired of him being in charge. Now go make your speech, get the policewoman in place, and then take me home."

McMartin was sitting in his car across the street from the police station when he saw Kristie and the cop come out and then get into a car. He started the engine and followed them into the traffic, taking care to stay a few cars behind. He guessed they were going back to the cop's apartment, but when they passed it and kept on going, he decided that they were on their way back to hers instead.

Smiling to himself, he turned left at the next stop-light and took another route to the apartment building, betting with himself that he would arrive before they did.

A short while later he wheeled into the parking garage and parked before hurrying toward the elevator. As he rounded a corner, he saw a slim, red-haired woman waiting for the elevator to arrive. For a moment, he thought it was Kristie and he smiled, but when she turned around and gave him a cool, studied look, he realized it was someone else. He nodded and smiled again, and after a moment the woman smiled back. As she turned, he got a glimpse of a shoulder holster and a gun beneath her coat and his eyes narrowed thoughtfully.

He'd bet a year of his life that she was a cop, and the fact that she looked an awful lot like his Kristie was suspicious. Suddenly his smile turned vicious. They were planning a switch. Yes, that was it. Well, two could play at this game, he thought.

When the elevator car finally arrived, McMartin rode it up alone.

Kristie opened the door to her apartment and then hesitated before going inside. The stalker had gotten in here once before. She had every reason to assume that he'd done it again.

Scott was under the same assumption, and made her wait just inside the doorway while he pulled his gun and did a thorough sweep of the entire place.

"It's clean," he said, holstering his weapon as he came back into the room. "I'll bring your things from my house in a couple of hours, as soon as I make sure Officer Franks is in place."

"I thought she'd already be here," Kristie said.

Scott nodded and frowned. "Yeah, so did I. Let me make a few calls while you settle in, okay?"

"I've got to call my mom. She called yesterday, so she'll worry if I don't."

"Yes, all right, but wait until I find out what's keeping Melissa Franks."

"Yes, of course," Kristie said, and then hung her coat up in the closet and began walking through the place that was her home. The only trouble was that it felt more like a cage than a place of rest and comfort.

By the time she returned to the living room, the frown was back on Scott's face.

"What's wrong?" she asked.

"Franks left the precinct before we did. She should have been here by now."

"Maybe she's stuck down in the garage in that stupid elevator," Kristie said.

"You mean, it stopped before?"

"Oh, but yes," Kristie said. "That's why I didn't panic when it stopped on me until I heard that man's voice."

Scott frowned. "I suppose it's worth checking out."

"So go," Kristie said. "I'll lock myself in and won't let anyone back in but you."

Scott hesitated, unwilling to leave her alone, even for that short of a time.

Kristie rolled her eyes. "Scott! For goodness' sake. It won't take five minutes, tops."

"Okay," he said, and opened the door. "But promise you won't let anyone in."

"Yes, yes, I promise."

He grinned at the frown on her face and then

grabbed her and kissed her soundly before she could object. They broke apart only after they heard a chuckle.

"Well, now...are you coming or going?"

They turned. Marjorie Petrowski, grinning from ear to ear, was laughing at them.

"Oh! Marjorie, we were just... I mean—"

She laughed again and patted Scott on the arm as she winked at Kristie.

"My dear...I can see what you were doing. However, that's beside the point. I was just on my way out to get some ice cream. I've been hungry for that Ben and Jerry's Chunky Monkey. Do you know the flavor?"

Kristie rolled her eyes and then groaned in appreciation.

"It's one of my favorites," she said.

"They're all your favorites," Scott teased.

Marjorie laughed. As she did, a door suddenly banged down the hall and they all turned toward the sound. It was the maintenance man, though he wasn't wearing his coveralls and was moving rather furtively as he hurried down the hall toward the stairs.

"Hey, you!" Scott called. "Wait!"

The man froze and then turned. When he saw Scott, he dropped his toolbox and bolted toward the stairs.

"Call the department. Tell them I need some backup," Scott told Kristie, then added, "And get inside and lock the door."

Scott took off down the hall after the man, leaving Marjorie and Kristie alone in the hall.

"Whatever's going on?" Marjorie asked.

"Oh...it's too complicated to explain," Kristie said. "You'll have to excuse me, I need to call the police."

"Then call, call," Marjorie said, waving Kristie toward the phone. "I'm staying with you until I'm sure you're okay."

Kristie hesitated, then shrugged. "Fine, but lock the door behind you," she said as she ran to the phone.

She dialed 911, relayed Scott's message, and then disconnected. She was about to replace the portable phone on the base when she looked up. From where she was standing, she could see Marjorie's reflection in the mirror just to her left. And in that moment when Marjorie believed herself not in view, her entire facial structure had changed. The prim purse of her mouth had relaxed into a thin-lipped, almost-masculine sneer. She'd taken off her coat, as well as the jacket to her jogging suit and as she turned toward the coffee table, Kristie realized Marjorie Petrowski didn't have any boobs. It wasn't as if she'd never seen a flat-chested woman before, but she'd never seen one with shoulders that broad and hips that flat.

Her heart started to pound, and instead of hanging up the phone, she slid her thumb back onto the speed dial, knowing that if her suspicious were correct, she was going to have to make another call to 911.

"May I get you something to drink?" Kristie asked. "Maybe a cup of coffee, or a soft drink?"

Marjorie turned around, and at that moment Kristie knew her fears had been true. Marjorie smiled at Kristie and shoved a hand through her hair and pulled. The hair came off in her hand, revealing a high forehead and a very bald head.

"Hello, my darling, Kristie. I've been waiting a very long time for this moment."

"Well, Andrew...I'm sorry to say I can't return the favor."

He was startled that she knew his name and it showed. A dull flush suffused his neck, then spread up his cheeks.

"So you think you're smart, do you?" he said, and took a step toward her.

Kristie pressed the speed dial button with the pad of her thumb and held the phone out toward McMartin, pointing it like a gun in hope that he would not notice what she'd done.

Seconds later, she heard the faint sound of the dispatcher's voice and started to talk loudly to him and in a threatening manner.

"So you're Andrew McMartin. I never thought I'd meet you hiding behind the proverbial woman's skirts."

His sneer faltered. "Shut up, bitch," he yelled, and picked up a lamp and threw it at the wall near her head.

Kristie screamed as she dodged and then ran to her left, quickly putting about twenty feet and a sofa between them.

"Stay away from me!" she screamed. "You won't get away with this, you know! Detective Wade is in the building. You can't kill me and expect to get away with it. Why don't you leave now, before he comes back?"

McMartin was furious. He started toward her, pulling a length of rope from his pocket as he ran.

Just the thought of wrapping it around her neck and stifling her lies made him hot.

Kristie was screaming for help as she ran, hoping that the dispatcher would get the message, relay it to Scott, and get her some help before it was too late. But just in case it didn't happen in timely fashion, she wasn't going down without a fight.

She made it to the kitchen a few yards ahead of him and grabbed a chef's knife from the knife block on the counter. It was large and awkward, but she figured if she ever connected, it would do the most damage.

McMartin made a dive toward her just as Kristie spun. The knife swiped through his shirt and into the flesh of his chest, leaving a good nine inches of skin exposed, along with a wash of fresh blood. He dropped the rope as he jumped back in shock, fingering the cut as the blood seeped through the thin, white fabric of the cotton knit shirt.

"You bitch."

The surprise in his voice made Kristie smile.

"What? Surely you didn't think I would just throw up my hands and lay down and die for you?" She waved the knife toward his face and took a small bit of pleasure in watching the pupils of his eyes widen as he stepped back in shock. "If you thought that, then you didn't know me as well as you thought, because I don't quit. Not on myself. Not ever."

He thrust his hand into his pocket, fingering the handle of his switchblade as he considered his options. Time was not on his side. That was a given. But after the way she'd come undone in the elevator, he'd been certain that she was a quitter—a victim who was too afraid to fight back. Lucy McKee had been such a woman. She'd begged for mercy, but hadn't lifted a finger in her own defense. She'd still been begging when he'd slit her throat.

"You're going to be sorry," he said as he pulled out the knife and popped the blade. "I was going to make it easy on you, but not now. Before I'm through with you, you're going to be praying to die."

"You don't have much time," she said. Then, to his horror, she laughed. "Of course, I've never known a man who needed much time for anything. If I was a betting woman, which of course I'm not. But...if I was...since you chose such a unique method of hiding from the police...and...you were so comfortable in a woman's shoes, then I'd be willing to bet you can't hold a climax any longer than you can hold that stupid temper of yours."

She made a tsk-tsking sound and grabbed the back of a kitchen chair, ready to use it as well as the knife to fend him off.

It was the taunt about his sexuality that sent him over the edge. He came toward her with a roar, flinging furniture aside as he ran.

Chapter 7

Scott's cell phone was ringing as he exited the stairwell at the garage level. He answered it without thinking, his focus still on the missing maintenance man, who'd somehow disappeared, and the whereabouts of Melissa Franks.

"This is Wade."

It was Tucker. "Kristie's in trouble," he said. "Where are you?"

Scott's heart dropped as he pivoted quickly and started running back up the stairs.

"I'm in the stairwell of her building. What are you talking about? I just left her with a neighbor lady."

"I don't understand it, but from what the 911 dispatcher could understand, the person with her is trying to kill her. 911 has dispatched some cars. I'm on my way, but you're her best bet. You better hurry. The dispatcher said it sounds bad."

"God help us both," Scott said, and dropped the phone into his pocket as he bounded up the stairs.

It wasn't the first time he'd run up several flights of stairs, but he was betting with himself that it was definitely the fastest. Less than a minute after getting the call, he exited the stairwell onto the fifth floor, and even though he was about fifty yards away, he could hear Kristie screaming as he ran. The door to her apartment was locked. Just as he started to try to kick it in, she screamed again. It was a shrill, blood-curdling sound that sent a chill throughout his body. In the next breath he had pulled his gun, shot out the lock, and kicked in the door.

McMartin was astride Kristie's legs, trying to stab her, but she had hold of his wrist with both hands and wouldn't let go. One second Kristie was certain this breath would be her last and the next McMartin was gone. She had a moment's impression of him flying backward through the air and then realized Scott had pulled him off of her and thrown him against the wall. Overwhelmed by the fact that she was no longer in danger, she started to shake.

Scott reached for his handcuffs and was in the act of cuffing McMartin when he tried to resist. Scott yanked him up by the shirt and stared him straight in the face.

"McMartin."

Andrew McMartin sneered and then grinned.

"Yeah, that's me." Then he lowered his voice to a slow, ugly taunt. "I had her, you know. I had her first."

"No, *I* had her first," Scott said. "When she was

sixteen years old and a junior in high school. She's not yours, you sick bastard. She never was and she never will be, she's mine."

McMartin's expression fell. It was the last thing he'd expected to hear.

"It doesn't matter. I—"

Scott shook him harshly. "Just shut up and listen. You have the right to remain silent. You have the right to an attorney." His voice slid into a lifeless monotone as he spoke until he'd informed McMartin of his constitutional rights, then ended with the inevitable. "Andrew McMartin, do you understand these rights as I have given them to you?"

"Yeah, yeah, I know my rights," McMartin mumbled.

"Good," Scott said, then doubled his fist and hit him on the chin as hard as he could.

McMartin's head snapped back as he dropped limply to the floor. It was all Scott could do not to take out his gun and shoot him where he lay. As soon as he had him cuffed, he shoved him out of the way and ran to Kristie. It wasn't until he knelt beside her that he realized there was blood all over her.

"Oh, God... Oh, honey...don't move," he said. "There's an ambulance on the way."

"It's not mine," she said, and then put her head between her knees. "I think I'm going to be sick."

Scott lifted her up and carried her to the bathroom. She dropped to her knees by the commode just as they heard a commotion in the other room.

"Sounds like help has arrived," Scott said. "Will you be all right for a minute?"

She nodded.

He started toward the door and then stopped, reluctant to leave her alone.

"Scotty...please," she begged, and laid her head on the closed lid of the commode. "Just leave me alone. I'll be all right."

He hurried back into the living room just as his partner and four uniformed officers were arriving.

"Looks like it's all over but the shouting," Tucker said, eyeing the bloody room and the handcuffed man. Then he noticed Kristie was nowhere in sight. "Where's Kristie? Is she all right?"

"I think so," Scott said. "But I want an EMT to look at her anyway. She's covered in blood and I can't tell what's hers and what's his."

A pair of EMTs came hurrying into the room and then began assessing the seriousness of McMartin's injuries.

"He doesn't look so good," Tucker said, toeing the bottom of the unconscious man's shoe with his boot.

"I think the cuts are superficial," Scott said, then added, "He's alive, which is more than he deserves."

When a second pair of EMTs arrived, he waved at them to follow him. "Come with me," he said, and led them toward the bathroom.

As they entered, Scott saw that Kristie was sitting on the side of the bathtub with her head in her hands. She was shaking so hard she couldn't stand up. Cursing himself for ever leaving her alone, he rushed to her.

"Honey, the paramedics are here. I want them to check you out, okay?"

She tried to lift her head, but her whole body felt heavy—too heavy to move.

"I told you, I'm okay," she said, and then slid to the floor in a faint.

Scott scooped her up into his arms and carried her next door to her bedroom where he laid her on the bed. Even after the EMT verified she had no injuries and was probably just in shock, Scott wouldn't let her out of his sight. The EMT suggested they contact her doctor for a sedative prescription, that after a trauma like this she would probably have trouble sleeping. He also recommended counseling, but it was nothing that Scott didn't already know. Once he was sure that she had not been physically injured, he actually let himself relax.

Tucker stepped into the bedroom long enough to let Scott know that everyone was finally leaving.

"I'll do the paperwork," he said.

Scott turned and looked at his partner, then raised an eyebrow in disgust.

"Hell, Tucker, you weren't even here. Tell the lieutenant that I'll be in later to do the report."

"Okay, but don't say I never offered to do you a favor."

"You'll thank me later," Scott said.

"For what?"

"For that suspension you didn't get for faking a report."

Tucker laughed. "Okay, you've made your point."

"Don't I always," Scott said. "So go get the bastard off the premises before Kristie wakes up."

"He's already on his way to booking, via a quick

visit to the emergency room to get some stitches.'' Then Tucker looked at Kristie, who was already showing signs of waking. ''For a frail little thing, she's damned good with a knife.''

''She might look fragile, but you've forgotten one thing,'' Scott said.

''What's that?'' Tucker asked.

''She's from Texas. We grow 'em pretty down there, but we also grow 'em tough.'' Then his voice softened as he looked at her. ''Thank God, she didn't quit on herself or I would have been too late to save her.''

Tucker thumped him on the back. ''You got yourself a good woman, there, buddy. Don't mess it up.''

''There's no way,'' Scott said softly. ''I lost her once. It isn't going to happen again.''

''You have to admit, he had a pretty good disguise,'' Tucker said, thinking of McMartin.

Scott grimaced. ''Yeah. We were looking for a man.'' Then he thought of something else. ''I keep thinking about McMartin's aunt who was supposed to live in the area. I wonder how she ties into this?''

''We got word this morning after you left the office that she's been dead for the last nine months. Cancer, I think. McMartin was her only living relative. She left him a big chunk of money and all her property.''

''So now we know where he got the wigs and clothes,'' Scott said, then added, ''And why he could devote all of his time to his sick stunts. He didn't have to work.''

''It's a good thing he's got some money. He's going to need it to pay for a lawyer.''

''Yeah, right,'' Scott said, and then added, ''Hey,

Tucker, do me a favor on your way out and tell the building super to get someone up here to replace Kristie's door and lock and tell him to do it today."

"Will do," Tucker said. He started to leave when he thought of one other thing he was curious about. "Hey, Scott."

"Yeah?"

"When I called you..."

"Yes?"

"Why were you in the stairwell?"

Scott groaned and then rolled his eyes. "Oh, hell...Melissa Franks."

"Who?"

"There was a female officer who was supposed to stay with Kristie. She wasn't here and I was going to look for her when I saw that maintenance man we'd been looking for. He started to run and I took off after him."

"Oh, that's another thing," Tucker said. "Another bit of info was tied up after you left. We found out that the maintenance man is a Croatian named Johan Blinzer. His green card ran out over a year ago and he's probably been dodging immigration ever since."

"No wonder he ran," Scott said. "But what about Franks?"

"I'll check it out and give you a call," Tucker said.

"Kristie says sometimes the elevator gets stuck."

Tucker grinned. "Then I'll take the stairs."

"Just make sure Franks is not trapped in the damned thing," Scott said.

"I'm on it," Tucker said, leaving Scott alone in the apartment with Kristie. He sat on the side of the bed and laid his hand on her forehead. Her skin felt clammy. He knew it was from the shock of what she'd experienced.

"Kristie...honey?"

She opened her eyes and looked at him.

"Scotty?"

"What, baby?"

"It *is* over, isn't it?"

"Yes. It's over."

She looked down at herself and at the blood all over her hands and clothes.

"I need a shower."

"You'll take a bath," he said. "You're too shaky to stand."

"Whatever. I just want it off," she muttered, then sat up on the side of the bed and started peeling off her clothes.

Scott went into the bathroom and started the water, adding a good dose of bath salts, then helped her into the tub.

"Call me when you're ready to get out," he said.

Kristie was already scrubbing at herself, desperate to get the blood off of her hands, when she stopped and looked up at him. Her chin started to tremble.

"You saved my life."

"Damn it, honey, don't cry," he begged, and then dropped to his knees, cupped her face in his hands and brushed his mouth across the center of her lips. "Just soak and relax."

She nodded, leaned back against the tub and let herself slide down until her chin was just above the water. She let out a small sigh and closed her eyes.

Scott stood and had just started out of the bathroom when she called him back.

"Scott."

"What, honey?"

"My clothes...the ones I had on."

"Yeah, what about them?"

"I don't ever want to see them again."

His shoulders slumped, as if the weight he was carrying was suddenly too heavy.

"I'll get rid of them for you."

"Okay," she said.

He started out of the room once more.

"Scotty?"

"What?"

"Thank you."

He nodded and kept on walking because if he stopped and looked at her again, he would cry, too.

Minutes later, his cell phone rang. It was Tucker.

"We found Melissa Franks. She's got a concussion, but she's going to be fine."

"Damn it, what happened?" Scott asked.

"He saw her in the parking garage. Franks said he started acting real weird, but before she could make a move, he'd coldcocked her. She came to, found herself tied and gagged and stuffed inside the trunk of his car. The way we figure it, he was probably going to dump her after doing away with Kristie."

"At least she's okay," Scott said. "Tell her I'm sorry."

"Will do. Her husband is on his way to the hospital, so you can give them a call there later if you like."

"Yeah, I'll do that," Scott said, and disconnected. Now all their questions were answered except for why someone like Andrew McMartin felt the need to terrorize innocent women, but he was guessing that was something they'd never find out.

Two hours later there was a repairman in the living room hanging a new door and locks. The banging and hammering was intermittent, but didn't seem to be bothering Kristie, who'd fallen asleep soon after getting out of her bath.

Scott was running interference while in the kitchen heating soup when the phone began to ring. Although it wasn't his phone, he feared the constant ringing would wake Kristie before the answering machine could pick up, so he answered the call.

"Hello? Samuels residence."

There was a moment of silence and then a woman spoke.

"Is Kristie there? This is her mother, Shelly."

Scott grinned. "Hi, Mrs. Samuels. This is Scott Wade. Yes, Kristie is here, but she's asleep."

"Scotty? Scotty Wade from Midland?"

He grinned again, only wider. "Yes, ma'am."

"Why, Scotty! I can't tell you how surprised I am to hear your voice. Kristie Ann didn't tell me she'd seen you again."

"It's been pretty recent," he said. "I ran into her the other day and stopped by to say hello."

"You live in Chicago?"

"Yes, ma'am. I'm a detective with the Chicago Police Department."

"Land sakes. Blaine will be pleased to know of you. I can't wait to tell him. I had no idea where you and your family had gotten off to. How are your parents?"

"Dad retired years ago and they moved to Florida. Mom didn't like the Chicago winters."

"I can't say as I blame her," she said, then got right to the point of her call. "Scotty, why is Kristie in bed? I called her office, but they told me she'd taken a few days off and now you tell me she's sleeping...and in the middle of the day. Is she ill?"

Scott hesitated. The story was Kristie's to tell, but he didn't want to lie.

"Well...no, ma'am, not exactly. When she wakes up, I'll have her call you herself, okay? Then she can tell you everything, but please know she's fine. Just worn out."

"Well...if you say so."

Scott could hear the worry in her voice. "Look, Mrs. Samuels, I promise you she's all right. She's had a hard time, but everything is over. And just for the record, I'll probably be seeing you soon."

"Oh?"

This time the lilt in her voice made Scott smile.

"Yes, ma'am. As soon as I can get some time off, I'll bring her home. I think she needs to be with you guys for a few days."

"I hope you'll be staying, too."

"Let me put it this way, ma'am. I'm not letting her out of my sight for at least the next seventy years. After that...we'll have to talk about it."

"Oh, Scotty...this is wonderful news. Did you know that I'm finally a grandmother? Loretta and Billy have a new baby boy."

His grin widened. Something told him that his future mother-in-law had just challenged him to make sure it wasn't her only grandbaby.

''Yes, ma'am. Kristie told me. She's pretty anxious to see her nephew.''

''Well, you just tell my girl to call me the minute she wakes up.''

''Yes, ma'am, I will.''

He disconnected, then turned to find Kristie looking at him from the doorway.

''Who was that?'' she asked.

''Your mother.''

Kristie's chin jutted. ''What were you talking about?''

''You.''

Her eyes widened. ''What did you tell her?''

''Just enough.'' He set the soup off the heat and held out his arms. ''Come here to me.''

She walked into his embrace.

''Kristie Ann?''

''Hmm?''

''Would you like to go home for a while?''

Her shoulders started to shake and Scott knew she was crying again. The way he figured it, after what she'd been through, she was due at least a month of good cries.

''Does that mean yes,'' he asked.

''Yes, please,'' she mumbled, and held him close. ''But only if you come with me.''

''That goes without saying. Of course I'm coming with you.''

''Good.''

There was a brief moment of silence while Scott argued with himself as to the wisdom of saying this now. But after what they'd been through, he had to get it said.

''Kristie?''

"Hmm?"

"I heated some soup. Are you hungry?"

"I guess. What kind is it?"

"Minestrone. It was all you had."

"Yes, I'll have some if you will."

She sat and watched as he dished up the soup. Once they were seated, Scott didn't eat, but watched her instead.

"Aren't you hungry?" she asked when she realized he wasn't eating.

"I have something to say to you."

She laid down her spoon. "Okay?"

"I'm in love with you all over again."

A smile started in her heart and spread all the way to her face.

"Oh, Scotty, I love you, too."

He went limp with relief. "Well, it's a good thing, because your mother is already planning our babies."

"She's *what?*"

The shock on Kristie's face made him laugh. "She mentioned Loretta and Billy had a baby and—"

"Good Lord," Kristie said. "I'm so sorry. I hope you weren't too embarrassed?"

"No…challenged a bit, but definitely not embarrassed."

She laughed out loud. "If you come with me to Texas, you know what they're going to think."

He took a deep breath. "That's what I was getting to."

"What? You don't want to go now?"

"No, on the contrary. How do you feel about long engagements?"

She grinned. "Don't like 'em."

"I knew there was a reason I still loved you," he drawled.

"So what are you saying?" she asked.

"That I think we should get married at your parents' house while we're in Midland. That I don't want to spend another night of my life without you in my arms and that I want to live with you and have babies with you and grow old with you, Kristie Ann. That's what I'm saying."

She got up from her seat, sat in his lap and wrapped her arms around his neck.

"So...this is a proposal, right?"

He nodded.

"And this is the twenty-eighth day of December, right?"

He nodded again.

"So, if we can get to Texas fast enough, we just might be able to get married on New Year's Day."

"Oh, honey...no way. How about the day after?"

She frowned. "But why not? It would be so romantic."

"You know how your family is about football. No one would come to the wedding. They'll all be watching the games."

She stared at him a moment, thinking of the lifelong tradition of Texas football, and then threw back her head and laughed. She laughed so hard and so long that, for a moment, Scott feared she was going to get hysterical. Finally she calmed down and managed to agree.

"Oh, God...I've been in Chicago too long. I'd completely forgotten about that. You're right...you're so right. Can you imagine the look on my daddy's face if I told him that he was going to have to walk me down the aisle instead of the annual day of eat, shout at the NFL umpires, and sleep?''

He laughed as she added, ''We'll figure it out after we get there.''

He grinned. ''Good thinking. In the meantime, did I mention that I love you?''

''Yes, but I'd like to hear it again, if you please.''

''I love you, Kristie Ann. I have loved you since the sixth grade and I love you even more today.''

''That's because I grew breasts,'' she said.

He looked startled for a moment and then it was his turn to laugh. When he could look at her without laughing all over again, he took her hand and put it on his heart.

''I don't know what the future will bring us, but I do know that whatever it is, we'll do it together.''

''Together,'' she said, and then leaned closer for his kiss.

Epilogue

It was New Year's Eve and Kristie was in her mother's kitchen getting glasses out of the cupboard. For as long as she could remember, Blaine Samuels had made a toast on New Year's Eve, and at the stroke of midnight when the new year was just beginning, they drank to good health and a good year. The fact that they were drinking Uncle John's homemade wine out of her mother's jelly glasses was immaterial to the situation. It was the gathering of family and the love that kept them bonded that mattered most.

Just as she started to pick up the tray, her mother came into the kitchen and stopped her with a look.

"I'll carry that, honey. You go on in with Scotty. He's looking for you."

Kristie sighed. She'd waited until she was home and face-to-face with her family before she'd told them what she'd endured. They'd cried with her and then thanked God on their knees that she was still alive to tell the tale. The fact that Scott had saved her life had only endeared him to them even more. They'd always liked him, but right now, in their eyes, he was as close to perfect as he would ever be.

"Mama, I'm okay."

"You might be," her mother said, "but I'm not. At least not yet. So you're going to have to bear with me while I baby you some more."

Kristie grinned. "You just let me know when I'm no longer delicate, okay?"

Her mother swatted her bottom with the flat of her hand.

"You go find that man of yours and get ready."

"Ready for what?"

Her mother's eyebrow arched. "Now I know I raised you smarter than that. For the kiss, Kristie Ann. I've kissed your daddy at the stroke of midnight on New Year's Eve ever since we've been married and the magic hasn't worn off yet."

Kristie grinned. "Oh…so it was magic was it? And all this time I thought it was about sex."

Her mother grinned. "I'm not talking to you about my sex life, now get out of my kitchen."

"Yes, ma'am. I'm on my way."

She was still grinning as she walked into the living room, and almost instantly her gaze centered on Scott. He was leaning against the mantel and laughing at something her father was saying. Breath caught in the back of her throat and then tears momentarily blurred her vision. She knew that there would be tough times ahead for them, just as there would be times of near perfection, but at this very moment, she knew the meaning of bliss.

Scott looked up, caught her staring at him, and lost all train of thought.

"Uh, excuse me," he muttered, and left Blaine in the middle of the punch line of a joke.

Kristie smiled as he put his arms around her. "I think you just abandoned my father."

"He's not as pretty as you," Scott said softly, and kissed the side of her cheek.

"Here, everyone, get a glass," her mother called. "It's almost midnight."

The room was full of family. Loretta and Billy. Kristie's mother and father. Her uncle John and aunt Patty. Her brother Justin and his wife, Marcie. Babies were sleeping in the bedrooms, while older children had bedded down on pallets down the hall. There was a strength within this house that had nothing to do with the sturdiness of the structure and everything to do with the family who'd gathered beneath its roof.

The television was on and a local television station began counting down the seconds as everyone turned toward Blaine Samuels and lifted their glasses.

"Here's to good health for us all and another good year." And then he looked at Kristie and she saw his eyes fill with tears before his gaze slid to Scott. "And here's to the man who saved my daughter's life."

Scott flushed, but lifted his glass and drank along with everyone else. At that moment the old clock on the mantel began to chime the hour and everyone knew that a new year had just begun.

Scott turned to Kristie and lowered his head for the traditional kiss.

Kristie sighed in satisfaction as Scott took her into his arms, and when she felt the warmth of his mouth on her lips, she knew her mother had been right all along.

It wasn't just about sex.

Love was magic after all.

* * * * *

FIGHTING FOR HIS WIFE

Paula Detmer Riggs

Dear Reader,

A secret admirer—what a great fantasy! It's not only archetypal, but also sheer fun to write. It reminded me of the days when I could recite entire passages of *Gone with the Wind* from memory. Of course, I was in love with Rhett Butler and thought Scarlett was a total idiot for not appreciating the terrific hero who adored her.

Although the hero of *this* book, Bryce Hunter, never read *GWTW* (or if he did, he would never admit it), at heart he is every bit as romantic and dashing as Rhett himself. At the same time he is a twenty-first-century knight determined to win back the love of his life.

Naturally, this knight's campaign wasn't without its bumps and detours, primarily of the passionate kind, but his resolve never wavered.

I certainly couldn't resist this hero, and neither could one Tia Kostas Hunter. I hope that you find him every bit as irresistible.

Sincerely,

Paula Detmer Riggs

Monday

"Hold the elevator, please!"

Inside the mahogany-and-brass compartment, security guard Barney Plotski shot out a hand, stopping the door an inch before it closed. Although accommodating the building's tenants and visitors was part of his job description, it could be a real pain in the posterior, especially during the morning rush.

As soon as he caught sight of the black-haired, dark-eyed cutie in one of those fake leopard-skin coats and fuzzy black hat hurrying toward him, however, his mood took a sudden spike upward. Normally, he wasn't much for career females. Had too much of a hard edge to 'em, but Ms. Tia Hunter always greeted him with a real genuine smile and a right friendly word.

Noticed things, too, she did, like how preoccupied he'd been one day last March when his Emmy had

had serious bypass surgery. On her way out that evening, Miz Hunter had handed him a potted orchid she'd bought on her lunch hour and asked him to give Emmy her best wishes. Emmy had been bowled over.

Word around the building had it that she was one of Shay, Tremaine and Weller's rising stars. Senior Account Executive is what it said on her office door. A few months back, one of her TV ads had won some big-time award, and the partners had thrown her a fancy party in that fancy meeting room in their office suite.

Her husband had been there that night, and from the things Barney'd overheard while standing in line at the coffee cart in the lobby the next morning, half the women at the party had hit on the man when Miz Hunter wasn't looking. Barney figured that was on account of Bryce Hunter being what his thirteen-year-old granddaughter called "major primo."

Reminded *him* of that actor Emmy liked so much, Kevin Costner. Only, Hunter looked bigger and broader—and younger. Early- to mid-thirties would be his guess. Twenty-five years a cop, Barney had automatically sized the guy up at six-five, two-ten, two-twenty—and all muscle.

Cryin' shame about him blowing out his knee his fourth year with the Bears—and hadn't that been a gruesome business to watch on national TV, with the camera right on the poor man's face and him in such terrible pain? Hired on as a coach after he retired, though, and darned if he hadn't turned out to be best offensive coordinator the Bears had had in a long time. Some of the plays he'd worked out made a man cry, they were that beautiful.

A few months back he'd heard that Miz Hunter had handed the coach his walking papers, although no one knew exactly why. He figured the poor guy had to be dying a slow death right about now. Leastwise, that's how *he* would feel if his darlin' Emmy up and tossed him out.

"Thanks, Barney," she said, huffing a little after her sprint across the lobby. "I'm running behind this morning."

"No problem, Miz Hunter." Whooee, but she smelled good, he thought as he punched the button for her floor. Like his mama always said, "Pretty is as pretty does." Only in Miz Hunter's case, with her shiny black hair, big, sparkling brown eyes and what Emmy called "classy" cheekbones, she was an honest-to-goodness knockout. Sexy enough to have an old man like him sucking in his gut, she was, too.

Tia caught the way Barney preened, and hid a smile. The youngest of six, she'd grown up watching her four big brothers swagger and strut and flaunt their bulging muscles and Greek arrogance for any female who happened to wander by. By the age of sixteen, when her fiercely protective papa had finally allowed her to date, she'd vowed to run at the first whiff of rampant testosterone. Instead, she'd taken one look at Bryce Hunter and melted.

"Have to admit I'm surprised to find you workin' today," Barney offered as the elevator passed the fourth floor. "It being the day after Christmas and S.T.&W. operating on holiday hours like most of the other tenants."

"I'm pitching a prospective client this morning. Today was the only date he was free until after the

New Year.'' Although she was fighting a rare case of nerves—pregame jitters Bryce would call it—her pride refused to let it show.

''Important deal, is it?''

''Major big. I've sweated blood for six weeks to come up with the perfect campaign.'' She felt her heart rate speed and made a mental note to carve out ten minutes to meditate before she made her presentation at ten. MegaVolt Cola was the most prestigious prospect she'd ever tackled. Landing it would take her to the next level in the S.T.&W. pecking order. A boost she desperately needed right now.

''You'll land 'em, no sweat.''

''I appreciate the thought, but I've learned never to count the money before the client's name is on the contract and the check has cleared the bank.''

''Maybe that's true about the others who do what you do, not with you, though. Ain't a man alive who wouldn't pull down the moon and lay it at your feet in exchange for one of your smiles.''

''Oh, I've known a few,'' she tossed off with a laugh. ''My soon-to-be ex, for example.'' After several false starts and some truly embarrassing outbursts of tears, she'd found that making jokes about her failed marriage provided a much-needed layer of insulation between her and a very dangerous caldron of emotions boiling away inside her.

Instead of laughing as most did, however, Barney grew thoughtful. ''Now that surprises me, Miz. Hunter. It really does. When I was still in uniform, I worked game day security and had me a coupla conversations with Coach Hunter. I don't pretend to be an expert, but he seemed more than average bright to me."

"You're right. He graduated cum laude from Notre Dame with a degree in finance." Which had helped make them—*him,* she corrected quickly—financially secure, if not yet rich.

"Seems to me a man that smart would know when he'd caught the brass ring and want to hang on to it."

"Things happen," she said, smiling through the stab of pain. "Our divorce is perfectly amicable."

The elevator arrived at her floor then, and the doors opened. Instead of stepping aside to let her exit, however, he held the door with his hand. "I'm not a betting man, but if I were, I'd bet my pension the right man will come along for you, too. Maybe sooner than you think."

Tia felt a lump forming in her throat. "It'll be a while before I'm ready for another relationship."

"You know best, of course," Barney said, stepping out of her way.

"If I don't see you before the weekend, happy New Year," she said as the doors started to close.

"Same to you—and kick some butt with those hotshot clients." Before she could thank him, the doors slid shut.

Heels clicking a no-nonsense rhythm, she crossed the elevator lobby to the gleaming walnut door bearing the distinctive Shay, Tremaine and Weller logo lettered in gold. Inside, the reception area with its thick carpeting, tush-pampering chairs, and lush accent plants was unusually quiet.

Instead of the usual receptionist, a Meg Ryan look-alike in a black turtleneck and red blazer sat behind the free-form marble-and-glass desk. A paralegal named Marilyn Lynch who usually worked in the contracts department, she reminded Tia of herself ten years ago when she'd come to S.T.&W. right out of the University of Chicago.

"Good morning, Ms. Hunter," she chirped, grinning. "How was your Christmas?"

"Hectic." Tia smiled. "And yours?"

"Wonderful!" Eyes sparkling, she held out her left hand. A tiny diamond set in a gold band sparkled on the third finger. "Kevin and I have finally set a date."

"It's lovely, Marilyn. Kevin has good taste."

"Oh, he didn't pick it out, I did." She dimpled. "But thanks for the compliment."

Laughing, Tia instinctively glanced down at the hand wrapped around the handle of her briefcase. Beneath the kid glove, her finger was bare. Pain stabbed hard, but thankfully not as deep as it had when she'd first removed the ring Bryce had placed on her finger when she'd been even younger than Marilyn. "My best wishes. I hope you'll be wonderfully happy."

Before Marilyn could respond, the door behind her swung open. Short, balding, and a thoroughly sweet man, Peter Goldstein was S.T.&W.'s chief accountant, and like Tia, a total workaholic. "Good morning, ladies." When he smiled, his entire face lit up, making him appear almost handsome.

"Morning, Pete," Tia said with a fond grin.

"Tia, I was hoping I'd run into you sometime this week."

"If it's about my expense account, I have copies of my receipts. In triplicate."

Pete laughed. "No, this is personal. I just wanted to tell you that Danny's crazy about the Bears' cap. Tell Bryce I owe him one."

Tia looked at him blankly. "Pardon me?"

"Since the Bears made the playoffs last year, Danny's gone football crazy. He was just fitted with new braces two months ago and he hates wearing them, so we made a deal. If he'd wear the braces for a month without complaining, I'd take him to a game. It took some doing, but I finally scored two tickets for Saturday's game." Noticing the puzzled look on Marilyn's face, he amplified, "My seven-year-old has spina bifida. The doctors think he'll eventually be able to walk with crutches and braces, but it's going to be a long haul."

A look of sympathy crossed Marilyn's face. "That must be rough on all of you."

"It can be, but Sue and I are determined to see that Danny has as normal a life as possible."

"Did he enjoy the game?" Tia asked, and Pete nodded.

"We went early, so Dan could watch the players warm up. One of the ushers stopped to chat, and I asked her if she'd give Bryce my card and a note explaining that we'd met at S.T.&W.'s New Year's Eve party three years ago and would he mind signing an autograph for my son." He grinned. "Next thing I know the usher took us down in a private elevator and onto the field. I have to admit I was a little nervous, what with Dan being in a wheelchair. Some people can't handle being around someone with a handicap, but Bryce treated Dan like any other starstruck kid. He introduced us around personally, and then arranged for us to stay on the sidelines during the game. One of the cameramen got a great close-up of Dan yelling his head off after the Bears scored, and now he's a real hero at his school. Helped his self-esteem enormously."

"Omigod, I watched that game," Marilyn said in an excited voice. "I remember seeing that little boy in a wheelchair! He's *adorable.*"

"Like his daddy," Pete boasted, and the two women burst into laughter. "I thought Bryce might have mentioned it to you," he said to Tia when the laughter died down.

"No, but I'm not surprised. Bryce has always had a soft spot for kids, especially those with special problems. A few years ago he and LaMar Lester set up a scholarship fund for disadvantaged kids, although no one but the foundation staff knows who established the original trust."

"He's a good man. One of the best."

Pete's praise only served to remind her of all the reasons why she'd fallen in love with Bryce. "I'll be sure to pass along your thanks," she said with a smile.

"Appreciate it," he said before heading down the hall toward his office.

Doing her best to ignore the butterflies multiplying in the pit of her stomach, Tia glanced at the clock on the marble wall forming the backdrop to the workstation.

"Marilyn, I'm expecting Harold Lewin from MegaVolt Cola and several of his staff at ten. Please show them into the small conference room when they arrive, and then buzz me."

The receptionist sat straighter. "Don't worry, I'll take very good care of them."

"Thanks, I appreciate it."

The phone rang then, and after saying a quick goodbye, Tia hurried toward the row of offices occupied by the art department, marketing research and account executives.

When she'd started, she'd been assigned a tiny cubicle in the bullpen with the rest of the interns. With each promotion, she'd moved closer to that coveted corner office. Last February, after landing the Granny Merryweather's Home-Style Bakery account, she'd scored an office with a panoramic view of the city, a perk only slightly less prestigious than the holy grail of corporate status: a corner suite.

A believer in subliminal messages, she'd redecorated with an eye toward putting her clients and prospective clients at ease while at the same time showcasing her professional status. To that end, she'd had the walls painted a quietly elegant ivory and had handpicked the furniture, mostly Art Deco revisited with an emphasis on comfort. On the wall opposite the window, she'd hung an eclectic selection of oils, watercolors and lithographs that were at once hip and high energy.

The door to the outer office was open, and her assistant Steph Gregory was already at her wraparound workstation, answering an e-mail message when Tia entered.

Tall, redheaded and irreverent, Steph was a firm believer in power naps, tarot cards and female empowerment. A perfect size sixteen and proud of it, she had exquisite taste, designed and sewed most of her own clothes, favoring vivid colors and sensuous fabrics. Although men flocked to her, she was extremely choosy, turning down four dates for every one she accepted.

"Nice hat and scarf," she said, glancing up from the screen to inspect Tia over the dark rims of her high-tech glasses. "Melina must be trying to quit smoking again."

Tia adored her older sister, but Melina Kostas was a bit of a flake. "Third time's a charm—we hope."

After depositing her briefcase and shoulder bag on an uncluttered corner of the workstation, she hung her coat on the brass rack in the corner. "I'd planned to be in by seven this morning, get a jump-start on the week, but the Cherokee refused to start again. I had to call the auto club, and it took them forever to arrive."

"I thought Bryce had set up an appointment to have the electrical system checked out."

"He set it up without consulting me," Tia said, shoving her gloves into her coat pockets for safe-keeping. "Since it wasn't at a convenient time for me, I canceled."

"That'll show the meddling so-and-so," Steph muttered before returning her attention to the screen.

Tia snatched off the mohair hat before whirling around to point a well-manicured finger directly at Steph's rather prominent nose. "I *swear,* if one more person tells me what a great guy Bryce Hunter is, I truly believe I will be driven to violence."

Steph typed another few words before hitting the send button. "One more person?" she asked, glancing Tia's way.

"Pete Goldstein just sang two choruses of praise, and yesterday I arrived at my folks' for Christmas dinner to discover that my *loyal* and *loving* parents had invited Bryce over for dinner—behind my back. After he left, my turncoat brothers took turns trying to convince me to reconsider the divorce.'' She hung up her hat before jerking the scarf free. ''I know why, of course,'' she continued darkly. ''The traitors don't want to lose those house tickets Bryce had been feeding them all these years.''

She turned around in time to catch Steph grinning. ''Stop that this instant. This is not funny. My Christmas was a total disaster, and it's all his fault.''

''Because?'' Steph prompted, a look of rapt curiosity on her face.

''Because he should have said no!'' She took a bracing breath before heading for the coffeepot on the credenza on the opposite wall. ''It's bad enough he refused to move out after I filed, like estranged husbands are *supposed* to.''

Because she couldn't bear to sell the Victorian town house they'd labored so hard to restore, he had agreed to let her buy him out—provided she made no objection to his continuing to live there until he'd found a suitable place to buy. Escrow on his town house was due to close on January second, the same day as their final court date.

''Having never been married or divorced, I didn't realize there was an actual rule book covering the dos and don'ts of breaking up,'' Steph commented in a wry tone that set Tia's teeth on edge.

''I thought you were on my side,'' she muttered, filling her mug.

''I *am* on your side. But I'm on Bryce's side, too.'' Steph smiled. ''I'm an equal opportunity pain in the rear.''

Tia laughed, but her amusement almost immediately faded into a familiar mix of resentment, sadness and regret. "Bryce still refuses to understand why I had to end things. He's utterly convinced he's the wounded party in all this."

"Men are really good at selective blindness. Gives them plausible deniability when the do-do hits the fan."

"I suspect his resistance has more to do with his nature. More than anything Bryce hates to lose, even at hearts. It took him two years of brutally hard work rehabbing his knee before he resigned himself to never playing again. After that, he shoved the dream he'd had since he was nine years old into a drawer in his head, locked it tight, and refused to talk about what might have been."

Tia uttered a humorless laugh. "From the first he's always been wary of sharing his feelings, but after he was forced to stop playing, he avoided anything that even approached emotional intimacy between us."

Steph glanced her way, her expression somber. "You do realize he'll treat you the same way, don't you? Once you sign those papers, it will be over between the two of you forever."

An unexpected chill ran through her. She hadn't really thought that far ahead, but now that she did, she realized Steph had called it exactly right. "It was over the moment he started walling himself off from me."

"Maybe he didn't want you to see how much he was hurting. A guy can get pretty prickly when his self-image undergoes a major meltdown."

"Trust me, with four brothers of the Greek persuasion I understand that all too well. But I meant it when I promised 'for better or worse.' I would have walked through fire to help him work through his disappointment and pain, but he wouldn't give me the chance. He didn't *trust* me enough to share his deepest emotions, which is the worst hurt of all." She inhaled in two fast jerks. "I could have handled the fact that he's a dud in the romance department if we'd been closer emotionally, but bottom line, I just can't go on feeling diminished, like I'm good enough to be his live-in lover, but not a real wife."

Compassion and understanding shimmered in Steph's eyes as she spoke. "I'm sorry, Tia. Truly."

"I know. So am I."

Resisting the urge to hug herself for warmth, she sipped coffee until the mug was half empty and the chill was gone.

Relieved, she mentally set aside the things she couldn't control for those she could. "I'd like to have the flash cards set up in the conference room as soon as possible so I can run through my presentation one last time," she said, refilling her mug.

Taking the hint, Steph swiveled back to face her computer. "It'll just take me a few seconds to check the rest of the mail," she said, her fingers already moving over the keyboard.

After slipping her purse and briefcase over one shoulder, Tia opened the door separating her private office from Steph's. Holding her mug in one hand, she flipped on the light with the other. Two steps into the room she stopped. Surprise rippled through her like an uncontrollable shiver.

"Oh, my!" she whispered out loud. Sitting dead center in the middle of her desk was a leaded-crystal vase filled with long-stemmed roses, several dozen at least, with velvety petals so deeply red they were almost black and so fresh, dew glistened on the deep green leaves. The scent that filled the room was delectably intoxicating.

"You sneak, why didn't you tell me?" Tia exclaimed as Steph entered.

"Because I'm as surprised as you are. The door was closed when I arrived. Only a window washer or Spider-Man could have gotten in here after that." Steph caught a dewdrop on the tip of her index finger. "These can't have been here more than a couple of hours, if that."

Tia agreed. "The florist must have checked in with Marilyn, although she didn't mention it." She glanced Steph's way. "Maybe they're for *you.*"

"There's a card," Steph offered, her tone eager. "See?"

"Don't rush me, I'm savoring the moment."

"Savor later, I'm having a cow here."

Taking a deep breath, Tia plucked a tiny vellum envelope from a nest of shiny leaves. "For Tia" had been typed on the front. The back was sealed.

Her heart rate took off like a shot. Could she be wrong about Bryce? Had he decided to fight for her after all? She felt her throat tighten. It was too late, of course. Or was it?

"Tia, open the damned envelope," Steph pleaded.

"I'm almost afraid to. What if they were sent by someone I don't like?"

"You'll thank him politely and refuse his phone calls."

"No, *you'll* refuse his phone calls," Tia corrected

before tearing open the envelope. Inside was a miniature card bearing no distinguishing marks to indicate the florist or manner of delivery. One side was blank. Something was typed on the reverse.

"For heaven's sake, Tia, what's it say?" Steph demanded, trying to see over her shoulder.

Tia breathed in the lovely scent before clearing her throat. "'This is going to be our year,'" she read out loud. "'Love, Your Secret Admirer.'"

Saturday's game with the Packers had been a nail-biter, as were most games between longtime rivals, Green Bay and Chicago. The lead had changed hands from quarter to quarter, but with only twelve seconds remaining, the Bears had kicked a field goal to win 39-38.

After spending Christmas Day nursing bruises and sore muscles, a goodly number of players had shown up early to hit the whirlpool before the team meeting set for ten. Bryce had arrived shortly after seven and, as was his habit on the day of a meeting, gone directly to his office to watch films of the game. A methodical man, he'd concentrated on the plays that had worked, then the ones that hadn't, rewinding and replaying a half dozen times while jotting down notes on a yellow tablet in his own shorthand.

Finally satisfied that he'd learned all he could, he'd strapped on his knee brace, changed into sweats and a T-shirt and headed downstairs to go ten rounds with the heavy bag used by the linemen to build arm strength and endurance. Now, less than forty minutes into his workout, the short jabs and body blows that had sung with demonic power twenty minutes earlier were now little more than powder-puff slaps. Hell, his niece Delfie had more of a punch, and she'd just turned six.

"Sure glad that ain't *my* body you're doin' your best to whomp up on." In the press guide put out by the Bears, defensive tackle LaMar Lester was listed as six feet five inches tall and two hundred and sixty-five pounds. The height was correct. The weight was thirty pounds light, give or take a couple of meals.

Too whipped to do more than grunt something obscene in response, Bryce put his entire two hundred and twelve pounds into one last left jab before stepping back. As he did, he felt pain corkscrewing his bad knee. He folded his wince into a scowl and hoped LaMar hadn't noticed.

"You're always bragging about being the meanest son of a gun ever to come out of N'Orleans," he tossed out between labored breaths. "How about pulling on a pair of gloves and proving it?"

"Now, I'd like to, bro, I surely would." As LaMar cruised closer, a grin rearranged his round face into a series of concentric folds. "Thing is, though, a man about to spend two ro-man-tic weeks in Gay Par-ee with his new bride would be ten times a fool to risk a coupla broken ribs putting him outta commission."

Bryce wiped his forearm over his damp forehead. "You have a point, there." Next to Tia, LaMar's fiancée, Deirdre Calhoun was the classiest woman he knew. "Besides, Dee would likely scald my butt for ruining her honeymoon."

Laughter danced across LaMar's face. "You got

that right! My lady ain't about to let anyone rain on her wedding parade. No, sir.''

Trying not to limp, Bryce walked to the weight bench where he'd left his gym bag and dropped the boxing gloves inside before uncapping his bottle of spring water and swallowing half the contents. ''Thing I can't figure, Lester, how'd you get so lucky? Dee being such a prize catch, and all?''

''Pure charm, bro. Something you ain't got much of.''

''Yeah, well, that's already been established,'' Bryce said in a terse voice before mopping his face and neck with the towel he'd hung over the bar at the end of the bench.

Now that his concentration had been broken, the hot-wired edginess had returned to turn his gut into a minefield. Turning his back on LaMar, he dug into his bag for the bottle of antacids he'd taken to tossing down like candy. He'd been nine years old and about to play in his first Pop Warner game when pregame jitters had hit him the first time. Once the game started, however, he was fine. But this plan he'd put into play this morning was way more than a game. It was his life.

Tia should have found the flowers by now, he thought as he shook out two tablets and chewed them up. Three dozen of those dark red suckers, guaranteed by the city's most prestigious florist to be the best the wholesaler had to offer. To make sure they'd be at the height of their beauty, the florist had had them flown in special by FedEx in the early morning hours.

Bryce had been prepared to talk his way in to Tia's office, but this time Lady Luck had been with him instead of blindsiding him the way she'd done these last few years. The rent-a-cop in the lobby had been ex-Chicago P.D. by the name of Plotski—and a rabid Bears fan. Once Bryce had explained why he'd shown up before daybreak with his arms full of sissy roses, Plotski had been happy to help, his silence guaranteed, no strings attached.

Since the stakes were so high, however, Bryce had hedged his bets by slipping him a C-note along with a promise to leave two tickets at the Soldier Field will-call window for the play-off game on January fourteenth.

That had been the easy part. The hard part was waiting to see if he would come out a winner this time—or spend the rest of his life regretting his stupid-ass mistakes.

"Yo, Hunt, you got a couple of those chalk tablets to spare?"

Silently, Bryce tossed LaMar the bottle.

"Thanks, bro." Looking sheepish, LaMar crunched down four before accepting a swig from Bryce's water bottle. "Gotta admit, this whole wedding thing is gettin' to me some. All the hoops Dee's got me jumping through, I'm tempted to throw her in the back of my 'Vette and haul her off to a Baptist preacher friend of mine down in Danville."

Bryce took another swig of water before capping the bottle. "Take it from a man who found out the hard way, she'd never forgive you if you screw up this fairy-tale wedding she has her heart set on. Next thing you know she'll be claiming you don't have a romantic bone in your body and suing you for divorce."

Dropping his gaze, LaMar kicked at the corner of the thick floor mat with the toe of his size fourteen high-tops. "Sorry to break it to you, Hunt, but takin' a classy lady like Tia on a fishing trip for her anniversary when she'd been hintin' about a romantic cruise for months was about as dumb as dumb can get." He grinned. "Hard for a woman to feel beautiful when she's swole up with mosquito bites and sleeping on sheets smelling like fish guts."

Bryce winced. No doubt that's exactly how Tia described to Deirdre their stay in head coach Ernie Biggs's cabin on one of the Minnesota lakes.

"Yeah, well, like the man says, hindsight is twenty-twenty," Bryce growled through a suddenly clenched jaw. "Besides, like I tried to explain to Tia, I get seasick on a damn ferry ride. How romantic would it have been if she spent two weeks listening to me heave up my guts?"

"You coulda taken her to Hawaii then or Paris, like me and Dee, someplace where she coulda worn all those imported nightgowns and fancy dresses Dee said she bought when you told her you were taking her someplace special."

Although LaMar meant well, the pointed jab hit deep and then flared into a barbed agony in his gut. It had taken him months to realize that his lack of romance was only a symptom of a larger problem—his inability to give Tia the closeness she craved. Looking back through a tunnel formed by a lot of sleepless nights and painful introspection, he cringed to remember how many times she'd sensed his suffering and tried to help. Instead of being grateful, he'd resented her questions and sympathy and, yeah, even her love. Because he couldn't really be certain he could keep that love once she realized he was no longer a hero, but just a regular guy. He still wasn't sure. He just knew he was miserable without her.

"I screwed up, I admit it," he rasped. "But I'm not letting her go without a fight."

LaMar hunched his shoulders. "You really think this secret admirer thing will work?"

"I think it has a shot, yeah. Dee does, too." Bryce wadded up his sodden towel and tossed it into one of the receptacles lined up against the wall. "Once Tia got it into her head she'd married a prize dud in the romance department she stopped listening and started convincing herself she'd be better off without me. It's my intention to prove to her she's wrong."

"Only she doesn't know it's you being romantic, so what's that gonna prove?"

"Once she falls in love with this fantasy guy, I'll step up and tell her the truth."

LaMar eyed him warily. "It's been my experience that ladies get honked off if they think a guy's playin' 'em for a fool."

"I thought about that, but Dee swears it doesn't work that way." Taking anything on faith had always been hard for him. Since he'd decided to fight to win Tia back, he'd sweated bullets trying to plan for any unexpected sideways stutter in his carefully crafted plan.

LaMar settled his bulk on the bench and splayed his hands, which were the size of catcher's mitts, on his knees. "If Dee says it, it's most likely true," he said after a moment's consideration. "Lord knows she's a whole lot smarter'n either one of us."

His grin flashed with pride and love. ''Like my grandmamma told me when she met Dee the first time, I must have done something powerfully special in another lifetime to be blessed with such a fine woman in this one.''

Bryce zipped his bag closed before slinging it over his shoulder. ''Whatever you do, my brother, don't ever take good fortune like that for granted. 'Cause if you do, you just might spend the rest of your life standing out in the cold, freezing to death—and knowing there's not a damn thing you can do about it.''

Ten minutes later Bryce stood alone and buck-naked at one end of the shower room, letting the steaming hot water pound the ache from his shoulders. Too bad LaMar hadn't taken him up on his challenge, he thought as he braced one hand against the slick tile. A couple of well-placed punches to the midsection would have gone a long way toward driving out some of the eels crawling around his belly.

Cool under pressure, the sportswriters had described him when he'd been playing. Oh, yeah, he was cool all right, he thought, disgusted at himself. Since Tia had dropped the hammer on him, he'd been a basket case.

He leaned forward until his head rested against the tile and water sluiced down his spine. *Irreconcilable differences,* it said on the legal papers. Meaning he hadn't measured up to the larger-than-life image she'd married. Not that she'd come right out and said the words. Tia hated to hurt anyone—

even her has-been husband—but that's what she'd meant.

You clueless dolt, can't you read between the lines? Dee had railed at him in the middle of what had to have been the worst hangover known to man. *This isn't about how she feels about you, it's about how you make her feel about herself.*

Although it had cost him a chunk of his pride, he'd admitted he hadn't a clue what Dee was talking about. *The woman wants to feel cherished and adored instead of taken for granted like...like that ratty old recliner in your den.*

He'd gotten that part okay. The next thing she'd laid on him had been the kicker. According to Dee, their marriage had gotten stale and the best way to fix it fast was to court her again.

It was the *again* part that had given him big trouble. From the age of thirteen when he'd suddenly shot past the girls in height and started developing muscles to go with his outsize shoulders and big feet, he'd had his pick of girlfriends. In high school and then at Notre Dame he'd never lacked for dates but had never found a woman he'd wanted as a permanent part of his life. Two weeks before his first preseason game with the Bears, he'd walked into a party given by Tia's roommate.

Yeah, it was a cliché, but as soon as Tia had smiled at him, he'd known that she was "the one and only." It had been the same for her. They'd made love that night and by morning were engaged. Six months later they were married.

Problem was, being raised from birth by his widowed dad the way he had, he hadn't a clue how a husband was supposed to act. After giving it some thought, he figured marriage was a lot like football, with its own set of rules and plays that could be mastered through practice and discipline.

Only in this case the usual plays turned out to be worse than useless. *You don't have a romantic bone in your body,* she'd said repeatedly. But whenever he asked her what kinds of things he should do to please her, she'd fallen back on that chick thing men hate: *If I have to tell you, it doesn't mean anything.*

So with Dee's help—and the pile of "chick" magazines she'd made him read as research—he'd come up with a whole new set of plays designed around an alter ego who would do all the things women seemed to find irresistible. As a guide he'd used the articles he'd devoured like the Snickers bars he kept hidden in his desk drawer.

In theory, it should work. In practice...no, damn it, it *had* to work, he repeated as he shut off the water. Because truth be told, he simply could not imagine a life without Tia in it.

Did houses mourn the loss of an inhabitant in the same way that a person mourned the loss of a family member or dear friend? Tia wondered as she hurried up the walk from the detached one-car garage to the back porch.

The spotlights Bryce had installed that first year elongated her shadow and dusted the bare branches of the lilac bushes with a ghostly light. Not-yet-melted remnants of last week's snowstorm outlined the bottom of the good-neighbor fence with white.

The house itself was Wedgwood blue with ivory trim and lilac accents. In summer, sweet-smelling alyssum and petunias spilled from the window boxes. Ten years ago when the Realtor had shepherded them up the crumbling front sidewalk toward the sagging porch, the patches of paint that had managed to cling to the shiplap siding had been a dingy pink. At first glance, it had reminded Tia of a doll's house she'd had once, ruined when she'd left it out in the rain.

Already impatient after days of house hunting, her big, tough bridegroom had looked horrified. *No way,* he had mouthed behind the Realtor's back. It had been too late. Tia had already fallen in love. Bryce had grumbled and scowled and sworn he didn't intend to spend a penny of his signing bonus on an eyesore that was one wind gust from firewood. His dad had a better-looking pig barn on his farm in northwestern Indiana.

The Realtor knew, even if Bryce hadn't figured it out yet, that he was sunk. All it had taken was a whispered plea in the dark and Bryce had given in. *If this derelict is what you really want, sweetheart, then I want you to have it.*

At twenty-one she'd been starry-eyed enough to take those words as a declaration of everlasting love. She'd been wrong. A man truly in love with his wife would have fought to save their marriage, she reminded herself as, juggling briefcase, purse and the garment bag containing her bridesmaid dress for Dee and LaMar's wedding on Friday night, she let herself into the small mudroom.

Bryce's huge snow boots lay where he'd left them last week after shoveling the walks. Her fur-lined boots—size six-and-a-half to his twelve-and-a-half—stood neatly side-by-side on a rubber mat. The much-used snow shovel had been propped against the wall by the water softener, and his down-filled vest hung next to the door along with his battered, sweat-stained cowboy hat and her gardening apron.

For weeks now he'd been promising to have everything packed and ready for the movers to pick up next Monday morning, but from what she'd been able to see, the boxes scattered in every room but the master bedroom were mostly empty. Since he hadn't contested the division of assets set up by her attorney, she felt guilty about complaining. Besides, he still had time.

After he moved out, the house would seem strange at first, the women in her support group who'd already been through it had warned. The rooms might appear painfully empty, especially the master bedroom where they'd placed the oversize mahogany bed that had belonged to his grandfather. Although she had loved it on sight, it should stay in his family, not hers. The house, though, had always been more hers than his, and in one week it would be hers alone, like her life. She intended to think of it as a thrilling new adventure.

This is going to be our year. Love, Your Secret Admirer.

Marilyn swore she hadn't seen a florist. No one else in the office admitted knowing anything. The follow-up phone call she'd halfway expected had never come. Steph was leaning toward an old boyfriend, someone who'd known her before Bryce had swept her off her feet. Tia had racked her brain, and she still didn't have a clue. Perhaps she would find out tomorrow, she consoled herself as she pulled open the door to the kitchen.

As she entered, Bryce turned away from the refrigerator door, a bottle of pineapple juice in one big hand. At twenty-three he'd been cocky, aggressive and wildly sexy, a world-class athlete with a powerful, hard-muscled body she'd immediately wanted to see naked. Then, as now, he'd been most comfortable in butt-hugging Levis, worn thin across the seat, thighs and knees, and an ancient Notre Dame sweatshirt with the sleeves pushed a few inches past wide forearms and strong wrists. Then, as now, she'd looked into his deep-gray eyes and experienced a violent surge of heat. Annoyed, and determined to overcome this unfortunate bump in the surprisingly smooth road to divorce, she offered a polite but cool greeting.

Eyes narrowing, he let the fridge door close behind him. "Did you remember to turn off the alarm?"

Before she could respond, the stupid thing screamed like a thousand banshees. Startled, she let out an abbreviated shriek of her own.

"Damn it to hell, Tia," Bryce growled, setting the bottle on the counter with a hard clunk before hurrying past her.

Blessed silence descended seconds later, although her ears continued to ring. When he returned, he ignored her as he grabbed up the portable phone from the holder and hit the speed dial button for the security company. After reciting their ID number—from memory Tia noticed with just the tiniest twinge of guilt—he explained that it was a false alarm.

"Yeah, she did it again." As he listened to the man's reply, his gaze meshed with hers. His lips twitched at the corners, a sure sign he was working hard not to smile. He wouldn't dare, she thought, tensing. "Believe me, I realize that, but my wife's a full-blooded Greek and inclined to overreact. I'm not real eager to get my skull bashed in with a frying pan."

"I do *not* overreact!" she said slowly and distinctly. "*I* am a cool and calm modern woman in total charge of her emotions."

His gray eyes darkened until they were the color of slate. Tiny laugh lines at the corners deepened an instant before he grinned. Part mischievous, part sexy and sizzling with testosterone, Bryce's smile had once rocked her world. Even now, she felt a distinct wobble deep down inside.

Reminding herself that residual feelings were to be expected, she set her briefcase and purse on an empty corner of the island and hung the garment bag over the back of one of the rattan bar stools.

"I'd appreciate it, thanks," he told the person on the other end. "We'll try to do better." He hung up, then leaned his backside against the counter and crossed both his arms and ankles. "Won't *we,* Tia?"

She nudged her chin higher. A Kostas always stood her ground, no matter how precarious. "I refuse to feel guilty about a false alarm now and then."

"Three this month, four last."

Oh, but she *hated* it when he backed her against a wall. If she had a failing, it was pride. More than anything she hated to admit she was wrong, but she was working on that, she reminded herself. "Perhaps you've forgotten that *you* were the one who had that…thing installed—over my strenuous objections."

The lazy amusement fled from his eyes. "I haven't forgotten anything, Tia—especially the rash of break-ins in this very neighborhood a few months back."

She waved her hand in a dismissive gesture before slipping out of her pumps. "Teenagers looking for money to buy pot. Once they were caught, the break-ins ended."

Bryce narrowed his eyes, obscuring their expression, but not before she'd seen something dangerous flash into the obsidian pupils. He had a temper to rival hers, but sports had helped him learn to control it. She was still working on hers.

"Tia, you were raised in this city. You read the papers and watch the news. You're also not in the least naive so stop acting like a spoiled brat who can't stand it when she doesn't get her way."

She sucked in a sharp breath. "I beg your pardon?" she asked, enunciating each word.

"You heard me. For ten years it's been your way or the highway. This time it's my way—at least for the next seven days. If you don't like it, find another place to stay until I'm outta here."

She shot him a look guaranteed to melt steel. "You can't order me out of my own house."

"No? You tried to order me out, and since I covered the down payment and most of the payments until you got your career in gear, technically it's more mine that yours."

Stunned, Tia stared at him. "Why are you behaving like this, Bryce?"

He shrugged. "Beats me. Could be I just got tired of always coming in second."

"What are you talking about?"

"Since the day we said 'I do', you've had your way on damn near everything including this money pit of a house. You wanted an *amicable* divorce, hey, no problem. You wanted to establish your career before having kids, okay. I respected your decision even though I would have preferred to start a family while my dad was still alive to enjoy his grandchildren."

"That's not fair! No one knew your dad had a bad heart."

Pain crossed his face. "I knew," he said, his voice flat and hard. "He asked me not to say anything to you because he didn't want to pressure you."

Tia felt a hole open in her stomach. "You should have said something."

"If I'd said something, you would have accused me of trying to use guilt to manipulate you, just like you accused me of being a 'throwback to the Ice Age' for worrying about your safety after I'm outta here."

Truth had to be respected, no matter how painful, so she swallowed the angry words that rose to her throat. "I appreciate your concern, I really do," she said, her tone stiffly polite, "but I don't need you or any other man to take care of me."

"Believe me, sweetheart, you've made that *real* clear." Without giving her a chance to answer, he pushed away from the counter and walked out of the kitchen.

"Don't call me sweetheart," she yelled after him. He answered by slamming the door hard enough to rattle the dishes in the dining room hutch. "Damn you, Br—"

The alarm suddenly shrieked, cutting off her words. Bryce had had the last word after all.

Tuesday

When the alarm clock went off at six, Tia woke up feeling jittery and out of sorts. The sheets that had been so crisp last night were now twisted around her like a mummy wrapping, all but cutting her hips in two. She was lying on her stomach, her arms hugging her pillow. Though she was still half asleep, it gradually came to her that she was moaning softly. In the next moment she realized that parts of her anatomy, primarily in the area of her pelvis, were *throbbing.*

Groaning out loud, she buried her hot face in the pillow. Waking up in the throes of the greatest dream sex she'd ever had wasn't intrinsically a bad thing, she supposed. As a tension reliever it was right up there with chocolate liqueur cordials and deep massage—unless the talented hands and mouth doing those wonderfully inventive and erotic things to her body belonged to her soon-to-be ex-husband.

For example, that thing he did with his tongue...

Her face went from hot to scorching, and then immediately cold and tingly. Adrenaline shot into her bloodstream, while at the same time her over-stimulated and pathetically susceptible hormones set her heart to racing. Instead of fight or flight, it was *Damn the divorce court, I want his hands on me now!*

Horrified, and worse, still far too aroused, she threw off the covers only to gasp at the sudden rush of frigid air from the open window. A run in the cold, that's what she needed! Maybe she couldn't control her hormonal surges, but she could over-power them with exercise endorphins.

Gritting her teeth against the chill—and her re-bellious emotions—she padded shivering to the walk-in closet where she stripped off her flannel nightshirt and hung it on the back of the door. Ig-noring the goose bumps racing over her naked body, she jerked open one of the built-in drawers, grabbed a sports bra and pulled it over her head. Sucking in, she realized her nipples were still distended and ach-ing. In her dream Bryce had suckled first one and then the other, using his teeth on the tip until she'd felt the sublime contractions all the way to the womb.

Do *not* go there, Tia Athena Kostas Hunter, she told herself firmly as she quickly threw on a thermal undershirt, bicycle shorts and sweats. Breathing hard, she pulled on two pairs of socks and her run-ning shoes before strapping on a fanny pack con-taining an ID card, extra house key and a just-in-case ten dollar bill.

After closing the window, she fished her cell

phone from her briefcase and tucked it into the fanny pack, as well. Her Walkman and earphones were in the entry closet, along with the down vest, stocking cap and gloves. Keeping in shape in Chicago in the winter was definitely not for sissies, she thought as she descended the stairs.

The aroma of strong coffee hit her a few steps before the first floor landing, which meant that Bryce had returned. When she'd opened the window just before climbing into bed around midnight, the spot at the curb near the front walk where he customarily parked his ten-year-old Porsche had been empty.

Bryce had always needed a safety valve for the complicated and sometimes volatile emotions he was so good at hiding under his "nice guy" persona. Sports had allowed him to blow off steam safely. When he hadn't been practicing or playing, he'd worked out and run. He could still work out as long as he protected his knee with a brace, but running was beyond him. Now when he was frustrated or angry or uptight, he drove to an abandoned road near the Bears practice field in Platsville, Wisconsin, and pushed the Carrera's powerful engine to the limit.

She'd gone with him once and had been terrified. On another level—one she suspected had to do with the more volatile DNA strands buried in her Kostas gene pool—she'd been utterly exhilarated.

He was in the kitchen when she entered, standing at the counter filling a bowl with about a thousand empty calories of a sugary kid's cereal. If memory served, this particular brand had a surprise in every box. Bryce collected them for her brother Nick's daughter Delfie, who was wild about her uncle Bryce.

A mug of steaming black coffee, a water glass of tomato juice and the *Tribune* sat at the place on the center island where he used to sit before the divorce reordered their daily lives. For the past six months he'd eaten his breakfast in front of the big-screen TV in the den, usually to the accompaniment of the latest game tape, while she'd grabbed something quick in the kitchen.

A definite uneasiness ran through her at this sudden change in routine. Bryce had never dealt well with change. When it had finally hit him that he would never run for glory again, he'd thrown his Heisman Trophy through the TV screen, destroyed boxes of irreplaceable memorabilia and smashed all the videos of his games.

Ignoring Tia's pleas, he'd left the house and disappeared for two days. When he'd returned, he'd been pale and unshaven, his eyes bloodshot from lack of sleep. They'd made love that night, and he'd been incredibly gentle. The next day he'd accepted the offer from the Bears to become an assistant coach and refused to even set foot on the Notre Dame campus again.

At the time Tia had believed he'd conquered his demons, but over the years she'd gotten glimpses of potentially explosive currents beneath the athlete's discipline and self-control that had led her to believe he'd only wrestled them into submission. It frightened her a little to think about the consequences if his control should falter.

"Good morning," she said politely.

He grunted something that sounded like, "Is it?"

before subjecting her to a bold, even arrogant inspection that set her teeth on edge. It was obvious from the way his mouth curled up at one corner that he was mentally undressing her. She refused to squirm.

"Going running?" he asked as she met his gaze defiantly.

"Obviously."

Her deliberate sarcasm went unacknowledged. "Might want to check the temperature before you head out. Wind chill's down to single digits."

Tia bristled. "After thirty-one Chicago winters I do know to take precautions."

He shrugged those enormous athlete's shoulders. "Just a suggestion." Turning his back on her, he returned the cereal box to the cupboard before digging out a spoon from the silverware drawer. "Your dad called."

Surprise sifted through her. "I didn't hear the phone."

"He called my cell. Wanted to know if you were all right."

"Why shouldn't I be?"

"Could be he read something into the way you kept glaring daggers at anyone who talked to me on Christmas."

She refused to feel guilty. "Do you blame me?"

"Do you care?"

"No." Bracing a hand on the back of one of the rattan stools, she launched into her warm-up stretches. From the corner of her eye she watched him walk to the island and slide onto one of the stools. He was limping slightly, a sign that he'd pushed himself too hard during his morning workout.

Part of the basement had been converted to an exercise area. When he wasn't traveling or at the field for an early practice, he worked out before breakfast. On weekends during the off-season Tia had often joined him, although she spent more time ogling his bulging and flexing muscles than toning her own.

More than once the ogling had rapidly escalated to fondling and groping and ultimately sweaty, primitive sex right there on the exercise mat. Once she'd even torn his shirt in her haste to get him naked. She still had the shirt hidden in her underwear drawer. It was, she realized with dismay, identical to the one he had on this morning, a regulation gray Property Of The Chicago Bears T-shirt washed so many times the thin cotton fit his wide, massively muscled chest and shoulders like a second skin.

On the other hand, the faded navy sweatpants, a relic from his years at Notre Dame, were just loose enough to mold his long muscular legs and hard butt to perfection without constricting his movements. The cotton fleece was damp where sweat had gathered in the hollow of his spine, just above the swell of his buttocks.

God, but she loved his butt.

Her mouth went dry, and her chest was suddenly filled with feathers. She wondered if her cheeks betrayed the sudden flare of heat.

''If you're waiting for an apology for last night, I'm fresh out,'' he said in a conversational tone before turning to the sports page.

Tia was still preoccupied with the erotic imagery

of the lean, cleanly defined musculature and cable-tough sinew of Bryce's lower body, so it took a moment for his words to register. This time the heat flooding through her had nothing to do with lust and everything to do with the Kostas temper.

"Fine, because I have no intention of apologizing to you, either," she snapped, glaring at him. On the night they'd met, Bryce had told her that her eyes could be more intimidating than a three-hundred-pound lineman with a homicidal streak. When he didn't so much as look up, she felt oddly deflated.

"I never thought you would," he said a bit absently, as though he were more interested in reading about Detroit's quarterback problems.

She forced herself to take an emotional step back. Suddenly it was vitally important to her that they not part enemies. "However, I am prepared to admit you have a point about the alarm. Since it's already installed, it only makes sense to use it." There, she thought. Even though she hadn't quite been able to pull off a smile, she'd managed a decent almost-apology.

"Like you said last night, it's your house." Careful to keep his expression one notch above bored, Bryce spooned cereal into his mouth and chewed.

At five this morning, when he'd headed downstairs to bleed off some of the sexual frustration slowly driving him out of his mind, he'd been a little shaky about the decision he'd made last night to play hardball for a change instead of worrying about hurting her damn feelings, but now he was beginning to enjoy himself. Getting Tia flustered had always been both a challenge and just plain fun.

His lady was as smart as she was gorgeous, and

so quick he had to stretch his dumb-jock brain to the limit to keep up with her. From the beginning, matching wits with Tia had always turned him on. Hell, who was he kidding, here? Just about *everything* about Tia turned him on.

During these past six months he'd done a lot of research on the female psyche. In the filing cabinet in his office were enough shiny magazines to supply half a dozen doctors's offices. Whenever he'd been able to carve out some spare time, he'd read every article in an effort to figure out what women wanted in a guy—and a relationship. Like honesty and commitment and communication. He was solid on the first two; the last one needed a lot of work.

Embarrassing as it was to admit it, some of the more graphic articles had had him squirming in his chair—especially the one entitled "Size or Skill? Which Is More Important In A Lover?" Best he could tell—and he seriously doubted any real man could be objective about his "equipment"—his was above average in size.

He wasn't real sure about the skill part, so he'd memorized some helpful tidbits, such as the "little known and underrated erogenous zones" guaranteed to produce orgasms of the cataclysmic kind.

Maybe he didn't fully understand all the nuances of a woman's mind, but he knew one hell of a lot more than he had when he'd agreed to this divorce she was so set on pushing through.

One thing had stood out, a kind of recurring theme that ought to be chiseled above every locker room door and imprinted on a male child's brain at birth—*Nice guys are boring losers. Smart-asses and bad boys get lucky—and stay lucky.*

He'd tried "nice." As nice as he'd known how to be, anyway. Now he intended to show her how bad he could be when pushed.

"Last night you said it was just as much your house," she challenged, her hands on her hips now. "In fact, you *claimed* it was more yours than mine."

"Did I?" He allowed himself a lazy grin. "Guess I did at that."

He took a sip of coffee before studying her through the steam. Her little cat's face with the fancy cheekbones and sassy chin was set in indignant lines. Her elegant brows were drawn into a V above deep brown almond-shaped eyes full of storm and fury. This was the adorable hellion who used to chase him around the house with a tennis racket, threatening to bash his head in because he'd found her hidden stash of marshmallow and chocolate pinwheels and eaten every last one.

The woman he loved more than life itself.

"Could be we need to renegotiate terms, Mrs. Hunter," he drawled finally.

He knew that "Mrs." bit would get to her, and it did, resulting in a patented Tia frown that should look fierce, but only served to draw a man's attention to her lips. Mind-scrambling, kissable lips they were, too. Suddenly the need to feel her mouth beneath his was so demanding it took every ounce of control he could muster to keep his butt in the chair.

"Define renegotiate," she demanded, her voice sharp with suspicion.

"Wheel and deal, darlin'. Upon further reflection, it seems real obvious I got hosed in this *amicable* settlement worked out by *your* attorney."

She sucked in a harsh breath. "You are clearly suffering some kind of brain anomaly," she said in a stiff tone. "Some esoteric football-related condition, no doubt caused by too many years sniffing smelly gym socks, resulting in a drastic decrease in your IQ."

Damn, she was good! Sparring with her was making him hot. Beneath the sweats, his body was definitely reacting. Much as he wanted to let this play out a little longer, he needed to call a halt before she noticed the damned inconvenient arousal he was powerless to prevent.

After refolding the paper, he chugged down his juice before carrying his bowl and glass to the sink. "By the way, the guy I bought my town house from was in an auto accident on Christmas Eve, and his wife's not sure he'll be up to moving right away."

He heard her quick intake of air and fought a grin. Maybe he should have hidden that tennis racket of hers. "That's too bad," she said in a tight voice, "but you agreed to move out on the second and I expect you to do just that."

Dishes rinsed, he put them in the dishwasher. He wiped his hands before turning to face her. "Way I see it, you can either charge me rent or I'll have my attorney call yours about rescheduling our court date. Your choice."

She shot her chin in the air. "You can go straight to hell," she enunciated with barely leashed anger. "And take your renegotiation *and* that stupid alarm system with you!"

He came within a muscle twitch of peeling her out of her clothes, dragging her to the floor and burying himself so deep she'd never forget the feeling of him inside her, but his instincts told him to wait. Seduction, like a perfectly executed draw play, was all about patience and timing.

"No can do, sweetheart," he said with a grin. "Hell's not on the schedule this season." Figuring that was as good an exit line as any, he grabbed his coffee mug and split.

Much as Tia hated to admit it, Bryce had been right about the cold. After running less than a block, her lungs had begun to burn, forcing her to return to the house. An hour later, when she'd arrived at the parking garage where she rented a space by the month, she'd discovered some poacher had taken her spot again, and had wasted twenty minutes tracking down the attendant.

When she'd finally hit her office, her morning had gone from frustrating to unproductive. Too many of the people she needed to reach were out until after the New Year. The still-gorgeous roses were the only bright spot in her otherwise gray day. Every time Steph put through a call, she'd expected to hear the voice of her secret admirer on the other end. A rich, sexy baritone, of course. Nothing else would do.

By noon, when he hadn't called, her mood had turned impatient. More than ever in need of a safety valve, she'd spent her lunch hour in the downstairs gym, sweating out the worst of the tension.

"Any messages?" Tia asked Steph the moment she returned to her office.

"Only two. It's been a slow morning, probably because of the holidays." Glancing down, Steph consulted the twin pink memo slips next to the phone console. "Mr. Lewin's assistant called to confirm your meeting with him and MegaVolt's CEO on January fourth. And Deirdre Calhoun called to remind you about the party at Pedro's tomorrow night. She's picking up one of her other attendants at the airport early afternoon, so she set the time for five-thirty, just to be safe."

Obviously Mr. Secret Admirer hadn't called. Disappointment ran through her, followed by a burst of irritation. Didn't this man...guy...person realize how important it was to follow up a positive first impression with another contact within twenty-four hours? Whoever he was, he was obviously not in sales or marketing or advertising, which eliminated just about every male she interacted with on a regular basis.

Of course, there was her brother Alex's firefighter buddy, Ryan, who'd been at her folks' place for Thanksgiving brunch. He'd seemed on the verge of asking her out more than once during the afternoon. Alex claimed she was too intimidating and should "tone it down" or she'd never attract another husband. She'd punched her big brother in the stomach instead.

Steph had lobbied on behalf of the computer consultant who'd revamped their network last October. Although the guy definitely had a nerd brain, the package was straight out of *GQ* with hints of fairly non-stuffy humor. A solid eight out of ten overall points on Steph's hunk-o-meter. Not the highest ever awarded—that had gone to Bryce who rated a solid twelve, but only because Steph had awarded extra points for his thick, dusty-blond hair and very masculine dimplelike creases grooving each cheek when he grinned.

Realizing she was in danger of obsessing—but over which unpredictable, disappointing male?—she poured herself a cup of coffee and took a sip. As she'd done all morning, she let her gaze drift toward the vivid bouquet visible through the open door to her office. The blooms were fully open now, and the provocative scent evoked images of moonlight on the sea, crystal flutes filled with vintage champagne and hot sex on satin sheets sprinkled with rose petals.

Noticing the direction of her gaze, Steph made a rude sound. "Some secret admirer, gets everyone all hot and bothered and then…nothing."

Great minds with similar thoughts. No wonder she and Steph worked so well together. "I told you it was probably a practical joke," she said with a stab at a philosophical shrug. "I need to go over the preliminary ideas for the new TV spots for Granny Merryweather's before tomorrow's lunch meeting, and then I think we'll call it a day."

"Sounds like a plan. Let me dig out the folder and a refill on coffee and I'll be right with you."

"Hand me your mug, I'll pour."

"Thanks."

Tia carried both cups into her office. Steph followed a moment later, file folder in hand.

"A limp noodle has more starch than my legs." Grimacing, Tia lowered herself into her desk chair. Her feet were swollen from the laps she'd run, causing her sexy new Italian pumps to pinch her instep.

Steph appeared unmoved. In her often expressed opinion, exercise was vastly overrated. "Think of it this way, boss, your buns are tightening to steel as we speak."

At the mention of steel buns, Tia's thoughts shot backward six hours to the farce she and Bryce had played out this morning in the kitchen. "Would you say I'm too invested in having my own way?" she blurted, surprising both herself and Steph.

"If I say yes, am I fired?"

Tia's jaw dropped before she recovered enough to exclaim, "No, of course not!"

"Just kidding," Steph said with a laugh before her expression turned thoughtful. "Does your asking me this now have anything to do with the take-no-prisoners mood you were in this morning when you arrived?"

Tia considered stonewalling, but that wouldn't be fair to Steph. Besides, she needed to settle this in her mind and Steph was the most up-front person she knew. "Last night Bryce accused me of being a spoiled brat. He said I insisted on having everything my own way."

"I assume you disagree."

"Emphatically!"

"Uh-huh. So, to sum up, what we have here is your basic Mexican standoff between the two of you, and I've been selected to pick the winner."

Tia couldn't help laughing. "No, you've been selected to tell me Bryce is a surly, bad-tempered, thick-headed jock who, for some inexplicable reason, has decided to do everything he can to annoy me."

"It does seem to be working," Steph offered in a droll tone.

"Damn him, he knows just what buttons to push

and I let him do it.'' Tia reached for her cup and took a sip. She'd seen the molten look that had flashed into his eyes as they'd faced each other across the width of the kitchen. He had wanted her. Worse, *she* had wanted *him* with a ferocity that had stunned her.

''In a perverse way it was very sexy,'' she admitted now and with great reluctance. ''Like...foreplay.''

Steph's eyebrows shot a full inch past the rims of her glasses. ''Oh-ho. Do I sense a reconciliation?''

''No, certainly not. Nothing has changed. I—''

The outer door opened to admit a young man dressed in a dark blue parka and a red stocking cap. Both bore the logo of a local courier firm. In one hand he carried a bulky parcel encased in opaque bubble wrap and an electronic signature pad in the other. His cheeks were ruddy from the cold, and droplets of water glistened on his shoulders.

After shooting Tia a speculative look, Steph scrambled to her feet and went to meet him. ''May I help you?''

The young man looked at Steph and then at Tia before addressing Steph directly, ''Executive Courier Service, ma'am. I have a delivery for Ms. Tia Hunter.''

''Thanks, I'll sign for it.'' When she finished, he took back the pad and handed her the package.

''Wait, I'll get my purse—''

''It's taken care of, ma'am.'' He tossed her a cocky grin before walking out the door and closing it behind him.

Tia's heart began to pound even before Steph set

the parcel on her desk. "What do you suppose it is?"

"I'll get my scissors," Steph said before disappearing.

Tia bit her lip and tried to contain her rising excitement. If this was a practical joke, someone was going to a tremendous amount of trouble.

"Here, you do the honors," Steph said, handing her the scissors.

"Close the door, just in case. If this is something embarrassing, I'd just as soon the entire office not know about it." Not that there were many of her fellow employees around to snoop, but even so, one couldn't be too careful.

"Good idea." Steph hastened to comply.

Tia turned the parcel this way and that before spying the strip of tape holding the wrap closed. She snipped, found another bit of tape, and snipped that. The bubble wrap fell open at the top, revealing a large satin bow the color of antique gold affixed to the handle of what appeared to be a large multicolored oval basket. A few more snips and she tugged the wrap free.

"Wow," Steph exclaimed softly. "I saw a basket exactly like that in Field's. According to the display, these are only made in one particular village in China and each one takes three months to weave. I have to tell you it costs more than I make in a week, including overtime."

"It's exquisite," Tia whispered, awestruck at the intricate design of the weave and the painstaking workmanship it must have required. Inside, nestled on a bed of sheerest silk the same color as the bow were intriguing goodies.

Feeling exactly like a six-year-old at her own birthday party, Tia set them on the desk one by one. First, the latest romantic suspense thriller by one of her favorite authors, then a bottle of outrageously expensive Pouilly Fuisse, followed by a sterling silver bowl containing fresh strawberries dipped in chocolate and wrapped in shimmering cellophane, a whispery soft robe of ivory satin and…fuzzy purple Barney the Dinosaur slippers!

"The man clearly has a sense of humor," Steph said, holding up the slippers.

"My favorite author, my favorite wine, the strawberries—how can he know me so well?" Tia wondered out loud. Romance and whimsy. "Whoever he is, he's clearly gone to a great deal of trouble."

"And expense," Steph added, fingering the label sewn inside the robe.

Tia had been in that particular lingerie boutique once, and although her soul had lusted, her practical nature had rebelled at paying so much for so little. Only once had she taken the plunge. The nightgown she'd bought had never been worn and was now tucked away in a drawer.

"There must be a card…" Tia searched through the swirls of silk until her fingers found another tiny vellum envelope. Inside, the card was again typewritten.

"'The weatherman predicts snow tonight,'" she read out loud. "'If we were together, I would make a warm fire, lay you down on a thick rug in front of the hearth and feed you strawberries dipped in wine. And then I would lick every part of your delectable body before making love to you in the firelight. Finally, when I was buried deep inside you, I would tell you how much I adore you.'"

"Now that's what I call hot," Steph murmured, fanning herself.

Unable to resist, Tia stroked the robe's embroidered lapel. The satin would feel slippery against her naked flesh and when Bryce— Her mind stuttered to a stop. No, when her *secret admirer* slipped it from her shoulders, it would slide down her body like warm spring rain.

"Do you think he'll call?" Steph asked.

"I don't know," Tia admitted. "But I think he has more planned, and I can hardly wait to find out what happens next."

Practice for next Monday night's game had been cut short by the icy squall that had swept in from Lake Michigan around two. By the time the players left the field the cold rain had turned to sleet. Coach Biggs had held a quick meeting with his four assistants to go over the injury reports from the trainer and the team doctor before calling it a day. Bryce had considered stopping by O'Casey's for a beer and a game of pool with LaMar and some of the other regulars. He was good at pool, better than most, and his ego could have used the boost, but with his nerves already rubbed raw, he figured he'd be lousy company and had headed home to a house he'd never particularly liked but couldn't bear to leave.

After checking the machine for messages and going through his personal mail, he'd grabbed a dark ale from the fridge and wandered into the den where he'd stacked some of the boxes he'd gotten from the transfer company. He liked packing about as much as he liked losing. In other words, he'd rather walk down Michigan Avenue in the middle of rush hour bare-butt naked.

His mood edging toward surly, he sucked down another mouthful and wondered if he dare stall another couple of days before he had to fill up a carton or two or risk Tia becoming suspicious. More than once these past few weeks he'd caught Tia checking out the contents of the boxes he'd scattered around. Each time her frown had gotten more impatient. Knowing Tia, he suspected it wouldn't be long before she started throwing his stuff into boxes herself.

It wasn't that he was superstitious, exactly. He preferred to think of his stonewalling as a form of positive thinking. If he cleared out drawers and closets and stripped his books and tapes from the shelves and cabinets, it would be tantamount to admitting he might actually lose this fight.

He rubbed at his belly, trying to loosen some of the knots. God, he was scared.

Leaning his head against the back of the chair, he let the bottle dangle from his fingertips and closed his eyes. The courier company had left a message on his cell phone voice mail confirming delivery to Tia's office. Would she bring any of the gifts he'd sent home with her tonight? he wondered. Be a great way to jerk his chain, show him what a lousy husband he'd been—especially after he'd given her a hard time this morning.

He frowned, and then shook his head. Even though she'd been spitting mad at him—and okay, maybe with good reason—Tia wasn't the type to indulge in petty revenge. She—

The doorbell rang, startling him into opening his eyes. Automatically glancing at his watch, he rose and walked into the small entry. After turning off the alarm, he unlocked the door and pulled it open.

Stark fear shot through him. Tia stood huddled on the doorstep, the sodden brim of her fuzzy black hat drooping pitifully over one eye.

"S-sorry, I couldn't f-find my k-key." Stumbling slightly, she stepped over the threshold.

He put his arm around her shoulders to steady her. Her teeth were chattering violently, and she was shivering uncontrollably. "My God, sweetheart, what happened?"

"J-Jeep just stopped in f-front of the g-grammar s-s-school. Wouldn't start again. I had to w-walk."

Two and half blocks in a sleet storm. He wanted to shake her until she rattled. "Why the hell didn't you call me?"

"Phone's still in my f-fanny pack."

Water dripped from the hem of her kick-ass jungle-cat coat to puddle on the parquet floor. She looked bedraggled and miserable, and her lips were blue. Panic coiled in his belly and beat in his head. "Hold still, honey. Let me get you out of these wet things."

She glanced down. "I c-can do it," she muttered, fumbling with the top button.

After impatiently pushing her hands aside, he made quick work of the buttons and slipped the coat over her shoulders. Taking a loop around his temper, he tossed the sodden coat into the corner, earning him a strangled protest.

"Don't go there, Tia," he grated in a voice made hoarse by emotions he didn't dare express. "I'm working hard at being thoughtful, but my control's pretty shaky right now.''

Jaw clenched tight against the words she wasn't ready to hear, he quickly stripped off her hat and then her gloves. Her hands were icy and streaked with black dye from the leather. Heart slamming, he chafed each hand in turn between his to stimulate the circulation. Her skin was frighteningly cold and clammy.

When he'd been thirteen, a girl visiting the farm next to his in the wind-swept dunes of Northwestern Indiana had gotten lost in the woods and died of hypothermia when a storm had hit unexpectedly. He'd been deer hunting and had been the one to find her. When he'd checked for a pulse, it had been like touching a block of ice.

''Why didn't you stop at somebody's damn house?'' he snapped, working to keep his terror under control.

Hard shudders began to rack her small body. Her face was so pale the freckles that were usually barely visible stood out like dots of gold ink, and her dark eyes seemed huge.

''B-because I was already wet and just wanted to get home, th-that's why. And s-stop yelling at me.'' She tried to push him away, but her arms had no strength.

''C'mon, we have to get you warmed up.'' Without waiting for a response, he scooped her up into his arms and headed toward the stairs.

''I can w-walk,'' Tia protested, but her head was already on his shoulder. Her body molded against him, soft and boneless. One hand rested on his shoulder, the other circled his neck. It was the first time she'd been in his arms in so many months he'd nearly forgotten how small and delicate she felt cradled next to his chest. An unnamed emotion pinched his throat. It felt like tenderness.

Moving quickly, he carried her through the master bedroom and into the adjoining bath. ''If I put you down, can you get yourself out of your wet things while I draw you a bath?''

When she nodded, he set her carefully on her feet. Swaying drunkenly, she clutched his arm for balance before steadying herself. Little by little she summoned the strength and will to stand apart from the need for his help—and from him.

When she removed her hand from his arm, he wanted to snatch it back. Instead, he watched intently for signs of renewed weakness. ''Okay now?'' he demanded when she took in a determined breath.

''Fine,'' she managed to say in a voice that was stronger now.

After making sure she had her feet solidly beneath her, he flipped on the light over the sink. Custom-made to accommodate his size and fitted with Jacuzzi jets to help him rehab his knee, the tub had been set into an alcove with a stained-glass window at one end. A small jungle of blooming plants sat on the wide lip at the other. Overhead, semi-frozen rain beat at the double skylight designed to provide light for Tia's garden.

His knee protested as he knelt to flip the stopper and turn on the taps. As steam billowed upward, rapidly filling the room, he opened the jar of fancy pink bubble bath Steph had given Tia for her birthday. Remembering how much his classy lady liked her bubbles, he dumped in a couple of handfuls. Almost immediately a pungent scent reminiscent of the roses he'd carried up in the elevator yesterday at dawn mingled with the steam to clog his nostrils, making him sneeze until his eyes watered.

By the time he caught his breath, Tia had managed to strip down to a shimmery black slip. A strip of filmy lace skimmed her breasts before dipping into a deep V. Another strip of lace kissed the tops of her thighs.

Horny bastard that he was, he felt his body stirring. "Don't even think about it, Hunter," he muttered, pushing up the sleeves of his sweatshirt to check the water temperature. Warm, not hot, he seemed to remember. Hoping to hell he was doing the right thing, he turned off the taps.

While he'd been preoccupied, Tia had removed the rest of her clothing and was now wrapped in a bath sheet. Wisps of glossy black hair clung to her cheeks and curled around her ears, giving her a waif-like appearance that tugged at his heart. Although her teeth were no longer chattering, she was still shivering. He grabbed another towel and did his best to dry her hair.

"Get in the tub," he ordered, holding out a hand to help her.

"Not while you're here."

"Stop acting like a lamebrain airhead. I know your body as well as you do."

Her eyes flashed fire, easing some of his fear. "I m-mean it, B-Bryce. Just g-go away."

"Hell." Bracing his weight on his good leg, he lifted her into his arms. As he did, the towel shifted, flashing a glimpse of lightly tanned inner thigh that had him sucking in hard.

"Put me down!" she ordered, grabbing a handful of his hair.

Pain ripped through his scalp. "Stop it, Tia, or I'll drop you on your cute little fanny!"

"D-don't you dare!"

Clearly the woman hadn't a clue how he was wired. In his entire life he'd never been able to resist a challenge. A dare was pretty much the same thing. Teeth gritted, he climbed into the tub and somehow managed to ease both of them into the mound of shimmering bubbles. He sneezed violently, cursed, sneezed again. Squinting against the steam, he slid down a few more inches until his back was against the sloping side of the tub and the bubbles had reached her chin.

"Relax and let the heat soak out the cold," he ordered when she stiffened. "You won't drown. I've got a good hold on you."

"That's the d-damn problem."

"Shut up and let the water do its job."

"Bully," she muttered, but the grit had gone out of her voice.

"Stubborn."

"Don't you forget it." Still clutching the towel, Tia closed her eyes and let out a sigh. Inch by inch she allowed herself to relax, until finally her head was tucked into the hollow of his shoulder.

The more she relaxed, however, the tenser he became. He'd missed cuddling with her almost as much as he'd missed making love to her. His hands itched to cup her breasts. Instead, he kept them loosely clasped around her waist.

"Don't ever c-call me a lamebrain airhead again," she muttered, her slurred voice more drowsy than angry.

He fought a smile. "No, ma'am."

"'Specially since you're the one wearing your clothes and sneakers in the bathtub."

"Clothes wash, but you have a point about the shoes. Bought 'em as a Christmas present to myself. Cost me a bundle, too."

"I'm not paying," she murmured—and let go of the towel.

The ends floated free before slowly sinking. His mouth went dry. Beneath the thick layer of suds she was naked. With each breath, bubbles shimmered and popped, thinning the shimmering armor between him and the body he longed to stroke. When she shifted her bottom against his already aching groin, he damn near strangled.

"Better now?" he asked, his voice rough.

"Yes, much." She eased forward far enough to turn to look at him. The shivering had stopped, and color was coming back into her cheeks and lips. Those sweet, soft lips that were only a few inches from his. His control began to unravel.

"I shouldn't have canceled the appointment to take the Jeep in for repair," she said with a weary smile. "You're entitled to say 'I told you so.'"

"Maybe someday. Like I tell the rookies, it's always good to keep something in reserve for the last few minutes of a close game."

Heaven help him, he wanted her. Worse, he was one muscle twitch from taking her. Reminding himself that winners planned while losers whined, he fought against the hot, urgent need consuming him.

Instead of a steamy, fragrant mist, he imagined himself stranded in the midst of a savage, blood-chilling blizzard.

It didn't work.

Suddenly her half-closed eyes opened wider. No doubt about it, she'd just discovered his distended groin. Her breathing accelerated. So did his. A bolus of heat shot straight to his rigid shaft. He wanted to shift away, but didn't dare.

"It's not my fault," he muttered, his voice strained. "You…wiggled against me."

She veiled her eyes with her lashes, cleared her throat. "It was unintentional, I assure you."

"Not a doubt in my mind."

She took a shaky breath. With each movement of her breasts, more bubbles popped until only a skiff of suds hid her nipples. "Sex is the last thing we need right now." Was that frustration he heard in her voice? Or was he projecting his own feelings on her?

"Speak for yourself," he muttered. He wouldn't beg. He'd be damned if he begged.

Lips curving into a sad-angel smile, she looked into his eyes. The pain of lost dreams shimmered in the depths, and a hole opened in his belly. "You're a nice guy, Bryce Hunter," she said in a soft voice. "A true gentleman."

"Yeah, just my luck." After easing her forward—and away from his screaming loins—he stood and climbed out of the tub. Grabbing a towel, he walked out and closed the door.

Fifteen minutes later, with his body still throbbing, he walked outside and stood in the icy rain until his teeth chattered and he had himself under control again.

Wednesday

The low-gear rumbling of a snowplow jerked him awake a few minutes past 3:00 a.m. After he'd checked on Tia around one, he'd poured himself a cup of coffee and settled down in the guest room bed to read. He must have fallen asleep.

Throwing on a flannel shirt over his T-shirt and sweatpants, he went down the hall to the master suite. Bathed in light from the hall, the large room with the twin dormers, sloping ceiling and antique furniture was comfortably warm. The air smelled of the sissy bath stuff and the distinctly feminine scent that was Tia.

For the first time since he'd known her, she hadn't insisted on opening a window before she'd drifted off to sleep around eleven. Now his tired little battler was sprawled on her stomach with her face buried in one of the pillows and her arms wound around the other. Although he'd tucked the covers to her chin less than two hours ago, the sheets and duvet were now tangled around her, as though she'd been wrestling monsters in her sleep.

Frowning, Bryce lowered himself carefully to the edge of the big sleigh bed that had belonged first to his grandfather and then his father. He'd been conceived in this same bed and when a blizzard had prevented his old man from getting his mother to the hospital, she had bled to death in the same spot where Tia lay now.

If it'd been his wife who'd died, he would have taken an ax to the century-old bedstead, burned the pieces and buried the ashes. That was just one more way in which he and his old man had differed. Like everything else touched by Mason Hunter's young wife, the bed where she'd died had become sacred—and a constant reminder to his only son that he needed to justify his existence every damn day he breathed.

After his father's death Bryce had planned to sell the ugly monstrosity, but Tia had fallen in love with it. Instead of explaining why he hated it, he'd caved, just like he always did. It was damned pathetic the way he'd tried to please her.

Guys had a filthy locker-room term for someone who loved his woman that much. Hell, he'd used it himself a time or two before he'd met Tia and gone down for the count. If he had any sense, he would split while he still had some self-respect left. Instead, he used his index finger to brush aside the thick lock of glossy black hair curling like a question mark over her cheekbone. Smooth as the cream-colored satin pillow beneath her head, her skin had lost the terrifyingly icy chill.

While she'd still been in the tub, he'd put in a quick call to the team doctor who'd warned him to listen for labored breathing and to check for fever every few hours. At the first sign of pneumonia, he intended to hustle her off to the nearest ER, no matter how hard she fought against it.

So far, so good, he thought, relieved. Didn't seem as though she would suffer any long-term damage. He should be so lucky, he thought, clenching his jaw. Living in the same house for months on end with the sexiest woman he'd ever known and not so much as touching her had been bearable only because he'd contrived to avoid her for long chunks of time. But now, with his plan calling for him to hang around more, he was fast approaching the record for cold showers.

It was so bad now he got hard at the faintest whiff of her perfume—and stayed hard. Even if he could figure out a way to make her want him again, with her feeling the way she did about him, sex would be a mistake. He wanted her, yes, more than was good for him, but he wanted her to come to him willingly and because she loved him, not because she had an itch. Although it galled him to admit it, having her use him that way would flat out kill him.

After edging his butt off the end of the duvet, he tugged it from beneath her hips. She mumbled something he couldn't understand before letting out a little huff of air that sounded far too much like a moan.

While he was trying to figure out what to do next, she turned over, dragging the covers with her. Her nightshirt was plaid, thick flannel and designed for warmth instead of seduction. It was also soft enough to outline her breasts much too clearly. His palms itched to mold and squeeze, and he felt a little dizzy. Beneath the plaid fabric were pebbly nipples rimmed with dusky color and—

"Bryce? Is that you?"

Feeling like an unwelcome intruder, he jerked his gaze to her face and kept it there. He might want her like hell, but he wasn't a damned voyeur. "Yeah, it's me. How are you feeling?"

"Very...cozy. And pampered." Her eyes were drowsy and seductive as she blinked up at him. He wanted to howl at his own stupidity for getting himself into this fix. He took another hitch around his control.

"Do you have a headache? Chills? Any trouble breathing?"

Her lashes dipped, covering her eyes as though she were taking stock. "My feet hurt, from running home in heels," she admitted in a rueful tone. "I think I have a couple of blisters."

He thought about offering to massage away the ache but decided he couldn't trust himself to stop with her feet. "So, uh, can I get you anything? Glass of water, Band-Aids, a couple of aspirins? Some more of your mom's cure-all tea?"

"Nothing, but thank you for offering." She frowned, ran her tongue over those sensational lips. He tightened his against a wild longing to take what he wanted and to hell with the consequences. "You look tired."

He was way beyond tired. "I'm okay."

Frowning, she used her elbows to push herself higher on the pillows. Her nightshirt pulled tighter against her breasts, sending an arrow of heat straight to his already white-hot groin. He realized his fingers were digging craters into his thigh muscles and made himself relax.

"You've been checking on me, haven't you?"

He shrugged. "A couple of times, yeah. Doc Marston thought it would be a good idea to make sure you're not coming down with something."

"Marston? You called the Bears' doctor?"

"Yeah, I called him. When you refused to go to the ER, it was either that or knock you out and haul you there unconscious."

Her lashes dipped again before lifting in one slow, sleepy sweep. Something far too close to laughter sparkled in those dark eyes. "Now that would have looked great on the sports pages. 'Coach Hunter clips wife on jaw in order to save her life.'"

His patience thinned to a razor's edge. "Yeah, great. The head office would love that."

Two little creases appeared over the bridge of her nose. "Bryce, I'm teasing."

"My mistake." He started to rise, only to freeze when she placed her hand atop his.

"I'm sorry I was so much trouble, Bryce. I didn't mean to be." The amusement faded from her eyes. "But thank you for taking care despite my, uh, lack of cooperation."

"That's one way of putting it." Because it had been so long since she'd touched him, it took every scrap of willpower left to him to slip his hand from beneath hers. "Go back to sleep, Tia. It's been a long day."

Tia heard the bleak note in his tone and felt something twist inside. Somehow, without meaning to, she'd hurt him again. "I hate what's happened to us, Bryce. We had so much going for us in the beginning. I only wish..." She let her voice trail off when she realized her feelings had become hopelessly tangled—and well beyond her ability to unravel in the middle of the night.

"What do you wish, Tia?" he asked, his gaze suddenly alert and focused, and yet, the intensity behind that gaze had sharp edges, the kind that could slice through the scar tissue that had only begun to form.

"I wish I'd listened to you about the Jeep," she said with a self-conscious laugh, knowing that she owed him more truth than she could give him right now.

His face closed up. "Go back to sleep, Tia," he said, and his voice was as cold and as bleak as the look that had flashed into his eyes before he'd turned and walked away.

Bryce had just hung up the phone when Tia entered the kitchen at a few minutes past six. She'd dressed warmly in wool slacks, silk shirt and cashmere blazer. Because it was snowing, she'd worn her knee-high calfskin boots.

Like her, he'd dressed for bad weather in thigh-hugging black cords and a thick Bears V-neck sweater over a beige Oxford-cloth shirt with a button-down collar and the heavy work boots he wore in the snow. His thick hair with its random sun streaks and unruly ways had fallen into an off-center part the way it usually did after he'd brushed it back from his face and allowed it to air dry. He looked tired, out-of-sorts and so gorgeous she sucked in an agitated breath. As she dropped her briefcase on the stool, he swept her with a critical gaze before turning away to fill a mug with steaming coffee.

"Might be better if you stayed home today," he said, holding out the mug, handle first.

She thanked him with a smile he didn't return. So they were back to being coolly polite, she thought, and felt disappointment tear at her stomach.

"I considered taking a personal day," she admitted after taking a greedy sip. "But I have revisions to the MegaVolt presentation to finalize before my pitch to the CEO on the fourth and a meeting with the people from Granny Merryweather's at noon today."

She took another sip of the industrial-strength breakfast blend and experienced the first licks of a much needed caffeine jolt. Feeling her engine revving made her aware that she was hungry. After grabbing another sip, she set about assembling the makings for a bagel with cream cheese and lox. "Want one?" she asked, holding up a bag of onion bagels.

"No thanks, I had a bowl of cereal after I worked out."

"How you can sustain life on zero nutrition is beyond me."

"The Hunters come from peasant stock. My ancestors learned to subsist on dandelions and salt pork."

"Ugh." Finished slicing the bagel, she popped it into the toaster oven. "Since you're wearing your coach clothes, I assume you don't intend to stay home, either."

"The team has practice at ten today." He lifted his mug to his mouth and drank.

"In the snow?" She treated herself to another look at those formfitting cords before taking the cream cheese and lox from the fridge.

"The players stay warm running drills. Only the coaches freeze their butts on the sidelines. When it gets too miserable, we hop up and down and call the players filthy names."

This time she did laugh. It had been a long time since they'd bantered like this, and she had missed it terribly. "What filthy name did you call Randall Jefferson when he fumbled the hand-off on that critical conversion in the last two minutes of the second half?"

Surprise flashed in his eyes, making him look both vulnerable and approachable. "You watched the game?"

"Of course, I always watch," she said as she went about slathering the bagel with a good half inch of cream cheese. "Just because we're getting divorced doesn't mean I've stopped being a Bears fan."

"When you stopped going to the games, I figured you'd lost interest."

"Technically, the ticket I used belongs to you, not me. I thought you might want to give it to...someone else."

His head came up quickly, and he studied her with those sometimes too penetrating gray eyes. "A woman, you mean."

"Well, yes. It occurred to me that you might have become involved with someone during the last six months." Putting her assumption into words sent a surprising pang through her.

"Would you care if I have?" His voice had gone quiet, a dead giveaway that the answer mattered. Because it did, she gave serious thought to her answer.

"I don't know," she said when she realized her thoughts refused to line up in a straight line. "I know I wouldn't have a right to complain since we're legally separated." Tia blew out a breath. "Strictly as a matter of curiosity, *are* you involved with someone?"

"No. Are you?"

This is our year. Love, Your Secret Admirer.

"No, I'm not involved." *Involved* implied mutual consent. Being courted was one-sided, so technically, she'd told the truth, so why did it feel like a lie? Or worse, a betrayal? Averting her gaze, she piled on more lox before taking a bite. Glancing up, she saw Bryce watching her.

"What?" she demanded far too curtly for her peace of mind. If he noticed, though, he gave no sign.

"Tow trucks are at a premium this morning because of the snow, but the auto club's dispatcher promised to have someone out by nine to pick up the Jeep. I told him we'd leave a key on top of the right front tire." He drank more coffee. "I also called the dealership and told the service manager to ride herd on his guys to have it back to you by quitting time. Best he'd do was promise to try, but the way things work these days, I wouldn't count on having wheels before tomorrow." He sounded frustrated, as though it annoyed him that he couldn't smooth the way for her. Despite her need to stay detached in order to think her way through the tangled strands tying her to this man, she found herself melting.

"Thanks for making the calls. Although I hate to admit it, a male voice sometimes works magic, especially with things having to do with motorized vehicles—and alarm company people."

"No problem," he said before turning around to pour himself a refill.

And that, she thought, was that. One more responsibility discharged, one less problem to solve. Her warm feeling evaporated.

Stepping past him, she plucked the cordless phone from the cradle. The number of the taxi company she preferred was on speed dial. Not surprisingly, she got the recording, asking her to hold. Resigned to waiting, she carried the phone to the fridge and took out a grapefruit.

"Excuse me, I need to get a knife," she said when Bryce showed no sign of moving out of her way.

He obliged her by stepping to the fridge for milk. "If you're calling for a taxi, don't bother, I'll drive you. We need to leave that key anyway."

"Oh, but—"

His expression turned stubborn. "I said I'm driving you. If you're smart, you won't argue." His mouth hitched up at one corner. "Or else, I really will say 'I told you so.'"

Although the plows had worked through the night, the streets were clogged and the commute was an exercise in patience—Tia's. Bryce handled it with his usual stoicism. By the time they reached the business district downtown, it was nearly nine.

"I'll be on the field in the morning, but I should be back in my office by one, two at the latest," he said, braking for yet another red light. "If you need a ride, give me a call."

"Thanks, but since I'm meeting Dee and her other attendants for drinks after work, I might as well take a taxi. Not that I expect to overindulge, you understand, but—" She stopped midsentence, her gaze locked on the advertising panel on the side of a Chicago Transit Authority bus in the next lane. A color photo of a larger-than-life woman smiled back at her.

"Oh...my...God," she whispered. "I must be hallucinating." Or looking in a very large mirror.

The photo was the one the photographer for *Chicago Style* had taken for the piece on the city's career women on the rise that had appeared in last July's issue. Beneath the photo, spelled out in bright red letters, was a quote from Byron: "She walks in beauty, like the night."

"Something wrong?"

Heart leaping to her throat, she turned to find Bryce watching her with a frown on his face. "I'm not sure," she said, more than a little dazed. "Look, on the side of the bus."

Leaning forward, he shot a quizzical look through the Porsche's passenger window. His sun-bleached eyebrows snapped together so violently she could almost hear the sound of a collision. "What the hell?" he grated, a muscle ticking alongside his jaw. "Whose idea was that? One of your bosses?"

"I don't think so." Wasn't that light ever going to change? she wondered, staring straight ahead.

"Whose then?" His voice had a chilled-blade edge she'd rarely heard before.

"I suspect it was my, uh, secret admirer."

"Your *what?*"

"The light's changed," she informed him a little too eagerly.

"The hell with the light," he muttered, but he shifted into first and set the sports car into motion—for about ten yards before traffic came to a standstill once again. Just her luck the bus had kept pace with them.

"I'm waiting, Tia," he said, turning slightly so that he could face her—and her image a scant ten feet away.

Beneath the luxurious circa 1930 muskrat coat that had belonged to her aunt Helen, she eased her shoulders back and sucked in a bracing breath. "Monday, when I got to work I found this rather...impressive bouquet of red roses on my desk. No one knew how they'd gotten there. The card said they were from someone who signed himself my secret admirer."

The word he used referred to a waste product generated by livestock on his father's farm. "What else did this card say?"

"That's private." The last thing she wanted to do was hurt his feelings.

"Guy has to be a loser or he'd have the guts to make his play face-to-face." The sneer in his voice had her teeth grinding together.

"His *play?* How very typical!" She stabbed a finger into his bicep, the one bearing the tattoo of the Notre Dame leprechaun. ''And you wonder why I gave up on you?''

His eyes mirrored the stormclouds overhead. ''So teach me how to make you happy, damn it! I'm not so dumb I can't learn!''

''I *tried,* Bryce. For years, I did everything I could think of, but it was like butting my head against one of those stone walls on your dad's farm.''

The light changed again, and a tense silence filled the luxury vehicle as he concentrated on not slamming them into the Lexus ahead. ''Let me tell you something, Tia, dramatic gestures are easy. All it takes is a checkbook. But what about the day-to-day stuff? Will this admirer of yours go the distance when the excitement wears off? Will he hang in during the boring parts? Keep loving you when you're PMSing and acting like some crazed lunatic?''

She made a strangled sound in her throat that won her an impatient look. ''Will this so-called admirer think you're still gorgeous and sexy when lines start to show up in your face and your body is no longer perfect?''

His expression stony, he pulled into the yellow zone in front of her building. Shifting into neutral, he let the engine idle as he turned a brooding gaze her way. ''Has this guy spent nights lying next to you picturing your belly swollen with his child and wanting you so badly he aches?''

Tia sucked in a breath. ''Why haven't you ever said these things to me before?'' she asked, her heart slamming.

''Hell if I know.'' He scooped his gloved hand

through his hair. "Maybe I thought you'd think it was corny."

"I think it's lovely," she said, her voice thick.

As though taking heart from her words, he straightened his shoulders and went on. "Look, you were right when you called me a loser in the romance department, but all my coaches have always said I'm a quick study. All I need is a chance to prove it."

Say the words, Tia told herself. Tell him that you want to try again.

"If you truly cared as much as you claim, why didn't you pay as much attention to me as you did to…to Polecat Atkins?"

His expression went blank for a moment, and then he frowned. "Tia, I've already said I'm sorry about that. I lost track of time and…" He stopped, and then heaved a frustrated sigh. "That's no excuse. You were sweet and thoughtful to plan a surprise for my birthday and I ruined it."

She'd reserved the bridal suite at the Drake, arranged for a candlelit dinner for two, and spent a fortune on an imported nightgown guaranteed by the boutique owner to drive a man wild. By the time Bryce arrived at the hotel—two hours late—the lobster tails had turned to rubber, and the imported champagne that had cost her half a month's salary had gone flat.

His excuse? First-round draft pick Polecat Atkins had suddenly developed a bad habit of running left when the quarterback expected him to run right. As assistant coach, it had been Bryce's responsibility to fix the problem, so he'd stayed after the regular practice to work with their high-ticket running back.

Whatever Bryce had done, it had worked. In every game since, Polecat had gained at least a hundred yards and was telling everyone who would listen that he owed it all to Coach Hunter.

"I wanted us to make a baby that night, Bryce," she said, staring at the dashboard dials for several frozen seconds before turning slowly to look at him. "I wanted that to be your birthday present."

He went still. When he spoke again, his voice was more sad than angry. "Is that where this is going now, Tia? I hurt you, so you get a free ride to hurt me?"

"We're not going anywhere, Bryce. That was part of the problem. I tried to open a dialogue, but you—"

"Screwed up. Yeah, I know. You've gone down the list of my faults often enough I have them memorized."

"You say you want me to teach you how to make me happy. Okay, lesson number one, stop playing 'Poor Me' and start acting like the strong, intellectually honest, courageous man I married."

Some powerful emotion flashed in his eyes before his face tightened and he reached past her to open the door. "Better get a move on, darlin'. Wouldn't want your secret lover to catch you talking to the loser you're divorcing, now would we?" he challenged.

"*Admirer,* not *lover!*" she shouted as she slammed out of the passenger seat. But he was already roaring away.

As the crow flew, O'Casey's was less than a mile from Soldier Field where the Bears had played their home games since 1971. Founded around that same time, the now-famous watering hole and restaurant occupied the ground floor of a narrow three-story, red-brick building that had once housed a fire station.

The patrons were a mix of fans, groupies, tourists, players and on occasion, sports reporters out to score a story. Bears memorabilia covered nearly every inch of the dark plank walls in the bar and, during the last several years, had begun making inroads on the rough whitewashed brick in the main dining room. Every item on the menu including the to-die-for Polish sausage calzone had been named for former Bears' greats, and during the NFL season, the big-screen TV in the bar replayed the team's last game over and over.

It'd been more than a month since Bryce had stopped by for a beer at the end of the day. Hanging out with the players was a luxury he'd been forced to limit after moving from the field to the sidelines. A coach needed to retain a certain distance to make the difficult decisions about a player's usefulness to the club. He hated it, but he accepted it.

After chatting with a couple of the guys playing pool, he'd taken a seat at one of the tables by the window in the bar and ordered a beer. He'd figured the imported ale would loosen the knots in his gut. He should have known better. Putting anything into his belly these days was risky. On this particular day, it was downright stupid.

Today was the third anniversary of his old man's death. A massive heart attack, they'd told him when he'd arrived at the hospital after breaking every speed record between Chicago and LaPorte, Indiana, some seventy-five miles away.

Turning his head, he looked out at the street. Although it wasn't quite five, it was already dark outside. Bathed in the glow of the streetlight, the snow piled by the plows against the curb appeared dingy and gray.

It had been below zero the day he'd gotten the call. Ice had coated the tree limbs and fence rails as he rocketed the Porsche along roads as familiar to him as the meandering surgical scars surrounding his knee. He'd found his dad in the cardiac care unit of the county medical center, hooked up to machines and tubes, his lean, work-toughened body lying motionless, his chest scarcely rising and falling. Despite the oxygen feeding into his lungs, each gasping breath had sounded like his last.

A kindhearted nurse had found the old man's only son a chair, and then had drawn the curtain around the bed to give them privacy. The laughter and chatter faded, and he felt himself slipping into the past.

Too jelly-legged to stand, Bryce sank down onto the chair. Rocks ground together in his chest as he took his father's calloused hand in his. In some distant part of himself, Bryce noticed that his hand was even bigger than his old man's and almost as rough.

"Pop, it's me, Bryce," he whispered around the greasy ball of fear stuck halfway down his throat. "Hang in, okay? You're tough, you can make it."

"Janie?"

"No, Pop. Not Mom. It's Bryce. Your son."

The old man's sparse lashes fluttered, then slowly lifted. Pain shimmered in eyes the same gray color as his own. "Too damn bad...about knee of... your'n. Really thought you'd...be in Hall of Fame... someday."

Bryce's eyes filled with tears, and his throat ached as he forced out the words he'd never once said out loud to this man. "I love you, Pop. All my life, everything I've done, I just wanted you to be proud of me."

And to love me.

His father's chest heaved upward, then sank heavily. Tears seemed to fill his eyes as he struggled to push words past bloodless lips. "Tried...love you. Swear I...wanted to. But...not even a son was...worth her dying."

Unable to do more than drag air into his lungs, Bryce stared at his father's haggard, pain-contorted features while an icy blade slashed him to ribbons inside. Never again would he allow anyone to get close enough to hurt him that way. Never again.

Bryce realized he'd clenched his fist so tightly around the bottle his tendons threatened to tear and forced himself to relax his grip. He supposed the shrinks would call that last conversation a defining moment, although, since he'd resisted Tia's pleas to spill his guts in front of a stranger, he would never know for sure.

Bottom line, whenever his feelings for Tia had threatened into the danger zone where he was vulnerable to a blindside hit, he'd retreated to the security of the sidelines. According to one of the articles he'd read, on a scale of one to ten, women rated a need to feel close to their partner emotionally higher than they rated great sex.

Close, meaning they wanted him to spill all his secrets like some New Age wimp.

To hell with the pain in his belly, Bryce thought savagely, lifting the bottle to his lips. He'd grown up shoving his anger and resentment against his old man into a deep, dark hole inside where no light ever shone. Just thinking about letting someone else see the ugliness buried there scared the hell out of him.

"Coach Hunter?"

Lost in his thoughts, it took him a couple of beats to realize the hot number in a short skirt and mile-long legs who'd taken his drink order had returned.

"Sorry, did you say something?" Hoping to head off the invitation he'd come to associate with that come-to-mama glint, he kept his voice cool.

Under the guise of making herself heard over the happy-hour babble, she leaned forward, giving him an up close and personal look at her obviously augmented breasts. He could smell her perfume, something musky and dark. Instead of turning him on, however, it only made him realize how much he missed burying his face between Tia's breasts and inhaling the clean scent of soap.

"The lady at the end of the bar would like to buy you another brewski," the waitress murmured. "She said to tell you she's had a crush on you since the first time she saw you on TV playing for Notre Dame, but I guess you hear that a lot."

"Not really." Most of the come-on lines he'd deflected over the years had been a heck of a lot more graphic.

"So what do you want me to tell her?" the waitress persisted.

The lady in the black power suit had the sleek, self-satisfied look of a woman who knew all too well the kind of sexual impact she made on a man. *Stop being a damn Boy Scout and take what's offered,* his horny body prodded. *Tia's divorcing you, remember? Tossing you out like yesterday's* Tribune.

This morning he'd damn near pleaded for another chance, and what did she do? Threw one of his many sins at his head.

"Coach?" the waitress pressed more urgently. "What do you want me to tell her?"

A former model, Deirdre Calhoun had become managing editor of *Chicago Style* magazine the same year that Bryce and LaMar had signed with the Bears. Over six feet, she had a regal bearing, killer bone structure and long willowy legs that Tia secretly coveted. Her face, with its flaring cheekbones and full lips, could have been crafted by Picasso in his early, non-weird period, and had been known to stop traffic. Her skin was a lovely, glowing chocolate-brown tinged with a hint of copper, a gift from an Indian great-grandmother.

No matter how together Tia felt or how carefully she'd applied her makeup and chosen her outfit, whenever she was with Ms. Deirdre Calhoun, she wanted to hide in a corner and obsess over her hideously obvious faults.

It was two days and counting until the wedding Dee had been planning for nearly a year. Since her four attendants were career women with jam-packed calendars, she had opted for a cocktail-hour bash instead of the traditional luncheon. For convenience sake, she had reserved a private room off the main dining room at Pedro's Corner Cantina where the margaritas were always frosty, the hors d'oeuvres spicy, and the conversation frank enough to send a timid male running home to mother.

Tia knew two of the other three women Dee had selected. She'd met Portia Devins three years ago when the former all-American basketball star from Purdue married Bears superstar wide receiver, Jackson Devins. A dusky, black-eyed goddess with close-cropped curls and an air of regal dignity Tia envied, Portia had turned down a professional career in the Women's National Basketball Association in order to earn a master's degree in special education. Two weeks ago she'd found out she was pregnant with their first child and had been glowing ever since.

Lis Raynes, senior fashion editor for *Chicago Style,* had a wind-blown mane of honey-blond hair, turquoise eyes, and a perfect size-two figure. Tia had tried to hate her on sight, but the woman was simply too darn nice.

The third woman, Shawnita Frontaneau, had a trendy buzz cut and huge green cat's eyes full of intelligence and humor. A high school principal, she and Dee had been friends since their grammar school days in Detroit. Like the others, Shawnita was eager to hear all about Tia's secret admirer. "Don't you dare leave out a thing," she ordered between sips of margarita.

"Especially the juicy parts," Lis added.

Unfortunately, despite Tia's best efforts, she hadn't dug up anything juicy or even interesting enough to share. After admitting she'd been as surprised and mystified as everyone else, Tia turned to Dee.

"The only real clue I have is the photo, which your photographer took nearly a year ago. So my question is this, Ms. Managing Editor, who at the magazine could have had access to the negative?"

Dee's nut-brown eyes regarded her with a mixture of affection and amusement. "Only the photographer, the photo editor, the entire layout staff and various other assorted personnel including, but not limited to, the janitorial and maintenance crews."

Tia groaned. "In other words, just about everyone who works for you."

"In a nutshell, yes."

"You didn't mention the managing editor," Tia said, narrowing her gaze.

Dee raised a haughty eyebrow, but her eyes were full of mischief. "Is that an accusation or a question?"

"No, the demented ramblings of a seriously stressed-out madwoman," Tia muttered before licking salt from the corner of her mouth.

Laughing, Dee scooped salsa. "You do realize that anyone with a scanner could copy the photo from the magazine and deliver it to the advertising firm selling space on those bus billboards."

Tia sighed. "Yes, and before you ask, I called C.T.A., their ad reps, and everyone else I could think of. Every single one of them stonewalled." Including the courier company and every florist she'd contacted during spare moments during the day. She'd managed to work her way down the list to the M's with absolutely no success. "I even resorted to offering bribes, but no one bit. I have a feeling this mystery man paid big bucks to ensure total secrecy."

"This mystery man also seems to have anticipated your moves and plugged all the holes in the line." Dee looked startled, as though her words had given rise to another thought. "Tell me I have not actually begun conversing in football analogies," she pleaded with mock horror.

"So far you're borderline," Tia said. "It helps to maintain contact with non-athletic types, preferably accountants and morticians."

Dee laughed. "In that case I'll have to widen my circle of acquaintances."

The others shared an affectionate laugh.

"So, how many calls did you get from people who recognized you from the picture?" Portia asked as the waiter arrived with another pitcher of margaritas.

Tia waited until he refilled her glass before answering. "My assistant, Steph, logged in thirty-six, and I lost count of the ones I took." She selected a chip and dug into Pedro's *salsa de diablo.* "So far I've turned down requests for radio and TV interviews and refused calls from both the *Trib* and *Sun-Times.* Everyone wants to know what, where, why, when, and especially who."

"What did you tell them?" Dee asked.

"No comment." Tia soothed her still-ragged nerves with several more sips while the ladies waxed eloquent on the subject of secret admirers.

"It has to be driving you crazy, not knowing who this guy is," Lis said before crunching into a taquito with perfect white teeth.

''Crazy is the operative word all right. Plus harried, hassled and, well, fairly intrigued.''

''What about Bryce?'' Portia asked. ''How's he dealing with this?''

''I'm not sure. He just found out this morning.''

Dee reached for a chip. ''According to LaMar, Bryce threatened to stuff Randall Jackson down the shower drain headfirst if he mentioned that photo one more time.''

Tia stared at her. ''He did?''

''Mmm-hmm. LaMar said even the veterans were walking on eggs around him all day, and some of those guys are flat-out scary. Weren't none of them willing to take on Coach Hunter when he was in a temper—and that's a direct quote from my honey lamb.''

The conversation turned to the wedding then, and Tia forced herself to join in, but her mind kept going back to the things Bryce had said to her that morning. By seven-thirty when Tia called for a taxi to take her home, she was pleasantly buzzed—and, she realized with a great deal of surprise, very eager to see Bryce again.

Bryce wasn't home. The house was dark when she let herself in through the front door. After flipping on the entry light, she diligently—and smugly—punched in the reset code. Feeling virtuous and just the teensiest bit off center, she hung her things in the coat closet before heading down the hall to the kitchen, hitting light switches as she went.

A hint of lemon-oil hung in the air as it did every Wednesday after her once-a-week housekeeper had worked her magic. The gray-stone countertops glistened, the smoked-glass fronts of the appliances showed nary a smudge, and the quarry-tile floor shone from a fresh coat of non-skid wax.

Although the house had only seven rooms and two occupants, Bryce had insisted she hire someone to do the routine cleaning and laundry so that she'd have more time to devote to her career—and to him, he'd added with that lopsided, impossibly sexy, irresistible grin that curled her toes and heated her blood.

Making a mental note to talk to Irene about cutting back to every other week after Bryce moved out, she headed for the den to check the answering machine. After sinking into the big leather chair behind Bryce's no-nonsense desk, she stabbed Play.

"You have fourteen messages," the digitalized voice informed her without a trace of emotion. Some were for Bryce, left by local sports reporters. Interspersed with his messages were calls for her from Melina and Mama, and from all four of her brothers. All demanded an immediate call back. Tia rubbed the spot on her temple where a dull headache had settled. No wonder Bryce fought so hard to guard his personal privacy.

Oh, God, was she the reason Bryce had gotten seven calls from the media? she wondered as the last message began.

Bryce, this is Shirley. Sorry to call you at home, but it couldn't be helped. I have my cell with me, so please call as soon as you get in.

It took Tia a moment to realize the caller hadn't bothered to leave her number. Meaning he must already have it. "Who the hell is Shirley?" she muttered, glaring at the machine as though it were a coiled rattlesnake.

"Jealous, sweetheart?"

Startled, she spun around in the chair to find Bryce leaning against the doorjamb, a large tawny-haired, gray-eyed, muscular predator contemplating potential prey. Only Bryce could make her feel both vulnerable and protected at the same time.

"I didn't hear the Porsche," she said, rising from her chair.

"Dare I hope my loving wife was anxiously waiting for me to come home?" The mockery in his tone had her chin shooting up.

"After you all but shoved me out into the street this morning, I couldn't care less when—or if—you come home."

He pushed away from the door and walked toward her with a graceful tight-hipped stride only marginally impeded by his bad knee. "I heard from LaMar that Dee was taking you ladies to Pedro's."

"So?"

His grin was lazy and calculated to undermine her defenses. "So the last time you had more than one of Pedro's margaritas, you came home and tore off my clothes." Grin slowly fading, he focused his gaze on her mouth. "How many margaritas did you have tonight, sweetheart?"

She wanted to punch him, but she would only bruise her knuckles. "I've asked you not to call me that," she said instead.

"Not asked, *sweetheart*. Ordered." He shook his head, sighed. "Damn but it makes me hot when you boss me around." Before she could reply, he lifted a hand to straighten the lapel of her silk shirt. When he let his fingers brush her throat, her skin turned hot and tingly beneath the slithery fabric.

"So take a cold shower," she snapped, meeting his smoldering gaze unflinchingly.

"I will, if you will—although I think we'd both enjoy a tub full of those pink bubbles a whole lot more."

"In your dreams, Hunter." Not for a moment would she give him the satisfaction of knowing just how easily he could get to her.

"Ah, Tia, a man can only dream so much before he has to have the real thing. For me, that's you, sweetheart. Only you."

"It's piling higher and deeper, farm boy."

His sudden grin was both abashed and wicked. Laugh lines framed eyes that had gone very dark and intense, and in the depths, treacherous currents swirled. The primitive woman inside the cosmopolitan suits and civilized persona longed to throw herself into those currents, to test herself against a danger that volatile and intense. Tempted, she found herself swaying toward him, only to catch herself before it was too late.

Awareness glinted in his eyes, along with a sharper, more disturbing emotion she couldn't read. "Who are you afraid of, sweetheart? Me or yourself?"

"Neither. I'm simply not interested in continuing this conversation." Fast losing control—and hating it—shc quickly stcppcd to onc sidc to cscapc, only to find herself trapped between the desk and his body.

"While the tub is filling, real slowlike, we'll get each other naked," he persisted as though she hadn't spoken, his husky whisper shivering along her nerve endings in a pleasure so intense it bordered on pain. "After a whole lot of soul-kissing, we'll sink down in those bubbles and after a lot more kissing, I'll rub you all over the way I wanted to last night." He gave her a bad-boy leer. "And you can rub me, 'cause I gotta tell you, sweetheart, I surely do miss the way you squeeze and stroke me with those talented hands of yours."

Her palms suddenly felt hot, and her insides were fast turning to pudding. "When dinosaurs return to earth," she muttered, more in self-defense than irritation.

"From that first night we've never been able to keep our hands off one another. Even while that slick attorney of yours was drawing up the papers, we were burning up the sheets."

"That's not true—"

"The hell it isn't. It wasn't more than three hours after I'd been inside you that a process server tracked me down on the practice field and slapped the damn divorce petition in my hand." A muscle ticked in his jaw. "The guy was good, I'll give him that. Made sure everyone within a dozen yards knew what was going on."

She winced. At least her agony had been private. His had been public—and to a man as proud as Bryce, miserably humiliating. "That wasn't the way I planned it, I swear."

"Guess you didn't plan the goodbye roll in the hay, either. Or did you?"

"No, it just...happened."

Remembering had a savage feeling of betrayal slamming through Bryce. Years of hard-won discipline allowed him to absorb it without so much as a flicker of an eyelash. "Since you hadn't laid your intentions on me yet, I didn't realize you were about to lock me out of my own bedroom."

Her eyes flashed fire. "If this is an attempt to lay some kind of guilt thing on me, you're wasting your time, Bryce. Yes, we had sex, and it was great. For years it gave me enough hope to keep trying. And you know why?"

He opened his mouth, but she blasted on. "Because when you were inside me, you were really *with* me. When you were looking at me during sex, I saw the man I married behind your eyes. The man I adored and respected and loved with all my heart and soul. For those few moments, you loved me, too. I saw it. I felt it. But as soon as the sex was over, you withdrew to that place inside yourself, and I was alone again." She stopped to take a breath, and a look of horror crossed her face. "I hate losing my temper. I really *hate* it." Lifting a hand, she impatiently brushed back a heavy lock of shiny jet-black hair that had fallen over her forehead. He thought her hand shook, and it seared his heart.

"Tia, you knew I wasn't a hearts and flowers kind of guy when you married me."

"But you were *present.* We talked and laughed together. We...played. But after you were hurt, you started to change. Not all at once, but little by little we stopped laughing. And after your father died, we even stopped talking."

"That's not true. We talked a lot." The words were out before he realized he was freaking defending himself, something he'd sworn never to do again when he'd been eight and about to get a whipping for leaving the pasture gate open.

Only whiners and little girls made excuses for their mistakes, boy. A man owns up and takes his punishment without complainin'.

"Yes, we talked," she admitted. "About the quarterback's sore arm or the guys you wanted management to take in the draft."

"You talked about your work, too. That's what couples do."

"Yes, but I also talked about how terrified I was when I pitched my first major account and how devastated I was when the client went with a different agency. When I was hurting, I went to you for comfort, and you were great about it, but you never once came to me. Not even when you were in the hospital and dealing with the loss of your most precious dream." Her eyes turned sad. "It hurt when you shut me out, Bryce. It hurt a lot."

Angry hornets were now dive-bombing his stomach lining. "I know that now, and I'm sorry." His voice came out harsh. He tried to gentle it. "I'm not sure I could have made it without you."

She shook her head. "You didn't need me, you only played at needing me."

"I needed you. Too much. That was the problem. I still need you." Stepping forward, he hauled her into his arms and sealed his mouth over hers.

It was still there, the craving that exploded inside him whenever he kissed her. She made a sound in her throat and then she was kissing him back, her hands convulsively opening and closing around fistfuls of his jacket.

Exultation sweeter than any he'd ever felt on the

football field swept through him, fogging his mind. Spreading his legs, he pushed her back against the desk. As eager as a hot-wired teenager, he rubbed his distended body against hers. Fire flashed through his groin and licked at his belly. His need was so great it frightened him, yet he was powerless to pull back.

Desperate now, driven by months of aching loneliness and savage longing, he slipped his hand between them and tore at the top button of her shirt. Her body bucked as his hand covered her breast. His mouth muffled her gasp as she thrust her pelvis hard against his fly.

Nearly strangling on a groan, he tore his mouth from hers. "God, sweetheart, don't or I'll lose it right now," he swore between ragged breaths.

"Hurry," she urged, her own breathing labored. "It...hurts."

Half-crazed, he buried his face in her throat, kissing her, licking her, tasting the salt on her skin. Her hands were in his hair now, tugging and kneading like kitten claws. His haste to feel more of her made him clumsy, and it took two tries to undo her belt and rip open the waistband.

She whimpered as he slid the zipper down and shoved his hand down between panties and skin. She shuddered and then shuddered again when his fingers slipped through the curls between her legs to the warm nest he sought.

His body quivered as he drove his tongue into her mouth and his fingers into the moist sheath. She gasped, convulsed, clutched at his shoulders.

"Please, oh, please," she cried, shaking.

"Please what, honey? Tell me what you want."

"You. Inside me. Now."

"Soon, sweetheart, soon."

Consumed with the need building inside her, Tia only dimly heard the words he rasped out. The sensations buffeting her were cruel, biting, glorious. She writhed, desperate for relief, but each time she was about to go over the edge, he seemed to sense it and stopped stroking her. She tried to move against his fingers, but he loomed over her, forcing her with his chest to fold backward until she lay helpless atop the desk.

His fingers moved again, teasing, taunting, driving her mad. This wasn't the considerate lover she knew, the man of infinite patience who treated her tenderly. This was the predator with violence lurking in the depths of piercing gray eyes, who took what he wanted, exactly the way he wanted. This was the brutally competitive warrior who'd fought for inches of turf, then fought some more. A man she'd only glimpsed, who both frightened and fascinated her.

"Do you want me to stop?" he demanded, his hot eyes fastened on hers. Angry, ruthless eyes full of dangerous currents and stark hunger. "Tell me to stop, Tia, and I will."

"I'll kill you if you do," she gasped, her body pinned beneath his hard thighs and massive chest.

"That's my little tiger," he crooned, his fingers taking her to the flash point again. Gasping, she strained for the climax, only to have him withdraw completely. Sobbing, she tore at his jacket as he moved backward. Quickly, impatiently, he jerked her slacks and panties over her thighs. Feeling the air on her heated flesh only served to excite her more.

"Now, make it now." She hated that she was begging him, but she couldn't help herself. It had been so long, and her need for him was greater than her pride.

"Soon, sweetheart," he crooned in an oddly gentle tone. "Soon."

Senses swimming, she was dimly aware of the rasp of zipper teeth, and the rustle of cloth over hard thighs. His arousal sprang free, thick and engorged. Hair-roughened thighs with muscles hardened to granite brushed hers, and she moaned. Curling his big, calloused hands around her knees, he spread her thighs wider.

"Look at me, Tia." His voice was rough, his expression savage. "Do you see how much I need you? *Do you?*"

She nodded, her thighs quivering beneath his stroking fingers.

"Tell me," he demanded.

"Yes. *Yes!*" Her voice ended on a keening cry as he thrust into her, embedding himself fully.

"Mine," he proclaimed in a thick voice as spasms shook her. "Tonight you're mine, and I'm yours, whether you want me or not." He withdrew, thrust again. "Say it!"

Still quivering, she heard the desperation in his voice to match her own—and so much need. She'd demanded that he reveal his feelings, and he had, pouring them over her in wave after wave, scalding and chilling her at the same time.

"Say it," he demanded again, thrusting harder. There was so much emotional agony trapped inside him, she realized, stunned, and all this time he'd borne it alone.

"Tonight, I'm yours," she managed to choke out through a tight throat. "And you're mine."

He let out a deep groan before withdrawing then thrusting deep once more. His hands held her hips as he worked her into a frenzy of need. Her hands clutched at him as she tossed her head side to side. Something fell from the desk. Her breathing began to rasp and then she was screaming as the greatest pleasure she'd ever known swept in a seething torrent through her.

He own release came in a silent, desperate shudder that rippled all the way through her. He collapsed atop her, his face buried in the hollow of her throat. Despite the discomfort of his weight, she was euphoric. Sated. Her mind drifted.

How long they remained joined, with his breathing mingling with hers, she couldn't say. Finally, after what seemed like centuries, he stirred and raised himself on his forearms to look into her face. Her guilt sharpened when she saw the tenderness shimmering like tears in his storm-gray eyes. "Are you all right, sweetheart? I didn't hurt you?"

She wanted to rage at him for exposing a darker, more primitive side of herself she never knew existed, but that would be unfair. At least, she owed him that.

"Except for something hard poking into my spine, I'm fine." She heard the stiffness in her voice, and saw that he'd heard it, too.

As he stood up, the lips that had seared hers with ardent kisses compressed in a dangerous line. He was still semi-aroused and wet from being inside her. ''If you're working up the nerve to tell me nothing's changed, don't bother. I already figured that out.'' Instead of the anger she expected, she heard only weariness in his voice.

Face stony, eyes hooded, he adjusted his briefs, zipped up his cords, and walked out of the room.

Thursday

"How come you've been ducking my calls, Tia Athena?" An injury to his vocal cords during his rookie year with the Chicago P.D. had left her big brother Nickolas with a distinctively raspy voice.

Tia shifted the phone to her other hand to delete the last paragraph of the proposal she'd been working on since returning from a late lunch. "I'm working, Nick. Unlike you cop-types, I have deadlines to meet."

"Then I'll keep it short. What's the deal with this secret admirer thing? And don't bother stonewalling, because I wormed the whole story out of Melina over lunch."

Tia made a mental note to have strong words with her blabbermouth sister at the earliest opportunity. "If you have the whole story, why ask me?"

"Do you know how many psychos there are on the loose in this city?"

"Don't start, Nick. I can take care of myself."

"Mama is worried."

She should have known Nick would pull out the big guns. "I talked with Mama this morning. Unlike my *brothers,* she has complete confidence in my judgment."

There was a tense pause. "Look, Tia, I realize you like to think of yourself as streetwise and tough, but—"

"Stop! I've already had the same lecture from Alex and Theo and Chris."

"Way I heard it you hung up on Theo and called Chris a dirty name, which hurt his feelings. I haven't talked to Alex yet, but I figure you were nasty to him, too."

She remembered now why she'd avoided Nick's calls. "I was not nasty, and 'thickheaded clodpole' is not a dirty name."

"Sounds like it to me."

"That's because you've never read Jane Austen or the Brontë sisters."

He made a rude sound. "It's those damn silly women's books that caused all the trouble between you and Bryce. No real man behaves like those wimps you and your girlfriends swooned over."

She sucked in an exasperated breath. "Like you know what's in those 'damn silly women's books.'"

"Hey, I read a couple, just to find out what you found so fascinating. Some of it was pretty hot, I have to admit, but the way those dudes behaved was way beyond real." He paused. "Although I remember one where this Scottish dude tossed this prissy little English virgin over his shoulder and carried her off to this big old ruined castle. Had her moaning and begging pretty good by the time he finished with her. Too bad I can't remember the name of that sucker, or I'd recommend it to Bryce. Might be just the thing—"

"That does it, Nickolas Aristotle. I'm hanging up now." The receiver made a satisfying crack when she slammed it down. She only hoped it was loud enough on the other end to give her idiot brother a headache.

"He thinks I'm being stalked by a psycho," she said when Steph walked in a few moments later with the coffeepot in hand. Gratefully, Tia moved her mug within easy pouring distance.

"Nick is a cop," Steph offered as she poured. "He has to think the worst. Still, it's nice to know he's watching out for you."

"I don't need a watchdog. I'm not a fool."

"No, but you are vulnerable right now. I read this article about con men preying on divorcées. Seems these lowlifes contrive to meet a likely 'mark' and then wine and dine her out of her settlement."

Tia held up her hand. "Don't start. I—"

She was interrupted when the door to the outer office suddenly swung open. "Hello, anyone here?" The voice was male and impatient.

"Relax, your faithful assistant will handle it," Steph said as she returned to her office.

Tia heard the murmur of voices before Steph reappeared, carrying an oversize cardboard envelope bearing the logo of the Windy City Courier Service. For Immediate Delivery was printed in red.

"Tah-dah!" Steph said with a flourish as she handed it over.

Tia's hand was steady as she pulled the strip along one end, but her insides were Jell-O. "We are operating a business here, Steph. It might be from a client."

"Wanna bet?"

"No." Inside the courier's envelope was another one approximately the size of a greeting card bearing her typewritten name.

"Hurry, I'm hyperventilating," Steph muttered as Tia reached for the silver letter opener given to her by her parents on the night before she started with S.T.&W. Tia's heart pounded as she extracted a smaller envelope and an engraved card.

"It's an invitation to a New Year's Eve party at The Drake," she said, handing it to Steph so that she could read it.

"Not *a* New Year's Eve party, Tia. *The* New Year's Eve party, the one that only the most elite of the elite score invitations to. Like His Honor the Mayor and the rest of the powers in City Hall and all sorts of Chicago's version of glitterati." Steph set the card carefully on the polished desk. "Dare we hope it's from you-know-who?"

"I can't think of anyone else who would be inviting me." Tia opened the second envelope. Inside was a single sheet of stationery. Of excellent quality, it bore no identifying marks. Once again, the message was typewritten.

> My dearest and most cherished Tia, I have told you that this is our year, but only if you wish it to be. I have dreamed of dancing with you in the moonlight, but this will have to do for

now. Look for me, my darling. I will be the man wearing a red rose in my buttonhole.

It was signed, "Your Secret Admirer." And there was a P.S.

I will stay until midnight, but not one minute longer. If you are not there, I will know you are not the daring and adventurous woman I believe you to be.

"It's Tia Hunter, Mr. Howlik. You said to call back at four about my Cherokee." The sudden silence on the other end was not a good sign. "Mr. Howlik? Are you still there?"

"Yes, ma'am, I'm here." The service manager cleared his throat. "About your Jeep, the part my guy needs was air-shipped from California on Wednesday afternoon. When it didn't arrive this morning, I put a trace on it. Seems the plane was grounded in Denver on account of bad weather. Provided the storm breaks up before morning, we'll have what we need by noon tomorrow."

"What if the storm doesn't break?"

"Then we wait till it does," he replied with a chuckle.

Tia bit back a pithy comment. "How do I go about arranging for a loaner?"

"You don't. Not from us anyway. The owner quit offering after our insurance went through the roof."

"All right, I'll *rent* one of your cars."

"I wish you could, Ms. Hunter, I surely do, but the same goes for rentals." He paused long enough for Tia to snap the pencil in her hand into two jagged halves. "Might be you could try one of them regular rental places."

"I'll do that," she said through a tight jaw before hanging up.

By five she'd called every agency in the book, only to discover the only vehicle available on such short notice was a Chevy Suburban. For the amount she would have to pay, she could hire a dozen taxis to ferry her home. In the end she settled for economy over convenience and called a cab.

LaMar's bachelor party was set for seven at O'Casey's. Bryce had made all the arrangements, such as they were. According to the etiquette book he'd read before going off to Notre Dame, acting as host was part of his job as best man.

Since he wasn't in the mood to battle traffic twice in one day, he took a change of clothes to practice and killed time in the weight room before hitting the shower. He'd just finished shaving when LaMar called in a panic, threatening to hop on the first flight out of O'Hare unless Bryce got his butt over to O'Casey's pronto. Bryce figured the pre-wedding jim-jams were just nature's way of testing the level of a man's commitment. Him, he'd puked for three days straight and lost so much weight the tux he'd laid out big bucks to have custom-tailored had hung on him like a cheap rental.

By six, when Bryce hit the door at O'Casey's, happy hour had merged into the dinner hour, and both the main dining room and the adjacent bar were jammed. A blend of laughter, conversation and good-natured arguing over last Saturday's Bears-

Packers game, the noise level was close to deafening.

At the tinkling of the bell over the door, Mama Rosalie stepped from behind the hostess station, a ready smile lighting a face that was both lovely and surprisingly youthful after nine children, thirty-six grandchildren and Bryce couldn't remember how many great-grandchildren.

"How's it going, Mama?"

"Richard hasn't finished stocking the bar in the private dining room, and the hot dishes aren't ready yet," she chided, offering her cheek for his kiss.

"Thought I'd better be here when the stripper arrives." He risked a grin. "In case she needs my help zipping up her costume or helping her with her pasties."

Mama narrowed her gaze. "You listen to me, Bryce Hunter. There will be no strippers or X-rated movies shown in this establishment tonight or any other night."

Hard-pressed not to laugh, Bryce had to work at offering her a meek look. "Now, Mama, I promised you we'd all be good boys, didn't I?"

"Bah! Rascals, that's what you are, the lot of you. You'll behave yourselves, or answer to me. Is that understood?"

"Yes, ma'am."

She glared at him for a moment longer before her lips curved into a fond smile. "LaMar is already here. The poor boy reminds me of my Nico before he married his darling Sofia."

Although he already knew the answer, he asked the question she expected. "Nervous, is he?"

Before she could answer, the door opened behind

him, admitting a middle-aged couple and sending frigid air blasting into the warmth. With her welcoming smile already blooming, Mama gave him a shove. "Go! Your friend needs you."

Unzipping his jacket as he walked, he headed for the accordion doors in the rear of the bar.

"Yo, Coach, stuff the Lions good on Monday!"

Bryce offered the burly speaker at the end of the bar a thumbs-up as he passed. By the time he slipped into the private dining room, he'd been subjected to a half dozen questions and comments. Not that it bothered him much. Being treated like public property went with the job.

A gangly, clean-cut young man wearing black slacks, white shirt and a bartender's green bowtie glanced up from the bottles he'd been arranging on a portable bar set up in one corner. "Sorry, Coach, I haven't finished bringing all the bottles from the main bar yet. Is there anything in particular you want? If it's not here, I'll get it from Nico in the front."

Bryce ran his gaze over the bottles. "Got anything soft?"

"Yeah, sure. Ginger ale, club soda, all kinds of diet stuff."

"Ginger ale will do fine. Don't bother with a glass."

The bartender bent to retrieve an icy can from a cooler and handed it over. "Anything you need, just let me know, okay? Mama gave orders to give you guys only the best of everything."

"Thanks." Bryce shoved a bill into the tip jar that he suspected had been set up first. "How long before the food's ready?"

"Uh, I'm not sure. I can check it out for you if you want."

"No hurry, but I'd appreciate it if you alert the kitchen we might get some early birds." He glanced toward the end of one of two long tables covered with white clothes where LaMar sat hunched over a can of beer, a half-empty bottle of rye and a shot glass. "Wouldn't be a good idea to let them get a jump on the booze without food."

"Gotcha," the barkeep said before hustling out.

"'Bout time you got here," LaMar muttered as Bryce approached. "I called over forty-five minutes ago."

It was more like thirty, but Bryce cut the poor guy slack. "Coaches actually work for a living, not like you pampered superstars."

"Pampered, my butt. You damn near tore Jefferson's head off this afternoon. Dude was sweating bullets before you finally turned loose of him."

Their bonus baby rookie had better learn to follow his blockers, or Bryce would find a way to convince Ernie Biggs to sit the kid down for a few games at the start of next season. "Jefferson needs to learn he can't freelance in this league. Too many veterans out there waiting to cut him off at the knees." Or destroy his career with an illegal hit—and take great pleasure doing it.

Keeping his expression controlled, Bryce set the ginger ale on the table before slipping out of his jacket and hanging it on the back of the chair. LaMar watched him glumly with those big brown bulldog eyes as he took his seat.

"For a man about to marry the second greatest woman in the world, you don't look real happy,"

Bryce said as he popped the top on the soda. "Want to talk about it?"

LaMar's features took on a look of stark panic. "Last night Dee started talking about names for our first kid, you know? Woman's not even pregnant and already she's getting all mushy over babies."

Bryce didn't dare think about his conversation with Tia yesterday morning. Every time he did he got mad as hell—and then sick inside. He'd come way too close to blowing it before he'd hauled himself back. "Seems to me I heard you say more than once you wanted a big family. At least a basketball team of Lesters."

"In the future, yeah. Like maybe when I hang it up, you know? Like five or six years from now."

"In five or six years Dee will be in her late thirties. Having babies isn't as easy then as it would be now. Especially if you're serious about filling up the backyard of that palace you have out in River Forest."

"We already agreed on kids, Dee and me, but—"

The bartender returned, carrying a tray of glasses, and glanced in their direction. LaMar shot him a glare that had the glasses rattling against one another. "This here's a private conversation, you dig?"

"Uh, right. Yes, sir, Mr. Lester." Shaken, the kid hastily set down the tray and rabbited.

"Hell, Hunt, what if I can't cut it?" LaMar grated in a harsh whisper when they were alone again. "What if I mess up like you did?" LaMar took several gulps of his beer before tossing down a shooter of rye. "I'm a strong man, but I swear, it'd flat out kill me if Dee tossed me out on my butt like...well, you know.''

''Yeah, like Tia did me.''

''Only good thing is, you two don't have kids. But if Dee has a baby right away, and things don't work out, the kid'll be in the middle.'' He shifted, looked down at the rings on the paper placemat left by the sweating beer bottle. ''Mama and Daddy were divorced when I was three. When I was five, Daddy left N'Orleans and moved to Cleveland. After that, the only time me and my three sisters saw him was when Mama made him and his new wife make time for us during summer vacation. After he had him more kids, it was like he couldn't be bothered with us, you hear what I'm saying? It was the worst kind of hell for a kid.''

No, growing up with a man who started every day remembering why the other side of his bed was empty was the worst. ''Way things are in the world these days, kids grow up tougher. Besides, you and Dee are solid. As long as you keep loving her right, she'll put up with you, no matter what kind of dumb-ass stunts you pull.''

''Yeah, except how am I gonna know if I'm loving her right?''

Bryce took a sip of ginger ale, but his throat remained tight. ''That's easy. Just do the opposite of what I did.''

Never one to make a rash decision, LaMar pondered, pursed his lips, blew out air. ''I never thought of it that way, but you got a real good point, my brother.'' Grinning, he straightened his shoulders, effectively shrugging off panic like it was an opposing guard dead set on removing his head from those same shoulders. "Yessir, a real good point. Thanks."

"Glad to be of service, bro. Always did want to be a good example for something."

Guilt flashed across the face that had been on the cover of *Sports Illustrated* last month. "Sorry, man, I know you're hurtin'. I didn't mean to lay this on you, but I figured that's part of a best man's job, right? Calming down the groom."

"Must be. I've been doing it for six weeks so far." Bryce leaned back and slowly stretched out his aching knee as far as it would go. Despite months of therapy, it still ached like a bad toothache after a long and physical day.

"Guess you know the media's been nosing around the players, trying to scope out the story behind those pictures," LaMar commented, studying him with open curiosity. "Since you made it real clear how you feel, everyone's afraid to talk."

"Actually I factored in the buzz since I figured it was inevitable anyway." He'd even counted on it. According to a couple of articles he'd read, women loved the idea of a man publicly proclaiming his love. A couple of times a year, at least, some guy paid to flash his proposal to his lady across the stadium scoreboard. He'd even thought of that himself, but nixed it when he couldn't figure out how to entice Tia to attend a game without tipping his hand. Besides, he wanted to prove to his brilliant lady that his jock's brain wasn't totally without imagination. At least, that had been his rationale. Now he wondered if maybe he'd ended up proving just the opposite.

"Would you believe her Cherokee ended up in the shop and I drove her into the city yesterday?"

"Lord a'mercy, does that mean you were with her when she saw herself grinning back from one of C.T.A.'s finest?"

"It does. She was speechless for at least five seconds, which goes a long way toward telling you how shocked she was."

LaMar laughed. "Are you kidding? With a firecracker like Tia, five seconds of silence has got to be worrisome." He sobered. "But was it a good speechless or a bad speechless?"

"I don't have a clue."

Bryce tossed down a couple of swallows before rolling the frosty can between his palms. His wedding band clinked against the thin aluminum, and he wondered why he still wore the damn thing. Habit, maybe. Or maybe he was avoiding the inevitable pain as long as he could. He supposed his skin would be as white as a fish's belly beneath the gold. Until he could spend a day or two in strong sunshine, the pale band of white would be as conspicuous as a brand.

"You're not the only one having second thoughts," he confided when he realized the silence had gone on too long. "I'm beginning to think this whole secret admirer thing is a train wreck waiting to happen."

Laughter exploded in the bar out front. LaMar flicked a glowering glance at the door, warning off anyone fool enough to enter.

"From what I got from Dee when she got home last night, Tia's real excited about being courted by this mystery man. Dee says it reminded her of the way girls act in high school when some real cool dude throws some interest their way.'' He leaned forward. ''Dee thinks it's a real positive sign.''

Bryce resisted the urge to squirm. These kinds of soul conversations made him want to bolt. ''Did you ever do something you knew was going to twist back on you wrong, but you couldn't make yourself stop?''

''You mean like smoking dope behind the bleachers in high school when you knew practice was about to start and it was a good bet the coach would come looking for you, but you couldn't stop because the high was just too good?''

Bryce studied the beads of moisture on the top of the can. ''It was good, all right. More than good. At least for me. I'm not sure about Tia.''

He felt LaMar's stare burning into his skin. ''Are you saying what I think you're saying? You and Tia got it on?''

Bryce winced. ''Yeah. Last night when I got home, she was in the den, and we got to sparring the way we've been doing lately. Next thing I know she's flat on her back on my damn desk.''

LaMar blinked. ''That ugly schoolteacher's desk in the den? The one Tia keeps trying to give to the Salvation Army?''

''Only one we have.''

''No wonder you were limping worse than usual this morning.''

Bryce shot him a killing look. Just his bad luck LaMar knew him well enough to remain unruffled. ''I promised myself to go slow. You know, do the courting thing like I should have the first time. Only, first chance I get, I blow it.''

"Is that why you're having second thoughts, 'cause you think it's not gonna happen the way you have it all planned out?"

"Something like that, yeah." He heard excited voices beyond the open door and suspected some of the guys had just shown up. "Way I feel right now, I'd just as soon toss the whole plan in the garbage and let Tia have her amicable divorce."

"Is that what you're going to do?"

Bryce shook his head. "No, the courier has already delivered the invitation. She might decide not to show up, but if she does, I have to be there." He finished his soda and put on his game face. "Besides, like the man said, it ain't over till it's over."

Or until he had absolutely no hope left. Not even a glimmer.

Friday

"Oh, my stars, it's her!" The shrill exclamation came from the woman who'd just been seated next to the table at The Bistro where Tia and Steph were having lunch. "Look, Glenn, it's the 'bus lady' you were asking the tour guide about yesterday."

Rotund and balding, with craggy features, Glenn gave the woman a sour-pickle look before picking up the menu the hostess had just set in front of him. "Don't look much like her to me," he rumbled in a nasal undertone.

Cursing herself for glancing up when they'd taken their seats, Tia dropped her gaze to her half-eaten Caesar salad and prayed fervently for a just-in-time rescue. Across the table, Steph was struggling not to laugh. This morning Tia had received a call from a boy she hadn't seen from high school asking her to have his children and another from a fraternity brother of Alex's inviting her to bankroll some get-rich-quick scheme.

"I know it's her," the woman persisted, her strident voice cutting through the popular restaurant's lunchtime buzz.

"Tell me she's not coming this way," Tia murmured through stiff lips.

"She's coming this way," Steph replied before lifting her coffee cup to hide her grin. "Brace yourself."

From the corner of her eye Tia caught sight of fuchsia slacks below a neon-blue parka. Nearly smothered by the woman's vanilla-scented perfume, she forced herself to look up. Although the bony, sharp-faced woman with the bad dye job looming over her had to be in her sixties, she had the same predatory look of the lean and hungry groupies who hung around Soldier Field before and after a game.

"Sorry to bother you while you're having your lunch, hon...but, Lordy, I just got to know. It was your picture me and Glenn seen on those buses, isn't it?" Behind the pink-tinged lenses of her glasses, the woman studied her intently.

"No, actually it's my older sister, Crystal Flame. People say we could be twins. I can't see it myself, though." All too aware that the woman had attracted the attention of nearby diners, Tia mustered a polite expression as she said in a low tone, "Actually Crys' boss is the one who arranged for the pictures to be on the buses."

"I knew it! He's filthy rich but real shy and has been in love with her forever, but she won't give him the time of day. I read a book just like that once."

Tia cleared her throat. "Actually, Crys is an exotic dancer and next week her boss plans to put up a photo of her in costume." She leaned forward and lowered her voice even more. "It's mostly just feathers and a few sequins—and, um, well, you know, tassels."

From the corner of her eye, Tia saw good old Glenn's head snap up. Refusing to feel guilty, she offered the woman a long-suffering sigh. "You can imagine how difficult this is for the rest of the family. First my other sister Charlotte has that sex change operation and is now our brother Charles, and now this. Dad can't show his face at the pool hall these days, and Mother is on serious medication. Personally, I'm thinking of leaving town."

The woman's eyes widened, and then went a little glassy. Her mouth opened and closed like a fish trolling the lake bottom, but she couldn't seem to find the right words.

"Sit down, Gladys, and let the poor woman eat her lunch." Tia heard the amusement in Glenn's voice and shot him a look. Humor glinted in his eyes for a moment before he shifted his attention back to his wife. "*Now,* Gladys, or we're leaving. I didn't let you drag me into this place to sit here with my belly growling while you make a pest of yourself."

"Well, I never," Gladys muttered, looking affronted, but to Tia's immense relief, she returned to her seat and sat.

Tia heard a choking sound coming from behind Steph's coffee cup and shot her a warning look. "Don't you dare laugh, Stephanie. I'm barely hanging on here."

"I have a pair of those Groucho glasses, the ones with the big nose and mustache if you'd like to borrow them," Steph said when she had herself under control again.

"I just might." Tia picked up her fork and stabbed an anchovy. "I thought for sure those pictures would be gone today."

Their server—*Hi-my-name-is-Tony*—arrived to refill their water glasses and apologize in a low tone for the invasion of privacy. "Marcel said to tell you he'll move you to one of the back booths if you prefer."

"Tell Marcel thanks, but we're fine," Tia replied before forking the anchovy into her mouth and chewing vigorously.

"Just give me the high sign if you change your mind," he said before taking himself off again.

"The price of fame," Steph said, watching Tony's butt with avid interest. Not bad, Tia decided after a moment's study, but not in the same mouthwatering class as Bryce's kick-ass buns.

How long, she wondered, until she stopped measuring every male she met against Bryce? Before the familiar depression set in, however, she thought of her secret admirer. In all the years she'd been married to Bryce, this nameless, faceless man had been the only one who'd aroused the same gut-level excitement. Even if it was only in the abstract, she reminded herself as she took a sip of water. Who knew what she would feel for him face-to-face? Or belly-to-belly?

Excitement spiraled through her insides at the intimate thought. Hard on its heels, though, came a nagging worry. She'd been wondering if he could measure up to her own personal fantasy, but until this moment it hadn't occurred to her to wonder if she would measure up to his.

Her stomach gave an annoying lurch. Okay, so she was thirty-one instead of twenty-one, and her thighs did have an annoying little jiggle, but all in all she was in decent enough shape. Besides, it was her soul that mattered more than the package. Right?

"Speaking of fame," Steph continued when Tony had disappeared into the kitchen, "I caught Bryce on *Wake Up Chicago* this morning. The new sports guy—I never can remember his name but he used to play for the Bulls—showed up at practice yesterday with a camera crew and asked Bryce flat-out about the rumor."

Tia froze, her fork halfway to her mouth. "What rumor?"

Steph concentrated on twirling red-pepper fettuccini around her fork. "The one about how after the Saints fired their head coach on Monday, they asked permission of the Bears to interview Bryce for the position." Glancing up, she lifted both eyebrows above her glasses. "So, is it true, or what?"

Tia's fingers tightened around her fork. "I have no idea. If it is, he didn't mention it to me."

If Steph noticed the sharp tone to her words, she gave no indication. "Well, I guess there's really no reason why he should, since the two of you are going your separate ways in—what, three days?"

Tia's stomach hit bottom and then began to churn. "No reason at all."

"Might even be the best thing for him, you know? Give him a fresh start in a new city without any painful memories.'' Steph chewed and swallowed before taking a sip of coffee. ''Might be a good thing for you, too, especially if you and Mr. Wonderful get something going.''

''There is that, yes.'' Realizing that her appetite had somehow disappeared, Tia put down her fork. ''So, what *did* Bryce have to say?'' she asked after blotting her lips in a deceptively casual gesture she suspected didn't fool Steph for even a millisecond.

''Essentially that he never commented on rumors.'' Steph speared a sliver of lemon chicken before glancing Tia's way. ''It was pretty obvious that he wasn't pleased to be asked, but to give him credit, he was very professional. Did the modest 'it would be an honor just to be considered bit,' of course, and then real casual-like mentioned how much he'd always looked forward to the red beans and rice LaMar's grandmother fixed him whenever the team was in town.'' Her eyes took on an interesting gleam as she added, ''And then he grinned real slowlike, you know the one I mean?''

Oh, yes, she knew. She'd fallen in love with that grin before they'd even exchanged a word. When he'd been playing, Bryce had been a media darling. His thousand-watt grin had been on the cover of countless sports magazines. After his playing days were over, however, the requests for interviews had fallen off to almost nothing. To his credit, he took the change in status philosophically.

Why should I complain? I've had more than my fifteen minutes in the sun—and besides, bein' famous got me you.

''I asked him once if he wanted to be a head

coach and he gave me this 'Are you crazy, of course I want it' look."

Not that he was counting on it. After he'd been forced to give up his playing career, Bryce never counted on anything. But Tia knew deep in heart that he desperately wanted to prove that he was the best again. She wanted it, too. Because she loved...*had* loved him so much.

This time when she finally caught the service manager at the Jeep dealership between phone calls, the harried man was even more apologetic. "I'm sorry, Ms. Hunter. Like I told the coach when he called a little while back, Tuesday's storm really messed up our parts deliveries."

"Bottom line, you're saying the Cherokee still isn't ready?"

"Well, yes, ma'am, guess that's about it in a nutshell."

Tia pressed her fingers against the sudden pinprick of pain in her right temple. Three hours before Dee and LaMar's wedding was definitely not an opportune time for a migraine. "Okay, best guess, when will I lay eyes on my Cherokee again?"

"Uh, best guess, Monday?"

Instead of screaming like a banshee, she restricted herself to a cathartic groan before wringing a promise from Howlik to call her the moment the part arrived. She'd just hung up and was reaching for the bottle of painkillers in her top drawer when she heard voices in the outer office.

An instant later Steph walked in, an odd look on her face. "Bryce is here. Want me to send him in?"

Tia blew out a confused breath. "Why not? My day's already totally out of control."

Interesting how one man could make an entire office shrink, Tia thought as Bryce stepped across the threshold. Yes, he was much larger than most men, but it was more than size. Presence was one word. Confidence another. And, heaven help her, sex appeal.

Beneath a beautifully tailored camel-colored cashmere overcoat he wore the black tux Dee had insisted on for LaMar and his groomsmen. Mason Hunter ought to see his son now, she thought with a jolt of both pride and sadness. The motherless farm boy who'd taught himself the finer points of etiquette from a book he'd borrowed from the library was at home in the most sophisticated circles of this city or any other.

Jaw tight, he took inventory of her office, pausing only to sneer at the roses and gifts on the built-in shelves holding the TV and VCR before aiming that same impatient gaze directly at her. "The cop on the beat gave me ten minutes grace period before he had to ticket me—and it took me three to get up here, so move those gorgeous buns, sweetheart."

It took her a moment to unlock her jaw. "Am I to deduce from this that you are under the erroneous impression I'm going somewhere with you?"

"You don't have a car, it's Friday on a lousy day and cabs are at a premium. Either you ride with me or take the bus, and since the church Dee picked is three blocks from the nearest bus stop, I figured you wouldn't be real thrilled to walk all that way carrying your dress."

Tia followed the direction of his pointed gaze to

the garment bag hanging on the hall tree along with her muskrat coat. As a matter of principle she really shouldn't let him bully her, but he had a point about those three blocks. Besides, she realized to her intense dismay, she wanted to be with him.

What was wrong with her? Fantasizing about one man while wanting to sleep with another. Her ambivalence was not only disturbing; it was totally out of character. Tell him no, she told herself. Make a clean break. Mind made up, she took a deep breath. "All right, I'll accept a ride, but on one condition."

He cocked his head. "What's that?"

"No conversation," she ordered, rising. "Not one word."

A white stretch limousine had just deposited LaMar in front of the church and was pulling away from the curb when Bryce slipped the Porsche into an empty parking space next to the loading zone. Looking both gallant and terrified, the groom opened the passenger door and helped her out.

"Just sent the car back for Dee and her folks," he said after nearly crushing her in a bear hug. "I had to stay in a hotel last night on account of her daddy the reverend insistin'."

"It's more romantic this way," she said as Bryce joined them, her garment bag folded over one muscular forearm.

"What is?" he asked, glancing from one to the other.

"Me, bein' locked out of my own bedroom by my bride's daddy," LaMar mumbled. "The man ain't within miles of here and I feel his eyeballs on the back of my neck."

"Try having damn near your every move watched by your bride's daddy *and* her four brothers for a solid month before the ceremony." Bryce grimaced. "Now that's pressure, son."

Remembering his frustration had Tia biting off a laugh. "It wasn't anywhere near a month, and you know it."

"I know I was ready to tear your clothes off in the limo on the way to O'Hare," he said, his mouth relaxing into a grin. It wasn't quite the killer smile she loved, but close. Those annoying lust flutters assaulted her insides again.

"Hey, I can get behind that tearing off clothes idea," LaMar said, his expression brightening. "I was thinkin' we were gonna have to wait until we got all the way to Paris."

"Where are you staying?" Tia asked as they walked toward the entrance.

"The Ritz. Dee hung out there once a long time ago and swore she was going back for her honeymoon." He grinned. "Like I told her she's lucky I got that new contract last year. Otherwise, I never coulda afforded it."

"I always figured that if you're really in love, the most important thing was being together, not where you were or how much it cost." Bryce glanced her way, his expression hooded. "Turned out I was wrong."

The church, with its vaulted ceiling and arched pillars, was lavishly bedecked with satin bows and flowers in Dee's colors of lilac and pale blue. Candles on the altar and in dozens of candelabra placed around the sanctuary provided the only illumination.

In the front of the sanctuary LaMar stood at rigid attention, his big chest rising and falling in short jerks. Bryce stood next to him, looking almost as nervous as the groom. Both looked immense and extremely proper in formal clothes.

Don't look at him, Tia told herself as she started down the aisle. *You'll be fine as long as you don't look at him.* Beneath the lilac silk her chest hurt. Her fingers were locked around the bouquet of lilies and carnations so tightly they ached. Ahead of her were the other three attendants, spaced evenly and walking with the same measured cadence, their long chiffon-over-silk skirts swishing around their ankles. One by one they reached the altar and turned to wait for the bride.

At the altar now, she smiled at LaMar who did his best to smile back. Close to tears, she didn't dare look at Bryce, or the dam would burst. Relieved that she hadn't disgraced herself, she took her place next to Lis and turned to gaze back the way she'd come.

The music ended, and a split second of silence swept over the packed pews before the organist began the familiar strains of Lohengrin's "Wedding March." Looking radiant, Dee had eyes only for LaMar as she glided forward on the arm of her older brother, Sergeant Major Willis Calhoun, U.S.M.C.

In the front pew Dee's mother pressed a lacy handkerchief to her lips while across the aisle both LaMar's mother and grandmother wept openly.

Tia's smile wobbled. Lis sighed. A baby gurgled. The music ended, and an expectant hush settled. Looking dignified, yet exultant, Reverend Dr. Shelton Calhoun stepped forward, his gaze full of pride and happiness. LaMar grabbed Dee's hand and grinned. As Tia took Dee's bouquet and turned toward the front, she caught Bryce's eye. Her throat closed. She had never seen him look so sad—or so alone.

After the ceremony, custom had required Bryce as best man to escort her to the rear of the church where they stood next to one another in the receiving line. When he had politely offered her a ride across town to Ma Maison Petite for the reception, she had just as politely refused. Someone—she suspected Dee—had arranged for the two of them to sit together during the wedding supper. To the casual observer, Bryce appeared relaxed, even attentive, but she'd caught the black look he'd given LaMar—and LaMar's apologetic shrug.

Once the toasts had been drunk and wedding cake consumed, Tia had been about to excuse herself from the head table when he'd beaten her to it. Since then she had avoided him. Or perhaps he avoided her.

Since the dancing had begun about an hour ago, she'd danced nearly every dance, most of them with Manny Chacon, the Bears' rookie placekicker. More streamlined than most of his teammates and at five-ten, the shortest man on the team, he was to-die-for handsome, with a wicked gleam in his brown eyes. He reminded her of her youngest brother, Alex.

"For an Anglo, you sure can dance Latin," he shouted over the pulsing salsa beat.

Pleased with the compliment, Tia sidestepped a lumbering lineman whose tiny date gave her an apologetic look over the man's beefy shoulder. "I spent a summer working in an orphanage in the Dominican Republic when I was in college. My roommate was Mexicana and she taught me.''

''I know this club in Cicero where the band is so hot they put asbestos on the walls,'' Manny shouted a few seconds later. ''How about I take you there sometime after the season ends?''

''Nice thought, but very bad timing,'' she shouted back with a grin.

Her face felt flushed and she was definitely becoming winded, but she hated to stop. The band was only five pieces, but the sound they made was huge. Since she'd been a little girl, she'd loved to dance, and Manny was a terrific partner. According to her big sister, the self-professed font of knowledge on all things sexual, a man's skill on the dance floor directly correlated to his skill in bed.

Although Tia usually deferred to Melina in such matters, in this case big sis was dead wrong. Although Bryce had been breathtakingly graceful sidestepping blocks and escaping tackles with a football tucked into the crook on his arm, he had two left feet on the dance floor, a fact she'd learned all too painfully when she'd finally coaxed him into waltzing with her at their reception. Her poor toes had been bruised for a week. On the other hand, in bed his timing had been impeccable.

The song ended on a soaring note from the trumpet, and Manny caught her up in an exuberant hug, only to stiffen and step back so hastily she nearly stumbled. ''No offense, Tia, but I think we'd better sit this one out.'' He sounded oddly nervous.

''Is something wrong?'' she asked as the band swung into vintage Johnny Mathis.

He glanced past her left ear. ''Not yet, but considering that homicidal look in Coach Hunter's eyes, things could get real wrong in a hurry if we don't cool it.''

Stiffening, Tia slowly turned. Bryce stood to one side of the room near a large ficus tree, a nearly full champagne flute in one big hand, watching her with eyes the color and texture of the wind-scoured Indiana boulders on his father's farm.

As their eyes clashed, her breath stuttered in. He looked ready to strangle her. *A dangerous man to cross,* her mind registered, even as a sensation very like a shiver raced through her.

The first time their eyes had connected across a dance floor, she'd felt that same visceral punch. It had been raw lust in its most primitive form, she knew now, but at the time, she'd been too busy keeping air moving in and out of her lungs to manage more than a few incoherent thoughts.

Less than four hours later, she had found herself in Bryce's brand-new high-rise apartment overlooking Lake Michigan, lying naked on a king-size bed in a bedroom filled with moonlight, about to be mated by a tawny warrior with a magnificent body and wonderfully talented hands. No other man had touched her since.

Beneath the slippery silk, her body responded to both the memory and the man with the hard eyes and even harder jaw. Wild and wanton, that's what she'd been in the den two nights ago. That's what she wanted to be now. And damn him, he knew it.

Unable to look away, she felt her breathing quickening. As she stood transfixed, the other guests receded into a blur. His mouth softened, and for a moment she felt as though he'd just kissed her. Both her body and her heart yearned for the real thing.

Jerking her gaze from his, she turned to offer Manny an apologetic smile. Leaning closer to be heard over the pulsating music, she said, "Don't worry about Bryce. The Bears need you healthy to win next week and cinch a playoff bid."

"Maybe, but the thing is, I've seen that look before, only it was in the eyes of a timber wolf on my uncle's hacienda in Mexico. One of Tio Miguel's vaqueros had been tracking this she-wolf and had her in his sights when out of nowhere an enormous male leapt for the vaquero's throat. My uncle had to kill the animal to save the man, but it sickened him, he told me later. The wolf had been a magnificent animal whose only sin had been to defend his mate." He shot a quick glance in Bryce's direction. When his gaze returned to her, she saw admiration glinting in the depths. "A love like that should be honored, Tio claimed. And envied."

With each hour that passed the party gathered momentum. Given permission by the coaches to blow off steam, the players—and their wives and dates—cut loose with all the exuberance of college kids on spring break. Before long, the men had shucked constricting suit coats and jackets, loosened their ties and rolled up their sleeves. The ladies slipped out of their shoes, and the dancing became more uninhibited.

After a little coaxing from her new son-in-law, Dee's mother had slipped out of her beaded jacket, kicked off her heels, and out-shimmied every other woman in the room. While his teammates shouted encouragement, LaMar did his best to keep up with her. By the time Reverend Calhoun cut in, the most feared tackle in the NFL was sweating profusely and gasping for air. To everyone's surprise, the austere minister turned into a wild man on the floor, matching his glamorous wife move for move.

Although the dancing was pure American instead of traditional Greek, the joy and exuberance of the participants reminded her of her own parents at her reception. Remembering made her want to cry. Instead, she decided to take her sore feet and strained nerves home to bed.

Spotting Dee at the dessert table, she hurried over to say her goodbyes. "I wanted to wish you 'bon voyage' before I head home."

"You can't leave yet!" Dee protested before adding a raspberry tart to the goodies on her plate. "The fun's just starting." Spying a couple of Bears approaching, she motioned for Tia to follow her to an empty table on the edge of the floor. As she settled into one of the chairs, she caught sight of Bryce seated with LaMar's elderly grandmother on the opposite side of the room.

He'd sandwiched Nana Lester's bony hand between both of his, and he was smiling at something she'd just told him. It occurred to Tia just how often during similar occasions he'd shown an equal thoughtfulness to other older ladies, making sure they weren't neglected or lonely.

"Nana Lester is crazy about that man," Dee said when she noticed the direction of Tia's gaze. "I think it's because he flirts with her as though she were still the prettiest girl in the room." Dee's expression softened. ''And darned if she isn't, in her own way.''

Tia saw the glow in Mrs. Lester's eyes and had to agree. ''My grandmother Kostas adored him, too. She left him her papa's gold and lapis cuff links.''

''According to LaMar, Bryce has had dozens of 'offers' from some very desirable ladies over the years, but he's always been so besotted with you he's never once wavered, even for a moment.''

Tia realized she could count a half dozen friends or acquaintances whose husbands had strayed. Even though all of them were bright, attractive, and interesting women with successful careers, infidelity had shaken their confidence and self-esteem. ''I know he's never cheated on me, Dee. He has a core of integrity I've never doubted.''

Dee accepted a flute of champagne from a passing waiter and allowed herself a taste before her expression turned somber again. ''I shouldn't tell you this. In fact, I promised myself I wouldn't, but now that I'm an old married lady, I've come to realize how important it is that us wives stick together.'' She glanced toward the head table where LaMar was hanging out with some of his teammates, laughing.

''The night you told Bryce you wanted a divorce, he took himself down to O'Casey's, laid down a C-note and told Nico to keep the boilermakers coming. LaMar and I had just gone to bed when he showed up at the flat and tried to punch a hole in our front door with his fist. He was pretty incoherent by then, but after pouring three cups of espresso down his throat, LaMar bullied him into saying enough for us put the pieces together.''

"Those pieces being what exactly?"

"That you'd finally figured out your all-American Prince Charming was really a boring has-been and decided to cut your losses." Dee glanced around to make sure no one was within earshot before adding, "And then he just put his head down on my brand-new breakfast table and cried."

Certain she'd misunderstood, Tia stared at her. "But...Bryce never cries. Not even when his father died."

Dee's eyes filled with sympathy. "When I put him to bed in the guest room, he told me that his heart was breaking. That he had taken his grandfather's double-barreled shotgun out from under the bed, loaded both barrels and then sat staring at it for he didn't know how long, trying to talk himself out of using it."

Stunned, Tia could only stare at her while her brain scrambled, then fought its way back to reason. "What stopped him?" she finally managed to articulate.

"Realizing you'd be the one to find him."

Afraid to move for fear she would shatter, she took in a long and careful breath and let it out the same way. "If he cared that much, why didn't he fight to win me back?"

"It's only a guess, but I suspect pride is a big part of it." Her voice grew pensive. "Think about it, Tia. From the time he was a kid, Bryce had been praised and fawned over for his physical ability, not for what was inside. Growing up poor the way he did, he might have been able to work his way through a local college, but no way could he have gone to Notre Dame without a full-ride scholarship.

It was the same with LaMar. Because they could play football better than most, all kinds of doors opened to them. Money, fame, power. Sex.'' Lips compressing, she swept the dance floor with a telling gaze before concentrating her attention on a flashy blonde with a lean and hungry look clinging to the arm of one of the running backs. Dee frowned as she looked at Tia again. ''When Bryce's playing days ended, a lot of those doors slammed shut.'' Dee hesitated before adding softly, ''Including the door to your bedroom.''

Dee's words weren't meant as an accusation, but Tia felt the sting as though they were. *I've had more than my fifteen minutes in the sun—and besides, bein' famous got me you.*

Tia sucked in a breath and let it out slowly. Music pounded through her head until it began to ache. ''I never cared about the fame or the money or any of those surface things. I would have willingly lived on a farm if that's what he wanted—although I admit that wouldn't have been my first preference.''

Laughing appreciatively, Dee shifted her gaze to the bubbles rising from the bottom of the delicate flute. ''Can you imagine what it must be like for him now, Tia? Standing on the sidelines watching others run for the glory he'd only begun to taste and wondering if his wife would rather have one of those other guys instead of him?''

Tia winced. ''If only I had known, I would have shown him it wasn't true.''

''You couldn't have known. Bryce isn't any more likely to share his secrets than he is to share his wife.''

"Are you saying I shouldn't keep my date with my mystery suitor tomorrow night?"

Dee's expression turned thoughtful. "I've been out there dating for a long time. I've met a lot of men, most of 'em nothing but little tin gods with too much ego and too few scruples. Bryce is gold, Tia—solid twenty-four carat. Plus he loves you." Dee shifted her gaze to the bubbles rising from the bottom of the delicate flute. "I guess what I'm saying is this. I'd think twice before throwing that away."

Impatient and restless by nature, Bryce had acquired patience the hard way—by getting his ass kicked hard whenever he messed up. First by his old man, and as he'd grown older, by a succession of coaches, who'd made him hone his skills in practice before allowing him off the bench.

During these past six hellish months, he'd been more patient with Tia than he'd ever been with anyone or anything else in his life—including himself. But now, as he watched her chatting with Dee, he realized he was close to his limit. As it was, he figured he'd achieved a personal best tonight. Hell, he damn well deserved a medal for standing there like a freaking statue while his wife had shimmied through dance after dance with that pipsqueak, Chacon.

Just young enough to be cocky and, as Bryce had noticed first thing, as sneaky as hell, Chacon probably figured no one would notice how he "accidentally" brushed his body against hers every chance he got.

The kid was lucky he had taken the hint and

backed off, Bryce thought grimly as he downed another mouthful of straight ginger ale. Otherwise, Chacon would be spitting out teeth and thanking his lucky stars Bryce made it a rule to pull his punches with guys he liked.

LaMar's grandmother touched his arm, pulling him back from his troubling thoughts. According to LaMar, the stately woman with the sharp eyes of a hawk and a huge heart had been a practicing Voodoo priestess in her younger days before passing on her skills to her daughter, LaMar's aunt. He was tempted to ask her to cast a spell over Tia, but that would be cheating.

"*Cher,* it appears your lady is fixin' to say goodnight."

"Yes, ma'am, it does."

"Go on with you, then, boy. Tell her all the sweet and loving things I see in your eyes when you look at her."

Bryce's collar was suddenly too tight. "I'm not much good at talking, Nana Lester," he mumbled, his face growing hot. "That's part of the problem."

"Then show her," Nana ordered, her accented voice suddenly sharp enough to etch glass. "Do it tonight, Bryce Hunter, while the stars are in your favor. Otherwise, I fear you will lose this dangerous game you are playing with the woman who is the other half of your being." Her fathomless black gaze cut through him before turning bleak. "And that, I fear, will kill you."

Tia had just slipped into her coat and was pulling on her gloves when Bryce walked into the cloakroom. Sometime during the evening he'd removed his tie and unbuttoned the starched collar, baring the vulnerable hollow of his strong, bronzed throat. Once, she could make him tremble just by exploring that sensitive triangle with her tongue. Desire shot into her system at the speed of light, making her momentarily light-headed.

His gaze swept over her before narrowing perceptively. "No arguing, Tia. I'm taking you home." His eyes were steely, his voice curt. Skilled in the use and importance of visual and auditory clues to sell a product or an idea, Tia read his without any trouble. No matter what, he intended to take care of her—right up to the moment when the judge put them forever asunder.

A truly independent and strong female should refuse. Instead, this particular female was touched. "I accept," she said with a smile.

He lifted an eyebrow. "What, no conditions this time?"

She laughed. "Well, I would like to get home safely."

His mouth quirked. "I'll do my best."

Lulled by the purr of the perfectly tuned engine, Tia was nearly asleep by the time they arrived home. "That was fast," she murmured, sitting up and blinking to clear her vision.

"Speed limit all the way." Although Bryce slipped the keys into his overcoat pocket, he made no move to open the door. Puzzled, she turned to look at him. Although the interior was dimly lit by the streetlight on the corner, his face was obscured by shadows.

"You look as beautiful tonight as you did on the

day I married you," he said in a low, rough voice that shivered over her skin like a caress. "I thought I'd prepared myself, but when you walked up the aisle, I nearly lost it."

Her fingers dug into her beaded evening bag before she forced them to relax. "Tonight brought up a lot of memories for me, too." A laugh tumbled free. "You were so nervous you dropped the ring."

"And you stumbled over your own name."

"At least I remembered yours," she quipped, grinning. "Charity prevents me from mentioning my bruised toes after our so-called waltz."

"Hey, I warned you, but you insisted."

"I admit it. I should have listened."

He shifted, and one hand closed around the wheel. "I should have listened, too, Tia. You tried to tell me how unhappy you were. I didn't want to hear, and I'll always regret that."

A lump formed in her throat. "Thank you for that anyway. It means a lot."

He cleared his throat. "If I asked you to give me another chance, would you consider it?"

Her pulse leaped. "*Are* you asking?"

"Let's say I'm considering it." This time his voice was lashed with the wry humor that had been sorely lacking for a very long time.

Emotions churning, she took a deep breath. "If and when you make up your mind, let me know," she told him not unkindly before reaching for the door handle.

"Stay put until I can help you out," he ordered, opening the driver side door. "It's still icy in places and those shoes are a sprained ankle waiting to happen."

It was also bitterly cold, and Tia was shivering by the time Bryce ushered her inside the house. "Don't forget the alarm," she teased as she plucked the mail from the basket under the brass slot, but he was already punching in the code.

It seemed so familiar, the two of them returning home after an evening out, hanging up their coats, turning on lights, glancing through the mail. With a relieved sigh, she slipped out of her shoes and wiggled her toes against the faux Persian rug protecting the hardwood floor in the entry.

Glancing up, she caught the wicked gleam in his eyes. "I'll massage your aching arches if you fix me a cup of your special hot chocolate and brandy." It was a bargain they'd made many times before. Almost without fail, they'd ended up making love before they'd even finished their drink.

"There's something you should know," she said, keeping her gaze steady on his. "It has to do with the man who signs himself my secret admirer." As she spoke, the gleam in his eyes faded into the same wariness she'd seen earlier.

"I'm listening."

It annoyed her that she had to clear her throat before continuing. "He's invited me to a party tomorrow night. I haven't decided whether or not to accept."

His jaw tightened and then relaxed, a sure sign he was clenching his teeth. "Is that it, or is there more you need to get off your conscience before you can admit you want to jump my bones?"

Outrage, pure and hot, poured through her. "About that second chance, forget it, buster! Nothing's changed. You're still—"

"A jealous ass."

She supposed a more gullible woman would find his abashed grin utterly adorable. Not Tia Kostas, she told herself, glaring up at him. "If that's supposed to soften me up, you've failed miserably."

Frustration flashed out at her, so strong it nearly sent her reeling backward. "Damn it, Tia, you said you wanted me to 'talk' to you. So okay, that's what I'm trying to do, only you're not helping."

She blinked. "It didn't sound like talk to me."

"All rookies have a learning curve. Could be mine is steeper than most."

He moved his shoulders as though shifting a heavy burden. Tia thought about the broken shell of a man who'd raised him and longed to soothe away the hurt, but he would reject even a hint of pity. "I admit you've made a valid point," she said briskly. "And in the interest of fairness, I'm prepared to cut you some slack." Feeling the need to validate her own power, she jabbed him in the chest with her index finger. He looked startled, then amused, which earned him one of the famous Kostas frowns. "Hear this, Bryce Hunter, and hear it well, my patience is not unlimited."

Something very like hope came into his eyes. "Some things I can change, and I will, but if you come back to me, I won't turn my head when some guy comes on to you."

Before she had time to blink, his mouth was on hers and she was in his arms. Helpless to resist, she leaned into him, her body reveling in the security offered by the solid length of him. Pressing her breasts against his unyielding chest, she arched upward, her mouth moving under his.

Heat flashed through his hot skin to sear hers. His mouth took possession, his lips molding hers, his tongue seeking and then withdrawing. His hands slowly stroked down the length of her back to knead her bottom.

The room swirled, and her blood sang. This was Bryce, her husband, her love. Nothing was more important than the pleasure he gave her with those big tough-tender hands. Eager now, even desperate, she rubbed against the rigid flesh straining the fly of his tuxedo trousers.

Heat flashed deep into Bryce's body, searing him with pleasure so intense he shuddered helplessly. He pulled back, needing to calm down. "Let's go upstairs while I still have enough control left to get you out of this dress without ruining it," he urged, his voice rubbed ragged by the need prowling deep in his groin.

"No, I don't want control. I want wild and wilder." Eyes glazed, she cupped her hands around his neck in an effort to pull his mouth back to hers. Her need for him, the desire that matched his own, humbled him.

"Tia, you deserve more than a fast five minutes—"

Her mouth slammed into his, and her impatient little growl thrilled him right down to the bone. It was like coming home to paradise after a long and lonely trek through an empty wasteland. Sensing her desire to take charge, he gave himself into her hands, trusting her as he'd never trusted anyone before.

With each kiss, she took him deeper until his head was swimming and his body begged to be inside her. Desperate, he searched for a way to free her from the dress he'd imagined stripping from her all during the ceremony. When he found a zipper running from neckline to the curve of her spine, he damn near cried in relief. Trembling with need, his hands stroked the warm skin he found beneath the silk.

She moaned, her fingers clutching at his shirt to free it from the cummerbund. When she couldn't, she stepped back to glare at him. "Damn it, help me get this off."

Reluctantly, he stopped touching her to strip naked while she stepped out of her dress. Her skin was creamy and smooth, her breasts spilling from filmy cups the color of flesh. Her panties were nothing more than a strip of elastic and bits of see-through lace. When he realized she was staring at him with the same rapt awe, he came close to embarrassing both of them. "Looks like we need to take a time-out, sweetheart."

Despite her protests, he swung her into his arms and carried her upstairs to the room where he'd slept alone for so many miserable nights. "I've imagined you here too many times," he explained when she questioned him with a look. "Tonight I need the reality."

Even as he laid her on the bed, she was reaching for him. He pressed her into the mattress, his mouth seeking and hot, hers wild and willing. His hands roamed, luxuriating in the enticing smoothness before easing his fingers beneath the flimsy panties. Finding her wet, he tore her panties free before straddling her.

''Open your legs for me, sweetheart,'' he ordered—begged? ''Wider, love. Invite me in.''

Thighs spread, totally vulnerable and aching, Tia arched upward to meet his first powerful thrust, her need beyond anything she'd ever felt before. Her breath hissed in as pleasure ripped through her.

The scent of passion filled the air as he drove her higher and higher until she shattered. Once, twice—and then, incredibly, a third time. Her cries mingled with words spoken in an urgent tone she only half understood. His hands roamed and kneaded and, finally, caressed her in places that sent the most sublime pleasure rippling through her. Even as she sobbed with the joy of it, she wanted more. Slick with sweat, muscles straining, teeth gritted, he gave her all she sought—and more.

It was only when she was limp and sated that he allowed himself relief. With a shuddering groan, he rolled to his back and wrapped his arms around her. With bodies still joined and her heart gradually matching the rhythm of his, they slept.

Saturday

Tia opened her eyes to find herself alone in Bryce's bed. It was disappointing, but not unexpected. After years of rising at dawn to do his share of the morning chores on the farm, he'd never been able to sleep in much past six, even on the weekends. Apparently that wasn't one of those things he'd promised to change.

Still, there were some lovely advantages to living with a morning person, she reminded herself. Sometime around dawn he had nuzzled her awake and made love to her again until she was a melted puddle.

Feeling like a new bride, she gathered the pillow he'd used close to her chest and took in the smell of soap and shampoo and some indefinable something that made her body tingle and her heart turn mushy.

Her goofy wasn't-it-wonderful smile turned to a

yawn as she shifted her gaze to the clock. Ten minutes to nine. A quick calculation told her she'd slept four hours, give or take a few minutes. The man still had the moves. Darn tricky ones, too.

Now she knew how opposing teams felt when he'd set his sights on the goal line. But was it really love that had her wanting to jump out of bed and phone her attorney to call off the divorce or simply afterglow? That was the question she had to answer before nine Monday morning. Right now, however, she wanted coffee, she decided, tossing off the covers. And then she and Bryce would talk.

Deciding to shower and dress after breakfast, she returned to her own room and slipped into her serviceable-bordering-on-frumpy robe and the old-fashioned slipper socks her mama had sent from Greece every year for her girls. After washing her face, she tried to run a brush through her badly rumpled hair, only to be defeated by the infamous Kostas curls. No doubt this is how Cinderella looked the morning after, she thought, laughing—until she remembered the silky, sexy robe and dinosaur slippers on the shelf in her office. After five days of nonstop obsessing, she had forgotten all about her secret admirer!

Biting off Papa's favorite curse, the one her mama forbade on pain of some unnamed, but bound-to-be-horrible consequence, she sank down on her bed and tried to think. Everyone knew that Melina Irena was the flake in the Kostas family while Tia Athena was the sensible one. Going to bed with Bryce six hours after meeting him had been the one and only time in her life she'd given in to impulse. *Melina* was the one who'd dropped out two weeks before finals her sophomore year to fly off to Aruba with a studly brat-pack actor who'd been in Chicago shooting a TV movie.

Two weeks after returning home, Mel had forgotten the guy's name. Tia took great pride in never forgetting anything—until now.

I have dreamed of dancing with you in the moonlight…

A shivery little thrill ran through her before pooling in her stomach where it set up jittery pain-pleasure ripples. It had to be some kind of less than admirable anomaly in her personality, she thought glumly. Otherwise, how could she be in love with Bryce and at the same time be so pathetically eager to meet another man? Recognizing the first telltale throb of a tension headache, she decided to eat first, think later.

Halfway down the stairs, Tia smelled something burning. Quickening her steps, she hurried into the kitchen just as Bryce dropped a smoking frying pan into the sink.

"Damnation!" he muttered, turning on the cold water. The pan's contents hissed and spattered, sending sizzling droplets flying. Uttering another barnyard curse, Bryce jumped backward. At the same time, he caught sight of her in the doorway with her hand pressed to her mouth. "Think this is funny, do you?" he challenged in an ominous tone.

Tia shook her head. "Uh-uh, absolutely not."

At the strangled quality to her voice, his eyes narrowed to ominous slits. "Keep laughing and you'll play hell getting coffee out of the cook."

Standing there in tight jeans and yet another

Bears T-shirt with hair still damp and tousled from his shower and his chin jutting pugnaciously, he was irresistible. She felt her insides melting.

"The cook being you, I take it?" It cost her, but she managed to keep a straight face.

"You have a problem with that?" he demanded, sounding deeply offended.

It was such a joy to be able to tease him again without feeling that wall slam down to shut her out. It occurred to her that it didn't really matter whether or not she'd had some temporary crush on a man she'd never even met. After all, every woman was entitled to an intense fantasy or two in her lifetime. Here was reality. Here was the kind of love that mattered.

"No problems at all," she declared, risking a tiny smile. "I'm simply surprised, that's all. In all the years we've been married, I don't recall you doing more than opening a can or nuking a frozen dinner."

"You've obviously forgotten all those egg sandwiches you scarfed down over the years. The ones I made and you *claimed* were the best you ever tasted."

Her lips twitched. "How could I have possibly forgotten such culinary masterpieces?"

"If that was supposed to be an apology, it needs work," he said, his voice silky. "After I made a special trip to the butcher's for those sausage patties you like so much."

Her stomach gave a happy leap. "You made sausage?"

"Yeah, I was planning to surprise you with breakfast in bed." Mouth quirking, he prowled closer. The soap he'd used still clung to his skin, and his jaw was shiny from a recent shave. "Now that you hurt my feelings, I'm out of the pampering mood."

God, how she wanted this closeness to last forever. "Would a kiss help?"

His gaze dropped to her mouth. When those gorgeous gray eyes melted into heat, she deliberately parted her lips. He swallowed hard, and when he spoke, his voice was satisfyingly raspy. "Be a good start anyway."

"In that case, brace yourself." Insides quivering, she linked her arms around his neck and arched upward to press her lips to his. He responded instantly, his arms closing around her. She gave herself up to the sheer delight of the moment, the instant jolt of need, the rapid escalation of pleasure.

He moaned against her mouth before dragging his mouth from hers. "I've tried to fall out of love with you, Tia. Night after night I told myself to find someone else, someone who didn't demand more than I could give. But you're dug in deep, and I can't get you out."

She saw the naked honesty in his eyes and felt compelled to match it. "I want to tell you I'm still in love with you, but the truth is I don't know how I feel," she admitted before laying her cheek against his chest. "It's all a muddle in my head, and if you think it's easy admitting that, you're dead wrong."

He choked a laugh. "Wouldn't be the first time I've been wrong about you, sweetheart."

His heart pounded beneath her ear, strong and steadfast, like the man himself. "Dee told me about your showing up on their doorstep drunk." When his heart rate suddenly jolted into a near violent rhythm, she pulled back to look at him. "I could just shake you for even thinking that I wanted out because you couldn't play a stupid kid's game any-more."

He took a breath. "A man thinks all kinds of things when he's being tossed out on his ass."

Although his eyes were wary, he wasn't shutting her out. But it was costing him, she realized. Still, because they had so little time, she decided to take a dangerous chance and push him harder. "Just be-cause your father withheld his love doesn't mean it was your fault or that you're not worth loving, be-cause you are."

He stiffened, and his face closed up. When he would have pulled away, she tightened her grip on his neck and held on. "If you shut me out now, there's no hope for us. None."

His eyes turned to granite. "If you want me to admit my old man was a cold bastard, you've got it. But that was between him and me. It has nothing to do with us now or what happened to our mar-riage."

"It has everything to do with why I fought so hard to make our marriage work for so long before I gave up."

At his puzzled look, she tightened her grip on his arms and tried to shake him. It was about as effec-tive as shaking a boulder. "You're the reason, Bryce, the person you are inside this gorgeous body. The kind of man you are. You could have ended up as selfish and cold as Mason, but you didn't. Not even close. More importantly, you would never do to a child of yours what he did to you."

Naked pain flashed across his face. "You can't know that. Neither can I."

"I do know. Delfie adores you and so does Danny Goldstein. Kids can sense kindness and a loving heart and respond to it."

His mouth twisted, and self-mockery replaced the pain. "Yeah, I'm a damn Boy Scout."

Because she'd seen the pain and understood how much of it he still kept hidden, Tia took a breath and vowed to be patient. "I admire and respect you very much," she said in a quiet voice. "Even when I was spitting angry with you, I wanted good things to happen for you."

"If your definition of good includes divorce, we need a lot more work on that communication thing than I figured."

Seeing the trapped look come into his eyes, she deliberately lightened the mood. "Good things meaning your being offered a head coaching job in the very, *very* near future." Ignoring his frown, she offered a guileless smile. "This is where you're supposed to tell me if the rumors are true," she prompted when he appeared to be struggling to shift gears.

When it came finally, his grin was slow and crooked and endearingly boyish. "Like I've told everyone else who's asked in the last forty-eight hours, I never comment on rumors." He slid his hands down her spine to cup her bottom, and she realized his body was already swelling against her. "On the other hand, since it's you doing the asking this time, sweetheart, I find I am definitely open to a bribe."

She was starting to hum inside. "That sounds like

a challenge, Hunter, and in case you've forgotten, a Kostas never passes up a challenge."

He leaned down to nip her earlobe before whispering, "I'm real glad to hear that, honey, because neither does a Hunter."

The actual bribery itself took place in what was fast becoming Tia's favorite place—his bed. The man's endurance was awesome, but she had been tenacious—and, as he'd been forced to admit between helpless groans sometime during the sensual torture she'd inflicted on him, utterly ruthless.

By the time he'd pleaded for a truce, they'd both been drenched with sweat and gasping for air. When he'd finally gotten his lungs working again, he'd admitted that he had indeed received an offer from the Saints, one he'd yet to accept or reject.

Then, while Tia dozed, Bryce carried through on his breakfast-in-bed thing. Without the sausage, though, since he doubted he had the strength to make it to the butcher shop and back.

When the first sharp pangs of hunger had been satisfied—both for food and for each other—they dawdled through dessert. Just like a happily married couple lazing away a Saturday morning, Tia thought as she swirled another plump strawberry in real whipped cream. While he'd been downstairs, she'd visited the bathroom and then pulled on the T-shirt she'd all but torn off him earlier. Although he still wore the jeans he'd slipped on when going downstairs again, his chest was still satisfyingly bare.

"Open up, coach," she teased, rubbing it against Bryce's lips. "You'll like this, I guarantee it."

"Hmm?" Lying with his head in her lap, Bryce

opened his eyes and smiled. "Did you say something?"

"This is the last strawberry. At great personal sacrifice I have decided to award it to you for your outstanding performance on this particular field of play."

He laughed, and she realized how much she'd missed that infectious sound. "A man has to do what a man has to do," he drawled before biting the ripe fruit in two.

Tia spied the drop of juice on his lower lip and swooped down to lap it up with her tongue before eating the rest of the fat berry.

A deep groan rumbled from his throat. "At this rate, I'll never get any packing done."

Tia's saucy grin faded. Talk about a mood killer. Right up there with a bucket of cold water in the face. She kept her voice even and cool. "Please don't let me keep you then."

Bryce saw the hurt bleed into her eyes and cursed himself for letting down his guard. No matter how many articles he read, he would never understand a woman's mind. "Tia, I don't want to leave, you know that. I've done everything I could to keep that from happening, but it's out of my hands now. You're the one who filed for divorce. You're the only one who can call it off."

He forced himself to sit up. He wanted to reach for her, to comfort her with his body instead of the words that came so hard and were usually clumsy or wrong anyway, but he reminded himself of the prize he hoped to win and settled back against the headboard instead.

"Is that what you want, for me to call it off?" she asked warily.

His mouth softened. "You know the answer to that, sweetheart."

"Then why haven't you asked me any questions about my secret admirer? Don't you *care* that I just might spend New Year's Eve with him?"

"I'd like to break his neck!" That pleased her, he noticed. He just hoped she wouldn't want to break his when she found out the truth.

"If you ask me not to go, I won't," she said, her gaze steady and searching on his.

"Not a chance, sweetheart. I love you, and I want you like hell. I can't imagine ever wanting another woman the way I want you, but our marriage will only work if you want me the same way." He took her hand and ran his thumb over the knuckles. "Knowing how much I'm risking here has my gut in a knot, but neither of us can know for sure how you really feel unless you meet this guy tonight. If he's the one you want, it'll flat out kill me, but at least I'll be able to make a clean break."

It wasn't the answer she wanted, but it was the only answer he could give. He counted it a victory when she didn't jerk her hand free. "What if I meet him and I still can't make up my mind? What happens then?"

His stomach was on fire again. "Then we keep that appointment with the judge on Monday."

It was a night for sparkle and flash. Tia didn't possess an overabundance of either, but what she had was quality. Bryce had insisted on it. For a farm boy turned football player, the man had infallible taste—and an open wallet.

An irritable frown darkened her features as she affixed a flawless diamond teardrop to her earlobe. True to his word, he'd spent the entire day throwing things in boxes. Reminding her how much was at stake, she thought, glaring at her mirror image. Warning her that he'd meant what he said. Blackmail, that's what it was, she ranted to herself as she removed the other earring from its velvet nest in her jewelry box. *My way or the highway.*

Tia's hand froze halfway to her ear. Beneath the low-cut black silk bodice, her chest felt squeezed. Bryce Hunter, master strategist, had suckered her into following a decoy to the right while all the time he'd been planning to blow by her on the left.

Well, it wasn't going to work, she vowed. Not this time. She was still in charge. He'd said it himself. She was the one who filed and she was the only one who could...unfile, damn it. As for tonight—

"Your ride's here."

Startled, she dropped the earring and spun around to find Bryce standing in the doorway, one big hand braced against the jamb, watching her. In dusty jeans and a tight T-shirt he looked disheveled, unshaven and grumpy. Her heart turned over in her chest—at least it felt that way.

She'd just spent the better part of an hour and a great deal of concentrated effort transforming sensible Tia Hunter into a ravishing temptress—and that didn't even count the money she'd spent on the dress and shoes—but one look at him and she wanted his hands tearing through her hair and his mouth on her breast, ruining the silk beyond repair. Her breath escaped in an embarrassing rush.

Alarm tightened his features. "Sweetheart? Is something wrong?"

"No, I'm fine." Shifting her gaze to the mirror, she managed to retrieve the earring and screw it into place without fumbling. "Did you say something about a ride?" she asked when she finished.

"Yep. Limo driver's waiting downstairs."

She blinked, frowned his way. "Did you say limo?"

He grinned. "Big sucker, too. Black, like the wise guys favor."

Wise guys? Gangsters? Good lord, surely not! "Is the driver...alone?"

"Says he is."

Relieved, she took a breath. "I've already arranged for a taxi. It's probably on the way."

"No problem. I'll take care of it."

"I appreciate it, thank you." Nervous, and hating it, she retrieved her beaded bag from the bed and checked to make sure she'd tucked her invitation inside. Glancing up, she caught the appreciative glint in his eyes.

"That's...some great dress," he said, his voice strained. "Might put you at risk for pneumonia, though."

"This old thing?" she teased. It had taken her the better part of an afternoon to find it and the better part of a month's pay when she had. Sleeveless, with thin rhinestone straps, no back and a skimpy bodice, it had been cut on the bias so that it would appear to float around her ankles as she walked.

"Guy's bound to be walking funny before you even make it to the buffet table."

"Don't be crude," she chided, but she couldn't help reveling in his blatant admiration.

"Honey, all men are down and dirty when it comes to sex. Some of us are just more honest about it." Grinning, he extended his arm. "Would the princess allow this poor peasant to escort her to her pumpkin?"

Aware that he watched her every move, she forced a smile as she hooked her arm through his. "Cinderella is the one who rides in the pumpkin."

"Yeah? Well, tonight, princess, it looks like you're going in style." At the bottom of the steps, he stopped and swung her around for a hard, quick kiss.

"Take care of yourself, sweetheart. Whatever happens tonight, always remember I loved you first." With that, he released her, nodded once to the driver, and then walked with that slightly hitching stride down the hall to the den.

The driver's name was Nigel. With his erect carriage and British accent, he was right out of central casting. After helping her into her fur coat, he escorted her down the front walk to the limo parked in front of the Porsche, every inch the proper gentleman.

"Watch your step, it's icy," he said as she hitched up her dress and prepared to climb into the passenger seat.

"Oh, roses!" she whispered. Waiting for her on the far side of the seat. Wrapped in a cone of gleaming silver paper that crinkled as she settled back in the cushy seat. "Of course there are roses," she murmured before lifting the bouquet to her nose. The scent swirled in her head and made it swim.

Expressionless, Nigel turned on the interior light before closing the passenger door. An instant later he was behind the wheel and the powerful engine purred to life. As he pulled out, she realized he hadn't inquired about her destination. But he wouldn't, she realized. She was simply a package he was to deliver.

At the thought, some of her anticipation faded. Maybe Bryce wasn't the most romantic guy in the world, but he'd always treated her as an equal partner and not a possession. Sighing, she put a mental checkmark on his side of the ledger.

So far, so good, she thought, laying her bag next to her. As she did, her hand brushed an object on the seat. It was an oval box covered with blue velvet. The jeweler's name imprinted in gold on the front had her sucking in. This was the crème de la crème to Chicago's elite. Women had been selling their souls for identical boxes for over a century.

Hands shaking, she lifted the lid. Flawless diamonds glittered on a bed of white silk, intricately set in the shape of a teardrop. It was the perfect necklace for the dress. Oh, hell, the perfect necklace, period. To her disgust, her soul really did plead rather piteously.

It didn't feel right to accept it, so she wouldn't, but she could *borrow* it for the evening. In fact, after her escort had gone to so much trouble, to do otherwise would be an unpardonable insult. Conscience satisfied, she carefully fastened the masterpiece around her neck. It was surprisingly heavy against her throat and slightly cool. Forget Cinderella, she thought, bemused. This was Tia in Wonderland.

She depressed the button to lower the tinted window separating her from the driver. "Nigel, did you put the flowers and jeweler's box on the seat?"

He lifted his gaze to the mirror long enough to make eye contact. "Yes, madam."

"Can you tell me who gave them to you?"

"A courier, madam. He was waiting for me at the agency."

So what else was new? "Thank you," she said, settling back to enjoy the ride.

A uniformed security guard politely checked her invitation and her bag before directing her to pass through the metal detector. A sad, but necessary sign of the times, she thought as she walked into a wall of color and sound.

The ballroom was so crowded Tia found herself wondering if the planners had slipped the fire marshal a bribe to look the other way. It was truly a crush, as the ladies used to say in Regency times. The high-profile guests were polished and shiny and just a little smug as they greeted one another with air kisses and too hearty handshakes.

The band was top-notch and the music was alternatively hot and mellow with a smattering of jazz and soft country thrown in. The champagne was imported and expensive, the food plentiful and tempting, although Tia was far too nervous to do more than nibble a spinach canapé.

As she wandered through the happy celebrants, her nervous gaze searching for a telltale red rose pinned to the lapel of a superbly tailored tuxedo jacket, she was hailed several times by both personal and business acquaintances. All of the men wore formal attire. None wore a rose.

Nor did His Honor the Mayor. One of his more media friendly aides did sport a carnation on his lapel, but it was white, and besides, a trophy-wife type had anchored herself firmly to his side. As Tia chatted with a woman she'd met once at an alumni banquet, a couple of congressmen drifted by, deep in conversation, while a blond anchorwoman from the local network outlet tracked them with cool and calculating eyes. It wasn't as interesting as the Mad Hatter's tea party, Tia decided, but it had possibilities.

By the time thirty more minutes had ticked by, however, she'd used up her quota of idle chatter and people watching. Although he hadn't actually said he would be at the party when she arrived, it had been implied.

I will stay until midnight, but not one minute longer. If you are not there, I will know you are not the daring and adventurous woman I believe you to be.

She'd show him daring and adventurous, the rat. Anger seething, she was working her way through the throng toward the cloakroom when she heard Bryce's voice calling her name.

Heart leaping, she caught a glimpse of him through the press of the crowd. Although he grinned at her obvious surprise, she noted a definite tension around his eyes. So he'd come to fight for her after all, she thought while her insides did a happy dance.

Okay, so he'd taken her fishing when she'd wanted to dance in the moonlight on the deck of an ocean liner. Big deal. At least he'd never deliberately played her for a fool like some other never-to-be-mentioned-again jerk.

"Excuse me, please," she murmured, slipping past a large man with a florid face and a booming laugh.

"Sure thing, little lady," he said, beaming at her.

The crowd had grown thicker, and she took an elbow in the ribs and had her toes mashed before she was finally face-to-face with Bryce. God, but he was gorgeous, she thought, her heart soaring. And unbelievably sexy in a midnight-blue tux.

"So, you want to dance?"

"Dance?" Surely she'd heard him wrong. Bryce would rather eat quiche in public than dance. "You mean, the two of us? You and me?"

"Yeah, you and me. Us. Just like we did at our wedding." A crooked grin creased his cheeks and crinkled his eyes. "Unless you're afraid to risk it in front of all these society types."

Afraid? In a pig's eye she was afraid. "I will if you will."

"Let's do it." Definitely Wonderland, she thought as she let him lead her onto the dance floor. Her heart sank when she saw how crowded it was, but at least the tempo was slow. Maybe he wouldn't do too much damage if he crashed into someone.

"Sure you trust me not to mangle something?" he asked, bending his head so that she could hear him over the music.

"Even if you do, I don't care," she said, looking into those eyes she loved. "I just want to be in your arms."

Instead of answering, he swallowed hard, as

though something had caught in his throat and he was struggling to work it free. Only then did he say gruffly, "Whatever happens in the next few minutes, remember that I love you more than my life." Without giving her a chance to answer, he pulled her into his arms.

Thinking to hang on tight and do the best she could to keep her feet from tangling with his, she found herself whirling in perfect rhythm to the music, his strong arms both guiding and supporting her effortlessly. Here was the graceful man who'd once shaken off a half dozen tacklers to run seventy yards in a freak gully-flooding storm to score the winning touchdown for Notre Dame in the Fiesta Bowl.

Mystified, she lifted her gaze to his. The eyes meeting hers were full of laughter—and youth. "Surprised?"

"Stunned." A nasty suspicion gradually took shape in her mind. "Either you played a really rotten joke on me at our reception or you've been taking lessons," she said when the dance ended moments later. "Which is it?"

"Lessons. Every Wednesday night at the Y." He took her hand and tucked it in the crook of his arm before leading her from the floor. "After the first session, the teacher threatened to quit unless she received hazardous duty pay."

Tia choked a laugh. "So how long did you take these lessons?"

"Six weeks with Gale. Six more with Shirley."

The name jolted her memory. "She of the answering machine message?"

He nodded. "She had to cancel a session, but I'd made her promise on pain of broken toes not to mention a thing about the dancing on the machine, if she ever had to call me.''

Tia realized he had led her to a cluster of folding chairs half hidden behind a huge floral arrangement. ''You took dancing lessons. I can hardly believe it.''

Bryce saw the soft smile playing over her mouth and wanted to pump both hands in the air and shout. He'd won, by God. Against long odds, too.

''Believe it, sweetheart. I'd do just about anything for you.'' Figuring it was now or never, he took the rosebud from his pocket where he'd stashed it and shoved it through his buttonhole.

Suddenly everything stopped, including the breath going in and out of her lungs. For one frozen moment she simply stood there staring at the crimson rosebud before her breath shuddered in. ''Where did you get that rose?'' she demanded, her eyes narrowing.

He shot a self-conscious look at the velvety bud. ''Pretty wimpy, huh?''

''Answer the question, Hunter.''

''I think you already know the answer to that, sweetheart.''

Her eyes suddenly flashed fire. ''You… you…jackass!'' she sputtered in a barely restrained voice. ''All that noble talk about wanting me to be sure was just hot air. You knew I would choose you, one way or another.''

Bryce caught the wary looks shooting their way. He was used to playing out the important moments of his life in front of a crowd, but Tia hadn't developed protective calluses the way he had. ''Tia, let's take this outside,'' he urged in a low voice.

Too incensed to be rational, she slapped away the

hand he extended. "You deliberately set out to humiliate me in front of everyone I know."

Bryce Hunter was always cool under pressure, he reminded himself, uncurling the fists he'd jammed against his hips. To get his wife back, he'd be a damned rock if that's what it took.

"You wanted romance, you got romance," he said in a reasonable tone. "Having a secret lover is every woman's fantasy."

"Admirer," she grated between clenched jaws.

"Same thing."

"Not quite." Her breath hitched in hard. "When I think about all the time and energy I spent calling florists and couriers trying to find out your name, and...and how I went on and on about you to Steph and my friends and how I argued with my brothers and put up with...with *tourists* ruining my lunch." Eyes flashing, she sucked in an agitated breath. "All the time I was mooning around about this wonderful man who knew me so well, you were *laughing* at me."

"I wasn't laughing at you. I was *courting* you."

"How? By making me a public laughingstock?"

He shot a warning look at a guy staring at her chest before moving closer. "Don't give me that, Tia," he said, thankful for the privacy provided by the music and raised voices. "You thought this guy hung the moon just because he quoted some dead poet and sent you stuff with fancy labels. He could have been a sociopath or a fortune hunter or simply a serial philanderer, but that didn't matter because he knew how to play the romance game and I didn't."

"We're not talking about a game. We're talking about my life, and you...messed with it."

Something snapped inside, and six months of suppressed doubt and pain and anger came boiling out. "I was trying to save my freaking marriage, damn it! Obviously that doesn't count, so the hell with it. Get your divorce."

To hell with patience and understanding. To hell with worrying and sleepless nights. To hell with her. If she didn't want his kind of courting, some other woman would. He spun around, but Tia caught his arm before he could escape.

"I don't want a divorce, you idiot," she shouted over the cheers and comments of the spectators. "I want a baby."

Bryce had been gut-punched and knocked on his can more times than he could count. He'd been fuzzy-headed with concussion and blind with pain, but he'd never been so close to fainting dead away as he was at this moment. "You do?" he managed to get out through lips that had gone numb.

Tia's smile was soft and gentle and best of all forgiving. He wanted to lay his head on her shoulder and weep for all the mistakes he'd made. "More than one, actually, but I prefer one at a time."

It wasn't dizziness he felt spinning in his head, although it was close. And it wasn't weakness turning his knees wobbly. It was...joy, an emotion he'd come close to feeling a few times before but not like this. Never like this.

Before she could change her mind, he pulled her into his arms and sealed his mouth over hers. Fire shot through him as she returned the kiss. When he felt himself sinking into quicksand, he pulled back.

His heart trembled at the melting look on her face. Later, he promised himself, when they were alone and it didn't matter if things got more intense than he could handle, he would tell her that she was everything to him. And more. Right now he had to nail down the deal before that quick mind of hers started zoning in on the details.

"About that baby, how would you feel about giving birth in N'Orleans?"

Her eyes lighted. "You're taking the job?"

"That depends on you. I don't believe in long-distance marriage, but your career is just as important as mine. Doesn't seem fair to advance mine at the expense of yours."

"But if you pass this up—"

"They'll be other offers, Tia. I'm good at what I do, and each day I get better. I'm not worried."

She touched his face with a hand that trembled. "I love the roses and the slippers and all the other things, but this…this freedom to choose is the best gift you've ever given me." Her smile went a long way toward warming the dark corners that still remained inside him. "And I choose you and our baby and New Orleans, if that's where you want to be."

God help him, he was about to bawl. Somehow he managed to suck it up. "Forgive me for screwing things up, sweetheart?" he asked with a grin that wasn't as cocky as it should be. "In the marriage and in this secret admirer thing?"

Her mouth pouted. "I suppose I'll have to, since I'm crazy in love with you. But not quite yet. I'm still furious with you."

"Hell, and after I sweated blood through all those lessons so I could dance with you in the moonlight on this cruise to Mazatlán I booked for your birthday."

A cagey look came into her eyes, and he nearly groaned out loud. "If I forgive you now, do I get to keep the necklace?"

Before he could answer, the bandleader started counting down to midnight. Couples called to one another or strangers glanced around, looking for someone to kiss. As the crowd exploded into sound and the band launched into "Auld Lang Syne," Tia nestled closer, her arms around his waist. "I love you, my sweet secret admirer," she said, lifting her face for his kiss.

"I love you," he said before lowering his mouth to hers.

When they pulled apart, he gazed down at her. She was so lovely, and she was his. It was almost more than he could handle. "So, you want to dance, Mrs. Hunter?"

Her lips slowly curved. "Actually, I seem to remember something about my secret admirer promising to lick me all over. Of course, he meant in front of a fire, but I read somewhere that it's wonderfully exciting—not to mention romantic—to make love in the back of a limo."

"Yeah?" It wasn't the most romantic of responses, but since he was having trouble breathing, it was the best he could do.

Clearly pleased with herself, Tia nodded. "Since I *am* a daring and adventurous woman, I think we ought to check it out."

Bryce slipped his arm around her shoulders and

decided to forgo a victory lap in favor of a fast run to the goal line. "Romantic guy that I am, how can I possibly refuse?"

* * * * *

IT HAD TO BE YOU

Peggy Moreland

Dear Reader,

It isn't every day that a writer gets the opportunity to work on a project with a dear friend. The invitation to contribute to this anthology provided me with that rare experience. Sharon Sala's and my friendship stretches back a decade or more to the years I spent in Oklahoma. Then we were fledgling writers with big dreams and a wagonload of stories to tell.

I've never met anyone quite like Sharon. She has a heart of gold, a smile with the power to spill sunshine over the darkest day and the most amazing positive outlook on life. I've traveled with Sharon, laughed with her and shed a few tears with her. Now I've worked with her. Life doesn't get much better than this.

Besides the chance to work with Sharon, this anthology has given me the opportunity to test my skills at writing a shorter story than the Silhouette Desire ones I normally write. You'd think shorter would be easier. Not so. Bringing these characters to life on the page and weaving the threads of their love story within such a short format was a challenge for me, but one I thoroughly enjoyed.

I hope you enjoy reading "It Had To Be You." Dreams do come true. Just ask my heroine Jamie. Or my friend Sharon. She's seen quite a few of her own dreams come true, too.

Sincerely,

Peggy Moreland

Chapter 1

"One day off for Christmas," Jamie muttered as she dug through her purse for her key to the office. Her boss had to be a distant relative of Ebenezer Scrooge.

How was a person supposed to celebrate Christmas in one measly day? Especially when that person's family lived more than a four-hour drive away, which meant over an eight-hour drive round-trip.

Well, a person couldn't. Jamie was living proof of that. Instead of gorging on turkey and dressing and her mother's homemade mincemeat pie and building snowmen with her nieces and nephews as she'd planned, she'd spent the day alone, curled up on her sofa, with nothing but a half-dead spruce and a Bing Crosby CD of holiday music to remind her it was Christmas. She hadn't even bothered to dress, but had moped around in her pajamas all day, feeling sorry for herself.

She just hoped the JBs—her acronym for the jealous biddies back home who'd called her a snob when she'd announced she was leaving the small rural farming community where they all lived and moving to Chicago—never got wind of how she'd spent her first holiday in Chicago. If they did...

Don't go there, she warned herself as she unlocked the door and gave it a push. She was in a bad enough mood as it was.

Holding the door ajar with a foot, she dropped her keys back into her purse, then frowned and lifted her head, sure that she smelled roses. She sniffed the air. Had the janitorial service come up with a new rose-scented air freshener to replace the pine fragrance they ordinarily used? If so, she told herself, she was getting a can. The scent was positively heavenly.

Inhaling deeply to savor it, she shouldered open the door and reached to flip on the lights. She stepped inside, but was stopped short by the sight of her desk. Dead-center sat a tall, crystal vase filled with the most spectacular bouquet of roses she'd ever seen.

"No way," she murmured as she started cautiously across the room. She reached out to touch a bloom—the equivalent of pinching herself—and all but melted when her fingertip brushed the petal's cool, velvety surface.

"Oh, man," she said, releasing the breath on a sigh. They were real, all right. And so romantic they made her heart ache.

But who would send her roses? Not a boyfriend,

that was for sure, since she didn't have one. Her boss? She snorted a laugh. If it was National Secretary's Day and not the day after Christmas, he *might* be a candidate. Since it wasn't...

Her parents, she decided, and sniffed back tears at the thoughtfulness in the gesture. It was so totally unlike them. A rose*bush,* maybe. Something practical and with a life expectancy of more than a few days. But roses? Shaking her head, she took the vase between her hands and slowly turned it, counting each bud. An even dozen, she thought. Wow.

Spying a card nestled among the roses, she set the roses down and slipped it from its plastic holder, anxious to read the message her parents had sent along with the flowers. "'This is going to be our year.'"

Puzzled by the oddity of the typed message, she dropped her gaze to the bottom of the card and read, "'Love, Your Secret Admirer.'"

Secret admirer! She slapped a hand against her desktop to keep her knees from buckling beneath her. With her mind reeling crazily, she scanned the message again to make sure she hadn't misread it.

But the words were there in bold black on white. She clapped the card against her chest, her heart thundering beneath her hand.

"Oh, my God," she whispered, her eyes wide as she stared at the bouquet of roses. This was what she had yearned for, prayed for, even begged for. This was what she'd left family and friends in search of. This was what she had suffered ridicule and condemnation from the JBs to find. Romance... Excitement...

She gulped, swallowed, then held the card out to

read the message a third time. A shiver of anticipation coursed through her as she focused on the phrase "our year." She closed her eyes, trying to imagine what the coming year would be like with a man in her life.

No more lonely nights at home or weekends spent exploring Chicago alone, that was for sure. "Her man" would take her out to dinner at exclusive and ridiculously expensive restaurants, to the theater where he'd reserved box seats for them to see the hottest off-Broadway plays. He'd take her for midnight sails on Lake Michigan in his private boat, and toast her with champagne beneath a crescent-shaped, silvery moon. He would—

She opened her eyes to narrow them at the card. He *who?* She didn't have a boyfriend. Heck, she didn't even have a close male friend! So who was this mysterious secret admirer, anyway?

She turned the card over to look at the other side, hoping to find a clue to her secret admirer's identity. But the back of the card was blank.

"Has the mail come yet?"

At the sound of her boss's voice, Jamie whipped the card behind her back and whirled to block his view of the roses, not wanting him to see the flowers or for her to have to explain.

She could've saved herself the trouble. As usual, he had his face buried in the morning paper as he passed through her office en route to his. She could've been dancing on top of her desk buck naked and he wouldn't have noticed. Michael Shay had a one-track mind. *Business.*

Which was part of the rub. She'd done everything but slap an *Available* sign on her forehead and he'd yet to take the hint that she'd like to go out with him.

"No," she said, trying to keep the resentment from her voice. "But yesterday was a holiday. Christmas. Remember? The mail will probably be late."

"Oh. Right." Reaching his door, he stopped with his hand on the knob and slowly turned to look back at the roses. He glanced her way, a frown gathering between his brows. "Yours?"

My, my, my, she thought. The man has eyes, after all. "I guess so," she replied, trying her best to act as if they were no big deal. "They were on my desk when I came in."

"You guess?" He started back across the room. "Wasn't there a card?"

Still holding it behind her back, she curled her fingers around it, praying he wouldn't ask to see it. If he thought she had a boyfriend, he'd never ask her out! "There was a card, but there wasn't a name."

"Let me see."

Wishing she'd just lied and told him the roses were from her parents, she pulled her hand from behind her back and laughed weakly. "It's probably someone's idea of a joke."

He tossed his newspaper onto the corner of her desk and took the card from her to read. "'Secret admirer'?" he said, and sputtered a laugh.

She snatched the card from his hand. "Well, *I* happen to think it's romantic."

"Oh, it is," he agreed, biting back a smile. "And who is this romantic devil?"

Jerking up her chin, she pushed the card back onto its plastic holder. "I don't know."

"Oh, come on," he wheedled. "You can tell me."

Irritated with him for ruining what had to be the most exciting and romantic thing that had happened to her since moving to Chicago, she picked up the vase and rounded her desk to set the arrangement on the credenza behind it. "I would if I knew, but I don't."

"Not even a clue?"

She turned to face him and folded her arms beneath her breasts. "Don't you need to be working on the Peterson presentation? That *is* why we all had to come into work today, isn't it?"

"Yeah, but first we need to solve the mystery of this secret admirer of yours."

"And how do you propose *we* do that?" she asked, resenting his interference.

"We'll call the florist and find out who sent the flowers."

Before she could stop him, he plucked the card from the holder and turned it over, examining both sides.

"That's odd," he said. "There's no florist's imprint. No address. Nothing."

She snatched the card from his hand. "I could have told you *that.*"

Ignoring her, he slid his hands into his pockets and rocked back on his heels to study the arrangement. "The building was locked over the holiday," he said, as if thinking out loud. "So no one could have gotten inside to make a delivery."

Jamie's eyes sharpened. She hadn't thought of that.

"Which means," he went on, "whoever left the roses had to have access to the building."

She huffed a breath. "Well that certainly narrows the possibilities, since everyone who works for Shay, Tremaine and Weller has a key to the building."

He cut a glance her way. "Are you dating anyone who works for the firm?"

She stiffened defensively. "No, why?"

"Anyone who's shown an interest in you?"

She pursed her lips. "Just exactly where are you going with all these questions?"

"Just trying to help you solve the mystery."

"Not that I recall asking for your assistance," she informed him coolly, "but the answer is no."

He turned to study the flowers again, then snapped his fingers. "Tremaine."

Her mouth dropped open. "Tremaine?"

"This is exactly the kind of thing he would do." He chuckled, shaking his head. "I swear. That guy is such a Romeo."

"Romeo?" she repeated, having difficulty associating the term with John Tremaine, one of the three partners in the firm and the head of the design department.

"What?" he asked, frowning at her. "You don't like Tremaine?"

"No," she said quickly, aware that the two men were not only partners, but close friends, as well. "It's not that. It's just that he's so...so..."

He nodded, his expression turning grim. "I know," he said, as if he understood her bewilderment. "But the behavior John's exhibited lately isn't the real John Tremaine. The divorce," he explained, at her blank look. "He took it pretty hard when his wife left him. Started drinking and staying out all hours of the night. Guess he just couldn't stand the thought of going home to an empty house."

"I imagine that would be difficult," she murmured, unsure what else to say.

"Yeah, I'm sure it would be." He picked up his newspaper from the corner of her desk and slapped it across the palm of his hand, his expression smug. "Well, now that we've solved the mystery, I guess we can get to work."

He headed for the door to his private office, but paused in the doorway to look back at the roses. "Secret Admirer," he said, then chuckled and shook his head. "Leave it to Tremaine to think of romancing a woman with an angle like that."

Michael waited an hour, then picked up his phone and punched in the extension for Ben Weller, the third partner of Shay, Tremaine and Weller.

When Ben answered the line, Michael glanced at his office door to make sure it was still closed, then said in a low voice, "You can stop worrying about Tremaine. I've got everything under control."

"You got him to go to an AA meeting?" Ben asked in surprise.

Pleased with himself and the plan he'd concocted, Michael spun his chair around to face the view of Lake Michigan out his office window. "No. I found him a woman."

"A woman!"

Wincing, Michael snatched the phone closer to his mouth. "For God's sake, Ben!" he whispered frantically. "Lower your voice. We don't want anyone to know that we have anything to do with this."

"We, nothing. *You're* the one who said John needed a woman. *I* said he needed AA."

Michael scowled at the reminder. "And I told you Tremaine wasn't an alcoholic."

"Could've fooled me."

Michael dragged a frustrated hand over his hair, having been down this road with Ben before. "Look, Ben," he said, struggling for patience. "I know that John's been drinking a lot lately and coming into the office hungover, but he's *not* an alcoholic."

"Then what is he?"

"Lonely. A man at loose ends. Hell, you know how Tremaine is," he reminded his partner. "He's a couple kind of guy. Always has been. What he needs is a good woman by his side, someone stable, reliable. Someone who can fill the gap Cindy left in his life when she divorced him."

"And you know a woman like that?"

"Yes, I do."

"Who?"

Michael glanced over his shoulder at his closed office door, imagining his very efficient secretary working at her desk on the other side. A slow smile spread across his face. "Jamie Tyson."

"Your secretary?"

"One and the same."

Ben snorted. "In case you haven't noticed, John's preference for women lately has leaned toward the loud-mouthed, big-busted-blond variety. I hate to be the one to tell you this, Shay, but your secretary is anything but.''

''Which is exactly why she's perfect for him,'' Michael insisted.

''I can't believe you'd be that coldhearted.''

''What do you mean?''

''Offering up your secretary as a sacrifice just to get John in line.''

''Now wait just a damn minute,'' Michael said, bristling at the implication. ''You know as well as I do that something has to be done to stop John before he self-destructs and takes the whole company down with him. You've seen the financial reports. Hell, you create them! The quality of work coming out of the design department has decreased considerably over the last six months, which is having a decided impact on sales. And company morale is at an all-time low. The employees are damn sick and tired of having to scramble just because John can't seem to meet his deadlines.''

''Maybe so,'' Ben conceded, ''but that doesn't give you the right to sacrifice your secretary to save the company.''

''I'm not sacrificing anyone!'' Michael shouted, then clamped his jaw together and shot a look over his shoulder, hoping to God his voice hadn't carried to the outer office. Inhaling deeply, he turned back to face the window and lowered his voice. ''I'm doing this as much for Jamie's benefit, as John's,'' he informed his friend tersely. ''She hasn't lived in Chicago all that long, doesn't have that many friends. Hell, the woman's only had two dates since she moved here!''

''She told you that?''

"Well, no," he admitted reluctantly. "Not directly. But I overheard her talking to one of the other secretaries at the Christmas party. Sounded to me as if she's all but starving for some romance in her life."

"I seriously doubt that John, in his present condition, is capable of romancing anyone."

"My thoughts exactly," Michael agreed, "which is why I plan to help things along."

"Help? How?"

"I've already started the ball rolling. I left a bouquet of roses on Jamie's desk this morning and signed the card, 'Love, Your Secret Admirer.'"

"And how is she supposed to know they're from Tremaine, if you signed the card 'secret admirer'?"

"The secret admirer angle is just to add a little mystique to the gift. You know how women are," he said. "They eat that kind of stuff up."

"Maybe so, but I still don't understand how she's supposed to know they're from Tremaine."

"The power of suggestion," Michael replied. "When she couldn't figure out who the roses were from, I told her that it looked like the kind of thing Tremaine would do."

"It does sound like the old John," Ben agreed, then asked hesitantly, "Does he know you're doing this?"

"Of course not," Michael snapped.

"Then how do you expect to get the two together?"

"It's no different than laying out an ad campaign for a new client," Michael explained. "First I tweak their interests, raise their awareness levels. You know, make each take a second look at the other.

Then I drop a few hints to John that Jamie is interested in him. Do the same for Jamie, while continuing to send her gifts from her secret admirer. By New Year's Eve, the two will be a couple, I guaran-damn-tee it.''

''I don't know,'' Ben said doubtfully.

''It'll work,'' Michael assured him confidently, then frowned when he considered the alternative. ''It has to or we're all going belly-up.''

Refusing to allow Ben's pessimism to daunt him, Michael prepared to set the second phase of his matchmaking scheme into motion. He knew that this step would require a little more finesse than the first, since Jamie might be a hard sell to Tremaine. As Ben had so graciously pointed out, Jamie wasn't the big-busted, loud-mouthed blond John seemed to prefer of late. But Michael was certain that, if anyone could pull off the match, he could do it.

He waited until just before noon to approach John, hoping that by that time of day, Tremaine would have made it to the office. Just as he'd suspected—and feared—he found his partner seated behind his desk, nursing a hangover.

Not bothering to knock, Michael strolled in. ''Rough night?''

Tremaine lifted his head to glare at him through bleary, bloodshot eyes. ''If you're here to lecture, save it. I'm not in the mood.''

If Michael had thought a lecture would resolve his friend's problem, he would have gladly delivered one—along with a couple of hard thumps upside his friend's head. But since he'd already tried that method without success, he dropped down into the chair opposite his friend's desk instead. "I'll leave the lecturing to Naomi. She's much better at it than I am."

Tremaine snorted. "The damn woman's a shrew. Lit into me the moment I walked in the door."

Michael bit back a smile. The shouting matches between Tremaine and his assistant were legendary around the office. Fifteen years his senior and totally devoted to the man, after John's divorce, Naomi had decided her boss needed mothering and had elected herself for the job. John was less than pleased with the new role she'd assumed in his life.

"You're the boss," Michael reminded his friend. "If you don't like her harping at you, why don't you fire her?"

"Believe me. I've tried. Repeatedly. She just ignores me."

Michael dropped back his head and laughed. "You love her and you know it."

"Yeah," Tremaine agreed, smiling a little. "The old bat has her moments."

Deciding the time was ripe, Michael reared back in his chair and folded his hands behind his head. "Tell me what you think of my secretary."

"Jamie?" Tremaine asked in confusion. At Michael's nod, he shrugged. "I don't really know her. Why? Is there a problem?"

"No. I'm just curious."

"Well, from what I've seen, she appears efficient enough. Seems to handle the stress of the advertising business well. And, according to the office grapevine, she's a geek when it comes to computers, which is damn lucky for you, since you're so technically challenged."

Michael scowled at the jab at his computer skills. "I'll pretend you didn't say that," he muttered, then dropped his hands and leaned forward, bracing his arms on his knees. "But what I really want to know is what you think of her physically."

Tremaine puckered his lips thoughtfully and stared off into space, as if trying to draw a mental image. "Shoulder-length light brown hair, curly but not kinky. Cornflower-blue eyes. Friendly smile. Fresh-scrubbed look." He turned his gaze back to Michael. "In a word, wholesome."

Michael pushed out a hand, urging him to continue. "What else?"

"Well, she's a conservative dresser, but manages to pull it off without looking mannish like some of the other women around here do. She's physically fit, from what I've seen of her figure. Has the legs of a cheerleader or possibly an amateur gymnast. Nice, firm—" He snapped his gaze to Michael's, his face paling. "Oh, no, Shay. Don't do it. Please. You know what happened when you dated Lydia."

Michael shuddered and shook his head, remembering too well the nightmare he'd created when he'd made the mistake of dating his last secretary. "Don't worry. I've learned my lesson. I'll never mix business and pleasure again. I was just curious to know what you thought of Jamie."

Tremaine wrinkled his brow in confusion. "Why?"

Bracing his hands on his thighs, Michael pushed to his feet. "Because I think she might have a crush on you."

"Me?" Tremaine said, looking up at him in surprise. "Why? Has she said something?"

Michael shook his head. "No, it's just a feeling I've got. I've seen the way she looks at you. Kind of moon-eyed."

Tremaine held up his hands. "Don't worry, buddy. I'll keep my distance. I wouldn't want to be responsible for you losing another secretary."

Michael waved away his concern. "Hell, if you're interested, go for it. She works for me, not you." He glanced over his shoulder, as if to make sure no one was listening, then stepped closer to Tremaine's desk and added in a low voice, "But you better make damn sure you've got some asbestos gloves on, if you do."

Tremaine peered at him curiously. "Why?"

"Because that is one *hot* woman."

Chapter 2

He hadn't exactly lied, Michael told himself as he walked back to his office. For all he knew, Jamie probably had looked at John with stars in her eyes. Most women did. John had that wild, untamed artist look that females went berserk over. Why, Michael wasn't sure.

And as to his claim that Jamie was hot…well, he might have stretched the truth a bit there. Hell, he didn't know if she was hot or not…although there was something about her that made him think, in the right setting and with the right man, she might be. He'd picked up on that something the day she'd applied for the job as his secretary and had seriously considered not offering her the position, just so he could ask her out and explore that something a little further. But common sense had ruled in the end, and he'd decided he needed a good secretary a whole hell of lot more than he needed a woman.

As he reached his suite of offices, he saw his secretary approaching from the opposite direction, carrying a large box. He waited, holding the door open for her.

"More supplies?" he asked.

Without looking up, she nodded and brushed past him. Michael frowned after her, wondering at her subdued mood. He followed her inside, letting the door close behind him. "Problem?"

She shook her head as she set the box on her desk. "No…at least, I hope there isn't."

He propped a hip on the corner of her desk and looked at her closely, noticing that she seemed a bit pale. "Why don't you tell me about it and let me decide?"

"It's probably nothing," she said, and began to unpack the box. "But I ran into Mary on my way to the supply room, and she told me that Kristie Samuels received a bouquet of roses today, too."

Michael lifted his hands. "So?"

"Kristie's been having trouble with a stalker."

He scowled at the reminder. "Yeah. So I've heard." He looked at her curiously. "But what does that have to do with you?"

Catching her lower lip between her teeth, she looked up at the roses sitting on her credenza. "What if her stalker has decided to stalk me, too?"

Damn, Michael swore silently, understanding now why she looked a little pale. Hell, she was scared! He knew he should put her mind at ease, tell her that Kristie's stalker hadn't sent Jamie the roses. But he couldn't do that without exposing his duplicity and destroying his matchmaking scheme.

"I don't think so," he said, stalling for time while

he tried to think of a way to resolve her fears without blowing his carefully made plans. "From what I've learned from the detective in charge of Kristie's case, stalkers are obsessive, single-minded individuals, who focus their attention on one victim at a time. Besides," he said, giving her a reassuring smile as he stood, "we've already decided that Tremaine is your secret admirer."

"We did?" she said, looking doubtful.

"Sure we did." Knowing that he had to get her mind off the stalker and focused back on Tremaine, he caught her by the elbow. "Tell you what," he said, and urged her toward the door. "Let's grab some lunch. My treat."

She hung back, looking over her shoulder at the work piled high on her desk. "But the Peterson presentation," she reminded him. "We've only got a couple of days left to finish it and there's still tons of work to do."

He unhooked her coat from the antique coat tree by the door and held it open for her. "We can discuss it over lunch. In fact," he said, all but forcing her arms through the sleeves, "I've got a couple of new ideas I'd like to run by you."

She hesitated a moment longer, then turned for the door with a shrug. "You're the boss."

Jamie sat opposite Michael in a rear booth at Luigi's, a plate of spaghetti and meatballs growing cold in front of her, trying to figure out what had come over her boss. Never once in the six months that she'd worked for him had he asked her to join him for lunch. Not that she considered this a date or anything. She wasn't foolish enough to assume that. But still…

And what was all this sudden interest in her love life? Insisting upon helping her figure out the identity of her secret admirer and asking her questions about who she was dating and who all had shown an interest in her. It was so unlike him. So totally out of character. He'd never asked about her personal life before, never seemed to care if she had a life outside the office.

Not that she had much of one.

Scowling, she stabbed her fork into a meatball. Which was partly his fault, she thought resentfully. From the moment she'd set eyes on Michael Shay, she'd had to redraw the scale she'd used to measure men in the past. No surprise there, since her experience with the male gender up to that point had been limited to farmers and dairymen who considered Carrhart overalls, mud-splattered Wolverine boots and sweat-stained give-me hats the ultimate in business fashion.

But appearance wasn't everything, she reminded herself. Michael Shay had his share of faults the same as the guys back home. Not that he was difficult to work for. He'd never yelled at her and was always quick to praise her when she'd done a good job. And he'd never used his position as her employer to demand sexual favors from her, as her mother had warned her that some employers might try to do.

Although, at times, she wished he would.

And that's pathetic, she told herself as she dragged the meatball through the thick tomato sauce filling her plate. Wishing for sexual harassment, when what she truly wanted was romance. And she sure as heck wouldn't find romance with Michael Shay. If he had a romantic or sentimental bone in his body, he hid it well behind his Brooks Brothers suits.

She stole a peek at him across the table. But darn, if he wasn't the best-looking man she'd ever seen. With that thick, black-brown, razor-cut hair that made a woman want to mess it up a little. And those eyes. Brown like his hair, but shades lighter and tinted with slivers of gold that glimmered when the light hit them just right. His cheekbones were high and sharply defined, which had made her wonder if there wasn't some Native American blood in his family, a theory that his lithe, lean physique seemed to support.

And his mouth. She focused on it and had to gulp to swallow a moan. It was fascinating, mesmerizing and just begging to be kissed. His lower lip was just a little fuller than the upper, and when he was talking about something that excited him, he had a habit of sweeping his tongue over the lower one that made her toes curl in her shoes. And when he smiled…well, it was all she could do to keep from tearing off her clothes and begging him to ravage her. Thankfully, he didn't smile that often. Which was a shame, she decided, now that she thought about it. Because when he did smile, he seemed more human, more approachable and, if possible, more handsome.

And, heaven knew, Michael Shay was handsome enough. The sad truth was he was drop-dead gorgeous.

And, at the moment, frowning at her.

Heat crawled up her neck as she realized he'd caught her staring at him.

"I'm sorry," she said, and lifted her fork as if to take a bite of the meatball speared on its end. "My mind strayed for a moment. What were you saying?"

He rested his arms on the table and leaned forward, his forehead creased in concern. "You're still worried about the stalker, aren't you?"

Lowering her fork back to her plate, Jamie dropped her gaze, not wanting him to see the lie in her eyes. "Maybe a little."

He reached across the table and covered her hand with his. She gulped, staring as heat seeped from his into hers. She was sure that she would combust at any moment and burst into flames.

"Would it make you feel better if I talked to the detective working on Kristie's case?"

She snapped up her head, as stunned by his offer as she was by the concern she heard in his voice. "You'd do that for me?"

"Of course I would." He gave her hand a quick squeeze, then released it and rose, tossing his napkin onto the table. "I'll give him a call now. Won't take but a minute."

Dazed, she watched him walk away. What's going on here? she wondered in bewilderment. Had he experienced some sort of epiphany over Christmas? Had the ghosts of Christmas past, present and future paid him a visit, as they had Scrooge in Dickens's tale? Had he undergone some kind of dramatic personality change as a result of their visits?

She dropped her hand to her lap and rubbed at the spot where his hand had covered hers. He'd touched her, she thought, still feeling the imprint of each of his fingers. Really touched her. In an intimate, caring sort of way. She wasn't sure if she wanted to laugh, cry or run after him and beg him to do it again. Fearing she'd give in to the latter, she gripped her hands over the edge of the booth's leather bench and held herself in place.

Was it possible that he had feelings? she wondered. Not for *her* necessarily, but...*feelings.* The kind that normal people had? The kind she'd never seen him exhibit before? She blew out a long breath and uncurled her fingers from the bench, sure that she could control herself now and not run after him.

Wow, she thought a little shakily. Imagine that? Michael Shay...kind. Perhaps even caring. And all along she'd thought he was emotionless, that he probably had a calculator or a computer where other people had a heart.

A laugh bubbled up her throat at the thought of Michael having a computer for a heart. If he did, she thought in amusement, he would more than likely crash it. The man was dangerous around computers. She couldn't count the number of times he'd crashed his system. After only a week as his secretary she'd learned to copy his files onto a disk at the end of each day and lock it in her desk drawer for safekeeping. Now when he crashed his system, instead of having to recreate the lost information from scratch, she had only to reformat his hard drive, reload his programs and insert her backup disk to get him up and running again. That little bit of added security had saved her hours of nerve-racking, eye-straining work.

"What's so funny?"

She glanced up, startled to see that he was already sliding back into the booth, and quickly wiped the smile off her face. ''Nothing. I...I was just thinking about computers.''

He scowled. ''There's nothing funny about computers.''

Oh, if only he knew! she thought, but decided it wise not to share the humor with him. ''Did you get a hold of the detective?'' she asked instead.

''Yeah. He said to tell you not to worry. Kristie's stalker didn't send you the roses.''

''How can he be sure?''

He lifted a hand to signal the waitress for their bill. ''He wouldn't say any more than that. You know how it is. Official police business.''

''No, I don't know how it is,'' she said, suddenly angry. ''I've never even met this Detective whatever-his-name-is, and I'm supposed to accept his word as gospel and just forget about the stalker?''

Michael pulled out his wallet. ''His name is Wade. Detective Scott Wade. I know him, and if he says the stalker isn't your secret admirer, then he's not. Besides,'' he said, and dropped a fifty dollar bill on top of the ticket the waitress had left on their table, ''Tremaine sent you the roses. I already told you that.''

She rolled her eyes.

''I swear,'' he said, and stood, gathering their coats. ''The guy's a real Casanova. You'll see.''

Grimacing, Jamie scooted from the booth and pushed her arms through the sleeves of the coat he held for her. ''Yeah,'' she muttered under breath, ''and I'm Cinderella.''

* * *

Jamie rarely visited the design department and when she did, she usually came away with a splitting headache. She didn't understand how anyone could possibly concentrate in such a chaotic environment. There was always loud music playing, usually heavy metal, which alone was enough to set her teeth on edge. Add to that the open office concept, with everyone milling around talking and laughing and carrying on, and the psychedelic paintings on the wall, created by the employees themselves during spurts of creative genius... Well, it was a wonder they ever got any work done, at all—which she supposed was the problem, since Michael had sent her to check on the artwork that was due in his office weeks before.

Bracing herself for the onslaught to her senses, she pushed open the glass door and headed straight for Naomi's desk.

"Hi, Naomi," she called, having to raise her voice to be heard over the ear-splitting Led Zeppelin music currently playing. "Michael sent me over to pick up whatever designs you have ready for the Peterson campaign."

Naomi huffed a breath. "And isn't that just like a man? You'd think he'd have picked them up himself when he was here earlier." She flapped a hand over her shoulder, indicating the glass-fronted office behind her. "He was in there talking to John for almost an hour."

At the mention of John, Jamie looked up at the glass...and almost jumped out of her skin. The man in question stood on the other side of the glass, his arms folded across his chest, staring straight at her. With his shoulder-length, coal-black hair pulled back in a ponytail, he looked more like a Harley rider than he did a successful businessman. The black crew neck sweater, black jeans and black boots he wore only added to the biker look.

"Here's all we've got," she heard Naomi saying.

With a shudder, Jamie tore her gaze from John's. "Thanks," she said, and forced a smile for Naomi's benefit as she accepted the portfolio from the woman.

"Tell Michael I'll stay on John's back until he finishes the rest."

"I'll tell him." Tucking the portfolio under her arm, Jamie turned and all but ran from the design department. Once out in the hall and out of view, she collapsed against the wall, flattening a hand over her heart.

"No, God, please," she prayed fervently. "I know I asked for romance and excitement, but I didn't mean *that!*" She gulped, swallowed, then, just to make sure He understood, added, "I meant someone like...well, like Michael?" She tipped her head back and looked up, her expression pleading. "I know Michael's not perfect and needs a lot of work, and I know I've asked a lot of favors lately, but if you could see your way clear to granting me this one last itty-bitty request, I'll—" She stopped and frowned, unsure what to offer in exchange. It had to be something big. Something *really* big to equal the size of the request she was making. She wrinkled her nose and looked up again. "What if I agree to forgive the JBs for all the grief they've given me?" she suggested hopefully. "Would that be enough?"

* * *

It was well after six when Jamie stepped from the elevator and into the parking garage, straining to see over the top of the bouquet of roses she carried. She'd debated a good twenty minutes whether she should leave the arrangement in her office, but in the end had decided to take it home with her. She didn't really want to suffer through another day of explaining to all who asked, that, no, she didn't have a new boyfriend and, no, she didn't know who had sent her the flowers.

And she didn't care what Michael Shay said to the contrary, she thought stubbornly. John Tremaine was *not* her secret admirer. Heck, she hardly knew the man! She rarely had the occasion to interact with him, and when she did, he certainly hadn't appeared the least bit interested in her.

Other than that afternoon, when she'd gone to the design department and caught him staring at her.

She shuddered, remembering the intensity of his gaze. He wasn't her type, she told herself. If nothing else, his antics at the firm's Christmas party two days before had proven that. He'd arrived more than a little drunk and looking as if he'd been on a week-long binge. Throughout the evening, he'd talked too loud, drank too much and attempted to hustle every woman in the room, in general making a spectacle of himself.

And *this* is the kind of man I attract? she asked herself. With a huff, she shifted the roses to one hip and struggled to fish her keys from her purse.

''Need some help?''

She whirled in alarm, then sagged against the side of her car when she saw that it was Michael who had walked up behind her and not the stalker her overactive imagination had envisioned. "You nearly scared the life out of me," she said, as irritated with herself at her reaction as she was with him for slipping up on her.

He took the bouquet from her. "Sorry. But you looked as if you needed some help."

Frowning, she dug the keys from her purse and unlocked her car door. "I did," she said, then added grudgingly, "Thanks."

He handed over the roses, then waited as she settled the arrangement on the passenger seat. "Think you can make it now?" he asked.

She slid behind the wheel and pushed the key into the ignition. "Yes, I—" She froze, her gaze snagging on the long-stemmed rose tucked beneath the wiper blade.

"What?" he asked, and followed her gaze to the windshield. Reaching over the open door, he eased the rose from beneath the blade, then hunkered down bedside her car and offered it to her. "Looks like your secret admirer strikes again," he said, biting back a smile.

"It's not Tremaine," she said tersely as she untied the note that dangled from its stem.

As she read the short message she slowly lifted her fingers to her lips, her anger melting. "Oh, how sweet," she murmured, touched by the sentiment.

"What does it say?"

"'I'm thinking of you. Are you thinking of me?' And its signed, 'Love, Your Secret Admirer,' just like before."

Chuckling, he braced his hand on the door's arm rest and hauled himself to his feet. "I told you John was a Casanova."

She shot him a withering look, then dropped the note into her purse. "John Tremaine is *not* my secret admirer."

"Then who is?"

"I don't know, but—"

"Uh-oh," Michael said, looking over the roof of her car. "Don't look now, but here he comes."

She glanced over her shoulder. "Here who com—" She broke off before finishing the question and swallowed a groan as she recognized the approaching car as John's. The Porsche slowed as it passed by, the driver's head angled their way. Her gaze met John's and he smiled, lifting a hand. Jamie returned the smile—hers much weaker than his—and waggled two fingers, watching as he accelerated and sped away.

"Now do you believe me?"

She glanced up at Michael and quickly looked away, irritated by his smug look. "Just because he's friendly, doesn't mean he's my secret admirer."

"Are you sure about that?"

She grabbed the door handle. "Positive." She gave him a pointed look, waiting for him to move so that she could close her door.

He stepped back. "Well, I'm not," he said, then laughed when she slammed the door between them.

Whoever her secret admirer was, Jamie thought, she had to give him credit. He certainly knew how to get a woman's attention.

Throughout the drive home, she kept stealing glances at the roses, trying to imagine the kind of man who would court a woman in such a romantic way. Definitely not the caveman type, she decided.

A man who would think of doing something like this would have to be sensitive and in tune with the emotional needs and desires of a woman.

And creative, she added as she turned onto her drive. He'd have to be, to think of such a clever way to court a woman. She slammed on the brakes, then had to slap an arm out to keep the vase of roses from pitching forward and hitting the dash. Creative? she thought, gulping. John Tremaine was creative. Heck, he had a degree in art and was head of the design department at the firm!

No, she told herself, and shoved the gearshift into park. John Tremaine might be creative, but he certainly wasn't the type of man who would know how to charm a woman. She'd heard the women in the break room whispering about how he would corner them and say the most outrageous things. Some of the women thought it was funny, but to Jamie it was gross.

No, she assured herself as she gathered the vase of roses into her arms. There was no way John Tremaine could be her secret admirer.

But it wasn't Michael, either, she thought, and slumped back against her seat to stare at the roses, saddened by the realization. She'd never seen Michael do or say anything that she'd consider sensitive or romantic. And she seriously doubted that he was in tune with the emotional needs of a woman. How could he be, when he thought this whole secret admirer deal was funny rather than romantic?

No, she thought with a disheartened sigh as she climbed from her car. Michael Shay wasn't her secret admirer, either.

But, darn, she wished he was.

* * *

Michael paced the length of his living room, his forehead furrowed in thought. The next gift had to be better. The roses had been good, he told himself, and mentally gave himself a pat on the back for thinking of the idea. But not good enough.

And certainly not original, he thought with a frown, since he'd heard that not only Kristie Samuels, but Tia Hunter, who also worked for the firm, had received roses that same day.

The next gift had to be something unique, something off-the-charts spectacular, something that would grab Jamie by the heart and make her fall head over heels for John.

He stopped and frowned at the view of Chicago's skyline out his loft window. But how was he going to do that? From every indication he'd seen, Jamie seemed less than excited at the prospect of John being her secret admirer.

Frustrated, Michael turned for the wet bar and poured himself a glass of wine. He could sell her on the idea, he told himself. He knew he could. It was just a matter of putting this whole deal in terms he was familiar with.

He'd think of it as an ad campaign for a new product, he told himself, just as he'd explained it was to Ben. Jamie the consumer and John the product he'd been hired to promote. It was perfect. Familiar. He began to pace again. Now, it was just a matter of putting his finger on the pulse of the consumer, figure out what made her tick, what buttons he'd need to push to turn her on to the product.

Literally.

Amused by the unintended pun, he stopped and

tossed back half the wine, then dragged his arm across his mouth.

Okay, he told himself, and began to pace again. The focus is on the consumer. Specifically, Jamie. He'd concentrate on that angle first. From her reaction to the roses, especially the single rose he'd left on her windshield, he could assume that the size or value of the gift wasn't what was important to her. It was the sentiment that counted most.

He laughed softly and shook his head, remembering her expression when she'd read the typed note.

How sweet, she'd said, all but teary-eyed over the sappy message he'd written. He could have used the old standby "roses are red, violets are blue" or some other juvenile verse and probably would have gotten the same reaction from her. The woman obviously was a pushover where romance was concerned.

"That's it," he murmured, his eyes sharpening as he spun to grab paper and pen from his briefcase. He'd give her romance. Hell, he'd give her a damn basketful of it! He jerked out a stool and sat at the bar, holding the pen poised over the paper, prepared to start the list of items he'd fill the basket with.

But his mind was blank. He couldn't think of a single thing to write down! "Come on," he muttered, tapping the pen against the side of his head, as if to jar his brain into action. What kinds of things would put a woman in a romantic mood?

Flowers? No, that was out. He'd done flowers already. Candles? Yeah, he thought and jotted it down. Candlelight was definitely romantic. And he'd buy the smelly kind. Maybe a rose scent, since

Jamie obviously liked roses so much. And champagne, he thought, adding it to the list. What woman wasn't impressed by champagne? And some fancy glasses to drink it out of. Waterford? Nah, he told himself. Too expensive. Then muttered, "What the hell," and jotted down a note to buy two stems of Waterford.

With only three items on the list, he frowned, stumped as to what else would put a woman in a romantic mood. Lingerie? Something really sexy and revealing? He added lingerie to the list, then remembered a talk show he'd seen where a panel of women had discussed the least favorite Valentine gifts they'd received from men. Lingerie had ranked number one. He quickly drew a line through the word.

Unable to think of anything else, he hopped down from the bar stool and headed for the stereo, hoping some music would inspire him. He punched on the power and spun the dial, seeking a decent radio station.

"This is Charles David Montgomery," a DJ with a husky, bedroom-bound voice was saying, "bringing you songs for lovers on a cold winter night."

Bingo, Michael thought, grinning. He adjusted the sound, then returned to the bar.

"The phone lines are still open, so give us a call with your dedications," the DJ said as Michael seated himself at the bar again. "Our next song tonight goes out to Sherry from Jack. Jack wants you to know he's sorry, Sherry, and he hopes this song will convince you how much you mean to him and that'll you give him another chance."

Michael snorted a laugh. Jack must've screwed

up big-time, if he had to use a DJ as a mediator. Curious to hear what song the guy had selected to get him out of the doghouse, Michael listened closely, recognizing the opening chords of "You're My Soul and Inspiration" by the Righteous Brothers.

Jack might be a screwup, he thought with a nod of approval, but the guy definitely had good taste in music. Michael had a fondness for Golden Oldies himself and the Righteous Brothers in particular.

Then it hit him. Music! That's what he could add to the basket. He'd throw in a couple dozen CDs of romantic music. Every couple had their own special song. Why not let Jamie select the one for her and John?

Hooting a laugh, he added music to the list.

Hell, he couldn't remember the last time he had this much fun!

Chapter 3

Keeping her eyes on the computer monitor, Jamie picked up the phone and tucked it between shoulder and ear. "Michael Shay's office," she said into the receiver. "Jamie speaking."

"My, but you sound professional."

Jamie caught the phone in her hand and spun her chair around to give her full attention to the caller. "Mom!" she said in surprise. "What are you doing calling me at work?"

"A mother can't call her daughter whenever she wants?"

Jamie laughed. "Of course, you can. You know that. It's just that you've never called me at the office before. There's nothing wrong, is there?"

"No. But I need a favor. A rather large one," her mother added hesitantly.

"What?"

"Your dad needs a part for his tractor and the

nearest one he can locate is at a dealership in Chicago. You know how I hate driving in the city," her mother added, her tone turning pleading. "I hoped you'd pick it up for me and bring it here."

"Today?" Jamie asked in dismay. "Oh, Mom," she said uneasily, glancing over at the stack of transparencies she still had to scan. "As much as I'd like to help you out, I can't. We're in the middle of a big project and I have to work late tonight."

"Oh, you don't have to bring it tonight, sweetheart. Tomorrow would be soon enough. Since we missed sharing Christmas with you, we're looking forward to spending the weekend with you. You don't have to work on Saturday, do you?"

Jamie caught her lower lip between her teeth and glanced at her boss's door. "I don't know. Michael hasn't said anything about working this weekend."

"Well, if he does, tell him you've already got plans. Oh, and honey, you'll need to pick up the part today. The dealership is closed on Saturdays."

Jamie heaved a sigh. "All right. But you owe me one."

"A chocolate pie?"

She laughed. "Yeah. But make that two."

After writing down the address of the dealership, Jamie hung up the phone, then glanced at her watch. She'd planned to skip lunch to get more work done on the presentation, but she could use a break. She'd barely lifted her head from her screen since she'd arrived for work that morning.

Placing a hand behind her neck, she stretched her head back, trying to ease the tensed muscles, then, with a sigh, turned to face the computer screen again. Just as she found the place where she'd last been working, the door to Michael's office flew open and he shot out.

"Do you know where the transparencies are?" he asked frantically.

"Which ones?"

"The ones with the design for the billboards. I swear I had them earlier and now they're gone."

Without moving her gaze from the screen, she dragged a folder from the top of her credenza and handed it to him.

"You left them there when you took the call from Mr. Jernigan at my desk," she explained before he could ask how the file had ended up in her office.

"Whew," he said, dragging a hand over his head in relief. "I thought for sure I'd lost them. Thanks, Jamie. You're a doll."

"You're welcome."

Instead of going back into his office, as she'd expected him to, he propped a hip on the side of her desk. "Heard from your secret admirer today?"

She chose to ignore the teasing in his voice and continued to work, keeping her gaze on the screen. "No. I guess he's over me."

"I wouldn't be too sure. It's early yet."

"True," she agreed, and pushed her chair to the right, lifting the lid to the scanner. As she slid a transparency over the glass, he leaned over and reached for her mouse. She slapped his hand away. "Don't you dare touch that."

He pulled back, frowning. "I just wanted to see how much progress you'd made on the presentation."

Rolling her chair back in front of her monitor, she clicked on the icon for the scanner software and started the scan. "You want to know? You ask. But don't touch my computer. You might mess something up."

He slumped back against her desk, bracing his hips against the edge, and folded his arms over his chest. "Would not."

She glanced his way and sputtered a laugh when she saw his expression.

"What?" he asked irritably.

"You look like a spoiled little boy who's pouting because he didn't get his way."

"I'm not little and I'm not spoiled."

"No, you're not little," she agreed, willing to concede on that one point.

"And I'm not spoiled," he insisted.

She looked at him, giving his folded arms a pointed look.

He dropped them and straightened. "I'm not pouting. I'm irritated. Everybody's always ragging on me about being technically challenged. It gets damn old."

"I imagine it would," she replied as she transferred the scanned image into the document she was working on.

"Not every one is blessed with the same talents and skills," he continued, obviously unwilling to let the subject drop, "any more than they share the same dreams and goals. And, if you ask me, it's downright cruel to make a person the butt of every joke, just because he or she is somehow different."

Yes, Jamie thought, thinking of the JBs and their treatment of her. People could be cruel.

Including her, it seemed.

Feeling badly for the comment she'd made, she

dropped her hand from the mouse and turned to face him. "I'm sorry, Michael. You have my word that I'll never again mention your shortcomings where computers are concerned."

"Apology accepted."

"But you have to promise me something in return."

He narrowed his eyes to slits. "What?"

"You have to promise to quit insisting that John Tremaine is my secret admirer."

He opened his mouth, as if to deny her request, then closed it with a click of teeth. "All right," he said. "Deal." He stuck out a hand. "Let's shake on it."

Jamie took his hand and shook. But when she tried to withdraw, he tightened his grip.

"Why do you refuse to believe that he's your secret admirer?" he asked.

She lifted a brow in warning.

He released her hand and held his up in surrender. "I didn't say his name. I merely asked a question."

Pursing her lips, she turned back to her screen and positioned her fingers over the keyboard. "Because he's not my type."

"What is your type?"

She hesitated a split second, tempted to tell him to go look in the mirror, then forced her fingers into motion before she made a complete fool of herself. "I don't know," she replied. "But whatever it is, John Tremaine isn't it."

When he didn't make a move to leave, she glanced his way. "Was there something else you wanted?"

''Are you going to the company's New Year's Eve party?''

Where did that come from? she wondered and looked away. ''No, I don't think so.''

''Why not? Everyone who works for the company is invited.''

Yes, and everyone was taking a date, which was exactly why Jamie had decided *not* to go. ''It's black tie,'' she said, choosing to hide behind that excuse rather than admit she didn't have anyone to ask.

''So?''

''So I don't have anything to wear,'' she said in frustration. ''Now, unless you have something else you're dying to ask me, I really need to get back to work.''

Before she could settle her fingers back over the keyboard, he'd grabbed her hand and was pulling her up from her chair.

''What are you doing?'' she cried, trying to tug free.

''Taking you shopping.''

She dug in her heels, her eyes rounding. ''What! You're not taking me anywhere. I've got work to do and so do you.''

''We'll get it done.''

She dug those heels in a little deeper. ''No. Really. I don't have time.''

''Consider it your lunch hour.''

''But I was going to use my lunch hour to run an errand for my mother.''

He unhooked her coat from the rack and held it open for her. ''Fine. We'll run it after we find you a dress.''

* * *

Jamie followed Michael through the shop, trying her best to keep her tongue in her mouth and not drool on anything. She'd heard about this kind of shop before, where the salesclerks spoke in soft, refined voices and served wine to their clientele, but she'd never been inside one.

A thick Aubusson carpet covered the floor beneath her feet, and she'd swear the oil painting on the wall was an original. The three velvet settees arranged in a cozy semicircle in the center of the room looked like something straight out of an Audrey Hepburn movie.

"Michael!" she heard a feminine voice call in surprise. "Don't tell me Barbie didn't like the cashmere sweater set we chose for her for Christmas?"

Michael laughed and extended his hand. "Don't worry, Marcie. Barbie loved the sweater set."

Barbie? Jamie thought in bewilderment. Who the heck is Barbie?

Before she could ask, he reached behind him and tugged her around to stand beside him. "I was hoping you could help my secretary find something for the company's New Year's Eve party."

The svelte blonde circled Jamie, looking her up and down. "Well, of course, darling. Formal or cocktail length?"

"It's black tie," he replied. "We'll leave the length up to you. Mind if I look around?"

Marcie waved him away. "Please do, darling," she said, then focused her attention on Jamie. "Something in about a size eight?" she asked, lifting a finely arched brow.

The hag, Jamie thought, but smiled sweetly. "No, a four."

"Really," the woman said, giving Jamie a doubtful look up and down. "Well, I'll see what we have."

Marcie had no sooner left her than Michael returned, carrying a fire-engine-red dress draped over his arm. He held it up for her to see. "What do you think of this one?" he asked.

It was all Jamie could do to keep her chin from hitting the floor. The dress—and classifying it as such was stretching it some—consisted of three triangles of fabric. One formed the front of the skirt, a second formed the back, and the third, joined to the first with a rhinestone-encrusted disc, was obviously supposed to cover the breasts. But Jamie doubted any of the three would cover much of anything.

"If it had about another five yards of fabric," she said wryly, "I might consider it."

Michael frowned at the dress, then shrugged and turned away.

"Here you go, dear," Marcie said, returning with an armload of dresses. "Let's get you set up in a dressing room so that you can try these on."

Jamie followed Marcie into a room larger than her bedroom and outfitted with a floor-length, gold-framed, three-way mirror and a velvet-upholstered slipper chair.

"Would you like some help?" Marcie offered as she hung the dresses on a brass hook on the wall.

Jamie shook her head. "No, thank you. I can manage."

"Well, just give me a call, if you find you should need anything."

"I will."

After the door closed behind Marcie, Jamie hurried to the dresses, anxious to look through them. "Oh, my gosh," she whispered as she pulled out a long, ice-blue gown. She turned the hanger left and right, watching in fascination as the light struck the fabric, making the silver threads woven through it shimmer like diamonds.

Dying to try it on, she quickly stripped out of her clothes and pulled the dress over her head. She shimmied the clinging fabric down over her hips, then turned toward the three-way mirror, her eyes widening when she saw her reflection. She eased closer to the mirror, unable to believe that was really her reflection in the glass. Amazed at how glamorous she looked, she adjusted the low cowl neck over her breasts, then turned around and looked over her shoulder to check out the rear view. Her mouth dropped open when she saw how low the dress draped in the back. One wrong move and the whole world would know she had a freckle on the left cheek of her butt.

Feeling like a movie star, she swept her hair up and away from her face and examined the results. Deciding the dress required the more sophisticated look, she bent to dig a clip from her purse.

"Everything okay in there?" Michael asked from the other side of the door.

"Fine," Jamie mumbled around the clip she held between her teeth. She slid the clip into her hair, then sighed dreamily when she looked at her reflection. "Perfect."

"Are you dressed?" he asked, sounding impatient.

"Yes."

He opened the door and stepped inside. "I found this—" He stopped short. "Wow," he said, staring.

"Do you like it?" she asked, suddenly feeling shy.

"Like it?" he repeated, shifting his gaze to hers. "Well, yeah. It's great. Why? Don't you?"

"Oh, no. I love it." She turned to look at her reflection again and smoothed her hands over her hips. "It looks like something a princess would wear."

"Good. I'll tell Marcie we'll take it."

Jamie glanced down at the price tag, then lunged to grab Michael by the arm, stopping him before he could leave. "I can't buy this dress!" she whispered frantically.

He looked at her in confusion. "But you said you liked it."

"I *do* like it. But it costs seven hundred dollars! I can't afford to spend that kind of money on a dress."

He pulled his arm free. "Then I'll buy it."

When he moved to leave again, she stepped in front of him, planting a hand against his chest. "You'll do no such thing," she whispered furiously, then glanced over her shoulder to make sure Marcie wasn't within hearing distance.

"Why not? I can afford it."

"Whether you can or not, is immaterial. If *I* can't afford it, then the dress remains here." She dropped her hand from his chest and stepped aside, lifting her chin a notch. "Now, if you'll excuse me, I'd like to change back into my own clothes."

Women, Michael thought, tossing his keys onto his desk in disgust. Who could figure them out? All he'd wanted to do was to buy her a dumb dress and she'd swelled up like a toad, all indignantlike, her face turning all red and blotchy. The way she'd reacted, a person would've thought he'd offered to set her up in an apartment as his mistress or something.

And she hadn't spoken two words to him after they'd left the damn store. When he'd asked about the errand she needed to run for her mother, she'd merely handed him a piece of paper with an address on it. Deciding that he could be as stubborn as she, he'd driven to the location—a tractor dealership, of all places—and waited in the car while she went inside. When she'd returned, she'd tossed a sack into the back seat and climbed back in, still without saying a word, and had ridden in tight-lipped silence all the way back to the office.

Hell, it was nothing but a dress! Where was the crime in a boss buying his secretary a gift, if he wanted to?

He set his jaw. There wasn't, he told himself, and reached for the phone. And if she pitched another fit because he'd bought the dress after she'd specifically told him not to, then he'd tell her to consider it a bonus for all the long hours she'd put in on the Peterson presentation.

It wasn't as if she hadn't earned it, he told himself as he waited for an answer. If they won the Peterson account, half the credit was hers anyway. She'd worked as hard as he had on the presentation. Maybe harder.

"Hey, Marcie," he said, lifting the receiver to his mouth when the clerk answered. "It's Michael. Yeah," he said, chuckling. "Long time no see. Listen," he said, and scratched his head as he turned to face his office window. "You know that blue number that Jamie had in the dressing room? Box that up for me, will you? And send it over to my loft, along with the bill."

Jamie quickly locked her car, then hurried for the front door of her house, anxious to get in out of the cold. It was after nine and dark as sin. Wishing she'd thought to leave her front porch light on that morning before she'd left for work, she cautiously felt her way up the porch steps. Once on solid footing again, she breathed a sigh of relief and headed for the front door. Two steps away, she stumbled and had to fling out a hand to brace against the door, to keep from falling. Frowning, she looked back to see what had tripped her. A basket sat on the planked floor behind her.

Another gift? she thought in surprise, then quickly unlocked the front door. After dumping her keys and purse on a chair inside, she ran back out and stooped to pick up the basket. Lifting it high, she tried to see what was in it as she hurried back inside the house.

Unable to make out anything through the layers of red cellophane wrapped around the basket, she set it on the coffee table, then dropped to her knees in front of it. Her heart racing in excitement, she untied the ribbon that held the cellophane wrap in place and tossed it aside. Careful not to dislodge anything, she peeled down the layers of paper, sank back on her heels and stared.

"Oh, my gosh," she murmured, then quickly sat up and began pulling items from the basket.

A bottle of champagne came first, followed by two crystal flutes and several stacks of CDs bound with a white satin ribbon. Next she found candles, fairly dozens of them, scented with roses. On the bottom of the basket, nestled in a nest of silver streamers, lay a white folded card.

She lifted it out and read.

Champagne. Candlelight. Music. All the ingredients to create a romantic evening. If this is to be our year, we'll need a song. Which one will it be?

Love,
Your Secret Admirer

She placed a hand over her heart and read the message again, then, with a dreamy sigh, set it aside to gaze at the items she'd lined up on her coffee table. Champagne, candlelight and romantic music. Those were definitely the ingredients needed to create a romantic evening.

Rising, she began placing the candles around the room. When she'd finished lighting them all, she went to the kitchen and dug through the cabinets until she found a bowl large enough to ice down the champagne. Wishing she had the sterling-silver bucket the champagne deserved, she packed ice around the bottle and carried it back to the living room. She set it in the center of the coffee table, fussed with it a moment until she had it positioned just right, then straightened and gazed around the room, admiring the results.

Anxious to see what music her secret admirer had sent, she unwrapped the first bundle of CDs and flipped through them as she hurried to her stereo. There was everything from the Righteous Brothers to Michael Bolton to Aerosmith. She inserted several of the CDs into the player, then stepped back and closed her eyes, listening as the first strains of Michael Bolton's ''Only a Woman Like You'' filled the room. It was silly. Sadistic really, but she couldn't help imagining she was the woman in the song and Michael Shay the man.

Then it hit her.

''Oh, my God!'' she cried, and whirled for the coffee table to read the card again. She scanned the message, her gaze darting from phrase to phrase. *Perfect romantic setting...we'll need a song... which one will it be?* She snapped her head up to stare at the front door. He's coming, she thought, panicked by the thought. Here. Tonight. Why else would he have sent the champagne, candles and romantic music? What would be the point of creating the perfect romantic setting, if he didn't plan to be there to enjoy it with her?

Convinced that tonight was the night that her secret admirer would reveal his identity—oh, God, please let it be Michael!—she raced for her bedroom to change her clothes. Something sexy, she told herself as she threw open the closet door. But understated. She didn't want to appear too anxious...or, worse, desperate.

She selected and discarded item after item, but

found nothing she considered suitable for a night of romance. Wild-eyed, she spun and headed for her dresser. Jerking open drawers, she dug for just the right outfit, the perfect piece of clothing that would knock her secret admirer's socks off.

Suddenly she remembered. The silk lounge set her parents had given her for Christmas! It would be perfect!

Running back to the living room, she dropped to her knees in front of the Christmas tree and dug through the packages beneath until she found the one she'd opened from her parents. Sure that it was fate that her mother had chosen silk, instead of the usual sensible flannel, she headed back for her room to change her clothes.

Chapter 4

By midnight the candles had burned to nubs, the ice had melted around the champagne bottle and the CDs had each replayed a half dozen or more times.

And still no sign of her secret admirer.

Standing at the window, Jamie let the corner of the drape fall back into place, then crossed to the sofa and flopped down, dropping her elbows to her knees and her chin to her hands. So much for a life filled with romance and excitement, she thought miserably. And she'd been so sure that the basket was a sign that her secret admirer planned to reveal his identity to her that night.

Disheartened, she dragged herself to her feet and leaned to blow out a candle. A knock at the door had her snapping up her head. She stared at the door, unable to move. Was it him? she wondered, her pulse leaping at the thought. Her secret admirer? Not knowing who else would be at her door at that hour, she quickly fluffed her hair, smoothed the tunic of her silk lounge set and hurried to the door. Rising to her toes to peer through the peephole, she flipped on the porch light.

A distorted view of Michael Shay's face filled her vision.

She dropped to her heels, her mouth gaped wide in a silent scream of disbelief. Michael Shay? Michael Shay! OhmyGod! OhmyGod! OhmyGod! It was really Michael Shay!

He'd lied, was all she could think. He'd purposely misled her, wanting her to believe that John Tremaine was her secret admirer, when all along it was *him*.

Breathe, she told herself, and pressed a hand against her chest to still her pounding heart. She had to appear calm, cool and collected when she opened the door, not like some lovesick teenager. When she was sure that she had herself under control and wouldn't make a fool of herself, she opened the door.

"Michael," she said, feigning surprise. "What are you doing here?"

He lifted his hands, indicating the laptop he held. "I was working on the Peterson presentation and the screen went blank. When it came back on, the file was gone. Do you think you can find it?"

She slid her gaze from his face to the computer he held, her heart sinking. Trying her best to hide her disappointment, she stepped back and opened the door wider. "Sure. Come on in and I'll see what I can do."

He brushed past her. "Thanks, Jamie," he said gratefully, then stopped short and looked around.

"Oh, damn," he said, and looked back at her. "I'm interrupting something."

Don't I wish, she thought irritably. "You're not," she said as she crossed to the sofa and sat. She held out her hands. "It seems my secret admirer struck again."

"No kidding?" He passed her the laptop, then peeled off his gloves and stuffed them into a pocket, before shrugging out of his coat and tossing it on a chair. He dropped down beside her. "What he'd give you this time?"

She flipped open the lid to his laptop. "A basket filled with candles, champagne and CDs."

He leaned to pull the bottle from the bowl and examined the label. Puckering his lips, he blew out an admiring whistle. "I'll say this for the guy. He's got excellent taste." He sank the bottle back into the bowl, then picked up the card and glanced back at her. "Mind if I read it?"

Her attention focused on the computer screen, she lifted a shoulder. "Why not? You've read all the others."

He scanned the card. "What CDs did he send?"

She frowned at the screen, studying the data there. "The Righteous Brothers, Michael Bolton and...I don't know. Some others." She fluttered a hand in the direction of the bookcase on the adjacent wall. "They're over there on top of the stereo. Take a look, if you want."

Michael stood. "Don't mind if I do." He sifted through the CDs, reading the songs listed, then replaced those currently in the machine, punched the play button and adjusted the sound. With the music playing low in the background, he returned to the sofa and sat. He leaned close to Jamie to peer at the screen. "Found it yet?" he asked.

She shook her head. "No, but I will."

"Need me to do anything?"

She shot him a warning look. "Touch one key and you die."

Holding up his hands, he withdrew. "Just trying to be helpful."

With nothing to do but wait while she searched for the file, Michael tapped his fingers on the ends of his knees and looked around.

"You've got a nice place," he offered conversationally.

She glanced up and looked around, then dropped her gaze back to the screen. "Thanks. I like it."

"Craftsman style," he said, recognizing some of the architectural features.

"Mmm-hmm."

He stood and crossed to the fireplace, dipping his head to peer up the flue. "Does it work?"

"What?" she murmured, her gaze on the screen.

"The fireplace," he said, and straightened to admire the stone work.

"No. The owner had it closed up years ago, when he converted the house into apartments."

"That's a shame."

"What's a shame?"

He turned to look at her, then chuckled and shook his head, realizing that she wasn't paying a bit of attention to him. The woman was in a zone. She'd pulled her feet up under her and was now sitting cross-legged on the sofa, her forehead knotted in concentration as she studied the screen.

Wholesome, Michael remembered, his thoughts

growing thoughtful as he recalled Tremaine's description of her. John had certainly hit the nail on the head with that one. She did have that freshly scrubbed, natural look that women spent hours and hundreds of dollars trying to create. But Jamie accomplished it without the use of any female artistry. She never wore makeup—or if she did, it was so minimal that he'd never detected it.

As he continued to study her, she slid an arm beneath her hair and dragged it up to hold it on top of her head while she contemplated the screen, her lips pursed in concentration.

Michael's groin tightened in reaction. God, what a mouth, he thought. Full, moist and naturally stained the color of overripe strawberries. No telltale lipstick-on-the-collar stains from this woman. And with her lips puckered as they were at the moment, the bow on the upper one sharply defined, he couldn't help wondering what her mouth would feel like beneath his. What she would taste like.

Startled by the direction his thoughts were taking him, he dropped his gaze and silently swore. What the hell was the matter with him? He'd handpicked this woman for Tremaine. Heaving a sigh, he crossed back to the sofa and sat beside her again, but was careful to leave a good arm's length between them this time.

But not so far away that he couldn't smell her. He took in a breath and held it, analyzing the fragrance. Subtle. Feminine. And with just a hint of something floral. He carefully released the breath, then leaned a fraction closer, trying to determine the exact location of the scent on her body. Behind the ears? Between the breasts? On the back of her wrists? Or possibly she'd used a scented soap, which would explain why the fragrance seemed to surround her like a cloud.

Whatever it was, he thought, carefully straightening, he knew it hadn't come from any expensive bottle of perfume. Jamie might be a lot of things, but extravagant definitely wasn't one of them. She'd proved that with her shock over the cost of the bottle of champagne.

He gave her a sideways glance, frowning, as he remembered the dress she'd tried on that afternoon and her panic when she'd discovered its price. She wouldn't even let him buy it for her, when he'd offered. What woman wouldn't allow a man to spend money on her?

One with pride, he concluded. He added that to the growing list of admirable traits he'd discovered about his secretary, then frowned when his gaze slid to her chest and snagged on the jut of nipples beneath the midnight-blue silk top. It was cold in the room, he thought, but not *that* cold. Mesmerized by the erotic sight, he imagined himself reaching out and curling his hand over one of the soft mounds, and that knot in his groin wound a little tighter.

Gulping, he tore his gaze away before he did something stupid—such as grope her—and lunged for the coffee table, grabbing the first thing he saw to fill his hands. Pretending interest, he flipped the champagne glass over and studied the trademark on the bottom.

"Waterford." He quickly cleared his throat to remove the huskiness from it, then glanced over his shoulder to see if she had noticed. "The secret admirer sent these, too?"

Without looking up from the screen, she mumbled a distracted, ''Uh-huh.''

He set the glass down, relieved that she hadn't seemed to notice his eyes' lustful straying, and picked up a book of matches. ''Like I said. The guy's got excellent taste.'' Determined not to look at her again, he tossed the matchbook in the air while humming an accompaniment to the song currently playing.

She stopped typing. ''Do you mind?''

He glanced back at her. ''Mind what?''

She tipped her head toward his hand.

He caught the matchbook in midtoss and laid it down. ''Sorry,'' he murmured.

''Why don't you read a book or something?''

''Isn't there anything I can do to help? I feel badly dumping this on you and letting you do all the work, while I sit here twiddling my thumbs.''

''I don't need your assistance, I assure you.''

Puffing his cheeks, he rose. ''Whatever you say,'' he muttered. Thinking a little distance between them might be wise, he slid his hands into his pockets and strolled over to the bookcase. He scanned the shelves, but didn't find a title that caught his interest. He zeroed in on a thick photo album and plucked it from the shelf.

He glanced her way. ''Mind if I look through this?'' he asked, holding up the album.

Her attention on the screen, she waved a hand in his direction, indicating her permission.

With a shrug, Michael crossed back to the sofa and opened the album over his knees. He sputtered a laugh at the picture displayed on the first page. ''Is that you?''

"Is what me?"

"This," he said, lifting the album for her to see.

She looked up and gasped, making a grab for the album. "What are you doing with that?"

Michael put up an arm, blocking her. "You said I could look at it."

She clamped her lips together. "Yes, but I didn't know you had *that.*"

"Is it you?" he asked again.

Jamie glanced at the picture, then away, mortified that of all the books stored in the bookcase, he'd chosen the scrapbook she'd put together of her high school years.

"Yes, it's me," she said, feeling the heat of embarrassment crawl up her neck.

"Vetch Queen," he said, reading the sign on the side of the float she was pictured riding on, then laughed. "I never knew there was such a thing as a Vetch Queen."

"Just shows how little you know," she said, then tried again to take the album from him.

He angled his shoulder, thwarting her, and turned the page. "Who's this?" he asked.

She peered over his arm to see what picture he was looking at. "George Weatherby," she said, and had to smile when she saw the photo of her first boyfriend.

"He looks young."

"He was. Sixteen to be exact."

He turned his head to peer at her, arching a brow in question. "Boyfriend?"

"My first. I was madly in love and sure we would marry someday."

"But you didn't," he said, stating the obvious.

"No. George married Debra Maguire. Last I heard, they were expecting their fifth."

"Child?" he asked, shocked by the number.

She shrugged. "Good Catholics."

He snorted a laugh. "Obviously."

Jamie wrinkled her nose as he turned another page. "You don't really want to look at that, do you? It's just a bunch of boring old pictures."

He turned another page. "As I matter of fact, I do." He studied the picture displayed there. "Well, I'll be damned. John was right."

Frowning, Jamie strained to see what he was looking at. "Right about what?"

"You were a cheerleader. John said you had the legs of a cheerleader."

Her mouth dropped open. "John said that?"

"Yeah. I told you the guy is nuts about you." He turned another page and tipped the book for her to see. "Who are these people?"

Her expression softened as she looked at the photo. "All my brothers and sisters. Except for Joe," she added, "the oldest. He was in the army when that was taken."

He turned to look at her in amazement. "You mean all these people are your brothers and sisters?"

She peered at him curiously. "What's so strange about that?"

He shook his head and turned to look at the picture again. "Eight," he said, doing a quick count.

"Nine with Joe," she corrected. "Five boys and four girls."

He dragged a shaky hand down his face. "Man. I can't imagine having that many brothers and sisters. Hell,'' he said, and laughed weakly, ''I can't even imagine having *one* sibling, much less eight.''

''You don't have any brothers and sisters?''

''Nope. Only child.''

''Well, that certainly explains a lot.''

He glanced over at her. ''What does?''

Jamie inwardly winced, not realizing that she'd spoken her thoughts out loud. ''Nothing,'' she said, then wet her lips. ''Would you mind getting us something to drink?'' she asked, hoping to distract him. ''I'm really thirsty.''

He closed the scrapbook and set it on the coffee table. ''It's the least I can do. What would you like?''

''It doesn't matter. Just something cold and wet.''

He plucked the bottle of champagne from the bowl of water. ''How about if I crack open this bottle of champagne?''

Jamie hesitated, wondering if she shouldn't save it to share with her secret admirer, then tossed up a hand. ''Why not,'' she said carelessly. ''If my secret admirer wanted champagne, he should've stuck around a little longer.''

With Michael now busy dealing with the wire and cork, Jamie focused her attention back on the laptop, determined to find the missing file. ''Could you have saved the file under a new name?'' she asked, frowning at the screen.

There was a grunt, a pop and a fizz. ''Could have, I guess,'' he said. He filled each of the glasses, then handed her one. ''To your secret admirer,'' he said, lifting his glass in a toast. ''May you find in him all the things you want in a man.''

Grimacing, she clinked her glass against his. "I'll drink to that."

She sipped, while scrolling through the long list of file names on the screen. "You said the Peterson file," she said. "But exactly which one were you were working on when the screen went black?"

He rounded the coffee table and sat beside her, peering over her arm. "The one with all the artwork. You know," he said in frustration. "The one you made of all the transparencies that flips from screen to screen."

She pulled back to look at him, trying not to laugh. "You mean the PowerPoint slide show I created?"

"Yeah," he said. "That one."

Shaking her head, she closed the window and opened another. "This should make finding it a lot easier." She typed in some letters, clicked enter, then scrolled down the screen that appeared. She clicked on a file name, and the first slide of the presentation popped onto the screen.

His eyes rounded as he stared at it. "Damn," he murmured, and turned to look at her. "How'd you do that?"

"The file extension," she explained. "Each program has its own unique group of letters to designate files created within it. I just typed in the letters designating a PowerPoint file, then—"

He held up a hand. "No, please." He sank back against the cushion and pressed the glass to his forehead. "You're making my head hurt."

Chuckling, she saved and closed the file, then shut down the laptop. "You're never going to learn to operate your computer if you don't at least try to listen when I explain things to you."

"As long as you're around, I don't need to."

"That's no excuse," she scolded as she slid the laptop onto the coffee table. Relieved that she wouldn't have to recreate the information he'd lost, she sat back with a sigh and took a sip of her champagne. "It's good, isn't it?" she said, sweeping her tongue over her lower lip to catch a drop.

"The best money can buy."

"It's expensive?"

He rolled his head to the side to look at her. "Dom Pérignon? You've gotta be kidding me."

She shrugged. "I don't know anything about champagne."

He gestured to the bottle. "Depends on where you buy it, but you can figure that bottle set your secret admirer back at least a hundred and fifty or so."

She sat bolt upright to look at him. "A hundred-and-fifty dollars?"

"Yeah," he said, and grinned. "I'm telling you the guy's crazy about you."

"A hundred-and-fifty dollars," she said again, then sank weakly against the cushions, staring at the liquid in her glass. "Wow," she murmured.

Pleased that his choice had impressed her, Michael closed his eyes, deciding to enjoy the music while he finished his wine. The Righteous Brothers's "You're My Soul and Inspiration" was currently playing. Hearing the song again made him wonder if Sherry had forgiven Jack-the-Screwup yet.

"Have you picked a song yet?" he asked.

"No. But doesn't it seem kind of odd to you that he'd want me to choose our song?"

He opened one eye to peer at her. "No. Does it you?"

She lifted a shoulder. "Well, yeah. A couple's song should be one that's special to them. You know, a song they experienced together. One that, when they hear it, makes them think of the other."

Michael settled his head back on the cushion and closed his eyes. "Must be a woman thing. Men don't think like that."

"Oh, yes they do," she argued stubbornly. "I'll bet even you have had a special song."

He snorted a laugh. "No way."

"Listen," she said, then waited quietly while one song ended and another began. "What does that song make you think of?"

"A 1985 black Corvette, a dark road and Suzanne Schillings."

"See?" she said, and gave him a smug poke in the ribs. "Even you relate a song to a special girl."

"No. To an event. The Vette wasn't mine and neither was the girl. But that was the song playing on the radio the night I found my dad parked on a dirt road behind the country club, humping his best friend's wife."

Jamie stared, her eyes wide in shock. "Your father?" she whispered in disbelief.

"Yes. My father."

She gulped, unable to imagine the kind of scars a son would be left with after witnessing a scene like that. "But—"

Michael quickly drained the champagne from his glass, unable to believe he'd shared that torrid bit of his past with her. She'd really be shocked if she knew that his mother hadn't been any more faithful to the marriage than her husband had been.

"I guess I better be going," he said, and heaved himself to his feet. "Thanks for finding the file for me."

Jamie stared up at him, a thousand questions she wanted to ask running through her mind. "You're welcome."

He scooped his jacket up from the chair and pulled it on. "I'll see you in the morning."

"Okay. I'll—" She tensed, realizing what he'd said. "But tomorrow is Saturday. You didn't say anything about us working over the weekend."

"I didn't?" He shrugged. "Well, we are. We have to or we won't finish the Peterson presentation on time."

Jamie pushed to her feet. "But I can't work tomorrow. I promised my mother that I'd bring her the part we picked up for her today."

"How long will that take?"

"Eight hours round-trip. And that's only if I turn around and drive straight back, without spending any time with my parents."

He raked his fingers through his hair. "Damn," he muttered. "I really need your help."

"If you had said something, I—"

"I'll go with you," he said, interrupting her. "We can take my laptop and whatever material you think we'll need. You can work on the presentation, while I drive."

Jamie stared, unable to believe he was suggesting such a thing. "Are you sure?"

"Positive. We'll get in eight hours of work and

your parents will get the part as promised. It's a win-win situation for everyone." He tucked the laptop under his arm and headed for the door. "Can you be ready by eight?"

"Well, yeah. I guess."

"Good. I'll pick you up then."

Jamie stared at the door, after he closed it behind him, then turned and ran for her room, panicked at what she should wear.

Chapter 5

Holding a towel over her head to hide her half-dried hair, Jamie flung open the door for Michael, then turned and ran back to her room.

"Make yourself comfortable," she called over her shoulder. "I'll just be a second."

Michael stared after her. "Women," he muttered, and stepped inside, closing the door behind him. "I thought you said you could be ready by eight," he said, raising his voice so that she could hear him.

"I did. But my hair dryer overheated. I won't be a minute, I swear."

With a snort of derision, he stuck his hands into his pockets, checking to make sure the little gold box was still there. He'd planned to leave the gift on her desk for her to find this morning when she came into work, but with the change of plans, he needed to think of somewhere else to stash it. He'd considered dropping it into her mailbox for her to find when they returned that night, but was afraid she'd forget to check her mail and someone would steal it. But where else could he leave the dang thing?

"I'm ready!"

He glanced back to see Jamie rushing from her room, her hair dry now, but her cheeks flushed and her eyes over-bright from the effort. Damn, he thought, giving her a quick look up and down as she tugged on her jacket. He'd never seen her dressed in anything but professional clothes—other than the night before when he'd barged in on her at midnight and caught her in what looked like her pajamas, and that dress she'd tried on at the boutique. He couldn't believe the change casual clothes made in her appearance. The brown leggings certainly showed off those cheerleader legs to the best advantage. He just wished the ski sweater wasn't quite so bulky. He'd barely been able to sleep the night before, for thinking about the glimpse he'd caught of her protruding nipples and wondering if the cold was responsible for their erect state or if they were like that all the time.

"Are you ready?"

He gave himself a shake. "Yeah," he said, and waved her toward the door. "I'm right behind you."

When she stepped out onto the porch, he pulled the box from his pocket, kept his gaze on her back while he dropped it discreetly onto the coffee table, then strode outside, whistling between his teeth.

"Enough," Jamie said wearily, and closed the cover on the laptop computer with a decided click. Holding a hand against the back of her neck, she leaned her head back, moaning as she stretched out the tensed muscles.

"It's really coming down now."

Glancing up at the windshield, she sat up straighter in her seat. The snow that had started a little more than an hour ago was coming down much harder. "How long do you think it's going to keep up?" she asked uneasily.

Michael dipped his head over the steering wheel to peer up at the sky. "Judging by the clouds, I'd say forever."

Jamie gave the sky a worried look, then shifted her gaze to the road ahead. "We've only got about another fifteen miles or so, but you might want to fill up with gas. If the weather gets any worse, the service stations may close. There's one on the right up ahead."

"Probably a good idea."

Spotting the station she'd mentioned, he slowed then turned onto the snow-covered drive and pulled to a stop in front of one of the pumps. When Jamie reached for her purse, he clamped a hand over her wrist. "Don't even think about it," he warned. "I'm paying for the gas."

Before she could argue, he'd flipped up his collar and hopped to the ground. A blast of snow and icy wind swept inside before he was able to close the door again.

Seconds later, he was sliding back behind the wheel, rubbing his gloved hands together and shivering.

"It's freezing out there!" he exclaimed.

Without thinking, Jamie reached to brush snow

from his hair and cheek. ''I'm sure it is. I'll bet it's snowed a good four inches already.''

''At least that,'' he agreed, then eyed the entrance to the service station. ''Do you think they'd have any hot coffee brewing?''

''Probably.'' She reached for her purse, but Michael stopped her, clamping a hand on her wrist again.

''I'll get it,'' he said, then shoved open the door and jumped out.

Once inside the store, Michael looked quickly around to get his bearings. He spotted a sign indicating the rest rooms and decided to take advantage of the facilities before hitting the road again.

After relieving himself, he headed straight for the coffee bar and poured two cups.

''Isn't that Jamie Tyson?'' he heard a woman ask.

''Sure looks like her,'' a second replied.

Curious, Michael craned his neck to look over the top of the coffeemaker and saw two women standing in front of the store window, looking out, their heads tipped closely together. Both women were wearing jeans so tight they gave new meaning to the term ''wedgie.''

''Get a load of that SUV, will you?'' the first woman was saying. ''A Lincoln Navigator. Fifty grand, if it cost a dime.''

''And did you see the coat the guy with her was wearing?'' the second woman said. ''Cashmere, and believe me, cashmere don't come cheap.''

Michael glanced down at the front of his coat and frowned. *What the hell did they care what his coat was made of or what it cost?* He lifted his head, wondering who the two women were.

"She obviously got what she wanted," the taller of the two women said.

"Yeah," the other replied, her tone sounding resentful to Michael. "A classy guy with money."

"She always was a snob," the first said. "Thought she was so much better than the rest of us."

Jamie a snob? He snorted. Not from what he'd seen. Deciding he'd heard enough of the women's petty gossip, he picked up the two cups and headed for the register by the front door. After paying for the coffee and gas, he shouldered open the door and stepped outside. The wind cut through him like a knife and he jogged for his Navigator, anxious to get out of the cold and back onto the road. Jamie must have seen him coming, because she leaned across the seat and pushed open his door, taking the cups from him as he climbed inside.

She inhaled deeply as she placed the steaming cups in the drink holders on the dash. "Oh, that smells wonderful," she said with a sigh.

Michael reached for the key, but noticed that the two women were still standing at the store window. He paused, frowning, remembering their snide comments. "Do you know those two ladies?"

She looked up. "What two—" She tensed, her face paling, then whipped around to face him. "Kiss me quick!"

He pulled back to look at her in surprise. "What?"

She grabbed him by the lapels of his coat. "Please don't ask questions," she begged. "I'll explain later. Just kiss me."

Not at all sure what was going on, Michael

looped an arm around her neck and pulled her toward him. "You better have a damn good explanation for this," he warned before closing his mouth over hers. He felt the tremble in her lips, tasted the desperation within her and wondered what it was about those women that frightened her so much, and why, when she'd seen them standing there, she'd demanded that he kiss her.

But then he felt the slow unfurling of her fingers on his lapels and the softening of her lips beneath his and he forgot all about the two women.

Damn, she tasted good, he thought, and deepened the kiss. And felt like sin. All firm and curvy. He could feel the soft mounds of her breasts pushing against his chest, those hard little nipples of hers at their centers. Anxious to feel more of her, he wrapped his arms around her, and dragged her over the console and onto his lap.

She was small, he realized in surprise, seemed to weigh almost nothing, in spite of the bulky winter clothing. But the hands that clutched at the back of his neck, holding his face to hers, were amazingly strong…and demanding. Her lips parted beneath his, an invitation he wasn't about to refuse.

He thrust his tongue inside, sweeping it across her teeth, then groaned as her taste sharpened, and he delved deeper. She shifted on his lap, her hip digging into his groin, then melted against his chest, pressing herself closer to him. His manhood hardened in response.

A moan started low in her throat, rose to slip past her lips, and he swallowed the sound, feeding the hunger that twisted inside him. He didn't care that he was in a public place or that two women were watching, monitoring his every move in bug-eyed fascination. His sole interest in females at the moment was the one on his lap. Jamie. Her taste. The feel of her hot little body pressed against his. She kept squirming, pushing her chest harder and harder against his, as if she couldn't get close enough. But that was fine by him. He wanted her closer. He wanted to absorb her, totally consume her.

God help him, he thought, what he really wanted was her naked beneath him and his sex buried to the hilt inside her.

The realization was a jolt to his system, the chilling dose of reality he needed to remember where he was, what he was doing. *Who* he was doing it with. He jerked back, all but tearing his mouth from hers. He stared at her, his chest heaving. In her eyes, he saw the same surprise, the same heat he knew must be mirrored in his.

He gulped, swallowed, not sure what had come over him, at a loss as to what to say. "Was that good enough?" was the best he could come up with.

Her eyes wide and round with wonder, she slowly nodded.

"So we can go now?"

She wet her lips, then nodded again, shifting off the console and back onto her seat to face the windshield again.

Michael started the engine and pulled the gearshift down into drive. Swearing, he shot it back up into park.

Startled, she looked over at him in surprise. "What?"

"I forgot to disconnect the damn hose," he muttered, and pushed open his door. He jerked his collar up to his ears to keep the stinging snow from sliding down his neck, then quickly ran to unhook the nozzle from the gas tank and return it to its slot on the side of the pump.

Once inside the Navigator again, he put the vehicle in gear and pulled back out onto the highway. He drove a mile in silence, trying to get his breathing back to normal. He drove a second, waiting for the explanation she'd promised. By the third, he'd worked himself into a temper.

"Well?" he said expectantly, glancing her way. "Are you going to tell me what that was all about?"

She groaned and closed her eyes. "I'm not sure I can."

"You can start by telling me who those two women were. They *were* who the show was for, right?"

She winced at the anger in his voice and looked down at her hands. "Shauna and Angela," she murmured. "Two of the JBs."

"JBs?"

"Jealous Biddies."

"Since I'm unfamiliar with an organization by that name, I'll assume that this club is unique to your hometown."

"Unique to me. I made it up."

He shot her a sideways glance. "Something tells me these women aren't aware they're members of this group."

Her chin bumped her chest. "No," she said miserably.

He waited for her to offer more, when she didn't, he said, "So who are they and why do you refer to them as the Jealous Biddies?"

She lifted her head to look out the windshield and he saw the sheen of tears in her eyes. He hoped she wasn't about to cry. If she did, he was afraid he might have to dump her on the side of the road, snow or no snow.

"This is so embarrassing," she said, gulping.

"I think I'm entitled to an explanation."

She glanced at him, then quickly away again, her cheeks turning a bright red. "Yes, you are," she said. She inhaled deeply, then released the breath on a rush of air and with it her explanation. "I was different, and because I was different, they made fun of me."

"Different, how?"

Grimacing, she caught the drawstring that ran through the hem of her jacket and twisted it around and around her finger. "I...I wasn't satisfied with my life here. I wanted more than a rural farming community could offer me."

"Like what?"

Curling her fingers into a fist around the drawstring, she turned her face to the passenger window. "Things you can find in the city. Theater. Museums. A career that had nothing to do with agriculture. I used to read fashion magazines all the time, practically lived on the Internet, exploring the places I wanted to visit, learning everything I could about life in the city.

"I was scared to death that if I stayed here, I would wind up marrying a farmer and spending the rest of my life scratching a living off the land. So while everyone else was out whooping it up and having a good time, I worked and planned and saved my money so that I could leave." She scowled at her reflection on the glass. "My girlfriends didn't understand. They thought I was stuck-up, a snob, when what all I really was...was different."

"Teenagers are inherently stupid."

"Yes," she agreed, then glanced his way. "But adults can be, too. I'm sorry for what happened back there. When I saw Shauna and Angela in the window, something inside me just snapped. All I could think was that I needed to prove to them that they'd been wrong, that I hadn't failed. That I was living my dream, just as I'd said I would."

"And kissing me proved that?"

"Yes." She blushed to the roots of her hair. "I mean, no."

"Well? Which is it?"

She pressed the heel of her hand against her forehead and shook her head, then lifted it to look at him. "I know this is probably difficult for you to understand, but most of the girls around here get married right after high school. They don't care anything about having a career or seeing another part of the world. They're totally satisfied to be someone's wife and have a passel of kids running around under their feet. Not that there's anything wrong with that," she added hurriedly. "Marriage and kids are fine. It's just that I wanted more."

She heaved a sigh. "That's what they never seemed to understand. To them, a woman without a man is a failure, and I didn't have one. That's why I asked you to kiss me."

Her explanation made sense to Michael...in a demented, twisted sort of way. But it also pissed him off. She had used him. Dragged him unknowingly into her little act for revenge.

Which wouldn't have made him mad, if he hadn't enjoyed the kiss so damn much. And all she seemed to have come away from the experience with was the satisfaction of proving that her girlfriends had been wrong about her.

"Forget it," he muttered, then asked, "Which turn do I take for your parents' house?"

Jamie tried the front door and frowned when she found it locked. Stooping, she lifted the corner of the door mat and pulled out a key.

"Now that's original," Michael commented dryly. "Bet a burglar would never dream of looking there."

Refusing to let his sour mood upset her—she had apologized, after all—Jamie shrugged and unlocked the door. "With nine of us, someone was always losing or forgetting their key, so Mom started leaving one under the mat to keep from getting awakened in the middle of the night."

She pushed open the door and stepped inside. "Mom! Dad!" she called. "We're here."

Michael followed her inside, closing the door behind him, and waited in the hallway while she went in search of her parents. The interior of the house, as far as he could see, looked much the same as his first impression of the exterior. Basic farm-style. Simple, yet clean and well-maintained. And warm and homey. A look his parents' home had never achieved.

He heard footsteps and glanced up to find Jamie walking back toward him, a piece of paper in her hand.

"What?"

"They're not here." She held up the paper. "They left a note, explaining that Aunt Lulu fell and broke her hip this morning and they've gone to Des Moines to take care of her."

"Aunt Lulu?" he repeated.

"My father's aunt," she explained. "We call her Aunt Lulu because she's a bit...well, a bit goofy." She did an about-face and headed back the way she'd come, motioning for him to follow. "I'm supposed to call Mom," she called over her shoulder. "Let her know we made it all right. Do you want anything to eat or drink?"

Michael followed her into the kitchen, but stopped just inside the doorway and gazed around. The glass-fronted cabinets and stained butcher-block countertops were obviously original to the structure, as probably was the scarred kitchen table. He felt as if he'd stepped onto the set of *The Waltons* and expected John Boy to come bursting in the back door at any moment. "Not right now," he said.

Jamie already had the phone in her hand and was punching in a number. She put the receiver to her ear and waved Michael toward a chair at the table, mouthing the word, "Sit."

Though his butt was numb from sitting, Michael sat, not knowing what else to do with himself.

"Mom?" he heard her say, then watched her sigh wearily. "Yes, we finally made it." She glanced over at him, then turned her back, as if embarrassed to be talking about him in his presence. "No, I didn't come alone. My boss is with me. Yes, Michael. The weather is terrible. That's what took us so long. How's Aunt Lulu?"

She wound the phone cord around her hand as she listened to her mother's reply. "Oh, dear," she murmured sympathetically. "That sounds painful. How long are you and Dad planning to stay with her?"

Michael found himself straining to hear the reply.

"Well, I know she must be grateful that you're both there with her. I don't know," she said, and shot an uneasy look over her shoulder at him. "We haven't discussed that yet."

She turned away and rubbed a finger at her temple. "Yes, I know the roads are dangerous, Mom, but we really need to get back to Chicago. We will," she promised to something her mother had requested, then exclaimed, "Feed the cattle! But why can't Jimmy feed them?" Her shoulders sagged as she listened to her mother's explanation. "No, I didn't know that. Yes, Mom, I know you wouldn't ask, if you had any other choice. Don't worry," she assured her mother. "I'll take care of it. Yes," she said, nodding, "I'll call and let you know our plans. I love you, too."

Michael watched as she hung the receiver back on its base on the wall. "Problem?" he asked.

"Aunt Lulu broke her hip."

"Yeah. You mentioned that. So what time are your parents due back home?"

"That's just it. They're not coming home. Evidently the storm hit Des Moines before it came this way. Mom said there's already about eight inches of snow on the ground and more expected tonight."

Michael glanced out the kitchen window and saw that the snow was coming down harder than ever.

"I have to feed the cattle," he heard her say, and

glanced back, watching as she crossed to the mud-room off the kitchen.

"By yourself?" he asked.

"It's no big deal," she replied, her voice sounding muffled. "I've done it before."

Michael rose and strode to peer into the room to see what she was doing and found her standing in front of an opened closet, her back to him, tugging on a pair of thermal coveralls over her clothes.

Though he'd never fed a cow in his life, couldn't remember ever being close enough to one to try, he heard himself saying, "I'll help."

She bent to drag a pair of rubber boots from the closet floor. "Thanks," she said, and gritted her teeth as she pushed her foot into one. "But I can handle it. You should stay inside where it's warm."

"While you're outside freezing your butt off?" Scowling, he shouldered her aside and yanked what looked like the longest pair of coveralls from a hanger. "I'm going with you."

She started to argue, but he silenced her with a quelling look.

Shrugging, she bent and pulled another pair of rubber boots from the closet. "These are Jimmy's," she said, then added, "My youngest brother. He's the one who's supposed to be feeding the cows, but he's at a livestock show with his steer and won't be home until tomorrow afternoon." She eyed his feet. "I think these should fit."

Michael shrugged out of his coat, tossed it aside. Holding open the coveralls, he stuck a foot into one leg, gave them a tug up, then stuffed his other leg inside. Fighting the stiff fabric, he worked the sleeves up his arms, then heaved the heavy suit up and over his shoulders. Winded by the effort, he dropped down onto a chair and pulled the boots in front of him.

"You really don't have to do this," Jamie said hesitantly.

Michael stomped the boot against the floor, forcing his foot inside, then stood and zipped up the too small suit. "I know I don't. But I am, so let's don't waste time arguing over it. Where are these cows, anyway?"

"In the pasture. Mom said the tractor and trailer are in the barn loaded and ready to go."

Michael started toward the back door, but Jamie caught him by the sleeve, stopping him. "What?" he asked impatiently.

"You'll need one of these." She chose a cap from a long rack of headgear hanging on the wall and tugged it over his head. After turning the fleece-lined flaps down to cover his ears, she clapped a hand over her mouth to smother a laugh.

Michael scowled.

"I'm sorry," she said. "But you look like Rocky from the Rocky and Bullwinkle cartoon show."

He caught her by the elbow and gave her a push toward the door. "I won't bother telling you what you look like," he muttered.

"What?" she asked, craning her neck to look back at him.

"Trust me. You don't want to know."

With Jamie behind the wheel of the tractor, Michael rode on top of the loaded trailer, his booted feet dangling off the stacks of baled hay. They'd argued about who would do what, the same as they seemed to argue about everything. Jamie had tried to convince him to drive the tractor, while she rode on the trailer and threw out the hay, claiming that the work involved would be too much for him to handle.

What does she think I am? he asked himself in frustration. Some kind of sissy? A weakling? He bent his arm, flexing his biceps, as if to prove that he had the muscle to do the job.

"You ready?"

He looked back, barely able to make out her shape through the blinding snow. "Whenever you are," he shouted. "Just say when."

"Have you got the wire cutters?"

He patted his pocket. "Right here."

"Okay. When I hit this next little rise, cut the wires on the first bale and throw it over the side. Work your way down the rows, so that the hay doesn't get top heavy and fall. Oh," she added as an afterthought, "and make sure you don't throw the wire out with the hay."

"What am I supposed to do with it?"

"Doesn't matter. Just make sure it stays on the trailer. I'll deal with it later."

"Fine," he muttered, seeing this as one more indication that she considered him less than adequate. "But hurry it up, will you? It's freezing out here."

By way of reply, she let off the clutch and stepped on the accelerator. The tractor jerked forward and the trailer followed with a lurch that almost unseated Michael. Grabbing at hay to hold on, he swore under his breath.

"This is it!" she yelled.

Michael pulled the wire cutters from his pocket

and snipped the first wire, a second, then gave the bale a shove, pushing it over the side of the trailer. Proud of himself and his accomplishment, he moved on to the next.

He felt something on the back of his thigh and kicked out, thinking a bale of hay had shifted and was rubbing against his leg. When he felt the sensation again, he glanced over his shoulder. His eyes shot wide, when he saw a big black cow, nibbling on his overalls. He looked quickly around and saw that more cows were trotting along beside the trailer, snatching mouthfuls of hay from the bales. There must be hundreds of them, he thought, then jerked his leg back, when another cow nipped at it, mistaking it for hay.

"Hey, Jamie!" he shouted. "Do something. These cows are all over me."

"They won't hurt you," she called back. "They just want the hay."

Michael picked up the wire cutters and frantically began cutting wire and pushing bales over the side. But the faster he worked, it seemed the more cows appeared, each one bolder and greedier than the one before.

"Give me a break," he yelled, pushing a cold, wet nose away from his cheek. "I'm throwing this stuff as fast as I can."

Thinking he'd outsmart the dumb beasts, he climbed to the opposite side of the trailer and pitched out a bale from that side. As if by magic, more cows appeared. One particularly impatient one butted its head against Michael's leg.

He kicked at the cow's head. "Get back," he shouted, "or I'll turn you into hamburger meat."

"I wouldn't mess with Junior, if I were you," Jamie warned.

"Why?"

"Because he's—"

Before she could complete her explanation, "Junior" took a running start and rammed his head against the side of the trailer, making it rock wildly from side to side.

Knocked off balance, Michael careened his arms, trying to remain upright, but failed. He pitched forward, landing face first on the hard-packed bales. He came up spitting bits of hay.

"—a mean-tempered bull," Jamie finished lamely.

Michael angled his head to scowl at her. "You said we were feeding *cows,*" he reminded her tersely.

"We are," she assured him. "Plus Junior. I guess I forgot to mention him."

Michael heaved himself to his feet, then stooped to pick up the wire cutters he'd dropped. Narrowing his eyes, he aimed the tool at Junior's nose. "Unless you want a certain portion of your anatomy to end up on the dinner table tonight, you best not do that again. *Comprende?*"

Chapter 6

By the time they returned to the house, Michael's feet and hands felt like blocks of ice.

He pulled open the back door and held it for Jamie. "What's frostbite feel like?"

She glanced at him as she passed by. "Why? Do you think you have it?"

He let the door slam behind him. "How would I know. I can't feel a damn thing." Which wasn't exactly true. He could feel his arm and leg muscles. They felt like knotted up balls of fire from all the bending and throwing he'd done.

"A good hot shower and you'll be fine," she assured him.

He watched her flop down on the floor to tug off her boots and was mortally afraid that he was going to have to ask her to remove his, as well. He wasn't at all sure he had the strength to pull them off himself.

He shuffled to the chair and slowly eased down, his quads screaming. Dropping his head back against the chair's high laddered back, he sighed wearily. "No wonder you wanted out of here. Very much of this kind of work would kill a person."

"It's not so bad when you're used to it."

He lifted his head to frown at her, just as she stood to shimmy the coveralls over her hips. In spite of his exhaustion, he found the sight unbelievably erotic. Which was nuts, he told himself crossly, and braced the toe of one boot against the heel of the other. It wasn't as if she was nude or anything. She was covered from neck to toe in ski pants and a sweater. Grunting and straining, he pried the boot off, then sagged back against the chair, his energy spent.

"Here," she said, "let me help you."

Before he could tell her he didn't need or want her help, she'd grabbed the heel of the remaining boot and tugged it off. "How do you do it?" he moaned pitifully. "You were out in the cold as long as I was."

"Like I said, you get used to it." She caught his hand and gave it a tug. "Come on. You need to get out of those wet clothes."

He tried to stand. He really did. But his body wouldn't cooperate.

Chuckling, she hauled him to his feet. "Man, you must really be out of shape."

She reached for the tab beneath his chin to unzip his coveralls, and he opened his mouth to tell her that he could undress himself. But he made the mistake of looking down at her to tell her so, and the words dried up on his tongue. She stood not six inches away, her head bent, the fingers of one hand braced spiderlike on his chest, as she slowly drew the zipper down with the other. She shouldn't be doing this, he told himself. It was too intimate an act. Too personal. Too sensual.

Her fingertips were burning holes through his coveralls. He was sure he could smell the scent of scorched cotton and searing flesh. And the suit seemed to be growing smaller—at least in one particular area. He needed to tell her to stop before he embarrassed himself. But before he could her knuckles bumped over his belt, dangerously close to his erection, and he tensed, slamming his eyes shut.

"Sorry," she murmured.

He opened his eyes to find her looking up at him, those blue eyes of hers all soft with apology and her cheeks still stained from the cold. She had the longest eyelashes, he thought, unable to look away. Still damp from the snow, they curled up to almost touch her eyebrows. And that mouth, he thought, focusing on it. Her lips were chapped from the wind, and the bow on the upper one, that tight little bow that he'd teased with his tongue only hours before, stood at attention, all but begging him to tease it again.

He wanted to kiss her, he realized. Wanted to drag his tongue across her lips and moisten them. More than his next breath, he wanted to crush his mouth over hers, forcing her head back, and expose the long graceful column of her throat to his hands, his teeth, his tongue. He wanted to rip that damn sweater off and fill his hands with her firm breasts.

Her hand came to an abrupt stop, the zipper at its end, and he sucked in a breath through his teeth. He saw the awareness that sharpened her eyes when she realized her hand's location, felt the tension that stiffened her fingers directly over his hardened manhood. She didn't move. Neither did he. They continued to stand in the chilly mudroom, with the snow piling up higher and higher along the deep windowsill and the wind whistling around the corners of the house, and her tensed fingers slowly burning a hole through the fabric that covered his erection.

He knew if he moved it would be to kiss her. And if he kissed her, he wouldn't be able to stop there. He wanted to make love to her. No, hell, he wanted to ravage her. He wanted his hands on her, feel her flesh heat and burn. Wanted to feel that hard little body of hers bowed beneath him.

And he wanted to taste her. Not just her mouth, though he could spend hours on it alone. He wanted his lips on her throat, on her breasts, on her belly. He wanted to drag his tongue down her thigh and back up again to taste the honeyed sweetness at her center.

He groaned, need becoming a sharp, twisting pain in his groin.

"Jamie..."

He heard the huskiness in his voice, the pitiful plea it carried, and would have turned away in shame if she hadn't lifted her hand and opened her fingers over his lips. Her touch was tentative, innocent, yet nearly dragged him to his knees.

Knowing he was fighting a losing battle with himself and knowing full well he'd probably hate himself later, he closed his hand over hers and pulled it down to hold against his heart.

"I want to kiss you," he said.

She nodded, never moving her gaze from his. "I know. I want to kiss you, too."

"It may not be enough," he warned, then wanted to kick himself for giving her an out.

She gulped, but slowly nodded. "I know. It's okay."

Before she had time to change her mind, he dropped his mouth over hers. Her taste shot through him like lightning, a jagged bolt of blue-white heat that had him releasing her hand to wrap his arms around her and drag her close. He felt the soft prod of her breasts against his chest, the silky twine of her fingers as she wrapped them around his neck and dipped his knees and put everything he had into the kiss, taking everything she offered in return. But it wasn't enough. Not nearly enough. Too many clothes separated them. He needed to touch her, feel her naked and writhing beneath him.

Using his mouth and his body to guide her, he urged her back, while he fought his arms free of the coveralls sleeves. Her shoulders hit the wall and he unwound her hands from his neck and pushed them up, pinning them against the wall above her head. He felt the shiver that shook her, the desperate arch of her body against his, and knew that she wanted him as badly as he wanted her.

Praying he was reading her signals right, he wedged a knee between her thighs. In spite of the thick layers of clothing, he could feel the heat of her body against his leg, the throbbing need that pulsed just for him.

Groaning, he dragged his mouth down her throat, then farther to open it over a breast. He heard her whimper, felt the painful dig of her nails in the back of his hands and sank lower still, dragging her hands down the wall until he was kneeling in front of her, his face buried against her belly.

He wrapped his arms around her waist, breathed in her scent, that musky fragrance that was all woman and red-hot desire, then curled his fingers over the elastic waistband of her pants and pulled them down, baring flesh inch by agonizing inch, until he'd exposed her mound. Lifting his head, he slid a hand between the vee of her legs and watched the flush of passion spread across her face, the heat darken her eyes. He found her center and her eyes shuttered close. He stroked her once, and she dropped her back against the wall, sobbing his name. Twice, and he sent her soaring, her back arching, her hands clawing at the wall.

"I want you," he said, his voice raw with need. "Here. Now."

Even as he offered the warning, he was tugging her pants from beneath her feet. He stood, his gaze on hers, and pushed his hands beneath the hem of her sweater and skimmed them up her ribs, stripping the sweater up and over her head. He tossed it aside and dropped his gaze to her bared breasts. With a low moan, he covered them with his hands and squeezed, his fingers sinking into the soft flesh.

"Beautiful," he murmured, and dipped his head to nip at a swollen nipple. He heard her whimper, felt her fingers knot in his hair, holding his face there, and opened his mouth and drew her in. Her flesh was like raw silk beneath his tongue, nubby and slick, her taste an aphrodisiac that made him want more and more and more. But the more he took, the more he wanted, the more he needed.

And he wanted all of her.

Flipping his belt open, he unfastened his pants and shoved them, along with the coveralls, to his ankles and kicked them aside. With his gaze fixed on hers, he slid his arms around her, cupping his hands low on her hips, then lifted her, holding her high against his chest.

He set his jaw, straining to hold her there, but muscles, fatigued from lifting and throwing hay, screamed in agony. Beads of perspiration popped out on his forehead and his arms and legs quivered like shaken Jell-O shots. Slowly, like a building imploding, he crumpled to his knees.

Jamie shrieked, clinging to his neck, as if afraid he was going to drop her.

"Maybe you were right," he gasped, settling her so that his thighs took most of her weight. "Maybe I am out of shape."

She pushed her face up to his and he was surprised to see the spark of anger in her eyes.

"You're not quitting on me now, buster," she warned. Reaching behind him, she spread out the coveralls he'd kicked aside, then gave his chest a shove. As weak as he was, that was all it took to send him tumbling to his back.

Sprawled as he was and with Jamie straddling him now, Michael wondered why he hadn't thought of this position from the start. Flat on his back, he certainly couldn't be expected to exert much effort, and he definitely couldn't complain about the view. Her breasts bobbed like ripe apples only inches from his face. And her butt… He groaned as she shifted, making herself more comfortable on his chest. A slight lift of the hips, he thought, and he was inside her.

"Hand me my slacks."

"Your slacks?" she repeated dully.

"Yes, damn it, my slacks!"

Frowning, she leaned over to nab them and

dragged them across his chest. He lifted his head high enough to dig his wallet from the back pocket, then tossed the slacks aside and pulled a gold foil packet from his wallet. He handed it to her.

"Since you're closer, you do the honors."

She huffed a breath. "How romantic," she muttered, then spun her bottom around on his stomach and bent over.

The view, he thought again, staring at her heart-shaped buttocks. No, he couldn't complain about the view. And she had the cutest little freckle on the left cheek. Smiling, he closed his eyes, listening to the tear of paper, then flinched as she fitted the condom over his sex. What hands, he thought, groaning. If he lasted more than five seconds, she'd be lucky.

She turned back around and stretched out over his length, propping her elbows on his chest. He opened his eyes a crack and found her frowning at him.

"What?" he said.

"Nothing," she muttered, and dropped her gaze.

"Well, there must be something bothering you or you wouldn't be looking so sour."

"Sour!" she said indignantly and sat up.

Regretting his choice of words, he looped his arms behind her neck and pulled her back down. "Maybe not sour. Unhappy," he offered, and waited to see her reaction.

Her mouth curved down in a frown. "It's just that...well, I thought it would be different."

"What would be different?"

"This," she said, waving a frustrated hand that encompassed them, the room and what they were doing.

Michael glanced around, noting the scattered

clothing, the drab little room with its concrete floor that he was much too aware of. He returned his gaze to hers. "I see what you mean."

"It's not that I expect candlelight and music or anything."

"No," he said, and pushed her up, so that he could sit up, too. "But a bed would be nice, wouldn't it?"

"Yeah," she mumbled. "That would be a start."

He sat her away from him and rose, then reached down and pulled her to her feet, as well. He slipped his arms around her waist and pulled her to him. "And some music wouldn't be that difficult to come up with, I'll bet."

"Well, no. My old stereo is still in my room."

He tucked his nose in the curve of her neck and nuzzled. "And your bed is still there, too?"

She let her head fall back, giving him better access to her throat. "Yeah, I think so."

He reached down, caught her beneath her knees and lifted her up. "So where is this old room of yours?"

She looped her arms around his neck. "Are you sure you can carry me?"

"Depends on how long we stand here talking about it."

Smiling, she laid her head on his shoulder. "Top of the stairs, second door on the left."

Chapter 7

Michael stumbled to a stop in the doorway of Jamie's room to catch his breath. A thick layer of frost covered the windows but allowed enough natural light to seep through for him to identify the shape of an iron bed on the opposite wall. Topped with two white pillows edged in eyelet lace and brightly patterned quilts, the bed was old, but like the rest of the house, warm and inviting. On the adjoining wall stood a wooden desk and chair. The stereo Jamie had mentioned occupied about half its scarred surface.

With the muscles in his arms threatening to revolt at any second, he headed straight for the desk. "You pick," he said, and shifted Jamie in his arms so that she could reach the stereo. With one arm hooked around his neck, she leaned to pluck a couple of CDs from the stack on top, slid them into the open slots, then punched the play button.

His strength nearly gone, he hobbled to the bed and shifted her weight to yank the quilts down. Laying her down, he followed, stretching himself out over her length with a sigh of relief. "Happy now?"

She reached to brush a lock of hair from his brow, her lips curving upwards in a lazy, if smug, Cheshire smile. "Mmm-hmm."

Following her hands movement with her gaze, she stroked her fingers over his forehead, then down over his cheek and rested the tips of her fingers against his lips. He closed his eyes, his chest tightening at the tenderness in the gesture. Curling his fingers around hers, he pressed a kiss to each fingertip, then shifted higher to cover her mouth with his.

She lifted her arms to wrap them around his neck, humming her pleasure as he swept his tongue over the bow of her lips. Beneath him, he could feel every curve, every swell, every dip of her body, each line and angle meshing perfectly with his.

In the background, Patsy Cline was singing "Crazy." Michael figured it was appropriate mood music, since he had to be certifiably insane to be where he was, doing what he was doing, with whom he was doing it with. It wasn't too late to stop, he reminded himself, even as he probed her lips apart with his tongue. But he knew he wouldn't. Not now. He'd lost the power to do so the moment she'd closed her fingers around the zipper of his coveralls in the mudroom downstairs.

Her hands slid down his back and he shivered as nerve endings he'd thought frozen sizzled and burned. He felt the slow undulation of her hips beneath his and blood surged into the erection that had grown soft during the agonizing climb up the stairs, making it hard again. But his desire to make love to her had never waned. He was beginning to wonder if it ever would.

Slipping a knee between her thighs, he gently wedged them apart, making a nest for himself, and pulled back far enough to look down at her. Her eyes were closed, her face tipped up to his, her lips glistening and swollen from the pressure of his.

"Jamie?" he whispered.

She blinked open her eyes to look at him and a slow smile curved her lips. She dragged her hands down to cup his hips. "Yes?"

Michael wasn't sure what it was at that moment that made him want her so badly. Maybe it was the way she was looking at him, her eyes glazed with passion. Or the slow, sensual curve of her lips. Or maybe it was the erotic glide of her hands moving over his buttocks and the soft dig of her fingers into his cheeks as she lifted her hips against his.

Whatever it was, he knew he couldn't wait any longer. He reached between them and guided his sex to hers.

"I know you were probably hoping for a couple of hours of cuddling and heavy petting," he said, breathing heavily. "To tell you the truth, so was I." He eased the tip inside and nearly lost it right then and there when she tensed, clamping around him. Gulping, he fisted his hands against the mattress, pushing himself up above her. "I swear I'll make it up to you," he promised, then thrust his hips against hers.

She arched high, her eyes widening, her nails digging into his buttocks. She remained suspended there a moment, her body quivering, then turned molten and sank slowly back against the mattress.

If Michael had thought he'd satisfied her, he would have been sadly mistaken. She lay still as death for about two full beats, barely long enough for him to draw a breath, then she lifted her hips and sent him deeper.

The breath whooshed out of him in a rush of air and he clamped his teeth together before his brains followed suit. Sensation after sensation exploded within him faster than he could discern them. Heat. He definitely recognized that one. And pleasure. That one, too. But he couldn't concentrate long enough to name any beyond that. Her hands seemed to be everywhere. Squeezing his buttocks; her nails scraping up his back; her palms sliding over his shoulders; the rake of her fingers over his nipples. Then he felt her hand push between them, her fingers circling him at the point where they joined.

He dropped his head to her chest on a groan. "Damn, Jamie," he gasped. "You're killing me."

Her hand stilled. "Is it your legs?" she asked in concern.

"No, no. It's—"

Before he could tell her that it wasn't his legs that were bothering him, she was pushing herself up and him over. With him flat on his back now, she straddled him and guided his sex back to hers.

"Poor baby," she murmured sympathetically, and stretched over him to brush a kiss over his lips. "You should have said something sooner."

Michael didn't say a word. Couldn't. Wouldn't! Not and take a chance on her misunderstanding again and stopping all together. At the moment, she was busy raining kisses over his face and doing something with her hips—he wasn't sure what exactly, but whatever it was, she was taking him along for the ride and the pleasure was unimaginable. Indescribable!

And her breasts. With her on top again, they were within easy reach. Taking advantage of the position, he cupped his hands around them, kneading them, then dragged his fingers out to pinch her nipples. She arched, moaning, and he lifted his head to catch one between his teeth. Taking her in, he suckled, watching her face, while moving his hips in rhythm with hers. Her lips were parted, her face flushed and her eyes closed in the most rapturous expression he'd ever seen.

"Oh, Michael," she gasped, dropping her head back. "Oh, Michael," she said again, more urgently. Then she yelled, "Michael!" and went stiff as a poker and ground her hips down against his.

All he could do was stare. He'd never seen anything like it. Experienced anything like it. She was gorgeous. Breathtaking. Surreal. With her face flushed with passion, her eyes all but aglow with it, and that hard, firm body of hers glistening with perspiration and spearing up from his, she looked like a goddess, a nymph, a siren.

Slowly her body unfurled and she stretched out over him again, purring like a cream-sated cat. "That was wonderful," she said, nuzzling her nose in the curve of his neck. "Delicious. Thank you."

He craned his neck back to look at her in disbelief. She'd thanked him? If there was any thanks needed, he should be the one thanking *her.* He'd never experienced such mind-blowing sex in his life!

But if she wanted to think he was responsible for that delicious experience, as she'd referred to it, who was he to tell her differently? Smiling, he cupped a hand behind her neck and placed a kiss on top of her head. "You're welcome."

She snuggled closer. "The weather's probably too bad to drive back to Chicago tonight."

He glanced at the window and the snow piled high on the sill. "Yeah. Probably is."

"Want to go to sleep?"

He reached down for the quilts and pulled them up over them, then turned on his side and curled his body around hers. "For a while, maybe."

She laughed, the sound vibrating against his chest. "Sounds good to me."

He closed his eyes, feeling warmer and more relaxed than he could remember ever feeling in his life.

"Michael?"

"Hmm?" he hummed sleepily.

"Who's Barbie?"

He pulled his head back to look at her. "My mother. Why?"

She snuggled her head back beneath his chin with a sigh. "I just wondered."

Michael stood at the window, naked, his hands braced high on the frame, staring out at the stark whiteness. The snow had stopped falling several hours before and the moon was out now, a sickle of silver suspended from a midnight-blue velvet sky.

It had been a hell of a storm, he thought, hypnotized by the sea of white. Snow lay a good eight inches deep on the ground and covered every surface, turning outbuildings into oddly shaped igloos. Remembering that he'd left his Navigator parked on the drive, he glanced down. It hadn't fared much better than the outbuildings. It looked like an albino dinosaur, with nothing to distinguish it from the rest of the landscape but two dark squares on the windshield that the northerly wind hadn't been able to reach.

He ought to be sleeping, he told himself. They had a long drive ahead of them in the morning. But who could sleep with all this quiet? he thought, frowning. He angled his head to look toward the bed. Well, obviously someone could. Jamie was buried beneath a mountain of blankets and sleeping like a baby.

Looking at her, even in sleep, was all it took to make him want her again. And, God knew, he'd have thought he'd eased that want by now. After the first time, they'd slept awhile, then awakened and made love again. Then again. And again. Each time different. Different positions, different pace, different mood. But after each, he'd been swamped with the same feeling of amazement. The same throat-tightening emotion.

He'd never had a woman do this to him before. He'd only been involved in a few serious relationships. Sexual relationships, yes. He'd had a lot of those. But serious? Not once he knew that was the direction they were headed. Serious for him spelled long-term, and long-term meant commitment and Michael had never cared enough about a woman to sign up for the long haul. Maybe it was because his parents' marriage had been so crappy. He'd had enough women tell him he needed counseling to suspect that he might be carrying around some excess baggage that he ought to unload or at least have examined.

But with Jamie things were different. Instead of trying to figure out a way to make a graceful exit, which was his normal after-sex reaction, he was thinking more along the lines of crawling back into bed with her and snuggling up beside her.

But maybe it was because *she* was different. She was natural and warm and funny. And seemingly insatiable when it came to sex.

You're not quitting on me now, buster.

Remembering her comment in the mudroom, he had to turn his mouth to his arm to smother a laugh.

And he'd worried that he'd stretched the truth a bit when he'd told Tremaine that Jamie was hot. She was that and—

He tensed, the blood slowly draining from his face.

Oh, God, he thought. *Tremaine. The secret admirer.*

Damn! he swore silently and pushed away from the window. *Damn, damn, triple damn, hell!* What was he supposed to do now? 'Fess up? Tell Jamie about his scheme to match her up with Tremaine? Admit that it was really him and not Tremaine who had sent her the gifts? That he, Michael, was really her secret admirer?

She'd never understand, he thought, wiping at the sweat that popped out on his forehead. Hell, what woman would?

But if he explained to her that he'd only done it

because he was worried about the company's future, how he was afraid that John was going to self-destruct and take the firm down with him. How he'd chosen her out of all the women he knew as the perfect one to settle John down and get his mind focused on business again... Well, surely she'd understand then. Perhaps even feel honored.

She wouldn't, he thought, suddenly feeling nauseous. She'd kill him. And if she didn't, Tremaine would.

It wouldn't matter that he'd had her best interests at heart, as well as those of the people employed by the firm who would lose their jobs if the company went under. She'd only see that he'd deceived her, that he was willing to sacrifice her, just as Ben had accused him of doing, to save the company. She'd feel used, cheated, abused. Worse, she'd hate him, think him selfish, heartless, cruel, all the things other women had accused him of in the past.

But in the past, he hadn't cared what others had thought of him. Succeeding was all that was important. Being number one. The head of the pack. And it didn't matter who he stepped on to get there or who he pushed away to remain there once he'd arrived.

But this time it did matter. Jamie mattered. And he'd screwed up big time.

He wouldn't tell her, he decided. It wouldn't be as if he was lying to her. By omission, maybe. But not an out-and-out lie. The secret admirer would just disappear, quit leaving gifts and romantic notes for her to find.

Then he remembered the little gold box he'd left on her coffee table, and swore.

Pushing a hand against his forehead, he inhaled deeply, forcing himself to calm down, to think clearly, rationally.

It'll be okay, he told himself. She'd find this last gift, then that was it. No more secret admirer. No more romantic notes. End of story.

And hopefully a beginning for them.

Michael pulled onto Jamie's drive and parked. "Home at last," he said, then turned to smile at her. "Going to invite me in?"

She leaned across the console, pushing her face only inches from his. "Will you make it worth my time?"

He laughed and dropped a kiss on her mouth. "You're insatiable."

She wrinkled her nose impishly and reached for her door handle. "Yeah, I know."

He climbed out, stretching as he waited for her to round the front of the Navigator. When she reached him, he hooked an arm around her waist and walked with her to the front door.

He took the key she offered, unlocked the door and pushed it wide. "I hope you have food," he said, following her inside. "I'm starving."

She shrugged out of her coat and tossed it over a chair. "I'll see what I've got." She started toward the kitchen, then stopped and backed up, staring down at the gold box sitting on her coffee table. "Michael?" she whispered.

Shrugging out of his coat, he swore silently when he saw the expression on her face. He knew what she was thinking, who she thought had entered her house while she was away and left the gift for her. The stalker.

He couldn't believe he'd been so stupid. So reckless. But he hadn't wanted to leave the gift in the mailbox or on her porch where someone could steal it.

Hiding his frustration behind what he hoped appeared as nonchalance, he crossed to the coffee table and picked up the box. "Well, well, well," he said, tossing it in his hand. "Looks as if your secret admirer has struck again."

Jamie lifted her gaze to his, her face as white as a sheet. "Oh, Michael," she murmured, her voice quavering. "He was here. In my house." She sank weakly to her knees and rocked back on her heels, squeezing her hands between her thighs. "The stalker," she said, her voice trembling, then looked up at him. "He was here in my house."

He hunkered down in front of her and sat the box aside to gather her hands between his. "Now don't start jumping to conclusions," he scolded gently. "Detective Wade assured me that Kristie's stalker isn't the one who's been sending you gifts."

She snatched her hands from his. "I don't care what Detective Wade says," she cried furiously. "No normal person would break into a person's home to leave them a gift. This guy is sick! He could be dangerous!" She clapped her hands over her face. "Oh, God," she moaned, rocking back and forth. "What if he comes back? What will I do?"

Michael couldn't stand it any longer. Seeing her fear...knowing he was the cause of it. He sat on the floor and pulled her onto his lap. He knew he had to tell her everything. Put her fears to rest. And when he did he knew she would probably hate him. Knowing that, he tucked her head beneath his chin and held her close.

"Jamie," he said quietly, searching for just the right words. "Kristie's stalker isn't your secret admirer."

She pushed angrily from his lap, her face streaked with tears. "Why do you keep saying that?" she cried. "There's no other explanation. No other—"

"There is an explanation," he said, cutting her off. He dropped his gaze, then made himself look her square in the eye. "It was me. I'm the one who's been sending you the gifts."

She stared, her eyes going round. "You?" she whispered. "But…you kept saying it was John."

"It's complicated," he said, rubbing uncomfortably at the back of his neck. "I was worried about him. And you," he added quickly.

She pressed her hands against her temples and shook her head. "You're not making any sense."

"I know," he said in frustration. "But if you'll hear me out, I think you'll understand." He took one of her hands in his and gave it a squeeze, needing that connection. "Since John's divorce, he's been acting crazy. Drinking and partying all the time. Coming into work hung over. Producing inferior designs, if he bothered to produce anything at all. And his actions are having a ripple effect throughout the company. Sales are down. Morale is low."

He sighed and looked down at their joined hands, remembering the gentleness in her touch, the sweetness, the heat, and wondered if he'd ever have the chance to experience it again. "I knew I had to do something to stop him. I'd tried talking to him, reasoning with him, but he wouldn't listen. Then I came up with an idea. I thought if I could find a woman for John, someone sensible and stable who could fill the gap his wife left in his life when she divorced him, then John would settle back down and focus on business again.''

''And *I* was that woman?''

He lifted his head, hearing the hurt in her voice, the resentment, and watched the fury burn to the surface.

''Yes,'' he said, tightening his grip on her hand. ''But you've got to understand. It wasn't like I was...well, sacrificing you, for the sake of the company. I knew you were unhappy, lonely, that you'd only had two dates since you moved to Chicago. Now, Jamie,'' he said, trying to reason with her when she snatched her hand from his.

''How did you know I had only two dates?'' she asked furiously. ''I never told you that.''

He dragged a hand down his face, knowing he'd just dug his hole a little deeper. ''I heard you talking to one of the other secretaries at the Christmas party.''

''So you felt sorry for me. Thought you could kill two birds with one stone, by putting John and I together. A win-win situation all the way around. Isn't that how you referred to our trip to my parents? You'd get another eight hours of work out of me and my parents would get the part they needed.'' She pushed to her feet and looked down at him, her eyes flat, cold, emotionless. ''You said you had only John and my best interests at heart. But it was *your* interest you were most worried about. *You* who came out the winner. And was that why you made love with me, too? Was that just another of your ways to kill two birds with one stone? You're horny and stuck and out in the boonies with your secretary, so why not just sleep with her?''

He shot to his feet. ''That's not true and you damn well know it,'' he said angrily.

She took a step back, wrapping her arms around her waist. ''I want you to leave.''

''But, Jamie—''

''Go!'' she screamed, then spun and ran into her bedroom, slamming the door behind her.

Michael stared after her, listening to the click of the lock. He was tempted to beat the damn door down and make her listen to reason.

But she'd already listened to reason. He had no other explanations, reasonable or not, to offer for his behavior. He was selfish, coldhearted, ruthless, just as she'd accused him of being.

Turning away, he dragged his coat from the chair and crossed to the front door. With his hand on the knob, he glanced back at the bedroom door she'd locked between them.

But she was wrong about one thing. He hadn't come out the winner on this deal. Not this time.

He was afraid he'd just lost the only chance he'd ever had for happiness.

Chapter 8

Jamie listened to the front door close, then waited until she heard the rev of the Navigator's engine before throwing herself facedown on her bed. She didn't cry—though she wanted to. Michael Shay didn't deserve her tears. He was a snake. A low-crawling, belly-dragging, slick-as-sin snake, and she'd be darned if she'd cry over something as despicable as a snake.

But, oh, she wanted to. The tears were there, tightening her chest, burning her throat and eyes, just waiting for her to open the floodgates and let them loose.

How could she have been such a fool? Such a naive and blind fool. How could she have fallen for such a heartless man? And to think she'd *slept* with him, both literally and figuratively. She'd given him her body, her heart, shared with him her bed. And what had he given her in return? Nothing but lies and deceit.

And the worst part was that she worked for the louse, which meant that she'd have to see him again.

She rolled onto her back and blinked furiously, trying to hold back the tears. She couldn't cry. Not now. She had to think. She'd quit, she decided, then squeezed her hand over her temples and shook her head. No, no. She couldn't quit. She couldn't afford the luxury. She needed the money too badly to give up her job. Besides, quitting would make this too easy for Michael, and she'd be darned if she'd let him off easy. *He* was the guilty party in this situation. All but selling her off to his best friend just to save his stupid company, then using her for his own physical pleasure.

Well, he'd picked the wrong woman, she told herself, and heaved herself from the bed. Nobody used Jamie Tyson, then shoved her aside. She didn't need him. Didn't want him. She didn't want any man. So what if she never experienced romance and excitement? She'd lived twenty-four years without it and had survived. She'd focus her energies on other things. She'd learn a foreign language or maybe take up oil painting. Belly dancing.

In the meantime, she needed chocolate. Pounds of it.

She headed for the kitchen, but stumbled to a stop in the living room, when she saw the gold box, lying on the floor.

A whimper slipped past her quivering lips. A part of her wanted to open it and see what was inside, just so she'd know what Michael had picked out for her. Another part told her to pitch the box in the trash.

It was a tough battle, but the latter part won.

Setting her jaw, she scooped the box from the floor, marched straight to the kitchen and tossed it into the garbage pail. In the pantry she found a bag of chocolate-chip cookies, then braced her hips against the countertop and tore open the top.

It wouldn't hurt to just take a peek, a little voice coaxed.

She pulled out a cookie and tipped up her chin. "I don't care what's inside. Whatever it is, it means nothing to me."

But what if it's something really valuable? the little voice prodded. *You can't just throw it away.*

"Oh, yeah? Watch me." She sank her teeth into the cookie and bit off a healthy-size bite. She chewed, swallowed, then took her another bite. As she chewed, her gaze strayed to the garbage pail. A banana peel, she remembered, gulping down the bite of cookie. The box had landed on the blackened banana peel she'd tossed in the garbage that morning. The box was probably stained now and reeked of banana.

As she continued to stare at the pail, a vision built slowly in her mind, rolling in vivid Technicolor with Dolby sound. She could see herself carrying her trash out to the street corner on pickup day, the little gold box sliding around inside the sack, surrounded by her household garbage. She could see the city garbage truck rolling up out front, and the men jumping down from the rear and pitching her sack into the back. She could hear the metallic grind and whir of the crusher, as one of the men flipped the lever that mobilized the unit, whisking her garbage out of sight and squashing it in with strangers' refuse. She could almost smell the truck's exhaust fumes as it roared away, carrying the little gold box to a landfill far, far away.

"Oh, for heaven's sake," she muttered, and tossed the bag of cookies aside. She stomped to the pail and stooped to fish the box out. It was light, she thought as she palmed it. She lifted it to her ear and gave it a little shake. Unable to identify the muffled sound, she took a deep breath and lifted the lid.

"Oh, my God!" she gasped, staring.

Her fingers trembling, she lifted a delicate necklace from the cotton padding it was nestled in. An emerald-cut blue topaz the size of her thumb dangled from the silver chain. She sank weakly back against the countertop. It was gorgeous and obviously expensive. Heavens! She couldn't just throw it away.

But she wasn't keeping it, either.

Firming her lips, she dropped the necklace back into the box and snapped the lid back into place. She wanted nothing from Michael Shay.

Not even the memories he'd left her with.

Hearing footsteps in the hallway, Jamie glanced up from the work on her desk and saw John Tremaine coming down the hall. Amazingly, he looked almost normal. Other than the ponytail, of course. She quickly looked away, hoping to avoid making eye contact.

"Good morning, Jamie."

She looked up to find him standing in the doorway. She pasted on a polite smile. ''Good morning, John. I'm sorry, but Michael hasn't made it in yet.''

He stepped inside. ''Actually, it was you I wanted to see.''

''Me?'' she said in surprise.

He dropped a hip on the corner of her desk and folded his hands on his knee. ''Yeah, you.''

She pulled back, wary. ''If you're worried about the Peterson account, we finished preparing the presentation over the weekend. Michael meets with their board tomorrow afternoon.''

''So that's why you didn't answer your phone this weekend. You were working.''

''You called me?''

''Yeah. Several times. I was hoping I could talk you into going to the New Year's Eve party with me tomorrow night.''

She narrowed her eyes. ''Did Michael put you up to this?''

He snorted a laugh. ''No. Why?''

''Swear?''

He held up a hand. ''If I'm lying, I'm dying.''

She eyed him a moment longer and finally decided he was telling the truth. ''I wasn't planning on going.''

''Oh, come on, Jamie. It's New Year's Eve. You don't want to miss all the fun.''

''What fun?''

They both looked up to see Michael striding into the office, wearing a dark scowl.

''The New Year's Eve party,'' John said, and stood. ''I was just asking Jamie if she'd go with me.''

Michael snapped his gaze to Jamie, his scowl

deepening. "I've already asked her. She said she's not going."

Jamie shot up from her chair. "You did not ask me!"

"I damn sure did, and you said you weren't going because you didn't have anything to wear."

"You asked me if I was *going* to the party. You didn't ask me if I'd go with you." Lifting her chin, she turned to John. "Yes, I'd love to go to the party with you."

John held up his hands. "Look. I don't want to create any problems. If Shay asked first..."

Jamie shot Michael a murderous look before replying. "He didn't, so there's no problem. What time would you like to pick me up?"

John looked uneasily from one to the other, then shrugged. "About eight?"

"Fine," Jamie said, and sat back down at her desk. "I'll be ready."

John turned for the door. "See you later, Shay."

"Yeah," Michael muttered.

Jamie wheeled her chair in front of her monitor and began to type. She could feel Michael's gaze burning into her back.

"Why did you agree to go to the party with him? You said yourself he isn't your type."

She kept right on typing. "I would think you'd be pleased. After all, you were the one who wanted John and I to get together."

"Oh, I'm pleased, all right," he muttered, then stomped past her desk and into his office, slamming the door behind him. Seconds later he stormed out.

"What is this doing on my desk?"

She continued to type, not bothering to look up.

She knew what he held. The little gold box. "I put it there."

"I don't want the damn thing!"

"Neither do I. I suppose you could return it and ask for a refund. Or perhaps you can find another woman to give it to." Pausing her fingers over the keys, she turned to smile sweetly at him and added, "Someone as desperate for a man as you thought I was."

He slammed his fist down on her desk. "Damn it, Jamie! I never said you were desperate."

She faced the monitor again and resumed her typing. "The inference was there."

She heard the grinding of teeth, the crumpling of cardboard. The next sound she heard was Michael's office door slamming between them again.

Michael chucked a rock across the water, then stuffed his hands into his coat pockets and hunched his shoulders to his ears, watching as it skipped across the surface and disappeared beneath the waves.

He should be out celebrating, he told himself. Tossing back tequila shots with some of the guys from the office, while they all patted themselves on the back for a job well done. Old Man Peterson himself had just signed on the dotted line, which meant that Shay, Tremaine and Weller had landed the advertising business for one of the largest corporations in the country, if not the world. Michael had personally spent months gathering data and preparing for the presentation, weeks sweating blood, worrying if Tremaine would come through with the artwork needed.

He should be jubilant, he told himself, riding high on adrenaline, whooping it up with his partners. Instead, he was standing on the banks of Lake Michigan alone, freezing his butt off, just because he couldn't stand the thought of going back to the office and chance seeing Jamie with John again.

"Damn it," he swore, and turned away from the water, raking a hand through his hair. He'd never even considered the possibility of falling for her while romancing her for John. Who would've? Matchmakers matched, they weren't supposed to fall.

But he'd fallen, all right. Hard.

And now she was going to the New Year's Eve party with John, an annual event hosted by all three partners of the firm.

I'm not going, he told himself. Watching her dance and flirt with Tremaine was a torture he didn't need. And at midnight, when the balloons were released from the ballroom ceiling and "Auld Lang Syne" was played, he sure as hell didn't want to be around if they were to kiss.

He swore again and kicked at an empty soda can left lying on the bank. Hell, she didn't even like John! She'd all but cringed every time Michael had brought up Tremaine's name. So what was all this sudden interest in John? Why had she agreed to go to the party with him, if she detested him so much?

He stopped, his heart seeming to stop, too, as his mind flashed back to the service station, the JBs and Jamie demanding that he kiss her. She'd wanted revenge, to prove something. Could that be why she'd accepted the date from John? Was she just trying to get even with Michael?

It was possible, he told himself, and headed for

the parking lot where he'd left his Navigator. But even if that wasn't the case, he wasn't going to just stand by and let John have her. It wasn't as if John had a prior claim. Michael had staked his claim first, and by God he wasn't going to walk away without putting up a fight.

"Why'd you have to pop off and say you'd go with him?" Jamie muttered as she reached behind her to fasten the waist of her black silk slacks. Why hadn't she simply told John she had other plans?

Pursing her lips, she snatched up the Angora sweater she'd laid out on her bed, shoved her arms through the sleeves, then pulled it down over her head. Because she'd wanted to get even with Michael, that's why. She flopped down onto the side of the bed. As if she could, she thought miserably.

And now, as her punishment for being vengeful, she had to go to a black tie party dressed in slacks and a sweater, escorted by John Tremaine, *GQ*'s version of a Hell's Angel.

The doorbell rang and she whipped around to look at the bedroom clock. It wasn't even seven-thirty yet, she thought in dismay. What was John doing here so early? She quickly stood and glanced in the dresser mirror, fluffing a hand at her towel-dried hair. Well, he was going to have to cool his heels for a while, she thought irritably as she headed for the living room. She hadn't even styled her hair yet.

At the front door, she paused a moment, offering up a silent prayer that John would at least be sober, then forced the corners of her lips up in a welcoming smile and opened the door.

But John wasn't there. No one was.

She stuck her head out and looked around. *That's weird,* she thought, frowning as she pulled her head back in to close the door. *I could have sworn I heard—*

The door struck something, keeping it from closing, and she looked down and saw the corner of a pink-and-white striped box trapped in the opening. Her frown deepening, she stooped to pick it up. Oh, God, she thought, recognizing the logo imprinted on the outside of the box. She quickly closed and locked the door, then hurried to her bedroom.

She dropped down on the side of her bed and set the box on her lap. Sure that she knew what she'd find inside, she took a deep breath, then lifted the lid.

The ice-blue evening gown she'd tried on at the boutique lay folded on a pink cloud of tissue paper.

Tears blurred her vision as she lifted the gown from the box. Shoving the box from her lap, she held the gown in front of her and moved to stand in front of the dresser mirror.

"Oh, Michael," she said tearfully as she stared at her reflection. "Why did you do this?"

Dragging a hand across her cheeks, she knelt and pulled the box to her, digging through the tissue, to see if he'd included a note. She found it tucked between the layers of tissue.

She hugged the dress at her waist as she read the typed message.

When I first saw you in this dress, you took my breath away. I remember you saying it looked like something a princess would wear. I couldn't agree more. Enjoy the ball tonight, princess.

Love,
Your Secret Admirer

"Damn you, Michael," she cried, fisting the card in her hand. "The game's over. There is no secret admirer. So why are you doing this to me?"

Because he's cruel, she thought tearfully, heartless. He'd gotten what he wanted. He'd matched her up with John. He'd even provided an appropriate dress for her to wear. He probably even thought she should thank him for it.

She'd kill him instead.

The doorbell rang and she dropped her head to her hand, knowing it was John. Well, she wasn't going to the party, she told herself, and stood. He'd just have to go alone. Snatching a tissue from a box beside the bed, she dabbed at her eyes as she hurried from her room.

"I'm sorry, John," she said as she opened the door, "but I'm not—" She stopped, her jaw dropping.

"Well?" he said, spreading his arms, to show off his black tux, white pleated shirt and black silk bow tie. "What do you think?"

Jamie put a hand to her head, unable to believe the transformation. "Oh, my gosh, John. You look...handsome." She opened the door wider and stepped back, staring as he strode inside.

He turned to face her and bit back a smile. "Do you plan to carry it or wear it?"

Puzzled by his odd comment, she glanced down and realized she was still clutching the dress to her waist. Tears spurted to her eyes. "Neither." She pressed the tissue to her nose. "I'm sorry, John, but I can't go to the party with you."

"What's wrong? Are you sick?"

Choked by the tears, she waved the tissue at him. "N-no, it's nothing like that."

He stepped closer. "Then what is it?"

She hiccuped up a sob. "It's Michael."

"Michael?" he repeated in alarm. "Has something happened to him?"

She pressed the tissue to her nose again and shook her head.

His forehead creased in concern, he took her by the elbow and guided her to the sofa. "Sit right here," he said, urging her down, "while I get you something to drink."

She caught his hand, stopping him. "I don't want anything to drink."

Frowning, he pinched his slacks up at the knee and sank down beside her on the sofa. "What's going on, Jamie?"

She gulped, then sucked in a shuddery breath in an effort to compose herself. "It's Michael." Just saying his name was all it took to bring the anger singing back. "Do you know what he did?" she cried, thrusting out the evening gown. "He bought me this dress and left it on my front porch for me to find."

"He did?"

She shot to her feet. "Yes, and that's not all he did." She flung a hand in the direction of the table and the vase of fading roses still sitting there. "He sent me those roses and a huge basket filled with candles and CDs and the most outrageously expensive champagne.''

''Michael?'' he said doubtfully.

''Yes, Michael! And he bought me a necklace, too. A blue topaz that perfectly matches this dress. And he wrote me all these really sweet notes.''

He snorted a laugh, shaking his head. ''Sorry. But I'm having a hard time imagining Michael doing all those things. Shay's not exactly what I'd call a touchy-feely kind of guy.''

''He didn't give them to me from himself,'' she said angrily. ''He gave them to me from *you!*''

He gave his head a hard shake. ''Now I'm really confused.''

''Here,'' Jamie said, and sat back down, smoothing the crumpled card across her thigh. ''Look at this. It's the note he sent along with the dress.''

John took the card and read it. ''Michael wrote this?'' he asked in amazement.

''Yes,'' she said, and rose to gather the others. She brought them back and handed them over to John. ''The one on top was the first he sent and was attached to a dozen red roses. The second he left on the windshield of my car. The third was in the basket.''

John read them all, then looked up at her, his expression skeptical. ''Are you sure Shay wrote these?''

''Positive. But he tried to make me believe that you did.''

''Me?''

''Yes, you.''

''But that's crazy.''

''Yeah, I know,'' she replied, scowling.

Frowning, he unfastened the button on his jacket and sat back, stretching his arms out along the back of the sofa. "Maybe you better start over from the very beginning. And don't try to spare my feelings," he added. "Something tells me I'm not going to like what I'm going to hear."

Jamie hesitated, knowing he probably wouldn't, then reluctantly began to detail Michael's scheme to match her up with John and his rationale for doing so. But she was careful to avoid any mention of the intimacy she and Michael had shared. There were some things better left untold.

When she'd finished, she looked at John. "Please don't be mad at him," she begged, fearing she may have destroyed a long-standing friendship between the two men. "He honestly believed he was doing us both a big favor."

Without replying, John picked up the cards from the sofa cushion beside him and looked at them again. "I'm sure he did," he said thoughtfully, then looked up at Jamie. "But something tells me he has since regretted his interference."

Jamie looked at him in puzzlement. "What do you mean?"

Instead of answering her, John glanced at his watch. "You better hurry and get dressed or we're going to miss the party."

"Oh, no, John," she said, backing away. "I can't go. Not now."

He arched a brow. "Why? Because Michael will be there?"

There was just enough of a challenge in his voice to put steel in her spine. If she tried to avoid Michael, he might construe it as a sign that she cared.

"Ten minutes," she said tersely, and turned for her room.

The party was already in full swing when Jamie and John arrived. Some couples were gathered around the buffet tables, talking and laughing while nibbling on hors d'oeuvres and sipping champagne. Others gyrated on the dance floor, dancing to music provided by a band set up on a tiered stage. Round, linen-topped tables circled the room, each centered with a black top hat that seemed to be exploding with silver streamers and a burst of twinkling stars.

Jamie was shaking like a leaf, and it wasn't because she'd just come in from the cold. This was a mistake, she thought as she looked out over the crowded ballroom. She should have stayed at home, regardless of how Michael interpreted her absence.

She felt John's hand on her arm and glanced his way.

"Would you like some champagne?" he asked.

She hesitated, fearing if she drank he would. And she didn't think she could deal with a drunk. Not tonight.

"I don't intend to get drunk, if that's what you're worried about."

She blushed, embarrassed to know that he'd read her thoughts so easily. Was she that transparent?

"I'm sorry," she murmured, dropping her gaze.

He placed a finger beneath her chin, forcing her face up to his. "No. I am. It seems that everyone realized I had a problem, but me." He smiled, then dropped his hand, looking her up and down. "Have I told you that you look beautiful tonight?"

Her blush deepened. "No, but thank you."

He shot her a wink. "You're welcome. Now, about that champagne..."

She squared her shoulders. "Yes, I'd love some."

"Wait right here," he said, "and I'll bring you a glass."

She watched him walk away and decided that John Tremaine wasn't such a bad guy, after all. Still not her type, but sober he was a different man, just as Michael had claimed he was.

She bit back a groan, furious with herself for thinking of Michael, and forced her mind on the party, determined not to think about him again.

She saw Naomi intercept John, and sputtered a laugh when the woman reached up to straighten his tie, then smile and give his cheek an affectionate pat. Another man might have resented the woman's fussing, but John didn't seem to mind. He dropped a kiss on her cheek, then said something and pointed toward Jamie. Frowning, Naomi glanced her way. Jamie smiled weakly and waggled a finger, wondering what the two were talking about.

As she watched, John said something else and Naomi's mouth dropped open. Laughing, John excused himself and headed back toward Jamie.

"What was that all about?" she asked, accepting the glass from him.

"Nothing. Just a private joke."

Before she could demand an explanation, he cupped a hand at her elbow and urged her forward. "Let's find a table, then I want to dance. I think they're playing our song."

Jamie looked at him curiously, but allowed him to propel her along at his side.

* * *

"Where the hell have you been?"

Michael swung his head around to find Ben bearing down on him, his hair wild, his tie askew. "What's the problem?"

"What's the problem?" Ben repeated, then flung out an arm to encompass the room. "This is the problem. In case you've forgotten, we're the hosts of this little shindig. You, me and Tremaine. And you jerks have left me to handle everything alone."

Michael tensed. "Tremaine's not here?"

"Oh, he's here all right," Ben replied wryly. "But he might as well be at home in bed for all the help he's been."

Michael scanned the room, looking for Tremaine, worried about Ben's reference to bed. "Is he drunk?"

Ben folded his arms and turned to stand beside Michael. "You tell me." He tipped his head in the direction of the dance floor. "Just look at him. You'd think he was Fred Astaire or something."

Michael started forward, unable to see the dance floor for the people crowding around it. He shouldered his way through and stopped at the edge, stunned to find Tremaine and Jamie on the dance floor alone. And they were putting on quite a show.

Salsa. That's what he thought they called this kind of dancing. Whatever it was, Tremaine had Jamie in his arms and was whirling around the room at a pace that made Michael's head spin just to watch. And the dance was seductive. Too seductive, Michael thought irritably as Tremaine bowed Jamie back, his mouth close enough to hers to share a cold. Ben had been right when he'd said that John might as well be at home in bed. But he'd failed to mention what John would be doing in that bed or who he'd be doing it with, if he were at home.

Just as his blood reached a slow boil, the song ended and the dancers straightened, laughing and hugging each other. The people crowded around watching burst into applause. Acknowledging the praise, Tremaine lifted his and Jamie's hands then bent in a low bow. He spun her around to face the opposite direction, and they bowed again.

It was then that Michael got a look at the back of Jamie's dress and remembered—belatedly—the darlingly low scoop of the gown's back.

Setting his jaw, he pushed through the crowd and onto the dance floor. He caught Jamie by the arm and whirled her around. Her eyes widened in surprise when she saw him.

"What do you think you're doing?" he whispered angrily. "You're making a fool of yourself."

Her eyes narrowed to slits and she jerked her arm from his. "No, I'm having fun. Now, if you'll excuse me, I'd like to get something to drink."

"Who died and elected you chaperone?"

Michael snapped his head around to glare at John. "Shut up."

John lifted a brow. "Shut up? Is that the best you can do?"

Michael whipped his arms back, fighting free of his tux jacket. "No," he said, balling his hands into fists. "I can do a lot better."

Having made her way to the edge of the dance floor, Jamie noticed the sudden hush that fell over the crowd and glanced back to see Michael and John squaring off for a fight. Horrified, she darted back across the floor and grabbed Michael's arm as he pulled back to throw a punch.

"Stop it!" she cried. "What is wrong with you two?"

Michael jerked free. "Why don't you ask him? He started it."

"Me?" John said incredulously, then laughed. "You're just mad because Jamie chose to come to the party with me and not you."

Michael gave him an angry shove. "That's a damn lie and you know it."

John stumbled back, but caught himself before falling. "Is it?" he asked, arching a brow.

"John, please," Jamie begged, aware that everyone in the room was listening to the two men argue. "Michael didn't invite me to the party. I told you that."

"Yeah, but he wanted to," John said.

"I did not!" Michael yelled.

Jamie snapped her head around to glare at Michael. "I think you've made that perfectly clear, not only to me but to everyone else in the room." Snatching up a fistful of her skirt, she whirled and stomped away.

John moved to stand beside Michael, clamping a hand on his friend's shoulder, as he watched Jamie's angry exit. "I'll say this for you, Shay," he said. "You really know how to charm the ladies."

"Just shut the hell up," Michael growled, then shouted, "Jamie! Wait!"

When she only quickened her step, he took off after her. He caught up with her just outside the door. He caught her arm, dragging her to a stop and moved to stand in front of her, blocking her escape.

"Jamie, please. I didn't mean that the way it sounded."

"Didn't you?" she demanded angrily. "Well, I happen to think your meaning was perfectly clear. You didn't ask me to the party. I'm not questioning the truth in that. But I *do* resent you informing the entire company of that fact in such a tasteless and thoughtless manner."

"I was mad."

"You were mad," she said, seething. "Well, I'm furious and you don't see me standing out in front of God and everybody screaming at the top of my lungs that you may not have wanted to invite me to the party but you sure as hell didn't mind sleeping with me."

"I think you just did."

"And I—" She blinked up at him. "What?"

He tipped his head and she glanced behind her to discover that John and the others had followed them into the hallway and had heard every word.

She grabbed Michael by the lapels, her grip desperate. "Please tell me this is all a bad dream."

"I would, but it would be a lie."

"Oh, God," she moaned, and dropped her forehead against his chest. "Is there any way to get out of this gracefully?"

"There might be."

"How?"

"You'll have to let go of me first."

She lifted her head to look at him. "Okay. But I'm not turning around. I'd die first."

"You don't have to."

She slowly unfurled her fingers from his lapel. "What are you going to do?"

He dropped a kiss to her mouth. "Just trust me."

He stepped around her, whispered something to John she couldn't hear, then returned, taking her hands in his.

"When you received the bouquet of roses, do you remember what was written on the card?"

She dropped her mouth open, then clamped her lips together and tried to tug her hands from his. "Michael," she whispered furiously. "This isn't funny."

He answered for her. "It said, 'This is going to be our year.' When I wrote that, I didn't realize that I was talking about you and me."

"Michael, please," she begged, knowing that everyone behind her could hear him.

"The second note said, 'I'm thinking of you. Are you thinking of me?' I can't answer for the last part, but the first part is definitely true. I was thinking about you. Still am."

"Michael," she moaned, dropping her gaze.

"And the basket? I spent hours trying to think of all the things you would consider romantic." He released one of her hands to push a knuckle beneath her chin and smiled when her gaze met his. "How'd I do?"

Tears burned her throat. "Perfect."

"And the necklace?" He shook his head sadly. "I must have screwed up there, because you returned it."

"No," she said quickly. "I loved it. I really did. It was just that—"

He pressed a finger against her lips, silencing her. "I know. And that was my fault. Why would you need the necklace without the dress?" He slid a hand into his pocket. ''But I bet you'd accept it now, wouldn't you?'' He pulled his hand out, dangling the necklace in front of her eyes.

Without waiting for her to reply, he clasped it around her neck, then pulled back, as if to appraise the results. ''You were right,'' he said, reaching to catch her hands again. ''It did need the dress.''

Her face crumpled. ''Oh, Michael,'' she said tearfully.

''And the note that was with the dress? The part about how you took my breath away? It was true. In fact, you take my breath away every time I look at you.''

She sniffed. ''I need to blow my nose.''

He pulled a handkerchief from his pocket and handed it to her, then cocked his head, listening. ''Do you hear that?''

She blotted at her nose. ''Hear what?''

''The music. Listen.''

She frowned, listening, then looked up at him, her eyes widening. '''Crazy.' That was the song that was playing the night we—''

He pressed a finger against her lips. ''Yes. You're right. They're playing our song.'' He held out a hand. ''Will you dance with me, princess?''

She laced her fingers through his. ''I'd love to.''

A collective ''ahh'' came from the group of onlookers as Michael pulled her into his arms.

Jamie tipped her head back to look at him. ''You know what?''

''What?''

''I knew it had to be you all along.''

He arched a brow. ''And how did you know that?''

"Because I made a deal with God."

"Really?"

She dragged a finger across the back of his neck. "Uh-huh. I promised Him that if He would make you be my secret admirer, I'd forgive the JBs for all the grief they gave me."

Michael tossed back his head and laughed. "I'm transferring you to legal," he said, hugging her to him. "You're one hell of a negotiator."

She drew back to look at him. "I love you, Michael," she whispered.

He was sure he'd never heard any words that filled him with such pleasure, such joy. "And I love you, Jamie. More than you'll ever know."

* * * * *